THE GAELIC

LETTERS

A Novel of the Almost Perfect Crime

D1596839

R. Thomas Roe

THE GAELIC LETTERS
A Novel of the Almost Perfect Crime

by R. Thomas Roe

Signalman Publishing   2010
Kissimmee, Florida

Interior layout and design by Signalman Publishing
http://www.signalmanpublishing.com
email: info@signalmanpublishing.com

Cover design by Duncan Long
http://www.duncanlong.com

ISBN-10: 0-9840614-4-4
ISBN-13: 978-0-9840614-4-0

Printed in the United States of America

ACKNOWLEDGEMENTS

I would be remiss in presenting this book if I did not credit certain persons for their contributions to the finished product. First of all my Mother, whose love for Ireland, the home of her family, inspired me with a great interest in the history and culture of that mystical place. Also my good friend, J.J. Rieder, also from my home State of Minnesota, for his many suggestions and helpful criticisms resulting from his review of various drafts of the novel. My publishing advisor, John McClure of Signalman Publishing, for guiding me through the somewhat complex course of getting the novel into print, and last but not least, Duncan Long, the cover artist for his splendid work and suggestions for improving the appearance of the finished product.

Now sweetly lies old Ireland
Emerald green beyond the foam,
Awakening sweet memories,
Calling the heart back home.

CHAPTER 1

Will Desmond stood in the darkened foyer for a moment to catch his breath. He hadn't been in the house for over two weeks, and he had thought it would have been easier for him by now, but his heart raced just the same as it always had whenever he entered his father's house. He looked over to the full length mirror by the coat stand and studied himself in it. He was not a pleasant sight. He looked much older than his forty years. He was thin as a post, and dark, visible bags had formed under his eyes. His ragged and ill-fitting clothes hung wet over his frail body from the long walk in the rain. Shaking the rain drops from his cap, he studied it for a moment and then thought otherwise and put it back on his head. "No need for that. I'm the only one here."

The contrast between this house and Will's crude stone hut was immeasurable. His father's house was huge, lavishly furnished, and decorated with hand-woven French tapestries and paintings by favored English artists. Slate flooring led from room to room. Will made his way into the living room, where he saw the ornately crafted, golden candelabra that extended from the well oiled, dark oak walls and the heavy timbers that rose upwards in support of the high, sculpted, plaster ceiling.

Will thought to himself, "All of this finery could not fail to impress any visitor with the wealth and power of the owner, much less one who eked out a bare subsistence from potatoes and corn raised on a small plot of ground."

It had been three weeks since his father had died, but Will could still smell the smoke from his father's pipe. Will half expected to see him walk out from one of the darkened rooms. As Will continued his way through the house, his footsteps echoed on the slate floors. The cold, damp air gave him an eerie feeling as he went, causing him to shiver and pull his jacket tight about him.

The house had always had a cold feeling to it, but especially now. It had been closed up since the funeral and there had not been a fire in the hearth since they took his father's body to the church for burial. Will resolved to do what he came to do, and then he would get out of there.

As he approached the darkened stairway leading to the second floor, he noticed a folder on top of the bookcase. He had somehow missed it before.

His fingers trembled slightly as he took it down and quickly scanned the contents. It contained only unpaid bills and nothing more. He placed it back on the bookshelf and started up the staircase.

When he reached the second floor, he heard the large, oak front door creak open. Standing breathless, he heard footsteps of someone entering the foyer.

"Who's down there?" he shouted.

"Solicitor Moore. Who's that?"

"Oh, it's me, Will, Mr. Moore. I was checking up on the house. Making sure no one's been in here."

"Now, Will, no one is supposed to be here. I'm taking inventory for the court and you're not supposed to be here either."

"Mr. Moore, you know the house is going to me or Michael or both of us, so what difference does it make anyway?"

Solicitor Moore appeared at the bottom of the staircase. "Don't be too sure about that, Will. Now, you had best be on your way." Solicitor Moore stared up at him.

Will exhaled heavily as he made his way down the stairs. "Mind explaining that to me? Just who else would the place go to other than us?" Will asked.

"Not for me to go into, Will. The Court handles that business, and I do mine."

It was obvious to Will that he would not have the opportunity today to find any additional information by searching the home or by questioning Moore. Will had been in the home one other time since his father's death and had searched through most of the rooms looking for any notes or documents that might tell him what was in his father's will, but he had found nothing. He had hoped to spend more time today going through files in his father's study one last time. Wondering what he was going to receive from his father's huge fortune had been driving him crazy. After all, he had worked hard, swallowed his pride, and even changed his religion, all with one thought in mind, to please his father and take over the estate.

"Why did Moore have to show up just this moment?" Will wondered. Ever since his father's death, Will had a growing sense that Moore didn't like him. He wasn't sure why and wondered if Moore was just keeping him in the dark to irritate him. Moore must have known that Will was worrying himself sick about what was going to happen to the Estate.

Will stopped at the bottom of the staircase. He studied Moore's face and thought, "Why the hell can't he just tell me? He knows. He was the one who had drawn up my father's final papers."

"You're just going to have to wait and hear what Judge Haverstock has to say," Moore said with a faint smile.

"The arrogant bastard," thought Will. "Some day I'll get even with him. I'll let him sweat for no good reason."

"Well, then, I'm just going to have to wait, aren't I, Mr. Moore?"

"Yes, Will, and I would advise you to remain off the premises until this matter is resolved."

*The future is not set,
there is no fate
but what we make for ourselves.*

Chapter 2

Tom Desmond had three sons, Will being the youngest. If his father's will had been written the way most in Ireland were, his chances of getting a major portion of the Estate were slim. On the other hand, if his efforts over the past ten years to gain favor with his father had paid off, he may very well have improved his chances of receiving a sizeable inheritance. Will had even prayed to God that his father would see the light and list him as the primary beneficiary. The fact that he had done that bothered him a bit, but those slight pangs of conscience soon passed.

Will's oldest brother, Jeremiah, had left Ireland for America years before when he was still in his teens. People all over Ireland were starving then, during the Famine in 1850, and Jeremiah, somehow, managed to get on a ship and leave. Under Irish custom, Jeremiah, as the eldest son, would become heir to his father's estate, but Jeremiah's relationship with his father was not normal. Solicitor Moore, who was handling his father's Estate, had asked Will about that and Will had told him that Jeremiah and his father had just never gotten along. Jeremiah was head strong, a little wild, and had some run-ins with the law.

Will went on to explain that even as a young boy, Jeremiah had a strong dislike for the Brits, and when the constable caught him stealing potatoes from bins owned by the Adam's family, the British jail guards beat the hell out of him. That turned him into a real Fenian at the young age of fourteen. With his father working for Sir Cecil Adams and holding many English views on Irish tenant farmers, the relationship between his father and Jeremiah suffered.

Then, when their mother died in the cholera epidemic, Jeremiah somehow managed to get passage to America. Will had always figured that Jeremiah had somehow stolen the money, since a passage ticket was nearly three pounds, a lot of money in those days. After Jeremiah emigrated, he rarely wrote home. That was almost thirty years ago. Needless to say, Will never mentioned the few letters he had received to anyone, especially to his father, Tom.

Tom Desmond had earned his wealth as a land agent for Sir Cecil Adams, who owned most of the land surrounding the town of Kinsale and was responsible for collecting the rents from the poverty stricken Irish tenant farmers. It was a responsibility that he seemed to handle with ease, even in the worst of times. He was known to be a cold-hearted agent for his English employer, and the only Irishman in Kinsale of whom it could be said that he had absolutely no friends. In recent years as famine again enveloped the land, Tom Desmond became even more of a hated symbol of British rule in the community. He treated the tenant farmers ruthlessly when they could not come up with the amount due to Sir Cecil, and he had evicted several poor, barefoot, tenant families from their dirt floor stone huts as winter winds, carrying sleet and ice cold rain off the Atlantic, howled outside of the only shelter they had.

In the winter of 1870, Sir Cecil Adams came down with a debilitating consumption that rapidly took his life. With no heirs born from his marriage to his wife Margaret, his entire estate went to her. She had absolutely no understanding of business, but, since Tom Desmond was so familiar with the management of their land holdings, she called upon him to see that their profitable operation continued. In time, Tom Desmond's interest in the business expanded. He began to take over all duties previously filled by Sir Cecil. Not long after that, Tom formalized his interest in the business, and in Margaret, with a simple, private marriage ceremony on the grounds of the Adam's Estate.

When Tom Desmond took up with Margaret Adams, he renounced his Catholic faith and became an Anglican. Will sent the news to Jeremiah in the States. The reason Will even wrote to Jeremiah was not due to any great affection for his estranged brother. Rather, Jeremiah would, every now and then, send money, and Will wanted that to continue. Apparently, Jeremiah had some guilt feelings over abandoning his siblings in their dire poverty. Will's letters would subtly remind Jeremiah of that, who would respond, when he could, with a few American dollars.

After his father's marriage, Jeremiah's letters sent a clear message to Will that he held his father in contempt for taking up with the English woman and turning his back on his Irish blood. Will soon realized that Jeremiah's distancing of himself from his father offered him a rare opportunity. From that time forward, Will took advantage of every opening that availed itself to further separate his father from his eldest son.

When Tom Desmond learned that he was being shunned by the Irish in Kinsale for taking up with the Englishwoman, Will told his father that it was the Fenians who had ordered the shunning. Tom was well aware from what Will had told him that Jeremiah was an active, stateside Fenian. Will took it a step further by cleverly implying that Jeremiah had somehow promoted the idea of shunning his father.

The shunning was a minor irritant to Tom now that he was living in comfort on the Adams Estate, yet hearing that his eldest son may have been party to it angered him further, and in time he refused to even mention Jeremiah by name.

Ever since his father married Margaret, Will made it a point to increase his contacts with his father. Without his other brother Michael's knowledge, Will would take what few vegetables the two of them had raised down the road to the Adam's Estate and deliver them to his father. His father would look up from his desk only long enough to waive Will towards the kitchen and tell him to give them to the cook. Will's father never invited him to stay for supper or even to come into his study for a chat. Nevertheless, he continued his campaign to win over his father and figured that given enough time he would wear down the wall that had always existed between them.

Will had long struggled with his loyalty to his father. Before Will began to realize that his father had stumbled into a very opportune relationship, taking up with the Englishwoman, it had made good sense for Will to distance himself from his father. His father had never been very popular in the community, not that Will could recall, and Will had learned early on, even as a child, never to mention his father in conversation with friends. Then, when the Irish began shunning his father, Will went through a confusing time. He saw little benefit in defending and siding with his father, who basically ignored him and treated him like any other tenant farmer. Yet, since the marriage, Will had begun to think that there could be something significant at stake for him, so he slowly and subtly began to publicly side with his father.

After Tom Desmond moved up the road to the Adam's Estate, he looked upon his sons as the individuals responsible for the annual lease payment on the small Desmond farm. There was never any question or discussion concerning their share of that payment. It was due in full and at the same time, even though Tom Desmond was now both lessor and lessee of the property. The fact that Will and Michael had to make that payment to the Adam's Estate, as did everyone else in Kinsale, kept them in the good graces of his neighbors. Nevertheless, the townsfolk kept an eye on both of them to see if they were benefiting from their father's very opportune change of status. Thus far there seemed to be no change in the material well being of either son and consequently, they continued to find acceptance in the community.

But there were some differences between the two. Michael's close ties with the Fenian activists in the Kinsale area garnered him generally higher regard than Will. On the contrary, Will had studiously avoided any such affiliation and that, combined with his new interest in his father made him somewhat suspect. Beyond their politics, Michael was outgoing, personable and easy going. Will, on the other hand, was very quiet, a loner, and considered a poor risk when it came to lending him tools. He was never shy about asking for assistance when struck by the slightest calamity but was hard to find when someone else needed help.

In normal times, the Desmond farm was sufficient to provide a bare sustenance for the two Desmond brothers, but it was not large enough for the two of them to peaceably live together, particularly after their father's marriage. The relationship between the brothers wasn't great before the marriage, but it rapidly deteriorated afterwards. Michael had become more and more active with a nationalist group called the Irish Republican Brotherhood, a group actively fighting for Home Rule, while Will had taken on more of the attitudes and interests of his pro-British father. Michael, like most of the young Catholic men in the Kinsale area, had become active in the IRB as soon as he could handle a weapon. His politics ran counter to Will's unexpressed dream of someday, taking over the reigns of what had been the Adams Estate to become the primary, if not sole, landlord in the Kinsale area.

In recent years, the Fenians in County Cork had become more strident in their demands for Home Rule and had begun actively pursuing the matter of rent abatements. Virtually all of the land in Ireland was owned by British interests. The rents were exorbitant compared to the revenues the land could produce, and in recent years, with the continuing famine, the tenants had been withholding rent payments in protest. The situation deteriorated with more and more Irish farmers withholding their rents, which prompted the British to evict large numbers of tenants for nonpayment. The tenant farmers retaliated by sabotaging British business interests and burning British homes. The Land Wars ensued and Fenian guerilla operations spread throughout Ireland, particularly in County Cork and southwest Ireland. Kinsale, located in southwest Cork, became a hotbed of this Fenian activity.

These events were taking place just as Will's father was distancing himself from his Irish roots and taking on the appearance and customs of the Englishman who had previously occupied his home. Tom seldom saw or spoke with his son, Michael, who had become deeply involved with the Fenian activists. The day finally arrived when Tom announced that Michael was no longer welcome in his home.

CHAPTER 3

Five years passed with absolutely no contact between Michael and his father. When Margaret Adams Desmond passed away, Michael did not attend the funeral service in the Anglican Church, and even if he had done so, his father, or others present, would most likely have requested that he leave. Michael's suspected involvement with Fenian attacks on British owned homes in the Kinsale area was well known among those in attendance at the funeral. Will, on the other hand, was close by his father throughout the church service and at the cemetery. Will offered sympathy and consoled him at every opportunity, particularly after he learned that Margaret had left the entire Adam's Estate to his father. Tom was now an extremely wealthy man, and no one was more aware of that fact than his son, Will. Regardless of Tom Desmond's new status, he and his son were the only two Desmonds present at the funeral. There were other relatives in the community, but they held no affection for Tom and were now, along with everyone else in the Irish community, beginning to question Will's motives.

Michael and Will continued to carry on the necessary chores at the farm, but they only spoke with one another when absolutely necessary or when they were involved in a heated argument over politics. It was obvious that living together on the same small plot of ground could not continue indefinitely. One evening, after the chores had been completed and the two were fixing their own separate dinner from their dwindling supply of potatoes, Will spoke to his brother with no visible sign of animosity.

"Michael, have you thought about emigrating?" Will had been after Michael to emigrate for years so that he could farm the Desmond holding by himself. He would then also be the only Desmond son left in Ireland and that could have some bearing on what might eventually happen to his father's Estate.

"I have thought about it, but there's work to be done here, and I would be leaving it for others, if I left."

"Michael, one of these days you're going to get shot or hung with that Fenian business."

An argument then ensued, sending Will over the edge and the two almost came to blows before Will finally picked up his coat and headed down the road to his father's house. Once inside the house and comfortably seated on a fine, embroidered couch before a peat fire, Will unburdened himself to his father about Michael's Fenian activities. Tom Desmond had heard it all before, many times, and only muttered, "They're going to bring nothing but trouble on Ireland. They ought to farm their fields and stay home at night. Michael's no better than the rest of them."

In the year or two before Tom Desmond died, he began to bring up Jeremiah in conversations with Will. These conversations unnerved Will, who had assumed that Jeremiah was well out of his father's thoughts. It seemed to Will that his father sensed that his days on earth were limited and that he wished to reconcile with his eldest son. In these conversations, Will told his father that he believed Jeremiah had been dead for some time because no one had heard from him in years. In truth, Will had been corresponding with him right along, and was continuing to receive funds that provided support to Will and his brother. The funds, in fact, had never left Will's possession.

Tom Desmond had been making inquiries about Jeremiah's well being with the few people in the community who had been in communication with him, but no one had heard from Jeremiah in years. In time, Tom concluded that Will was right. Jeremiah must have passed away some years previous.

In the months leading up to his father's death, Will rarely left his side. In the final month, Will stayed in the large stone house with his father to be in constant attendance. Michael tried to visit his father on a number of occasions, but Will managed to keep him away through one artifice or another. Finally, Will told Michael that his father had requested that he not even attempt a visit in view of the fact their relationship had ended long ago. Had Michael known the truth, he would have learned that his father had asked why it was that Michael had not come to visit him in his last days. Will explained to his father on those occasions that Michael was too occupied with his Fenian activities and had expressed no interest in seeing his father even when he had been urged to do so.

Whenever the opportunity presented itself, Will discreetly asked his father about his will, but his father would only reply, "Don't worry about it. Moore has taken care of that business."

Whenever his father slept, Will would pour through the papers in his desk, searching for a copy of his will or some evidence of how he planned to dispose of the property that he had inherited from Margaret. As his father's condition deteriorated and he slipped into comas with increasing frequency, Will could hear him calling out for Jeremiah. He even heard him ask for Michael but never did he hear his father call out his own name. He knew it was possible that he would inherit nothing and spend the rest of his life trying to survive on the small plot of land he farmed. Thinking further about that, he realized that he could lose even that if his father's property went to someone else.

With his father lingering between life and death, the emotional toll on Will began to show. Associates of his father assumed his haggard look was due to the son's close affection for his father. Rather, known only to him, it was due to the increasing tension playing on Will's nerves over the question of the inheritance.

In the last week of his father's life, Will received a letter from Jeremiah inquiring about his father. Apparently, time had soothed Jeremiah's anger towards his father, and this caused considerable concern to Will. He feared that if Jeremiah again appeared on the scene he could disrupt all of Will's efforts to gain control of his father's fortune. Will thought long and hard about how to handle Jeremiah. He finally wrote a response informing Jeremiah that his father wanted nothing to do with him due to his involvement in the Irish Republican Brotherhood in the States. Will further explained to Jeremiah that their father had become a staunch Unionist using his new found wealth and influence to push for extended and continuous British control of Ireland. Will closed the letter by stating that it would be best for all concerned for Jeremiah to completely sever ties with the family. A few days later their father died.

Following his father's death, Will expected to quickly learn about the disposition of the huge Adams Estate. Regretfully for him, Solicitor Moore informed him that it could be weeks or even months before the will was made public. In the meantime, the court was in charge of the property and no one was to enter the house or grounds, much less remove any property belonging to the Estate. Rumor had it that Judge Haverstock was purposely waiting to see if any shirttail Adams Family relatives would surface to claim the huge Estate. It was very unusual for an English family to lose control of such a large holding, particularly to Irish tenant farmers, and Judge Haverstock, of English blood himself, did not want to be seen as favoring an Irish farmer over a claimant from a titled English family. He would see that the Estate remained open as long as possible.

The three sharpest things in the world:
a thorn in the mud,
a hemp rope,
a fool's word.

Chapter 4

Three months after Tom Desmond died, the Surrogate Court posted a notice in area newspapers giving the time, date, and location of the reading of Thomas Desmond's will. Solicitor Moore had contacted both Will and Michael a few days ahead of the general public regarding the forthcoming publication of the notice. Solicitor Moore informed them that the only persons making claims on the estate were a few small creditors seeking payment of bills incurred for various repairs made to the house. That was welcome news to Will as he had feared that some previously unknown Adam's family heir would surface with a claim superior to that of his own. He also continued to worry that Jeremiah may yet appear and spoil everything.

Will arrived at the court house a few minutes early to find a good seat. When he entered the court room, he was surprised to see only a few people present. They all seemed to be court staff, with the exception of Solicitor Moore who was seated at the Counsel's Bench. There was no sign of Michael or anyone else who might claim an interest in the Estate. By the time Will sat down in the benches reserved for the public, he had run the gamut of emotions and had resigned himself to accepting anything or nothing.

Finally the judge, wearing a white wig and flowing black robes, entered the court room. The clerk struck his gavel and those in attendance rose to their feet. Upon rising, Will's composure immediately disappeared. His heart began to race and sweat broke out on his upper lip. He felt nauseous and had to grip the railing in front of him to steady himself. He looked around to see if others had noticed, but no one seemed to. After preliminary matters were completed, the judge directed the clerk to read the Last Testament of Thomas Desmond, Deceased. Will listened intently as the clerk read from what appeared to be a five or six page document. The first two pages contained legal definitions and explanatory comments for what was to follow. When the clerk finally came to the paragraphs detailing how the estate was to be distributed, Will thought he might faint.

"Title and interest . . . in and to my entire Estate . . . to my beloved son, Jeremiah," the clerk read.

That was all Will heard. The words struck him like a club. All of his efforts had produced nothing but the hatred of his neighbors. Will was numb. He wasn't angry, he was afraid. He could not imagine how he was going to survive, now hated by his own townspeople for having forsaken his culture and publicly renounced his Catholic faith. He heard the clerk drone on but the words didn't register. He was penniless before the reading and he was penniless now.

An annoying hammering sound disturbed him, and he quickly came to his senses when he saw the clerk pounding the gavel and scowling directly at him. Will realized the proceedings had concluded and the Judge was leaving the courtroom. Then realizing why the clerk was continuing to glare at him, he sprung to his feet and stood in deference to the departing Judge.

Solicitor Moore then approached him and suggested they discuss the will in the conference room. Will could see little to discuss but followed him into a room off the courtroom where they both took their seats.

Moore had a copy of the will with him, and he first explained the procedure for distributing assets of the estate and the time frame within which this would normally be accomplished. He then looked up at Will and said, "Now we're going to need a death certificate on Jeremiah. We can't transfer title of the Estate to you and Michael until that is filed and approved by the court."

Will looked at him and suddenly realized that he was the only person in Kinsale, or Ireland for that matter, who knew that Jeremiah was not dead. No one else had heard from him in years, including Michael. Will himself had not heard from Jeremiah since he had told him it would be best if he severed ties with the family. He sat dumbly listening to Solicitor Moore explain why the death certificate was required and how Will could go about obtaining one. His father's will had stated that the property went to Jeremiah only on the condition that he was living at the time of Thomas Desmond's death. But if he was not living, the property would then go to Will and Michael.

"Consequently," Moore explained, "it will be necessary to contact the court house in the town where Jeremiah lived and obtain the necessary document."

Will made no comment. He only nodded as Moore explained the procedure. When Moore finished, he asked if Will had any questions.

"No... I don't think so. I'll have to get that certificate... Ah, is there some way I can have a copy of the will?"

Moore handed him the copy he had been reading from and said, "This is your copy. I have another in my office. If you have any questions, you know where to find me."

Will walked out of the court house in a daze. "What am I going to do about Jeremiah?" he thought to himself. "If I can satisfy the court that Jeremiah is dead, I will still have to deal with Michael. He and I would then equally share the Estate, including the small farm."

As Will walked back to the farm, his thoughts ran in circles, but he knew that he could not deal with Michael on a long term basis. He would have to do something about him. As long as Michael was alive, Will knew that it would be a bitter contest between the two for control of the property. When he reached his hut, he had his answer. Michael would have to go.

Ireland is where strange tales begin
and happy endings are possible.

CHAPTER 5

The Land War had accelerated in Ireland with considerable blood being shed between the Irish peasants and the British troops, many of whom were of Irish extraction. Homes were being burned and there were frequent assassinations occurring on both sides.

Michael Desmond was known to be involved in the burning of British owned buildings and homes. Due to his involvement, he was a likely target of British death squad reprisals, which afforded Will a golden opportunity. On the night of August 14, 1879, while leaving his small hut on the Desmond farm, Michael was shot to death by an unknown assailant. When his body was discovered by a passerby, he was found with a rifle, ammunition, and documents that indicated he was on his way to participate in an IRB military operation. His death surprised nobody, and the matter was quickly closed by the British authorities. Will had an ironclad alibi, too; he was traveling to Bandon at the time of the murder to purchase farm equipment and was not considered a suspect.

In the days following Michael's death and burial in the Catholic cemetery, Will concentrated his thoughts on what to do about Jeremiah. His immediate reaction after talking with Moore in the court house was to file the necessary document attesting to the death of his brother, Jeremiah. But if Jeremiah subsequently surfaced, Will would lose everything and, most likely, be sent to prison. On the other hand, if he didn't try to capitalize on the fact that everyone thought Jeremiah was dead anyway, he would be doomed to living a life of abject poverty as a common Irish peasant. He decided to take the gamble.

The letter he wrote to Jeremiah explained that his father had passed away and that Michael had been murdered, apparently by Fenians. Will had never mentioned Michael's association with the IRB in any of his letters. He added that both he and Michael had converted to Anglicanism to please their father before he died. Their father, in return, had rewarded Will's faithfulness by leaving him the entire Estate. Will closed the letter by criticizing Jeremiah for leaving the family to seek his fortune in the United States and for taking up with Fenian interests there. Will told Jeremiah never to contact him again. As far as Will was concerned, Jeremiah was dead. As he sealed the letter, Will knew there was always the risk that

Jeremiah might return to Ireland for a visit, and if he did, he would learn the truth of what had taken place. Fortunately, the odds of that occurring were very slim. Will personally knew of only one person who had left the Kinsale area and returned, and that person was wealthy and could afford it. The trip involved an arduous, expensive voyage and Jeremiah's letters indicated he enjoyed only very modest means. Will would assume the risk.

Before mailing the letter to Jeremiah, Will had taken steps to obtain Jeremiah's death certificate. He had obtained the name and address of an attorney in Chicago, Illinois, and had written him a letter requesting his services in locating the death certificate of his brother, Jeremiah Desmond, born sometime around 1835 and believed to have passed away sometime before May 12, 1879, somewhere in Illinois or Wisconsin. In order for the property to pass to Will, it was necessary to find a Jeremiah Desmond that had died sometime before his father died. With the millions of Irish that had emigrated during the Famine of the forties, there had to be hundreds of Jeremiah Desmonds in the States. That was a very common Irish name. All Will needed was one Jeremiah Desmond who fit the approximate age of his brother and who had conveniently died before May 12, 1879.

After mailing the letter to the attorney, Will waited several weeks before receiving a reply. The return letter stated that the attorney had located six possible deceased Jeremiah Desmonds within the presumed age group. The likely candidate's dates of death were listed. After reviewing the information provided, Will circled the name of one. He then wrote back to the attorney, included the required fee for services, and requested the death certificate for the Jeremiah Desmond who had passed away in Columbus, Wisconsin, February 20, 1879. He stated that an additional five dollars, U.S., would be sent forthwith upon prompt receipt of the certificate.

After a delay of several weeks, Will received the requested death certificate, properly authenticated and stamped by the Columbia County Probate Court. Without delay, Will delivered it to Solicitor Moore. On May 12, 1880, the Surrogate Court of County Cork, under the signature of Judge Haverstock, issued its decree transferring all property listed in the Estate of Thomas Desmond to his sole living heir and beneficiary, his son, William Desmond.

Will Desmond opened the main entry door to his new, huge home in the late afternoon of the same day that he had signed the decree. He placed the few personal belongings he wished to retain from his former life on the couch in the foyer. He stripped off his worn, tattered work clothes and stood naked, laughing and then dancing through the rooms on the ground floor. Out of breath, he washed himself using the fragrant soap lying in the dish and then walked through the large kitchen, which was five times the size of his former hut, and out onto the cool grass. He was beside himself with his success at having taken over the Estate.

He stood there, naked, urinating and surveying the vast grounds of what was now the Will Desmond Estate. He walked back in the home, threw his clothes into the trash and went to his father's closet. He selected the finest shirt and trousers he could find and topped it off with an expensive felt hat that was one of many on the upper shelf in the closet. He then searched through the large cabinets in his father's dressing room and found stockings, which he had never worn in his life. He put these on and found a pair of expensive shoes to complete his wardrobe. Everything he wore was a bit too large for him, but his exuberance overcame such minor problems. Later, sitting in the study and surveying the large collection of bound books on the shelves surrounding the room, he smoked one of his father's fine American cigars. A treat he had never experienced. He found a bottle of Irish whiskey, filled a glass tumbler, leaned back in the soft leather chair, and tried to relax. He would have, except the image of Jeremiah Desmond kept interrupting his reverie.

CHAPTER 6

Quinn looked out the window of the aircraft but could see nothing but black sky overhead and a gray mass appearing below. "At least it's not storming out. If it was, I would be a nervous wreck," Quinn thought.

The pilot came over the intercom and announced that they would be landing in Dublin in just under three hours. The flight from Atlanta was scheduled for seven and a half hours, and they were running ahead of schedule by at least a half an hour. "The west winds must have been stronger than they anticipated. Well, the sooner the better," Quinn thought.

He had tried to get some sleep on the plane but could not get comfortable enough with his long legs pushing up against the seat in front of him, and he was stiff and sore from sitting in the same position so long. He had run farther and faster than usual that morning and was now paying the price. "Not bad, though, I'm sixty-five and still at it," he thought. His regular running program had paid off. He was proud of himself that he had regularly maintained his tall, thin build and felt fortunate that he still had a full head of silver-gray hair. One of his lady friends had said that it gave him a very distinguished look.

Quinn had resolved to enjoy life to the fullest ever since he had closed his law office in Atlanta and had retired from the profession. The trip to Ireland was his first overseas vacation in what he called "the good life." He had practiced law by himself in a small office above a hardware store since he was a young man. He referred to himself, among friends, as a member of a dying breed, the sole practitioner who handled a variety of small cases and who did not fill out a time sheet at the end of the day. He had never made much money but that was not important to Quinn. He was more interested in living life as he wanted rather than having his schedule dictated by the pursuit of the American dollar.

He was not said to be a hard worker, but he was certainly not lazy. He just had a variety of interests and constant work was not one of them. He was a lifelong avid reader and had always thoroughly enjoyed his running program. Had his parent's estate not provided him with a modest income, he would not have been able to retire, even at sixty-five.

The woman sitting next to him folded her newspaper and put it into the seat pocket. Turning off her reading lamp, she looked over at Quinn. "Is this a business trip for you or otherwise?"

"Just sort of a tourist thing," Quinn replied with a smile.

He had told only a few friends what the real purpose of his trip was. To everyone else he simply said that he was taking a vacation to Ireland and that he may travel over to London if time permitted. He was embarrassed to tell them that he was going to Ireland to learn what had happened to family members who had not made the passage to America during the famine of the mid-1800s. He did not know why such a trip sounded like a foolish notion to him, but it did.

The woman returned the smile and added, "You'll enjoy Ireland. I have a son there. He works for Intel, so I come and visit him about once a year. Have you been there before?"

"No. It's my first trip. I'm looking forward to it."

The woman persisted, "Do you have family in Ireland? So many Americans do, you know?"

"My mother's family all came from Ireland, so maybe I do. I have no idea."

"Oh, that's interesting. You should find that out. I don't know how you go about doing that, but I'm sure there are people there who could help."

"Maybe I'll look into that." Quinn smiled again recalling the hundreds of hours of research he had done over the past year.

"What part of Ireland was her family from?" she continued.

"Down in Cork somewhere. I'm not sure. I was told they were from the area around Kinsale on the coastline of County Cork, but I'm not totally sure if that's correct." He had learned this from Sean, and until he found out otherwise he would assume that his friend was correct.

Thinking about Sean brought back painful memories of the evening he was killed. Quinn and Sean had been in the Irish Pub in Atlanta, just off Peachtree Street. Quinn could see Sean now, sitting next to him at their table just off the stage during one of the band's breaks. Sean had lit another cigarette just after he had snuffed out the last one in the ash tray. Quinn could re-envision every detail of Sean's appearance that night, his thick black hair in disarray like usual, his wrinkled, dingy, white shirt frayed at the collar, his only tie knotted loosely at the collar. Quinn smiled to himself when he thought about Sean's thick glasses with the badly scratched lenses and the broken frame repaired with a narrow strip of duct tape securing the left temple. Sean's characteristically deceptive comic appearance masked his very sharp mind. In the empty chair alongside Sean lay his pride and joy, a beautifully crafted fiddle, his sole possession in life that may have actually had some value.

Aside from his obvious disrespect for material well being, Quinn saw Sean as one deeply entrenched in the pursuit of justice for the truly downtrodden of the world. Unlike many with similar interests, he did not seem to harbor any desire to benefit himself by what he called an "equal distribution of economic resources." Sean had always seemed to be quite content with what he had been able to acquire in his thirty plus years of living on the planet.

Sean's politics were another matter. There were no limits to the energy he was willing to expend in the pursuit of his political goals. Irish Nationalism was no doubt much dearer to him than any other interest in his life and, as Quinn had come to realize, the very driving force of his existence. Quinn had known about Sean's strong Republican views from the start, but over time he had come to the further conclusion that Sean was not just an expatriate Irishman teaching Gaelic at the University and playing his fiddle at a small pub in Atlanta for a few bucks. His politics was another side to Sean that Quinn slowly became aware of as their friendship grew.

Not until their last conversation did Quinn grasp the depth of Sean's dark side. Sean had never admitted or implied in any way that he had any involvements in Atlanta other than his open and obvious pursuits at the University and the Pub. Quinn had spent a great deal of time with Sean over the past year talking about virtually everything from politics to music to sports and not infrequently to women, but now, and ever since that last night, he wasn't sure that he had ever known the real Sean.

Quinn now knew at least that Sean had tried to keep their friendship separate from his other life. Quinn had only caught hints of another side to Sean through very occasional lapses in his conversation or from what he had seen when they were both in the Pub. Young Irishmen would occasionally come up to Sean and whisper something into his ear or hand him notes that quickly disappeared into his pockets. Quinn considered it none of his business, whatever it was. He enjoyed the intelligent, musical side of his friend and ignored the rest.

Quinn sat back in the comfortable airplane seat, relaxed by the soothing hum of the airplane's engines, but he couldn't sleep. He kept going over his last conversation with Sean in the pub, as he had so many times since. He could remember almost word for word what they had said to each other.

As the band's first break came to an end and the band members began reassembling on the small stage, Sean had taken a final drag from his cigarette, snuffed it out in the ash tray, and finished off the stout that remained in his glass. He checked his watch and looked over at Quinn. "You're not going to blow out of here right away are you?"

"Fairly soon. It's getting late. Almost nine-thirty. Not as young as you, my friend."

"Well, hang around until the next break. There's something I want to go over with you."

"What the hell's that?" Quinn asked.

"Just hang around. Won't be over thirty minutes. Get another beer. You could use the weight anyway."

Sean stood up and carefully lifted his fiddle and bow from the chair. He took his position up on the stage with the other three fellows who were preparing their instruments, the concertina, drums, and pipe. Soon they were underway as the rapid triple time beat of an old Irish jig replaced table conversation, and everyone in the pub began clapping along to the rhythm of the music.

Quinn ordered another pint of Guinness, which he nursed through a set of traditional Irish music. After the set, Sean returned to the table. He carefully stored his fiddle and bow on the empty chair and sat down as the bartender brought him a pint.

"Ok, Sean. What is it that you wanted to tell me?"

Just then, one of Sean's fellow Irishmen came to the table and the two engaged in a whispered conversation for the next few minutes. At one point in the conversation, Sean paused for a moment, stared at the wall, and tapped his finger on the table as he apparently mulled over what he had just been told.

This was not a particularly unusual occurrence for Quinn to witness. It was these rather mysterious communications that would occur once or twice an evening when Quinn was at the table with Sean that had convinced Quinn that Sean and his Irish born friends were involved in activities that he, Quinn, would be better off not knowing about.

When it became apparent to Quinn that the break time was rapidly running out, he spoke up. "Sean, I've got to get going. What was it you were going to tell me?"

"Oh, I'm sorry Quinn. Business you know." Sean waved off the Irishman. "If it isn't one thing, it's another." Looking at his watch, Sean continued, "Now, I'm a little short on time. Let me just say . . . I don't know how to bring this up. I've been hearing some things that I should talk to you about."

"Like what?" Quinn asked.

Sean straightened up in his chair, looked over to a group of his friends, and said, "This family history project of yours is . . . ah . . . it's causing some people some concern."

"You've got to be kidding?" Quinn stared at Sean in amused disbelief.

"I'm not, but I don't have time to go into it right now."

"What the hell are you talking about, Sean?"

Sean bit his lips as he thought how to best answer Quinn's question. "Sometimes innocent appearing things can be risky, and we don't know it. That might be the case here. I don't know. I just don't have time to go into it right now. Let's talk about it tomorrow."

Quinn moved his pint aside and leaned closer to Sean. "Sean, I want to talk about it tonight. Does this have anything to do with the break in at my house or having my computer ripped off? I've been wondering about that."

Sean just sat in his chair without responding. One of the other band members walked over to the table and tapped him on the shoulder to let him know they were over time on their break. Sean stood up and picked up his fiddle and bow, but he was obviously thinking of how to reply to Quinn. He finally said, "Quinn, in my line of work, there are many things going on that I just can't talk about. That's just the way things are. I hope you understand."

Then Sean leaned down very close to Quinn and whispered, "When I'm done here, I'll call you from a pay phone, and I'll . . . ah . . . I'll tell you why you are a matter of interest to some people and why you have to be careful. Gotta go."

Quinn had gone over Sean's last words hundreds of times since then, searching for clues as to what he was going to tell him. Whatever it was must have been so sensitive that he didn't want to use his house phone. He was obviously concerned about a tap.

Quinn was deeply concerned about a connection between what Sean was going to tell him that night and his murder just a few hours later. Quinn was fairly sure that Sean was heavily involved with what was left of the Irish Nationalist Party and, God knows, they still had their problems over there. Quinn had believed that the so called "Irish Problem" had been solved but was aware that there were still radical fringe elements still active and that Sean must have been a part of one. He was probably playing with fire and may have been burned in the process.

Regardless of the reason behind his friend's murder, Quinn would miss him. They had become good friends since meeting almost a year ago, and Quinn had enjoyed the evenings spent in the pub listening to Sean play the fiddle. He remembered that he had to call Sean's former wife when he arrived in Ireland. Quinn had set aside time to visit with her and Sean's two boys when he was in Dublin. He knew Sean would have wanted him to do that.

CHAPTER 7

It was several years after his grandfather had died when Quinn became somewhat curious about life in the old country. By then, his grandfather's family had all moved out of Minnesota, and his mother was living at her own house in Atlanta, near where Quinn practiced law. When Quinn had questioned her about her parent's lives in Ireland, his mother could not remember many of the details. She was up in years and could not recall even where they had lived, other than to say it was somewhere in County Cork. It was only some years later when he was getting close to retirement that a conversation with his then widowed mother, living in a nursing home at the time, sparked his interest and set him off on his journey to learn about his family's past.

It happened on one of Quinn's last visits to the nursing home before his mother died. She was lying in her bed, and they were talking about her family. She said she regretted that she did not know more about her parent's life in Ireland and those left behind. She mentioned that there were other Desmonds that had stayed behind in Ireland. This triggered an interest in Quinn's mind and set him on a course of learning about his Desmond family line. Quinn could not draw on other Desmonds in the States for assistance because his mother, just like Quinn, was an only child. He was now the sole remaining descendant of his grandfather, Jeremiah Desmond.

After his mother passed away, Quinn inherited his parent's very modest estate, which included the home he was now living in as well as a small mutual fund account. This, combined with the very limited savings he had accumulated over the years and his Social Security payment, afforded him a reasonable amount of freedom to do what he liked provided that he used a reasonable amount of common sense. It was this freedom that enabled him to pursue the inquiry into his past and satisfy a curiosity that had been building over a period of time.

Just as the hum of the airplane's huge, jet engines were beginning to put him to sleep, Quinn thought about the fact that it had been almost a year to the day since he had begun his search into his family's past. Since then, he had scoured the local genealogy libraries for information that might relate to the Desmond family, and he had accumulated quite a bit of information on Irish emigration but had found nothing in the libraries that could tie him specifically into Jeremiah Desmond's family in Ireland. It was a stroke of luck and possibly foresight on the part of Jeremiah and his mother that he came into possession of some papers that would provide him with many of the answers he had so desperately sought.

When his mother moved into the nursing home and Quinn moved into her house, she left him all of her possessions, including many boxes of photographs and personal items that she had accumulated through the years. Included among these items was an old wooden crate with leather hinges and faded stenciled lettering on the side. The crate contained personal papers and photographs. After noticing the crate in the basement one day, mostly because of its obvious age, Quinn made it a point to go through the contents in the following days. But it was not until several weeks after his mother had died that Quinn again came across the crate.

When Quinn wiped off the dust and opened the crate, he was struck by the musty odor of the old letters and papers that had apparently been placed there by his Grandpa Jeremiah and passed down to Quinn's mother.

One packet of letters especially caught his eye. They were tied together with a brown string that was stiff and easily broken when Quinn untied the knot. The letters were brittle and discolored from age, but all were still legible and, from what Quinn could determine, seemed to be addressed to "Jerm." Quinn assumed this meant his grandfather, Jeremiah. Quinn struggled to read the signature because of the broad ink flourishes of the handwriting, but the signature was the same on all the letters. He presumed that the language the letters were written in was Gaelic, because, with the exception of a few English words, he could not understand a word of what was written. The letters were undated, not enclosed in envelopes, and did not appear to evidence any return address of any kind.

Quinn handled the packet of old letters very carefully. He slowly unfolded each letter so as not to break apart the brittle paper on which the strange words were written. He knew this was a rare find, one that could potentially bring him answers to the many questions running through his mind. The letters most certainly had to have been written by Desmonds in the old country. He could only estimate their age from the appearance and condition of the paper, but they were obviously written a very long time ago. He set the letters aside with care, thinking that he would locate a translator in the morning.

Most of the other items in the crate were of no particular interest to Quinn, but a few were. He found his mother's diary, her marriage record from St.Patrick's Church in Birch Coulee, Minnesota, Quinn's birth announcement, and obituary notices on the deaths of his father, John Parker, his grandfather, Jeremiah Desmond, and one for his grandmother, Eileen Farrell Desmond. He found these to be of considerable interest and set them aside for future reference.

He sat in the basement going over the papers until the late afternoon light began to fade, at which time he replaced the contents of the box, put his mother's diary in his jacket pocket, and carefully carried the packet of old letters up to his study. He set the letters on his bookcase and continued to read his mother's diary until the early morning hours.

The day after his initial review of his mother's collected papers; Quinn went on a run around the lakes, thinking the whole time about his family's history. The conversation with his mother and the mysterious contents found in the packet of old letters had caused the seed of curiosity about his ancestors to take root. He knew very little about how one went about tracing family history, but he would learn. It would be interesting and, if need be, he could always take a trip over to Ireland and find someone there who could help him locate his family. It could turn out to be a most memorable experience.

In the following days he drafted a summary of his family history as he understood it and closed with a comment that he was his grandfather's only living descendant and that his grandfather had come from County Cork. That was all that was known about Jeremiah Desmond's life in Ireland, other than the fact that he had emigrated during the Great Irish Famine. No other relatives had emigrated with Jeremiah, as far as Quinn knew. He thought that these few facts might be of some assistance to an interpreter of the letters if, and when, Quinn was able to find one.

Two weeks passed before Quinn located a Gaelic speaking interpreter at the University. The following day, he gave the letters and the family history summary he had prepared to the language department secretary, because the translator was busy teaching a class. Quinn felt a little nervous about leaving the letters with a third person, but she assured him they would be delivered safely to Mr. Flanagan. While he was at the University library, Quinn found a gazetteer of townships in Minnesota and learned that the community of Birch Coulee no longer existed other than as a geographic boundary in Renville County, so the chances of finding any families still residing there was not at all likely.

Seeing the reference to Renville County gave Quinn an idea. In no time he was on the phone with one of the volunteers in the Renville Historical Society office. She advised Quinn that they had extensive collections of various family materials from the Birch Coulee area and that he was welcome to visit any time to go through the files. Quinn wasted no time in accepting the invitation and by the next afternoon, he was on a Delta flight to Minneapolis. The following morning, after a long drive in a rental car, he was in the Olivia Public Library where he was directed to the Renville County Historical Society's Genealogy Room. The room was small, not much more than ten by ten feet, but as he soon found out, it contained a wealth of information. He was greeted by a kindly appearing, grey haired woman, who introduced herself as Helen Smith.

"Can I help you find anything?" Helen asked.

"Yes, I hope you can." Quinn explained to Mrs. Smith who he was and that he was interested in the Desmond family who had lived in Birch Coulee Township back in the mid to late 1800s.

Mrs. Smith was silent for a moment as she tried to recall the Desmond name to determine if she had anything on it that may have been compiled by other researchers. She shook her head, "No, the Desmond name is not familiar to me, but I could be wrong. We might have something on it. Let me show you what we do have and then you can get comfortable and see what you can find."

Mrs. Smith explained the filing system to him and then assisted him in locating the files dealing with families in the Birch Coulee area. She also showed Quinn the reference file on old newspaper clippings containing anything relating to the residents then living in the County. In a very short period of time, Quinn had enough materials awaiting his review to keep him occupied for a couple of days. He settled back in the chair and began reading one of the local histories that was type written, single-spaced, on yellowed, dried out paper entitled, "The First Settlers."

After two days spent poring over manuscripts, musty old newspapers, and other materials that had very likely not seen the light of day for many years, Quinn's eyes had about given out as had his writing hand. With his notebook almost filled and his briefcase stuffed with Xerox copies of newspaper obituaries, birth and death notices, marriage announcements, and other references to anyone bearing the name Desmond, Quinn thanked Mrs. Smith, left a donation for the Society, checked out of his motel, and headed for Minneapolis.

On the drive back from Olivia to Minneapolis, Quinn's mind was numb from absorbing so much information, some relevant to what he was looking for but most undoubtedly bearing no connection whatsoever to his Desmond family history. Unfortunately, he had to review each and every piece of paper to be sure they were not the all-encompassing treasure that would answer every one of his questions. He had commented on that to

Mrs. Smith, and she affirmed that it was the search for the golden egg with all the answers that kept genealogists returning. She told Quinn that she could tell that he was now hooked on a hobby that he would thoroughly enjoy.

In the coming days, Quinn systematized his efforts by computerizing the information he had collected that seemed to be the most relevant so far. He had purchased a laptop computer and software that greatly simplified his record keeping and contributed to a more efficient use of his time in the library. In order to be on the safe side, he transcribed everything to two identical floppy discs that he stored in different locations in the event that someone might choose to borrow the laptop on a permanent basis. He was also able to obtain Federal census records through the 1800s from the Mormon Library in Atlanta, and that was a tremendous help because he was able to follow his grandfather's census data from the time of his arrival in New York to his death in Minnesota.

In reviewing the materials he had obtained in the Renville County Library, he realized that virtually all of the Irish families in the Birch Coulee area had emigrated from Ireland in the late 1840s, during the Famine years. They came into Renville County and settled in close proximity to one another in Birch Coulee Township. Quinn concluded that it was not a coincidence that the Irish settled so close to one another, rather they had done so by design. They more than likely knew one another from the old country and had sought out familiar faces in deciding where to live in the new country. Following this assumption, Quinn made note of their names in the hopes that it would assist him in locating the homeland of his grandfather in Ireland. If he could determine the town or village the others had come from, that could provide him with the answer to his grandfather's birthplace.

It had been over a month since Quinn had dropped the packet of Gaelic letters off at the University, but he still did not have the results back from the translator. He was informed by the secretary at the University that the Gaelic language instructor had taken a sabbatical to Ireland shortly after receiving the assignment and had neglected to tell Quinn. By the time the translator returned, Quinn was more than eager to find out what information the letters contained and, furthermore, he was very concerned that the letters had not been misplaced in the interim.

When he called the translator, Quinn had difficulty understanding his heavy Irish brogue, but he assured Quinn that the letters were safe and that the translations would be complete the following Wednesday at the latest. Concluding the call, the translator said, "These are very interesting letters,

Mr. Parker. They raise some questions that I'm sure you're going to want to check out. I don't have time to go into that now because I have a class in just a few minutes. See you Wednesday."

In the intervening days, as Quinn waited for Wednesday to arrive, he became more and more anxious to know what was written in the letters. What could this Flanagan be talking about that he would want to check out? Quinn could only hope that the letters would connect him to his grandfather's townland in Ireland. Unless they provided a clue, he knew there was little chance of ever learning anything about his grandfather's life before his arrival in the States in 1850.

Quinn had learned from his research in the libraries that if he did not know the townland or parish that his grandfather had emigrated from, there was virtually no way to find him in any of the old Irish records. The only exception to that rule was a particularly unique surname, and, unfortunately, Desmond was a very common Irish name. As Quinn waited for Wednesday to come around, his curiosity regarding the contents of the letters grew. He could only hope that they would provide him with the information that he needed to go forward with his research.

CHAPTER 8

The two men sat at a small table in the corner of the pub farthest from the noise of the crowd gathered at the bar. They spoke in hushed tones so that others seated at tables nearby could not hear what they were saying. Even if they had, one would need to understand Gaelic to follow the conversation.

"How did the trip go? Did you get the job done, Sean?"

"Of course. Look at these." Sean took a packet of letters from his brief case and handed them to his companion. "Be careful, they are very brittle. Tell me which ones are not genuine. I will tell you. Four of the ten are forgeries. Can you tell me which ones?"

His companion carefully compared all ten of the letters. "They all appear to me to have been written by the same person. I am certainly not an expert, but there seems to be no difference whatsoever in the paper, ink, or handwriting. Even the flourishes in the capital letters are absolutely identical. How did you do this?"

"Our people lined up everyone we needed even before I arrived in Dublin with the originals. First of all, three of the guys in the Dublin office and I figured out what we wanted the letters to say, to bring about the desired effect. I knew a lot of the background, having grown up down there, but we had to get the basic facts confirmed and that was all done before I got there. Then we gave that information to our contacts, who have knowledge of the customs and practices prevalent in Kinsale and Cork in the 1880s time frame. Those people put what we wanted the letters to say into the proper words, phrases, dialect, idiom, that sort of stuff, so that what went into the letters would ring true to an expert who knew what to look for. At the same time our staff people located paper that we could use to write the letters."

"Where the hell did you get that?"

Sean laughed. "Joe, let me tell you. That was the hardest part. They finally found it in London. A collector there had some sheets of paper that seemed to me to have come off the same run as the originals. They made paper differently back then and you can't just duplicate paper. We were lucky there. Look at it. You can't tell the difference. The ink was a problem too, but we could mix and match that a bit. We had to be careful on that too because you can chemically compare inks and we had to be sure the forgeries would pass that test. I am told ours will pass. They look the same to me. Then we got to the hard part."

Joe interrupted, "I was wondering about that. Where did you find the guy that did the writing?"

"Let me tell you, Joe. The Dublin office has people they can call on to do anything. I was impressed. Apparently, they have a number of guys that can reproduce virtually anything and no one can tell the writing is not genuine. But first, for this job, you need to duplicate the pen, or whatever they called it in 1880. I learned something here. They didn't have fountain pens in 1880. They came later. They did have ink pens, you know, that you dip. Our guys had to actually make an ink pen that would compare favorably to that used on the original letters. Now an expert can examine the tracings of the pen under a scope and note the difference between the originals and the forgeries, but, so what. You can always say the writer just used a different pen. That argument might also cover any minor noted differences in the paper or the ink. The handwriting, though, has to be identical."

Joe looked carefully at the writing on the letters that Sean identified as forgeries. "Whoever wrote these had a cool hand. No tremors show up and even the pressure on the pen for the various letters is identical with the originals. Where'd he come from?"

"Joe, would you believe he has a cigar shop on O'Connell Street. Sort of a hobby. The INA uses him all the time for this sort of thing. Perfect job, eh?"

"Yeah, Sean, talent lies in strange places. You know, Sean, this guy's grandfather could be the right one. His letters don't preclude that possibility."

"Right on. That's what makes it so perfect. The original letters use the right names for the brothers but don't give the father's name, or the two wives names or the Englishman's name. Nor is there any mention of Kinsale, or even Cork. Only that the writer's father married an Englishman's wife and inherited some property. No description. They do say the one brother was an Anglican and was killed by Fenians. That doesn't match with what we know about the family. What got my attention when I first read the letters was the similarity of the brother's names and the fact the old man got some property from marrying an English widow. I figured it was something we could run with and so did the guys in Dublin."

"Looks good to me, Sean. When do you meet your guy?"

"Tomorrow at three."

CHAPTER 9

It was 3 o'clock sharp, Wednesday afternoon, when Quinn rapped on the door to the language office cubicle with the name Sean Flanagan scrawled with a black felt marker across the top of the frosted window. A voice with a distinct Irish accent came from the other side of the door, "Come in."

Quinn opened the door to the minuscule office piled to the ceiling with books, papers and cardboard boxes of varying sizes presumably filled with more books and papers. He was immediately struck by the acrid smell of old tobacco smoke that exuded out of the walls.

As small as the office was, Quinn could hardly see Sean Flanagan sitting behind what Quinn assumed was a desk piled high with books on top and more books stacked all around it from the floor up. He appeared to have carved out a small cave for himself, surrounded by books with bindings turned this way and that. Order was apparently not important. Quinn estimated Sean's age at around forty, give or take a few years. He was clearly not one to place too much attention on his appearance or on his physical well being. He had a pale, thin look about him that suggested to Quinn that physical exercise was not one of his interests, and the nicotine stains on Sean's fingers confirmed that opinion.

Quinn's survey of the room and its occupant was interrupted by a surprisingly strong voice coming from the mouth of the book cave. "Have a chair. You must be Mr. Parker?"

Without waiting for Quinn's response, Flanagan continued, "Interesting letters. I don't get to read old Gaelic that often and some of the words and phrases were a bit of a problem. Everybody thinks Gaelic is Gaelic and it may have been that way years ago, but the Irish changed all that."

Flanagan spoke with a clipped, rapid pace, as though he was in a hurry to get the words out, which forced Quinn to stand with his head cocked so as not to miss what it was the speaker was telling him.

"Every region made its own changes to the language so that someone from Galway couldn't understand someone from Cork. Probably did it on purpose. Who knows? Better yet, who cares? Anyway, I think I have what you wanted me to do, more or less anyway."

Quinn stood in front of the professor's desk, not saying anything but absorbing what was in his own mind a living confirmation of his concept of the typical college professor. Hair all over the place, large glasses with the broken temple of the frame taped, a gaunt look on his face, which further bespoke his lack of interest in healthy living. He was most likely tenured, but his workplace was in total disarray. He was probably very intelligent and overpaid for the amount of work he did, which also allowed him to make a little extra on the side. Sean Flanagan interrupted Quinn's reverie, "Well, are you going to stand there, sit, or what? Have a chair and get out your check book. The kids have to eat, you know."

Quinn sat down, somewhat taken aback. "Sure. What do I owe you?"

Sean Flanagan leaned back in his chair and adjusted his glasses, which kept slipping down his nose due to the fact the duct tape was unwinding from the broken temple. "Well, let's see. Being your typical European socialist, I like to charge what the market will bear, but. . . ." Flanagan eyed Quinn's worn tweed jacket with the faded leather elbow patches and went on, "Sometimes that just doesn't hack it."

Quinn caught the jab and with an appraising look at Flanagan's soup stained, antiquated tie, he returned to filling out the check, and said, "Nice tie."

Sean Flanagan gave a hearty laugh, apparently having received similar comments in the past.

"Touché. It's my survival tie. I could live for weeks with this thing. You know they make us wear a tie when we teach here? Who the hell cares? I could go into the classroom without my pants on as long as I'm wearing a tie. I swear to God, if they didn't pay me I wouldn't do it."

With that, Flanagan again rolled his head back and let out another hearty laugh. As he did so, his glasses fell down over his nose, but with a quick, expert jerk of his head, he snapped them back into their proper location.

Quinn could not suppress a smile as he stared at the professor while trying to evaluate whether this fellow knew what he was doing or not. He was sort of a strange acting guy, but there was something likeable and, to some extent, even reliable about him. Maybe it was his office that gave him credibility. He either read a lot or just liked to keep books piled high in his office. Quinn would give him the benefit of the doubt, and assuming he had read just a fraction of the books and materials stacked on the floor, desk, and what were presumably tables, this guy was definitely a reader. That impressed Quinn, regardless of everything else that he was observing about Sean Flanagan.

Quinn loved books. He liked the feel of the pages and the smell of the bindings. He enjoyed books so much that he could spot a true book lover by the careful, almost caressing way they turned the pages. He did note that most of the books, whose bindings he could see stacked about the room, had a political tone. *The Life of a Rebel: Che Guevara* and *Redefining Democracy* both had bookmarks about half way through them, as did many of the other books stacked around the room. Quinn surmised that maybe he was one of those people who liked to read a number of books at one time.

Glancing at his watch for the date, Quinn filled the check blank out with the exception of the amount.

"Well, moving right along, what are the damages," Quinn asked.

Sean Flanagan leaned forward with an almost serious look on his face. "I take it you are in a hurry. That is unfortunate, because I found your letters very interesting. The summary was interesting as well. If you have a minute or two, and, if you don't mind sharing the information, where did the letters come from?"

Flanagan peered over the top of his glasses, which had slid down the slope of his nose, giving him a bit of a comical appearance. But the look of intense interest in his eyes left no doubt that he was very eager to learn the answer to his question.

Quinn paused for a moment as he leaned back in his chair and reflected on how to respond. He was in no hurry whatsoever, but he was not inclined to converse openly with others, particularly strangers, regarding his new interest. He was a bit embarrassed to admit that he was studying his family history, as though it was something only grey-haired, old ladies did after their husbands passed away. While he collected his thoughts, Quinn explained to Flanagan that he had found the letters in a box of his mother's things and was merely curious about what they said. He assumed they were addressed to his grandfather, but from whom he did not know. His curiosity had led him to bring the packet to Flanagan for translation. As his voice trailed off, he said that aside from that he had no particular reason for pursuing the matter.

Flanagan seemed to be far more interested in Quinn's family history than Quinn expected. Answering question after question, Quinn related to Flanagan virtually every fact concerning his mother's family in Ireland that he was aware of up to that point. Flanagan pressed him for detail after detail concerning the Desmond family and seemed to have little, if any, interest in the Parker line. Flanagan repeatedly asked questions concerning the fact that Quinn Parker was the sole living descendant of Jeremiah Desmond and that there was absolutely nothing known regarding his grandfather's life in Ireland other than what was in the summary. He almost appeared relieved by Quinn's responses. Finally, Quinn asked him if he had Desmond relatives since he seemed so curious about them. Flanagan seemed to flush and stammer a bit, then referred to the packet of Gaelic letters, saying that they had raised some issues that brought the Desmond Clan to mind. Quinn wondered what that was but figured he could look at that in the translations.

Flanagan eyed Quinn for a moment and adjusting his glasses said, "Here are the translations attached to each letter. You can go through them and form your own opinions regarding their contents. But if you want, I'll explain how I reviewed them and what it looks like to me."

Quinn nodded, agreeing to Flanagan's suggestion. Obviously the professor, being familiar with the history and culture of Ireland, would be better equipped to read between the lines and would not miss whatever meanings were lost in translation. "Yes, by all means. Please do."

Flanagan leaned back in his chair, opened a drawer and took out a battered pipe, a bag of tobacco, and a metal tool of some sort that Quinn assumed had something to do with the pipe. "Do you mind?" Sean asked.

Quinn shook his head. He had smoked for years himself and still missed the smell of tobacco smoke. He figured something else would get him sooner or later anyway. He watched as Flanagan carefully went through the ritual of loading his pipe and tamping the tobacco down with the flat end of the metal tool.

The pipe itself had a well used look about it, and the way its owner handled the device, it was apparent that he held it in high esteem.

"You know, this is a genuine brier pipe. Most of those you see nowadays are look-alikes, like everything else, fakes. A good brier pipe is made from the root of the shrub in the Mediterranean, and that is where this one came from many years ago. It belonged to my great grandfather, and it may even be older than that. Maybe he got it from his grandfather. Anyway, it's one of my three enjoyable vices, my pipe, a pint, and Colleen, whoever she may be."

Again, a hearty laugh followed, along with a snap of the head to readjust the glasses. With that, Flanagan placed the stem of the pipe in his mouth, lit a wooden match, waited for the sulfur to burn off, held it close to the bowl, made a sucking sound through the pipe, and blew out a cloud of blue smoke that filled the small cubicle with the sweet aroma of fine tobacco.

"Ah, that's better. Well, let's see, where to start?" With that, Flanagan set the flat-bottomed bowl of the pipe on the one open spot on his desk barely large enough to accommodate it and picked up the letters.

"Very interesting letters, very interesting." Flanagan then went on and explained that because the letters were all undated, he had to make some assumptions regarding their sequence, which he believed he had done correctly. He then labeled each letter and its corresponding translation with a sequential number, one being the earliest written. He presumed from the content that the first three or four were written in the years immediately following Jeremiah Desmond's emigration from Ireland, and the rest of the letters were written years later. This was assuming that Jeremiah had come over in the mid-1800s as Quinn had written in the summary he had sent along with the letters. Flanagan said that he believed Quinn would have the same impression when he read them.

Flanagan asked Quinn again what he knew about his grandfather Jeremiah's father, as though to reconfirm that Quinn had no information on him whatsoever.

"My grandfather, yes. My great grandfather, no. I have nothing on him at all. No name, nothing."

Flanagan thought it over and said, "It's strange your mother didn't mention him, but on the other hand, there may be a fairly good reason for it. The letters tell us that your great grandfather was a land agent for an Englishman with extensive holdings. Sorry to tell you that, but at least he wasn't in jail for child molestation."

Again, a hearty laugh followed by a snap of the head repositioning the glasses. He went on, "That was not a popular occupation back in those days. Irish land agents were not very well liked, even by their own families. They were more closely tied to the English than to the Irish, and most of them were as ruthless with their own kinfolk as with anyone else who was not paying their rent. In the mid-1800s, not too many people were able to pay their rent on time, if at all, and furthermore you could almost presume that your kinfolk were lessees and not land owners. Very few of the Irish families owned their land. Almost everything was leased from English owners."

Quinn was aware of some of this from his reading of Irish history and merely nodded in agreement.

"Anyway, your great grandmother, wife of the land agent, died sometime when your great grandfather, the land agent, was still a relatively young man. The letters don't show a date, but it seems as though she died about the same time your grandfather emigrated to the States. That was not unusual back then with all the disease and everything associated with the Famine, but anyway . . . she apparently died fairly early on as the letters discuss that at some length. Your great grandfather remarried it seems a number of years after your grandfather emigrated. Again, a lot of the details are just not here. This marriage was very profitable it appears... since the new wife was the widow of the English landowner for whom your great grandfather was the agent. Good move on his part I would say."

Flanagan again let out a hearty chuckle, readjusted his glasses and went on, "So guess who becomes the big landowner? The new wife of your great grandfather. Now from reading the letters, I think this happened around the late 1800s, maybe 1880 or so. In any event, the letters are from your grandfather's brother, William. They are all signed "Wilm," but that is the way they did things back then."

Quinn wondered how Flanagan had deciphered the scrawl on the letters to pick that out, but he let him go on without interruption.

"The first letters talk about life on the farm, how they missed your great grandmother who had died fairly recently, and then the later letters mention the marriage to the English widow and how the Irish community shunned the guy. From the wording of the early letters, I get the impression that this William does not communicate with his father either. There seem to be extended breaks between the letters, and I assume your grandfather, Jeremiah, is sending him letters bringing up other more mundane issues that some of these letters deal with. But, in all of the early letters there is something or other mentioned about the father, your great grandfather, usually something disparaging in those first letters. Then in about the sixth or seventh letter, William announces that the Englishwoman has passed away and in the next letter comes word that your great grandfather is the sole heir."

Sean took a long draw on his pipe and discovering that the flame had gone out. He paused for a moment to relight the tobacco. Having accomplished that, he said, "With this letter, William's attitude towards his father suddenly changes."

Sean chuckled and said, "I wonder why?" He then continued, "The next letters imply a newly found close bond of love with his father, as though that is what the relationship between your great grandfather and his son William had always been. William is also criticizing Jeremiah in these later letters for abandoning William and his father by leaving Ireland to seek his own fortune in the States. There then appears to be a long break in time between all these letters and the last two.

The first of the final two letters lays out in tearful terms the fact that William's dearly beloved father has passed away and also that the brother, Michael, was killed in the Land War between the Irish peasants and the British. There is no mention of what is happening to all the property his father owned when he died. The next letter, again written some time after the previous one, states that William is now the sole heir to the land holdings, and that he therewith severs all ties with Jeremiah for having left William and his father to suffer the wrath of the English on their own."

With that, Flanagan laughed freely. "I don't know what the hell he's talking about. It seems the English were pretty damn good to the old man." Flanagan paused and shook his head as a visible comment on what he had said.

"Oh, yes . . . one thing I didn't mention, the land your great grandfather apparently got a hold of . . . that is very good land. It's not used for farming anymore but for residential and commercial use. It virtually surrounds Kinsale. Have you ever heard of Kinsale?"

Quinn recalled reading that the English had landed at one time around Kinsale in order to establish English owned colonies somewhere, but that was the extent of his knowledge. Quinn shook his head and said, "No, not really."

Flanagan went on, rolling his eyes to emphasize what he was saying, "It's very high buck turf. It is the French Riviera of Ireland. Not quite the same but needless to say, it is pricey land to own in quantity if your long lost family still owns it. Seems that there was somewhere in the area of over three thousand hectares, that's around eight thousand acres to you Yankees, and it was all right along the coast. It's beautiful country down there, the eastern side of southwest Cork. I would assume that your grandfather came from the same area. He more than likely worked some of that land before he boarded the ship for New York or Quebec or wherever the hell he landed."

Quinn was fascinated by what Sean Flanagan was telling him. The letters were proving even more interesting than he had ever anticipated and he was also beginning to look upon Sean Flanagan as a newfound resource in tracing his family history. Best of all, Flanagan appeared to have some interest in the genealogy aspect, but that may have been related solely to the letters. Quinn was not sure what all of this meant and could not read into what Flanagan had said to pick out his take on the contents of the letters. Quinn waited for Flanagan to go on with more insight into the communications, but he just sat there, impassively, apparently deep in thought but not sharing anything with his guest.

After a while, Quinn drummed his fingers on the desk top and said, "Well, this is fascinating. I was hoping for a tie-in to some specific part of County Cork, but this is much more than I ever hoped to get. Maybe now I can find some family over there after all?"

Sean Flanagan raised an eyebrow, leaned forward, and spoke as though to a child who did not get the big picture, "It seems to me there's a hell of a lot more than that involved here. If it were me, I know what I would do. Something happened to a hell of a lot of money, and I would want to know what did. Seems your grandfather was the older brother of the two, and normally he would have received all or at least half of the land your great grandfather inherited. That's the way it worked back then. I would wonder why he didn't, or maybe he did and somebody took it from him. For openers, I would have some attorney in Ireland do a title search on the land and also check out the wills."

Quinn said nothing since all of this was coming so fast. He would need time to take it all in. He just said, "Interesting."

With that Sean Flanagan looked at his watch and said, "I had better run to teach a class or else I am going to be in big trouble."

Flanagan took down Quinn's address and phone number, and the two men were about to go their separate ways when Quinn realized he had not paid for the translation. Flanagan told him it was on the house because it had been interesting going through the letters. He added, "That is, provided you keep me informed on what happens. This could be interesting. I gotta go."

With that the professor picked up his briefcase and walked towards the door to his office. As he did so, he glanced down at Quinn's shoes. "My God, white bucks. I haven't seen those in a long time. You must have "em specially made." Again Sean let out the high nasal laugh that Quinn was beginning to consider Flanagan's trademark.

Quinn just laughed and replied, "Yeah, if I had your tie, I would have the perfect ensemble."

Flanagan gave a wave as he sped off towards his classroom deftly grabbing his glasses in midair as they were plunging towards the floor.

Quinn immediately returned to his home and began reading the translations. The letters were not long, and Quinn read and reread each letter a number of times, carefully examining every thought that was being conveyed. It appeared to Quinn that the relationship between Jeremiah and William was a strained one right from the first letter. That they were brothers was made clear a number of times in the letters where William spoke of "our father" and addressed Jeremiah every now and then as "brother," but there was never any warmth shown to Jeremiah.

The first letters coldly related facts that the writer apparently felt some obligation to convey to his older brother. There was mention of having received Jeremiah's draft, which may account for William's need to advise Jeremiah on certain business matters related to the homestead back in Ireland. In fact, the first few letters requested additional financial assistance. Quinn knew that it was customary during the great emigration of the Famine period, and in the following years for those who had emigrated to the States, to send money back to family members who had chosen to stay or who had to stay because they lacked the funds to purchase the ticket to leave. It was possible that William, for one reason or another, had to stay in Ireland while the others all emigrated. Jeremiah's description of the good life in the States could have created a barrier between the two.

Whatever the cause, William's letters were cold recitals of facts concerning his activities on "the farm." From the wording of the letters, Quinn presumed that the two brothers had worked a small parcel of land that did not earn enough profit to support the two of them or to make the lease payments. That was primarily what generated the need for funds from Jeremiah. Quinn could not tell how long Jeremiah had been sending money to William, but from a review of all the letters they did appear to span a considerable number of years as Sean Flanagan had suggested.

After reading all of the letters a number of times, Quinn agreed with Flanagan's comments regarding the change of attitude of William towards his father. Before the death of his English wife, William's references consisted of only very occasional snide comments, such as, "Your old man went to Dublin with 'the Queen', so I won't have to make the lease payment until he gets back next week. I hope your draft arrives before then." After the Englishwoman died and it was discovered that "the old man" had inherited the extensive real estate holdings, the letters spoke in glowing terms of what "father and I did over Holiday."

Quinn chuckled at what appeared to be a blatant display of pandering to wealth and thought to himself that it was as old as humankind. People just never change. He found it interesting that his own grandfather's brother would have that flaw, but he immediately took solace in the fact that William was not one of his direct ancestors. He also gave some thought to the terrible conditions under which people, such as William, lived their lives and how easy it was to criticize them for having taken steps to survive that were not necessary to take in this day and age of adequate food and shelter for virtually everyone.

In the letters discussing the inheritance received by Quinn's great grandfather, there were references to the land area involved being on both sides of the Bandon River and running out to the Head of Kinsale. He made a note of the description, intending to check it out at the library. Quinn went over the letters a number of times looking for some reference to the Desmond name but could find none. He was very curious as to what connection Sean Flanagan was talking about that triggered his curiosity about the Desmond family name. He would have to ask him about that if and when they met again.

The thought that kept running through Quinn's mind as he read the letters was Sean's comment that if it were him, he would hire a lawyer over in Ireland and check everything out. Quinn had another idea that was rapidly taking hold. Why not go over there and do the research himself? It would give him a chance to check out Catholic Church records on the Desmond family that did not appear to be readily available anywhere else, including in the Mormon Library.

Quinn knew that the Mormons were collecting Catholic records from Ireland, but they were not yet complete, and if one wanted to be sure he was examining the total record then he had to go to Ireland to see the originals. He could also check land records, wills, census records, birth and death notices, and other records not available anywhere in the States.

Quinn had been doing real estate law in Georgia for years and was well aware that the basic systems were the same in the States as in Ireland. He would probably be as well qualified as anyone once he figured out the filing systems and methods of record keeping that the Irish used. The more he thought about it, the more interested he became in taking the trip and doing the research.

CHAPTER 10

Sitting behind a large oak desk in the Desmond Enterprises president's office in Belfast, Patrick Desmond read over the latest financial reports that his secretary Martha had just laid before him.

"Well, Martha, how are we doing this quarter?"

It was an ongoing joke between the two of them. Patrick knew full well that Martha scanned the reports before bringing them into his office, and Martha knew that he expected her to review them. He appreciated her take on what was going on financially in the company, and he would usually ask for her thoughts.

"Very well, Patrick. Sales are up and so is the net. That's what counts. Would you like some tea?"

"Yes, please."

Martha poured her employer a cup of tea, laid it before him on the desk, and quietly retreated from the office. The relationship between Patrick and Martha was not what one would normally find in the president's office of a large corporation.

When Martha was stationed at her desk within view of the other employees in the Executive Offices of Desmond Enterprises she served as the efficient model of secretarial decorum, typing, pouring the tea, answering the telephone, and performing the usual duties of a top level executive secretary. When in the privacy of Patrick's office, her conduct would vary, depending upon the tone set by the president. That could range from very formal to very informal. When she was not at work and out of the view of her co-employees, Martha was companion, paramour, and confidant to Patrick and had been so for a number of years. Her position in Desmond Enterprises was solid, just as long as Patrick Desmond was the president.

When Martha had closed the door behind her, leaving Patrick alone in the office, he reviewed the financials to see how the various profit centers of the corporation were doing. Retail sales at the Desmond Stores in Northern Ireland and in the Republic were both up substantially. There was also an increase in sales of Desmond merchandise marketed through other retail chains under their own labels, with the only negative figures coming from the operations of Desmond Farms in County Cork.

Desmond Farms had never operated at a profit as far back as Patrick could recall. They were kept in existence as an operating entity solely for the reason that they had been in the Desmond family since time immemorial. The Desmond Clan had lived on the land long before his great grandfather had married into wealth and changed the lifestyle of the Desmond Family for generations to come. Patrick had spent much of his youth on the old Desmond homestead, primarily because his father, Dennis, enjoyed spending time there. Patrick would have preferred to be at the Desmond estate in Belfast, but his father thought it would be better if he grew up in the pastoral setting that had nurtured the Desmonds for generations.

As a child, on the Desmond Farms, in Kinsale, located on the south coast of the Republic, Patrick's friends were all Anglicans, as was he. The Desmonds did not mix with others of differing religious or political views in that primarily Catholic community, so Patrick's exposure to other political opinions was limited to say the least. When he attended Royal Crest, in Belfast as a boarder, he was a ready recipient for the pro-British view that was aggressively taught at the school, a view that he held for the rest of his life.

Patrick's children, Adam and Ellen, were direct opposites in their view of Desmond Farms. His son Adam, who was in his last year of college at Royal Crest, had no desire to visit the old farms, much less spend time there. His interests were not that mundane and he was aware that the Kinsale youth made fun of his effeminate mannerisms. Adam had not turned out the way Patrick would have liked, and no matter how hard he tried Patrick was unable to change his only son. Patrick had looked forward to having a son who would eventually take over Desmond Enterprises and be a driving force for the company, but it was apparent that Adam was not going to be the man for the job.

Patrick's daughter, Ellen, on the other hand, had an innate reverence for the Desmond homelands and made it a point to spend time there whenever her busy schedule allowed. Ellen had only recently completed her four years at Queen's College in Belfast and had taken a position with the Desmond Enterprise's Dublin Office, in Ballsbridge, starting as a clerical assistant. There was little doubt among those who knew her and respected her talents that she would move rapidly through the ranks of employees to assume a top management position in the company. Ellen was intelligent, ambitious, energetic, and personable. She was beyond a doubt Patrick's favorite in the family.

Patrick had always been careful about exposing his children to the risks of the world in view of the family's very sizeable wealth. But there were other reasons for his concern. His long time involvement as a major contributor to Unity, the preeminent political organization favoring continued British control of Northern Ireland, made his family somewhat vulnerable to reprisal from the Nationalist elements in the south as well as their agents in the north. The safety of his daughter Ellen, living in the south was always a matter of concern for Patrick. Fortunately, she had a wealth of common sense that provided a measure of assurance for Patrick.

Adam, on the other hand, was the one who could wander, blindly, into a bad situation and even then not recognize that he was in the wrong place at the wrong time. Fortunately for him, he was in Belfast and living either a generally protected life at Royal Crest or at his home at Park Ridge.

Patrick's wife and the mother of his children, Hillary Fairchild Desmond, held Desmond Farms in even lower esteem than did Adam. At least the reason for her opinion had more substance than his. The Farms had been running in the red ever since she took an active role in managing Desmond affairs. Furthermore, there was no love of the past on Hillary's part to counterbalance the status of the Farms in her mind. Hillary was a Fairchild. She was English, through and through, and she was embarrassed to admit that she had married an Irishman. While she found Patrick's financial statement to be very acceptable, she could never forgive him for not being English.

Hillary's opinion of the rank and file Irish, whether in Northern Ireland or in the Republic, was that they were a quarrelsome, untrustworthy lot who drank to excess and who severely lacked social graces. Hillary looked upon the conflict going on in Northern Ireland as "just further evidence of the damaged gene pool among the Irish people." When in London, she would constantly put down the Irish in the presence of her husband with one of her latest "Paddy" jokes. Her friends would all laugh, and soon Patrick would join in the laughter because he was too humiliated to do otherwise.

Unfortunately, Hillary had one anecdote that caused Patrick great embarrassment and that she would retell at every opportunity when she was back in her homeland. On the occasions when she had a bit too much to drink, she would say, "Old William Desmond went from tilling the field to filling the till very suddenly, to everyone's surprise." She would then laugh and shake her head to demonstrate her opinion of how the Desmonds had acquired their wealth.

Unfortunately, these occurrences seemed to be on the increase in recent years commensurate with the increase in both her age and her drinking. Now that she was edging fifty, just a touch overweight, and, frankly, a bit over-stressed from her social and business activities, she did not have the same endurance on the barstool that she had displayed when Patrick first met her.

Aside from Hillary's deficiencies as a wife and companion for her husband, she was a brilliant manager and entrepreneur, whose management style and input had produced a long history of profits for Desmond Enterprises. She had a natural instinct when it came to predicting future trends in retail clothing, the main source of income for the company. Desmond Stores had flourished not only in the north but also in the Republic from the time that she took an active role in decision making at the company.

The benefits that Hillary brought to the Desmond Family came with a price. She was incapable of being satisfied in her various interests, be they personal or business related. She spent virtually all of her working hours in consultation with her own staff of advisors and accountants, developing business strategies and new ideas for making profits for Desmond Enterprises.

Her own Fairchild Family fortune dated back to Henry the Eighth, as she put it, and, as she so often said, "I can buy and sell Desmond Enterprises five times over, anytime I want." From the time that Hillary was a young woman, she had participated in management of Fairchild Investments. Over the years, as her parent's only child, she eventually assumed sole ownership and control of the various funds operating under the umbrella of Fairchild Investments. She brought in her own managing agents to handle business affairs with offices throughout the world, all acting under her immediate direction. That did not mean for a moment that she was out of touch with anything that was going on anywhere in the company. She had a frightening knack for looking at a financial statement and ferreting out a problem area no matter how deeply buried in the columns of income and expense.

Consequently, those who worked for her soon learned that they had better be totally candid about what was happening in the company, regardless of how high up the executive ladder they had climbed, or they would be rapidly replaced. She wouldn't shed a tear over firing an executive who had been with the company for years if she discovered they had been trying to cover up a screw up, regardless of how minor it was. In fact, Patrick had commented to his friends that Hillary was almost enjoyable to be around when she was in the process of firing a long term employee of Fairchild Investments.

The relationship between Patrick and Hillary was basically one of convenience. The two of them allowed one another their own space to conduct their lives as they saw fit. Patrick had little if any interest in how Hillary led her life as long as she continued to make the business judgments that produced profits for Desmond Enterprises. Their marriage had become more of a business venture than anything else. Virtually all of the inventory items from Southeast Asia going to Desmond Stores were carried in vessels owned and operated by Fairchild Investments, and this mutually beneficial relationship provided the primary if not the sole basis for peace in the family.

While Patrick served as the figurehead president of Desmond Enterprises, it was his wife, Hillary, who made the management decisions that determined the course the company followed in dealing with the competition. Patrick did have certain areas of responsibility that he was primarily responsible for. One of these was in dealing with the Unity representatives who were constantly seeking ever larger contributions to their political organization.

Negotiating contributions with Unity was no small task. The relationship between the two entities, the company and the political party, dated back to the years when Patrick's father ran the company. Desmond Enterprises had always contributed substantially to Protestant political groups in the north, and Patrick's father strongly advised his son to continue the practice for both business and political reasons.

With the emergence of Unity as the political force that dictated government policies and practices in the North, it became an absolute necessity for any large company to be viewed in a favorable light by Unity. Furthermore, Unity's power base was its union, with virtually every Protestant laborer and tradesman in the North belonging to the Unity Labor Union.

When Desmond Enterprises had problems with government regulatory agencies, a phone call to the proper party official usually smoothed the way. Likewise, when wage negotiations became difficult between management and union employees of Desmond Enterprises, a well placed contribution to party officials would work miracles. Furthermore, the shadowy, paramilitary wing of Unity, popularly known as the Provos, provided protection for not only Desmond interests throughout the island of Ireland but also for Hillary's far flung investments that reached around the world. It was a known fact in the north and the south that the Desmond

Stores were under the protection of the Provos, and this was sufficient to dissuade even the youngest petty thief from exercising his talents.

Patrick did not publicize his role as one of the main sources of financial support for Unity, and while that fact was not considered an issue of major importance among the members of the Belfast business community, it was known and discussed in the INA, the radical arm of the Irish Nationalist Party. This organization was the polar opposite of the Unity Provos, and much of the armed conflict that had taken place in the north of Ireland involved these two organizations.

In recent years Patrick had considered distancing himself from Unity for his own good health and that of his children, but unfortunately he discovered that he had become too important to the group and they could no longer afford to lose his support. The members of Unity had never threatened him when he had alluded to ending his support for the Party, but they had let him know that there could be adverse consequences. Patrick took that to mean that some of the easy access for his company's products and services would suddenly disappear, but he did not know if it could also mean something worse.

When Patrick had reviewed the financials, he set them aside and enjoyed the view of the Belfast shipyards and harbor through the floor to ceiling glass windows of his corner office. Patrick's office in the Port Towers overlooked the dry docks where ocean going ships were being built and repaired. He looked down on the hundreds of workers, who resembled a colony of ants, as they crawled around the half finished outlines of ships under construction. As he looked down at the teams of workers, he thought, "Unity members, right to a man. If you're not a Unity man, you don't get a job building the big boats."

He looked beyond the shipyard and out into the mist shrouded bay. It wasn't a good day to be working out in the open with light rain falling and temperatures in the low fifties. In other words, it was just another typical late October day in Belfast.

Patrick reread the note that had been hand delivered to him by the courier from Unity. What information could they have that he would find interesting? That's what the note said, and it instructed him to call Tony Carter and arrange a time and place to get together with him. Patrick swore. He did not like to advertise his association with Carter, and they had just had lunch a few days ago.

Patrick placed the call to Carter's office on his secure line and informed Carter's secretary that he would meet Carter at two that afternoon at The Bull, a restaurant in the heart of Belfast.

As the time drew near for his meeting with Tony Carter, Patrick became increasingly nervous. He hated the meetings with Carter. He was never able to relax around the man. Whenever they met, Carter would just stare at him with those beady eyes, and Patrick would get the feeling that Carter could tell exactly what he was thinking. It was obvious that both men were well aware that each held the other in contempt, and the mysterious nature of the call for today's meeting only added to Patrick's anxiety.

Patrick told Martha that he would be out for a couple of hours. He didn't have to explain since she knew who he was meeting with. She was more aware of his contacts with Unity than Hillary, and she was the person who actually drew up the drafts that were then deposited in a series of bank accounts under rather nondescript titles. The two favorites were Erin Antiquities and Ulster Commodities Limited, both shell corporations. Funds would then be drawn out of those accounts and transferred to Unity. Occasionally, funds would be drawn on accounts of operating Desmond Subsidiaries and issued directly to Unity, but that was the exception and not the rule. Martha was the only person involved in handling fund transfers to Unity, and records of those payments were never identified as such in corporate financials.

Martha had been Patrick's secretary for twenty years and had provided more services for him than merely typing his letters and handling his appointments. He had discovered years before that Martha's talents were not limited to the typewriter, and he had never grown tired of having her around. Patrick and Hillary had long ago stopped trying to carry on the appearance of a happily married yet successful couple. Their bedrooms were at opposite ends of their huge estate home, Park Ridge, and both of them ignored whatever affairs the other was currently involved with, unless it somehow became overly embarrassing to the less guilty party. Hillary was fully aware that Patrick had his long term relationship with Martha, and as far as Hillary was concerned Martha was doing her a favor.

In the meantime, Hillary was busy servicing the latest gardener, chauffeur, or yard boy who pleased her fancy. She did not go in for long-term relationships, because her overly active libido was constantly seeking a new challenge or a new diversion. Patrick did not take offense at her rather robust sexual appetite so long as it did not involve him, but he had chastised her on more than one occasion for not exercising a bit more discretion.

Fortunately for their mother, Ellen and Adam were seldom on the property, so Hillary did not have to exercise discretion too often. One of the reasons that Patrick went along with Ellen working in Dublin was to shield her from her mother's overly amorous activities. Unbeknownst to him, Ellen had long ago picked up on the personal habits of each of her parents and had not let it bother her. Adam, on the other hand, was totally oblivious to the fact that his parent's relationship was other than that of the typical husband and wife, although Patrick doubted if Adam had any interest in his parent's relationships, one way or the other.

As he made his way to the restaurant, Patrick counseled himself to be careful about what he said, because he always assumed that Carter carried a wire. Anything said could be filed away for future use. In this respect, Patrick had good reason for his insecurity. He had known Carter for a number of years and knew him for what he was. Carter was loyal only to Unity and had no scruples whatsoever when it came to anyone else, most certainly including Patrick Desmond.

Patrick entered the restaurant filled with customers and spotted Carter sitting at a table towards the back of the room off to the side. Carter was apparently reading the Irish Times and did not appear to notice Patrick as he came up to the table, but Patrick knew he had been observed. That was just Carter's way. Patrick sat down at the table as Carter continued reading his paper. Patrick observed him, waiting for Carter to make the first move. Patrick didn't want to appear too anxious to know what Carter had on his mind. That would put him at a disadvantage. The two sat at the table silently for some time.

Patrick sat studying Carter as he devoured some article in the paper that had captured his interest. Patrick was always impressed with the appearance of personal strength of Tony Carter. Carter had the build and appearance of a professional boxer. He had square shoulders, a thick neck, and large, heavy hands. He was obviously in excellent condition for his forty some years. His somewhat flattened nose evidenced more than one violent encounter with either a fist or a club sometime in the past. Combined with other signs of damage on his face from pockmarks, cuts, or abrasions, Carter gave off the impression that he had led a very tough life.

Finally, Carter set the paper aside, glanced around the room, and, when it appeared he was certain no one was interested in their conversation, turned to Patrick and said nothing while he studied his companion for a moment, as was his habit. This unnerved Patrick, who nervously pulled a ballpoint pen from his inside pocket and twisted it in his now perspiring hands to relieve his building tension.

Carter was the first to speak. "You know, Patrick, Unity goes through a lot of trouble to see that you and your company are well taken care of."

He paused, waiting for the appropriate acknowledgment of the truth of this statement.

Patrick thought, "God, why in the hell do we have to play these games?" Feeling compelled to respond, Patrick mumbled, "I know." At the same time he wondered if the perspiration he felt growing on his upper lip was visible to Carter.

"We have agents working all around the world and particularly in the United States, as you well know."

Again, the pause, and again Patrick made the appropriate response, "I know."

Carter continued, "Well, without going into the details, we have been picking up some information regarding the Nationalist movement in the States that surprisingly relates to you. We generally just keep our ears tuned to what they are up to in the area of fund raising. Of course, funds buy weapons, and that is our main interest but low and behold, up comes the name Patrick Desmond."

Carter paused to let the import of what he was about to say sink in. Patrick was obviously surprised by what he was already hearing, because he could not imagine how anything he did or was connected with could come to the attention of Unity agents in the States.

"It seems that you have relatives in the State of Georgia who have been in contact with Nationalist reps there. These cousins, or whatever they are, have an interest in learning whether you exist or not. They're not geology buffs, or whatever they're called, and no political interests that we know of." With a chuckle, Carter went on, "Just interested in learning about their Irish roots."

Patrick was now listening intently to what Carter was saying. He had never before thought about what had happened to the brother of his grandfather who had emigrated to the States many years before. His own father, Dennis Desmond, knew nothing about him and could barely recall his name, because his own father, Patrick's grandfather, never spoke of the brother who had emigrated during the Famine. Patrick had been told by someone, presumably his own father, that there was some bad blood between the two brothers and that contact between them was consequently lost. Sometime later the emigrating brother had died.

Carter had paused, waiting for Patrick, who he considered naive, if not a bit mentally slow, to absorb what he was saying.

Carter had grown up in the poorer tenements of Belfast living as a street tough, or as he put it, "Rocking the Catholics for entertainment." At one point, he did some time for theft and assault. He viewed Patrick as a typical spoiled, fat, rich weakling without a brain and certainly without real life experience. Carter also knew that Unity needed Patrick because, among other things, he had the cash to fund the operations of Unity. Carter despised Patrick but found it entertaining to play mind games with him, because he knew that he made the president of Desmond Enterprises nervous. He could see that Patrick was not enjoying their little talk today, because there was already a sheen of sweat building on his lip. Usually it took a bit longer for that to come into view.

Patrick put the ballpoint pen back in his pocket, now very interested in what was being said. He folded his hands together and, steadying his voice, replied that some of his family had emigrated in years past, but that he knew nothing of them other than that. Feeling he had made an appropriate response to Carter's opening remarks, he waited for him to continue.

After a suitably painful pause, Carter continued, "It seems that the Nationalist rep in the States who came into contact with your cousin, or whatever he is, was somewhat familiar with your family background down in Kinsale, so that when he met this guy and found out what his interests were, the rep saw the potential to create problems for us."

Carter again paused, waiting to see if Patrick was getting the picture. Studying the blank expression on Patrick's face, Carter decided to go on, "It seems as though there are rumors your grandfather may have played some dirty tricks in order to acquire the Desmond family fortune. Have you heard that?"

Now Carter could not suppress the grin that was beginning to build on his face. He had been looking forward to this meeting all morning to see how Patrick would handle the news that he might have an old buried family problem coming to life in the States.

Patrick thought for a moment and then being careful because he did not trust Carter for a moment, said "I never heard of anything like that."

Carter chuckled, fairly certain that Patrick must have known more than he was letting on.

"It seems as though the rep had heard the rumors years before when he was a kid down in the Kinsale area, and also when he was in the Cork area, later on, preparing information files on Unity donors. Your family's name was one that had been assigned to him to research and in the course of his work, he recalled some of the rumors and did a little more investigation. I would think you would have heard them yourself. You grew up down there in Kinsale, didn't you?"

With that Patrick flushed, because his statement that he didn't know about this rumor was an obvious lie. He did not enjoy having this Belfast sewer rat know that he had to lie about something as unimportant as his family history.

Again, twisting the pen in his hand, Patrick responded, "Oh, you hear anything over time. Who the hell cares? I never paid any attention to that sort of thing. People are jealous and they come up with all sorts of stories. If they hadn't come up with that, they would have said we robbed a bank some place. The crap people come up with."

Carter thought to himself, not bad. That's what I would have said. He then glanced at his watch and noted that he had to get down to business. Play time was over.

"This may be a bit more serious than it would at first appear. We were told that the Nationalist Party's Dublin office was taking this very seriously, and at that point we got concerned. We wondered why they were so interested, so we did some checking of our own and guess what?"

Carter could not help playing the game of throw out the bait and wait for the big fat fish to come and put the shiny hook in his puffy cheeks. After a moment, Patrick dutifully complied and asked the proper question, "What is that?"

"The story they are working on goes like this. It seems that your grandfather may have come up with a phony scheme to disinherit his brother who had gone to the States. The Desmond inheritance was to go to your grandfather's brother in the States, who was the first born son in the family. It looks to us, and we are still checking this out, that your grandfather may have done a little "hokus pokus" of some sort so that he would be the sole heir, not his brother. I don't know what or how that was to have been done or, for that matter, if there really was something done. Anyway, we're following the story, and we don't want to be surprised to find out that there is some truth to it. There was another brother in Ireland, but he had an untimely passing at about the same time. We are also trying to check that one out."

Patrick did not enjoy hearing these unseemly allegations against his grandfather. Nothing that he was hearing now seemed to relate to the old fellow who didn't seem to have a bad bone in his body. Nevertheless, Patrick knew how thorough the Unity people were when it came to investigating matters that affected their pocket book. He had little doubt that what Carter was telling him was true, at least up to this point in time. They were still checking on the story and in time it might be proven to be false, but regardless of that, what was Unity's position in this business and how did they intend to follow up on it. Patrick raised the question with

Carter.

Carter leaned back in his chair with a wry smile on his face, and as a teacher to a student, replied, "We don't quite know what it might mean, Patrick, but we look at you as one of our primary benefactors."

Carter was trying his best to appear appreciative even though he was not. He continued, "We don't want anything to interfere with your ability to continue your substantial gifts to the Party."

He then paused to let it sink in that this phony inheritance business could cause financial problems for Patrick Desmond and his continued support of Unity. Obviously Carter did not give a damn about what it might mean for Patrick or his family.

Carter's cavalier attitude angered Patrick, but he said nothing and instead concentrated on how to respond. He had learned long ago that when he was in this state of mind, confused about the best course of action, that it was best to say nothing and see where the cards fell.

"Interesting," he finally said. He then thought, "Let Carter blab on. He's the one who seems more worried about this than I am."

Patrick could not imagine that after all of these years anyone could come in and strip the Desmonds of their wealth based on some claim that was well over a hundred years old. As that thought gave him some reassurance, Carter immediately ruined it.

"If you're thinking that they don't have a claim on the Estate, you may be wrong. Our attorneys tell us that fraud tolls all statutes of limitations. It makes no difference if all of this happened yesterday or in the year one. What is key here is if the funds are traceable, and it appears they may well be. We think you just might have a problem."

The last statement unnerved Patrick, but he did a credible job of appearing somewhat calm as he asked, "Assuming that this person could present a problem, what do your people think we should do about it?"

Carter again looked at his watch and noted that he had a meeting he had to go to.

"That is the question. This may be nothing, or it may become a much more serious problem. For now we are monitoring the situation. We are keeping a watch on things and trying to find out what is developing. Now, this relative, a guy named Parker, apparently is the only living descendant of the one who emigrated, and if he were to have an untimely demise, there would be no one to pursue whatever claim there is, for whatever that's worth, but for the time being, we are of the opinion that we will just watch and wait to see what happens. The fellow that we have on him came to us from the East German Secret Police, the Stazi. Very professional and very effective."

Carter did not want to go into detail on what he meant by that statement, but the implication of it was quite clear to Patrick. Carter was amused to see that his companion was visibly shaken. The sweat on his upper lip had accumulated and was about to drop. Carter was quite used to the application of extreme measures when they proved to be necessary for the security of Unity and had, in fact, been involved in such operations earlier in his career. At times, such as this, he wished that he was back on the street doing the hit rather than sitting here with this bumbling bag of shit that had spent his entire life with a silver spoon in his mouth.

Again checking his watch, Carter said he had other business to attend to, implying that Patrick did not. Before they left the room, Carter went into his usual propaganda routine of explaining to Patrick the great need that Unity had for financial assistance. They had operations around the world, some above board, some not, and they all required a great amount of money to stay in operation.

"This full-time guy on your cousin is not cheap. It seems that your cousin likes to travel around a bit and also likes to drink Guinness at some Irish pub in Atlanta. You should have more boring relatives. It wouldn't be so expensive to follow them around. We also need your help, Patrick, with the elections coming up. Unity still has a majority in the assembly, but we have been losing a couple of seats every election. If you have been reading the papers, our politicians are not as popular today as they used to be. We need to get the people out and that takes money. If you could increase the contributions, we could afford to increase our efforts to see that you don't have any problems."

Patrick concluded that he was going to have to speak to someone higher up in the Unity chain of command about replacing his contact point. He could not take much more crap from this Belfast alley rat. Patrick thought for a moment and concluded that this will be the new game we play. If I don't boost the contribution, they will turn the screws on me. For all I know, they may be bullshitting me on this entire story. Patrick told himself that wherever the truth might lie, he would go along with what Carter was telling him until he learned otherwise. That would be the wisest course of action to follow.

The two men left the restaurant and within ten minutes, Patrick was back at his desk at Desmond Enterprises, staring at the wall, twisting the letter opener in his perspiring hands, and wondering where all of this was going to lead.

CHAPTER 11

D riving to the Atlanta library, Quinn Parker began questioning what his own motives were in connection with his growing curiosity about his great grandfather's inheritance. Was he subject to the same criticism that he was aiming at his grandfather's brother, William Desmond, for his quick change of attitude towards his father when money came into the picture? He didn't think he was since wealth and property had never been a motivating factor for Quinn, but he was a bit curious to know what had happened to the large estate after it went to William. The main questions remained, however. Were there relatives in Cork that he would enjoy meeting and, if so, would they wish to meet him?

Quinn considered it highly unlikely that he had any viable legal claim to any property in Ireland at this late date. All of this took place over a hundred years ago and the property had, beyond a doubt, been sold ten times over to potentially hundreds of people since his grandfather's brother took over the estate. Nevertheless, it would be interesting to find out what did happen. As he thought about it, his mind focused on the family line of descent from Jeremiah. His grandfather only had one child that lived and she, Quinn's mother, was his only heir. Quinn was the only heir of his parents, and unless he was missing something, he stood alone in the legal shoes of Jeremiah Desmond with respect to any claims his grandfather may have had.

Quinn dismissed the thought and mentally scolded himself for what had made him think of the opportunities that stood before him. He again pondered what had been his main reason for exploring his family history, and that was to better know himself. That was his real motivation, but all the same, Sean Flanagan's comment that "something happened to a hell of a lot of money, and I would want to know what did" kept coming back into his thoughts. He knew that satisfying his curiosity for the answer to that question, dictated that he check that out as well.

In the library, Quinn found the maps of Ireland and after locating the Kinsale area in the southern part of County Cork, he made a number of copies for his files and also copied other, more detailed, maps of County Cork that showed the villages and townlands that could aid him in his search for the old homesteads. He was assuming that Jeremiah Desmond had lived in the area around Kinsale inherited by his great grandfather, or very nearby, because his father would not have been a land agent on properties far removed from his own home, wherever it was.

Later, as he was driving home, he passed the Peachtree Mall and by chance noticed a bright green sign, Murphy's Irish Pub, buried in an array of neon lights advertising restaurants, retail stores, theaters and other establishments. He had driven by there many times in the past, but had never before noticed the pub.

With his new found interest dictating his moves, he swung into the next mall entry lane and back tracked to the point where the pub was located. The pub was a relatively small storefront, advertising "Authentic Irish Music," which Quinn could hear as soon as he stepped out of the car. Upon entering the pub, he held the door for a young man who had come in behind him and received an Irish accented "Thank you" for his services. As soon as he was inside the bar, he was immersed in a sea of people, primarily young men, all talking loudly over the sound of a band playing somewhere in the back of the bar.

Quinn could barely see across the length of the room due to the dim lighting and the haze from tobacco smoke. It was some time before he could make out that there was in fact a group of four musicians playing on a stage at the far end. Not a large band but in the confines of the small bar the volume of the music produced by the group made conversation difficult. Quinn had heard their style of music many times before when his mother played the old records she guarded so carefully in their home. He had always enjoyed Irish music, having grown up with it.

As he stood in the bar listening to the sound of the music with its distinctively driving Celtic beat, he thought what a fitting complement it was to the events of the day. He decided to stay, have a beer, and listen to the music for a while. He ordered a glass of beer and watched as the bartender drew a pint of Guinness, which was a bit of a process. The bartender would fill a pint glass, let the foam settle, fill again, and repeat until he had a fair measure of Guinness in the mug.

While Quinn waited for his pint, he studied the clientele of the bar. They appeared to be a mix of people, professional types with their suits and ties as well as laborers and tradesmen, all of whom probably stopped in for a pint after work and just never left. They were all engaged for the most part in small group conversations with usually more than one talking at a time. While he was watching the crowd, the bartender expertly slid the frosted glass full of the dark ale under an acceptable layer of white foam down the bar so that it came to a stop directly in front of him. Quinn acknowledged the skill of the bartender with a nod, which was returned. He left a five dollar bill for services rendered.

Quinn took his beer and worked his way towards the back of the bar so that he could better hear the band playing above the roar of the crowd. A customer was relinquishing a small table off to the side of what was probably the dance floor on other evenings, and Quinn edged his way through the crowd of standing, talking customers to lay claim to the prize before others became aware that it had become available. He sat down, resting his legs, which were a bit sore from the longer than usual run in the morning, followed by hours of standing and looking over maps and other materials at the library.

As Quinn stretched his legs and tried to get comfortable in the straight backed, wooden chair, he saw that every table in this part of the room as well as every available space at the bar was filled. The table was perfectly situated because the noise level of the music was a bit uncomfortable for the tables closer to the band, and to hold conversation there must have been difficult at best. That did not seem to bother the patrons, though, as most of them engaged in conversation with great enthusiasm and would only occasionally pause, sip from their mug of beer, and then cast a brief, appreciative glance towards the band members, whose music they all seemed to know.

As Quinn listened to the music, enjoying the tempo, he watched the drummer set the pace. He was an older fellow, but that did not prevent him from exercising complete control of the task at hand. He and the concertina player were in the center of the group facing the crowd, and the two other band members played the fiddle and pipe on either side, more or less facing each other so that their timing was perfectly coordinated with the others. Quinn then focused on the fiddle player whose back was slightly to his position so that he could not see his face. He could only see his heavy shock of thick black hair that was whipped back and forth by the rapid movement of the bow in his right hand. He made lightning quick strokes ever so lightly over the strings, creating a harmonic sound that was Irish fiddle playing at its finest.

He was clearly an accomplished musician and the best of the group. As the band finished the set, Quinn set his beer mug down so that he could show his appreciation by joining the other bar patrons in standing and applauding the performance. He was about to sit back down in his chair when the fiddle player set his instrument down, picked up his pint, which he had stashed on a shelf behind him, and stepped towards a table of patrons at the foot of the bandstand.

When Quinn had a decent look at the fellow, he was surprised to see that it was Sean Flanagan, the Irish interpreter, without his glasses, attired exactly the same as when Quinn was in his office except that his tie was now even more loosely attached. He was perspiring heavily from the exertion and taking great gulps of beer between comments to those at the table. It all made sense to Quinn after a moment. There aren't too many bars around Atlanta with an Irish flavor, and why wouldn't he be here. As far as the fiddle went, all of the Irish were supposed to be musically inclined, according to his mother, but this fellow was more than just adept at the fiddle. He had some solid talent with the instrument. Quinn thought that he may look and act a bit bizarre, but he certainly knew what he was doing with the fiddle.

Sean finished his conversation with the couple at the front table, put his glasses on, having taken them from his shirt pocket, and headed in the direction of the bar when he caught sight of Quinn. He waved and made his way through the crowd towards Quinn.

"Well, look who's here. Is this part of your research project, checking out local Irish bars, or did the wife throw you out of the house?"

Quinn motioned to Sean Flanagan to have a seat at the empty chair at the table, then stood and shook hands with him.

"Wrong on both counts," said Quinn. "Frankly I didn't know this place was here, but I may be a regular customer in the future." Quinn then stressed that he was very impressed with Sean's fiddle playing but hadn't recognized him without his glasses on.

Sean thanked him and said, "Fiddle playing, if done correctly, is too vigorous a sport for wearing glasses. Don't leave. I'll be right back as soon as I reload this mug."

The bartender had already filled a fresh mug of Guinness when he saw Sean leave the stage, so he soon returned to the table.

When Sean took his seat, Quinn said, "I was surprised to see you playing with the group, but on second thought maybe I shouldn't have been." Sean assured him that not quite everyone in Ireland played a musical instrument but quite a few did.

Sean then told him how he had learned to play the fiddle from his father who was an avid musician and that he played in the pub basically for the fun of it.

"Trust me, you don't get paid much to perform on this stage. It's basically a volunteer deal; in fact, nearly anyone here could get up and do almost anything he wants for this crowd. If they don't like what you're doing, they'll let you know."

The two men talked for a few minutes about the club until Sean had to again take the stage with the other members of the band. He told Quinn to hang around if he could, that he would be finished for the evening after the next set. Quinn was enjoying himself and found the music entertaining, so he assured Sean that he would be there for a while.

When Sean came back to the table after the set, he wiped the fiddle down with a soft, clean rag and then carefully secured the instrument in a battered, weather beaten case, with the bow alongside of it and placed the case on the empty chair beside him. From the careful manner in which Sean treated the fiddle, it was obvious to Quinn that he valued it highly. Sean later told him that it had been handed down to him by his father and had been in the family for a number of generations.

As the two men started in on their third pint of Guinness, they had exhausted the small talk, and Sean began talking about the history of Ireland, a subject obviously dear to his heart. He mentioned that the country had only gained its independence at the beginning of the twentieth century, having been suppressed by "those English bastards" for some seven to eight hundred years. Quinn was somewhat familiar with the history of Ireland but had never really given the relationship with England much thought. As Sean went on, it was clear that he had very intense opinions concerning the manner in which England had dealt with the Irish over the years, and he would periodically inquire of Quinn as to what he thought of this or that particularly dastardly act.

The first few times the relationship with England came up in the conversation, Quinn nodded in confirmation of Sean's particular indictment of whatever it was the English had done. But, after the third or fourth time, Quinn explained to Sean that he, like many Irish Americans, were embarrassingly deficient with respect to Irish history, to which Sean merely replied, "No shit."

Quinn ignored the comment and went on, "As a result, Sean, very few Irish Americans, including myself, have really given it much thought."

He told Sean that his own mother knew virtually nothing of her own father's life in Ireland.

"She couldn't even remember where he had come from, and I didn't know anything about where he may have come from until you mentioned Kinsale. That was very interesting news to me, because all I knew was that Jeremiah Desmond had come from somewhere in County Cork, Ireland. That was it."

Sean thought for a moment or two and replied that it had always astonished him that the Irish in America, many of whom had just as much

Irish blood in their veins as he did, knew so little about their homeland. He sat quietly for a moment or two, shaking his head, and then began quizzing Quinn on everything he knew about his family. He asked about other relatives that may have emigrated at the same time and gone to the States, but Quinn had nothing to add to what he had already said. Quinn said that he assumed other relatives had emigrated as well, but he knew nothing about them.

Sean's questions again reminded Quinn that Sean had said the Gaelic letters were the source of his curiosity about the Desmonds. Quinn told him that he had reviewed the translations and saw nothing in there that would key in on the Desmond name. He asked what Sean saw that drew his attention to the Desmond family. This seemed to cause Sean to fluster a bit which Quinn thought strange, but then Sean went on to say that there were quite a few Desmonds around Kinsale and maybe that was what had interested him in the name.

The talk then focused on how Quinn was planning to go about his family research project, and he told Sean that he was going to get as much information as he could at local libraries and the Mormon Church library in Salt Lake and then possibly travel to Ireland for a few weeks. He had purchased some books on how to trace family history in Ireland, and he planned on using them as guides while visiting the National Library and the Archives in Dublin. Sean nodded, very intently listening as Quinn explained what he intended to do.

When Quinn finished, with the comment that he had just decided that day to make the trip and would obviously have to give the matter a great deal more thought, Sean again surprised him by offering to assist him in anyway he could. He also mentioned for the first time that he was going back to Dublin himself in the near future.

"Well, if we are over there at the same time maybe you can show me around the town a bit, if you don't mind?"

"I would be glad to do that, and maybe I could help you with your research as well."

As the two men talked, others in the Pub would stop by the table to say hello to Sean and to congratulate him on his fine fiddling. It appeared to Quinn that his table mate was well known to the patrons in the bar as more than just a band member. Most of them spoke with a distinctly Irish accent, and the brief conversations that they had with Sean involved a meeting of some sort that was taking place later in the week. It seemed that when the matter of the meeting came up, they would continue the conversation in Gaelic, which was totally unintelligible to Quinn. Sean introduced Quinn to a few of the men who Sean explained had lived with him in the Liberties section of Dublin. That meant nothing to Quinn, but Sean told him he would show him the area if they were in the city together.

As the hour drew late, Quinn looked at his watch. "I have to call it a day, or else I'll drink another beer and have to hire a cab." Sean rose out of his chair as Quinn stood, put his hand on Quinn's shoulder, and, in a very serious manner, restated his interest in Quinn's family history project.

"I would very much enjoy working with you and would appreciate it if you would let me help."

In a voice evidencing disbelief in what he was hearing, Quinn responded, "You are asking if I will let you help me? Hell yes you can help me. I'll take all the help I can get. I would very much appreciate that."

"Good," Sean said and shook Quinn's hand. "Stay in touch, and I will give some thought as to how you might proceed over in Dublin."

With that the two men separated, and, as Quinn was leaving the bar, he noticed that a number of the Irishmen who had come by the table were now sitting down with Sean in what appeared to be a serious discussion. As Quinn drove home, he thought about his good luck in finding Sean and his willingness to help him sort out his family history. He thought it a bit unusual that someone would take an interest in such a mundane matter as somebody else's genealogy, but maybe Sean was just one of those overly helpful guys or a history nut. Still it was a little strange. Whatever it was, Quinn could use the help, and as long as there were no strings attached he would accept Sean's assistance. It was about eleven thirty by the time Quinn arrived at his home, and when he pulled his car into the garage he told himself that he was going to go a bit easier on the Guinness next time. He didn't know if he could have passed a Breathalyzer test, but he didn't want to find out the hard way.

CHAPTER 12

In the following weeks, Quinn devoted most of his time to projects related to his planned trip to Ireland. He had booked the trip well in advance in order to have time in the interim to flesh out what information he did have on the Desmond family before doing his research in Ireland. He had been told that nothing was computerized over there and that, if at all possible, he should first try to get to Salt Lake City and go through the Mormon records. He decided he would talk with Sean about that on Wednesday evening, Irish music night, when Sean would be there playing his fiddle with the band.

That Wednesday, as Quinn walked into the Pub, he could see his friend on the stage with his fiddle pressed firmly against his shoulder and the bow actively engaged in producing the familiar sound. Quinn again sought out a table close to the bandstand and ordered a beer while he waited for the next break. In time, the set was completed and when Sean Flanagan spotted Quinn, he came right over to the table and sat down, and one of the bartenders brought a pint over to him.

The two men talked about Quinn's plan to visit the Mormon library in Salt Lake City, which Sean thought was a good idea, because the records in both the National Library and in the Archives were hand filed and, it was true, nothing was computerized. Sean also commented that he had been talking with some friends of his about Quinn's plan to visit Ireland, and that it was possible he might be able to locate a fellow in Dublin who was very familiar with tracing ancestral records. This fellow could also give Quinn some help.

Upon hearing this news, Quinn became a bit nervous, and he explained to Sean that he was trying to keep costs down on the trip and would not have funds available to pay anyone. That was why he was going over there himself and not hiring someone in Dublin to do the work for him.

Sean held his hands up and said, "Wait a minute. Who said anything about charging? If I find somebody to give you a hand, there will be no charge."

Quinn thought this was too good to be true. He knew the Irish were very friendly towards the American tourists, but he did not expect this, and he said so to Sean. Quinn did not want to impose himself on anyone, but as Sean continued to insist that his friend would help him and did not expect to be paid, Quinn finally relented and agreed to work with whoever this fellow was with the understanding that Quinn would not seek his help unless he ran into a brick wall. That was agreeable with Sean, and he said he would set everything up when Quinn had his plans all worked out.

As they sat talking about Quinn's progress on gathering information and about Sean's teaching duties at the University, various people again came by the table and passed envelopes to Sean or made comments about meetings, locations, and times. Quinn did not want to get nosey about Sean's business, but he could not resist asking if these guys were also associated with the University. Sean just nodded and said, "Some of them are." Quinn figured that Sean did not want to go into it, and he was not going to press him.

CHAPTER 13

The following morning, Quinn woke up before dawn and drove over to the lakes for his morning run. After going through his stretching routine, he walked a bit and then took off at a good pace. The lake was flat, no wind, and no other runners in sight. As he came up on the north end of the lake, he noticed a solitary runner coming towards him. This was a bit uncommon before sunrise. He seldom ran into anyone before he had finished his run and before the sky had begun to brighten. As the other runner passed by, Quinn raised his arm to acknowledge him, and the other fellow did the same. He looked familiar and Quinn could not place where he had seen him before, but as he thought about it he realized that it may have been the Pub.

The runner was not one of the men that came over to the table, and, in fact, if Quinn was right, he was the tall blond fellow that had made Quinn a bit uncomfortable one evening, because from where he was standing on the other side of the bar, he seemed to be staring at either or both Quinn or Sean the whole time Quinn was in the bar. Quinn had first noticed him because he was very athletic looking, and Quinn had thought he somehow looked familiar, maybe from a running meet or from the track.

At the time, he had dropped the matter from his mind after concluding that the fellow most likely was staring at Sean. That was not overly strange in view of the fact that Sean was a very popular personality in the Pub, and it was not unusual for people to come over to him just to introduce themselves and tell him how much they enjoyed his playing. If Quinn saw him in the Pub again, and he was fairly sure it was the same guy, he would go up to him and mention that they had passed on the lake trail. Quinn never saw the fellow again on his morning runs, and after a time he forgot about the incident.

CHAPTER 14

Quinn flew into Salt Lake City and took the city bus from the airport to Temple Square. He checked into the Travel Motel, stashed his small bag, and walked over to the Mormon Library. It was a modern building, about five stories in height. As he walked in, he was greeted by a Mormon volunteer who gave him directions to the computer room, which he had been told was the best place to start. He was fortunate to avail himself of a computer and was already somewhat familiar with the computer program in use at the Library from prior visits to the Atlanta Mormon library, which was tied into the same system.

Quinn selected the option for the International records, highlighted "Ireland" and then keyed in "Kinsale." The computer buzzed and whirred and then presented him with a long list of documents and resource materials relating to Kinsale in County Cork. He pulled out his notebook and began writing down the film numbers for the vital statistics records that were available in the archives on the next floor. As he was writing, he noticed that he could print out the information depicted on the screen, saving him the time and energy of writing everything down. After he had printed out the data from the computer, he sat down at one of the tables to lay out his research plans. Looking over the printouts from the computer, he saw that there were no Catholic parish records, only some vital statistics, but these were from a time well after his Grandfather had emigrated.

Quinn had noted from studying the maps of the Kinsale area and from Catholic parish boundary maps in the Atlanta Library that Kinsale Parish was relatively small, and while his people may have lived in the area, it may have been in an adjoining Catholic Parish, yet close to the community of Kinsale. The other parishes bordering Kinsale Parish were Clonthead, Innishannon and Courcey's Country Parish. He would start with the films for Kinsale Parish and hope that he would find some information that would be helpful. If he ran into a brick wall, he would then search the other parish records for Catholic Church entries.

As Quinn thought about how he would do his research, he was aware of Sean's comment that Desmond was a common name in Kinsale. What if he found hundreds of Desmonds? That would almost be worse than finding none. He went back to the computer and searched the list of parish records available on microfilm and found films for Catholic records in all of the other three parishes that he had noted. He had been told that some of the parish records had not been released by the Catholic Church to the general public, and one had to go to the diocese to obtain them. He figured that was the case with respect to the absence of any Catholic record entries under "Kinsale" in the computer, at least he hoped that was the case and not an indication that they did not exist.

Quinn printed out the film numbers for the surrounding parishes and planned to review them later. After he had accumulated a number of computer entries on the church records from the communities surrounding Kinsale, he wrote down the film numbers on the Tithe and Griffiths records that were used to establish taxes administered in the early 1800s. This data listed every householder in the country and was broken down by townland, of which there were approximately twelve thousand total on the island of Ireland, so that the area encompassed by each was relatively small. According to Sean, that was an excellent way to begin locating family names, because the data was indexed alphabetically by household family name.

After recording film numbers in his notebook, Quinn went to the basement area of the building where the records for Ireland were kept. He was then directed by a volunteer to the Tithe index books that gave an alphabetical listing of family names and the townland in which they were located when the survey was taken. In reviewing the Tithe book for the Kinsale area, he was surprised to see that there were only two Desmonds listed and not the large number that Sean had led him to believe he would find. He was quite pleased to see that Sean was in error as this could possibly ease his search.

Following the instructions given to him by the Mormon volunteer, Quinn located the film numbers for the Griffith Valuations of the townlands in the Kinsale Parish area. He then pulled the films out of the bins, located a microfilm reader and began scrolling through the film along with hundreds of other people busily engaged in the same activity in adjoining carrels. As he rolled through the film, he saw that the photos of the pages of valuation data varied greatly in clarity. Some of the pages were difficult or impossible to read due to bad lighting in the filming or faulty processing of the film, while other pages were perfectly clear and easy to read. Hopefully the names of the people that he was interested in would be legible.

Quinn closely examined every page on the film, looking for a Desmond or anything resembling the name. He had been told that spellings of names could vary greatly, something he had already discovered in his review of Minnesota Census reports. He carefully reviewed the film but after searching the record for two hours found no entries for Desmonds. Nevertheless, he kept staring at the film entries as he wound his way through the reel, feeling fairly confident that in time he would find something. He was assuming that Jeremiah Desmond was born around 1830, meaning he should find his parents somewhere in the neighborhood.

Quinn kept working through the films and finally came to the two Desmond households located in the same townland, named Ballinacurra. Quinn's pulse quickened as he saw that one of the householders was named Jeremiah Desmond, and he at first thought he had found his grandfather but then realized that this Jeremiah Desmond would have been too young when the record was made to have owned the leasehold. The Griffiths Valuations were drawn up in the 1840s and his grandfather would have been just a child then. As he thought about it further, he recalled Sean's comment that in the old days, the first born male was named after his paternal grandfather. This could well be Jeremiah's grandfather, Quinn's great-great grandfather, and, as he thought about it, the relative ages seemed to work out for that. The other Desmond was a Cornelius Desmond, and that meant nothing in particular to Quinn other than the fact that he was very probably related to the Jeremiah Desmond shown residing on the adjoining lot.

As Quinn read down the list of householders in the townland of Ballinacurra, he noticed that a family by the name of O'Farrell lived just two numbered lots below Jeremiah Desmond. His grandmother, Eileen Farrell Desmond, was said to have come from the same townland as his grandfather. This was more than likely her grandparent's leasehold, because Jeremiah, like virtually all of the Irish back then, married very close to home. Quinn was ecstatic at this early find and wanted to call Sean with the good news. He again thought how fortunate he was to have run into Sean and received his assistance. Without the Gaelic letters and the information they contained, Quinn realized that tracing his Irish ancestors to their homelands would have been virtually impossible. He had been told early on in his quest to trace Irish ancestors that if he did not know the townland where they had come from, he did not stand much of a chance of finding them.

Quinn was in Salt Lake City for only three days, but after his initial success at locating what appeared to be the Desmond townland further progress was very limited. He was lacking the church records from the Catholic parish that encompassed the townland of Ballinacurra and could only hope that the records would be available in the National Library in

Ireland. The Mormons had filmed many, if not most, of the Catholic parish records in the Republic of Ireland but certainly not all of them. The fact that the Kinsale Parish records were not in Salt Lake City did not mean that they would not be in Dublin. Assuming the worst case scenario that the National Library of Ireland did not have the records, they should still be available in the diocese or the local Ballinacurra church. He would worry about that when he was in Ireland.

Quinn believed that others who had emigrated from Ireland and settled in Birch Coulee, Minnesota, at the same time Jeremiah had settled there had more than likely came from the Catholic parish that was just to the west of Ballinacurra, named Inishannon. Quinn based that assumption on the fact that the Griffiths records showed a small townland community in that parish named Ballywin that had a number of family names familiar to Quinn from his Minnesota research. This particular townland, which was situated within five miles of Ballinacurra, was more than likely the homeland of the other Birch Coulee immigrants. It only made sense to Quinn that his Grandfather would at least attempt to emigrate in the company of people familiar to him.

When Quinn tried to review the Innishannon Parish records, he soon became lost in literally hundreds of baptisms and marriages of people with the same surnames as those who had emigrated with his grandfather. If the similarity of the last names was not bad enough, the Inishannon records showed that they all named their children Patrick or Jeremiah or Cornelius. It soon became clear to Quinn that exploring these other family names from his Birch Coulee records would be a fruitless waste of his time in the library. Unless he obtained additional information on these emigrants who had taken up their domicile in Birch Coulee along with Jeremiah Desmond, he would have to restrict his efforts to the Desmond family line.

When Quinn returned to Atlanta, he had not brought back a great volume of information but he was very satisfied with the trip, having a reasonable basis for believing that he had accomplished a major goal, identifying the Desmond townland. When he arrived in Dublin, he would visit the National Archives, go through the census reports, and hopefully be able to trace the Ballinacurra Desmonds to the present day descendants, if there were any. On his flight back from Salt Lake, he had thought about what the experience would be like to meet cousins of his that had lived such a different life from his own. He was not even sure if they would have any interest in meeting him, but he assumed they would want to know what happened to the part of their family that had left Ireland to seek a new life elsewhere.

As soon as Quinn had unpacked and sat down at his desk, he called Sean. It was early in the afternoon when he left a message with Sean's office secretary to give him a call when he returned. Quinn left his home number and within a couple of hours his phone rang. It was Sean. Quinn told him what he had found and that he believed he had located the townland of the Desmonds at Ballinacurra. After explaining to Sean that there were only two Desmonds in the Griffiths materials for the Kinsale area and that one of them was named Jeremiah, Sean had to agree that he had most likely located the correct townland. The church records would validate his opinion, and Sean was almost certain that he would be able to find the Kinsale records in the National Library.

"So when are you planning on going over there?" Sean asked.

"I have a tentative reservation for late October, but I may try to go earlier. I'm beginning to think that I've about exhausted search materials in the States, and I may only find what I need in Ireland."

"Let me know the exact dates when you can. I would be glad to show you around Dublin if I can go at the same time, and remember, I've got a buddy over there that will help you with the research in the National Library," Sean said.

Quinn and Sean then made plans to meet at the Pub on Wednesday evening to go over the rest of what Quinn had found on his trip to Salt Lake.

CHAPTER 15

By the time Sean finished the set, there wasn't an empty seat in the pub. Many in the crowd had by now begun to look familiar to Quinn. He had become acquainted with a few of the Irishmen who Sean had introduced him to, at least to the point where they would greet him when he came in the door. Aside from a few casual friends of Sean's, there were four or five who seemed to Quinn to have some sort of business relationship with Sean, because he had seen them frequently engaged in serious discussions in a corner of the bar.

As of late, Quinn had begun to realize that nearly all of the native born Irishmen in the bar were strong supporters of a united Ireland, to say the least. Their conversations would heat up whenever they talked about British control of Northern Ireland, and they were unanimous in their solution. "Kick the bastards out of our land," they would frequently say. Quinn knew that was the definitive goal of the National Republican political organization, and one night in the pub Quinn mentioned to Sean that he assumed he was a member of the Nationalist Party.

"Of course," Sean answered.

Sean looked at Quinn with a bit of a surprised look on his face that seemed to ask, "What else would I be? All true Irishmen are Nationalists." Sean then paused, seeming to think about what he had said.

He went on, "I'm just not as involved over here as I was in Ireland. I used to spend quite a bit of time with the party when I was there, but being over here puts a damper on all of that."

Sean sat silently for a few moments as though he was thinking over the question and his response. He took a drag on his cigarette and then asked Quinn, "What are your views on what's going on over there?"

Quinn leaned back in his chair and asked, "What do you mean?"

"What do you think I mean? The Troubles. The Irish political scene."

"Well, I'm still putting it together. I'll confess. It hasn't exactly been on my front burner. I thought it had been settled some time ago, but lately I have been reading that it is not settled. Beyond that, I don't know much about it."

"It's not settled and won't be until the Brits are out of the north", Sean said as he crushed his cigarette out in the ash tray. "Geez, you're Irish aren't you? You should be up on this."

Quinn brushed off the remark. He felt he had his own national politics to follow, and he had enough trouble getting his interest up for that. While politics was not the only subject on Sean's mind when they sat talking in the pub, it was certainly the one that came up most frequently. Fortunately, it was not his sole interest.

The two men also talked about the type of work that each of them had done during the course of their lives, with most of the talking being done by Sean because he had held a great variety of jobs. Quinn soon became tired of asking, "What did you do then?" every time Sean said he had been canned or quit a job. He just let Sean ramble on into the next job, the next, and so on. Teaching Gaelic at the University was only the most recent job, and he hadn't been at that very long. As far as Quinn was concerned, Sean was just one of those guys who didn't get into the concept of long-term employment. It wasn't his style. It was clear to Quinn that he used work only as a necessary means to support himself while he actively pursued his real interests. Quinn just wasn't sure what they were.

"Well, Sean, do you like teaching at the 'U'?"

"Do I like it? Good question. I would have to say yes, I do. I like the students. When you work with young people, you learn to like how they're more direct, you know? No bullshit. They don't care about crap like whether you're wearing a tie or those fifties shoes that you seem to enjoy. By the way, I don't think my department head would approve of those. Speaking of that bastard, if he would get off my ass I would probably stay for a while."

Quinn had the distinct impression that this job too would be ending in the not too distant future. Quinn's opinion of Sean had changed considerably since he had first met him at his office. At first, Quinn considered Sean to be a bit of a flake. Intelligent, yes, but a flake. Quinn could now see that Sean's life was not the haphazard, scatterbrained existence that he had first labeled it, and furthermore, Sean seemed to have high respect from everyone of any consequence who frequented the club. What most impressed Quinn about Sean was that he seemed to use his free time to the utmost to nourish his very active mind. He was very well read and very capable of expressing himself on many subjects, which he was prone to do whenever the opportunity arose.

Quinn enjoyed his discussions with Sean, which covered a wide variety of subjects but mostly centered on political issues. They frequently started off a discussion when Sean said something like, "Americans seem to enjoy the Death Penalty."

Quinn would then look at him with a half smile on his face and say, "Now isn't that the kettle calling the pot black?"

"What do you mean?" Sean would counter.

"Well, what are you Irish doing to one another over there other than killing each other?"

"That's different."

Then the arguments back and forth would progress through the break and continue when Sean had his next break. They were lively discussions but done in a friendly manner. Sean argued very logically, but, in Quinn's view, he argued from a very liberal, or even socialist point of view. Sean tended to weight his side of any argument with concepts of what, in his opinion, was good for humanity. That was one area where the discussions would heat up, because Quinn did not believe that providing people with anything over and above bare sustenance was good for their motivation, and, in his mind, individual motivation was necessary for social progress. That argument would tend to get Sean going and almost keep him from rejoining his band mates when the break was over.

"You ever been married, Sean?" Quinn asked one evening at the pub.

"Sure, for a while," Sean answered and took a drink of his beer.

"Got any kids?"

"Two boys," Sean answered. Seeing that Quinn was interested in this and not about to drop the subject, Sean continued, "They all live in Dublin. Wife's name is Annie. Good gal actually. I see them all when ever I get back to Dublin. Kids are 8, 9, 10, thereabouts. I have to stop and think how old they are every now and then, you know, when I don't see them that often."

Quinn pressed on, "What type of work does she do, or is she working?"

Sean lit another cigarette. "Oh, yeah, she works part time in an office in the city center for RTE, the television operation in Ireland. I send them something every now and then to help out."

Sean paused because it was obvious to both of the men that what he sent wasn't much.

"We were separated for a long time, but now we are divorced. Ireland, you know. They put up the road blocks on that. I don't care, though, because I'd never get married again anyway, so what the hell's the difference."

He took another drink of his Guinness and drew on his cigarette while he looked around the pub to see who was there. This conversation made him a bit uneasy and his body language suggested a change of topic, but Quinn was curious about this aspect of his friend's life.

"Have you thought about trying to work over there instead of here?"

"I can make more money over here, and that's what they need. Between what I send and what she makes, there is barely enough to get them through."

Quinn had told Sean that he, too, was divorced, and the two men discussed what a lousy experience the breakups had been. In Sean's case, his wife could not deal with his lifestyle. They had lived together for a few years before getting married, but when they did and the kids came, the fun was over. She took on a whole new attitude. He tried the nine to five routine for a while, but it about killed him, and he just couldn't live his life that way. Actually, she sort of understood, but she just didn't want to stay married with him out and about half the time with very little money coming in. Sean said that he still had sort of a relationship with Annie and called her at least once a week.

"Who knows, maybe someday we can put it back together. When I'm in Dublin, I spend every available minute with her and the boys."

Quinn sat and looked at his friend, not particularly feeling sorry for him, but understanding that the path in life that he had chosen to follow was not always an easy one. Sean took his glasses off and rubbed his eyes. He looked older to Quinn. His eyes had a tired look about them when they were not hidden behind large glass ovals with the busted frame. His obvious lack of exercise did not enhance his appearance, with his rounded shoulders and the start of a paunch on his otherwise thin body.

Quinn thought to himself, "Christ, what this guy needs is a good running program." He had brought it up before, but it did not receive much of a reception. Sean's only comment had been, "I don't have time for that crap. You live and then you die. Make the best of the time you've got." Quinn could not convince him that if he took care of himself, he would possibly have more time to do the things he wanted to do. Sean didn't buy the argument.

CHAPTER 16

That evening, Quinn returned to his home and pulled up the National Republican homepage on the Internet. The page depicted a large, black eagle with claws clutching a globe and Gaelic wording with an English transcription under it that read, "One Nation, One People."

"Impressive," thought Quinn.

He read the party platform and some of the posted material, including a number of past editions of "Our People," the National Republican News," the official publication of the party. Quinn was somewhat familiar with the Nationalist organization as was anyone that paid any attention whatsoever to the news, and he was also aware that it was considered by many to be the legitimate political arm of the illegitimate Irish Nationalist Army.

With his limited knowledge as to what the real issues were over there, he had mixed feelings regarding them. He could understand the antagonism against the English but had difficulty understanding why the separate Irish groups could not seem to resolve their differences. He had a real problem seeing any justification in military operations that seemed to be aimed, for the most part, at innocent people. He decided to discuss that with Sean some time, but that was probably a touchy issue, and he would have to use some discretion when approaching the subject.

CHAPTER 17

P atrick sat in his office for some time with the door closed, digesting what Carter had said at lunch. He thought it was interesting that there were other Desmonds in the States, offspring, apparently, of the brother who had emigrated. He wondered what they were like and what their intentions were. As he thought about it, he realized that he didn't care what they were like as long as they were not interested in Desmond Enterprises or any of his property. He thought about discussing the matter with Hillary but knew it would be a mistake. He knew that Hillary would drop him like a hot brick if his financial situation suddenly reversed. He needed her brains in the business. She had about as much loyalty towards him as Tony Carter, maybe less. He would have to go slow in deciding how to handle this business and not proceed with undue haste.

In the meantime, he would get back to company concerns. He called Martha on the interphone and told her to come into his office. She walked in and stood in front of his desk with pen and note pad in hand. Patrick told her to boost the contribution this month in the Erin Antiquities account by a fourth. Martha raised an eyebrow, made a notation on the pad, leaned over the desk to display her ample bosom to her employer, and asked, "When do I get a raise?"

Patrick paid her little attention, staring off into space and twisting the pencil in his sweating palms.

That evening, sitting in his study, sipping Benedictine from his favorite brandy snifter, Patrick thought over what Carter had said. The sun was setting and Patrick had not bothered to turn on the lights, which added to the dismal thoughts that were passing through his mind. Sitting at his desk, he faced a large window on the other side of the study that provided a view of the rolling, well manicured lawns of the estate. The house, the acreage, and the lawn treatments suggested great wealth, but as Patrick sat staring out the window, he found it a depressing sight. He had come to take all of this for granted, as though providence had ordained this for him alone and for no one else. Now, it seemed, someone was stepping out of the past, threatening to take it all away. The thought chilled him to the bone, and he took another sip of the Benedictine to dull the pain.

Patrick could not imagine having to part with the home that had been in the family for the last three generations. The house and grounds had belonged to the Desmond family ever since his great grandfather, Thomas Desmond, managed to insert himself into the Adams family fortune by marrying the widow of his employer. Patrick pondered for a moment the horrible possibility that his great grandfather had the old Englishman rubbed out just so he could take his place at the dinner table. No, he thought, things are bad enough, with grandfather William being accused of absconding with the inheritance. Fortunately, we're only dealing with fraud or theft and not murder, which is way too far beneath the dignity of the Desmond family. Patrick chuckled and said, "Way beneath the dignity."

The Benedictine was now working on Patrick to the extent that he was beginning to find some elements of black humor in his situation. "God, what if Hillary had to go to work? No, forget that. She has the Fairchild fortune to play with, and she would laugh her ass off if I had to give up Park Ridge."

Patrick dwelled on that for a moment. After taking another drink of his Benedictine, he concluded that Hillary would sit back and watch Park Ridge sell to the highest bidder and then announce, after the divorce, that she had, in fact, been the highest bidder.

He envisioned her saying, "Now get the rest of your crap out of here, Desmond."

His vision was eerily real, as if she were in the room at that moment. Just then, as he was staring out the window, he watched as her Rolls Silver Shadow came through the entry gate and drove up the circular drive to the front of the house. Their houseman would be holding the door for her, and she would be entering his study within, he glanced at his watch, the next three minutes.

Hillary always came looking for him in the study because that was his favorite room in the entire house. He had his television set, a bottle of Benedictine, the London Times, and the other trappings that made his life somewhat enjoyable. She never checked in on him because she missed him or wanted to be with him. Her purpose was to amuse herself by informing him of his latest screw up in Desmond Enterprises, the one that she had managed to correct in the nick of time, or, if she lacked some such hot item, she would criticize something in his personal life, his clothing, friends, or personal habits.

Patrick could always tell what her day was like depending on the line of attack she chose, whether she had had a particularly good day, stock prices were up, a good earnings report had arrived, or she had sacked some poor old devil that would now be in the unemployment lines. And she never forgot to comment on Patrick's unfortunate background, his being born Irish. He poured himself another tumbler of Benedictine and chuckled to himself at the thought that he had actually married the bitch. She was right, he was occasionally very stupid.

The door to his study swung open, and Hillary flung herself into the room. That was another form of entertainment for her. She enjoyed scaring the hell out of Patrick with sudden unexpected moves, and the look on her face displayed the pleasure she received from this game of hers, the half open smiling mouth, the wide open eyes, the joy of catching her husband's every jerk and twitch of reverie suddenly, violently disturbed. This time he had known she would be making her traditional entry and was prepared for the sudden disturbance of his peace.

"Well, I see you're busy with your booze. A little early isn't it? You usually wait at least until half five."

She stood in front of his chair, a little closer than he would have preferred, wearing her color coordinated tennis outfit with the very short skirt that she enjoyed, because it showed off her one remaining physical asset, a rather perfectly formed rear end. Patrick had thought for some time that her active social life placed demands on certain parts of her anatomy.

Patrick was now somewhat mellowed by the Benedictine and was not about to be cowed by his wife.

"And I see that you've been quite busy today," Patrick retorted. "You may be pleased to hear that the children are coming here this weekend, so I thought we could all have a nice family get together."

He knew this would shut her up faster than anything. She had absolutely no more interest in spending time with Ellen and Adam than with him. This sudden announcement that had the possibility of interfering with her more enjoyable plans brought Hillary up short. She was silent for a moment, but Patrick admired the fact that she was able to maintain the same false smile she had on her face upon entering the room. There was a momentary pause in the conversation while Hillary rummaged through her bag of excuses to come up with a suitable reply.

"Bad timing," she finally said. "We're having a Board meeting on Saturday, and I have to be there to kick some ass. I also have plans for that geek you hired to run the retail stores. Have you looked at the financials yet on that operation, or have you been too busy with Martha?"

Patrick ignored the jab about his secretary and responded, "I did... see the financials, and we are doing quite well. We're in the black showing a seventeen percent profit, so what's your problem?"

Hillary laughed sarcastically while looking down at Patrick. "Take out the income from the sale of your Dublin vacant land, and you will see that you have about a ten percent loss. I would suggest you consider doing something before the entire business goes under."

Hillary paused and thought for a moment. "Forget it. I'll take care of it myself. You may see quite a few new faces in the executive offices next time you go down there, if you ever do."

Patrick glumly sipped the Benedictine, pondering how he had found himself in this situation, while Hillary stood there prattling away. He chuckled to himself at this thought. How could he have been so stupid as to let this happen?

"What's so funny Mr. President? Maybe it's the booze that's getting to you. Benedictine, that's a great drink for you Irish. The monks are the ones that came up with it, you know. It's a real, Catholic drink. Anyway, you sit here and finish off that bottle. I've got to clean up and get moving. I'm meeting some people at the Club in one hour."

With that, Hillary spun around and left the study, slamming the door behind her as she left. Patrick's chuckle soured.

"Meeting some people at the club, my ass!" he thought to himself. "She's got that tennis pro working overtime tonight."

Patrick tried to reconstruct in his mind the numbers on the profit and loss sheet for the retail stores.

"Maybe she was right," he thought. "What the hell, maybe she was right? She's always right."

This thought further depressed him and he refilled the glass. He would divorce the bitch, but on second thought he knew that he couldn't afford to do that. "She does have a golden touch in running the business, or is it a black club with a nail in it?"

Hillary had always been tough and he hadn't. Desmond Enterprises needed someone at the helm who had the balls to do the dirty work. With her it wasn't a matter of having the balls. She just plainly enjoyed handling the dirty work.

CHAPTER 18

Patrick sat in his study enjoying the quiet, watching as Hillary's Rolls drove down the driveway towards the gate. As her car entered the main road and disappeared from sight, he sank more comfortably into his soft leather cushioned chair and breathed a sigh of relief.

He looked over at the Benedictine bottle and spoke to it as though to a friend, "I've got to lay off of you, old Buddy. I've got problems in my lousy ass life that are going to require whatever brain cells I have left to figure out how to get out of all these messes. But, before we do that, I'll have one last drink, at least for today."

With that, Patrick poured himself half a glass, swirled it around, sniffed the sweet aroma, and took just enough to wet the inside of his mouth. He then set the glass down and a warm sense of euphoria came over him, settling him further back into his favorite chair as he rather absentmindedly surveyed the contents of his study.

The book shelves were filled with old leather bound books from days and generations past with a few current best sellers in the bookcase closest to the desk. He had read only a few of the books on the shelves, those of recent publication. As he surveyed the collection, he thought to himself that he should read more and not waste as much time as he did. As he sat looking at the old volumes in the shelves around the room, he realized that they had all been in exactly the same location his entire life and quite probably the entire life of his father and maybe even the life of his grandfather. He had never known of anyone in his family who had actually read these books.

The collection had originally belonged to the Adams family and his grandfather William had inherited it. The maid would occasionally run a feather duster over the bindings, or at least the part that she could reach, but that was the only attention they ever received. The books just might contain some gems of wisdom. He would have to put that on his to do list, along with everything else. Maybe next week he would at least survey the books. He had no idea what they might contain, and that could be interesting.

As Patrick continued his survey of the room, his eyes came to the large oil portrait of his grandfather. He hated the picture because no matter where he was in the room, his grandfather's eyes seemed to follow him, and he had a look of disdain on his face as though he were about to chastise Patrick for being such a lousy custodian of the Desmond family fortune. Patrick looked away from the picture, resolving to have it removed one of these days and thought about how his own father, Dennis, had commented on the painting. The painting had probably given him the same feelings of guilt that Patrick was experiencing, but as he thought further about his father, he knew that guilt had never entered his mind.

Patrick turned his gaze back to the picture of his grandfather and thought to himself, "You are the guy who caused this problem, that is, if I have a problem. I could be happily farming someplace down in the Republic, eating potatoes from my garden, but instead I'm up here sweating my balls off because I might lose this easy life that I've grown so, so used to. It's all your fault, damn it."

Patrick thought about that for a moment and concluded that it was a bit harsh, "Just kidding gramps, beats the hell out of working." With that, Patrick raised his glass in a salute to his ancestor, downed the remaining liquid, leaned back in the chair, and promptly fell asleep.

On Saturday morning, Ellen arrived on the train at the Belfast station at noon. Patrick and Adam were waiting in the lobby for her after she made her way through security. When she saw her father and brother, she rushed up to give them both a hug. Patrick had picked up Adam at Royal Crest on his way to the station, and his son was looking forward to the weekend away from the close supervision of the dorm monitors. Patrick explained to his son and daughter that their mother was unable to be with them this morning because of the Board meeting, but that she would see them at dinner that evening.

When they got in the car, Ellen brought her father up to date on what was happening at the Desmond offices in Dublin. Patrick had spoken with the Dublin office manager who was quite taken with Ellen's abilities to handle some of the more difficult problems that cropped up with shipments of merchandise that for one reason or another had been delayed or lost en route.

Patrick thought, "She's a chip off the old block," referring not to himself, but to Hillary. He hoped that Ellen did not take on all of the characteristics of her mother and so far his daughter seemed to be keeping her social life within reasonable bounds. Ellen, being the older of the two, somewhat dominated the conversation as Adam occasionally snuck a comment in here or there about how difficult his life was at Royal Crest.

Ellen had talked about training for a marathon the following spring in

Dublin, but Patrick had been trying to talk her out of doing that, saying that he thought it was too strenuous. Ellen laughed at his concern and suggested that he should think about doing something like that himself, as she made a point of staring down at his paunch. He went along with the joke and said, "Well, I just may do that."

Adam, sitting quietly in the backseat, had adopted his normally sullen attitude as he stared morosely out the car window, surveying the bleak Belfast street scenes. Adam seemed oblivious to the lack of affection emanating from either parent. Most of the time, he was deep in his own thoughts, pondering a current intellectual pursuit or dreaming up some suitably painful torture for the boys at Royal Crest who continuously made him the brunt of their jokes. He hated the school, the teachers, administrators, dorm prefects, and most of all his classmates. He considered them far beneath him on the social scale, inferiors academically and without any of the cultural attributes of one with noble blood, such as himself.

Adam had somehow conjured up in his own mind that the Adam's family, who were in his ancestral chain, had an ample enough amount of royal blood running through their veins to overcome the pollution stemming from his Irish ancestry. He ignored the fact that his relationship to the Adams family was by marriage and not by descent. He had studied the family relationships running back to his great-great-grandfather, Thomas Desmond, who had married into the Adams family, and had noted the parentage of all contributors to his own existence, concluding, rather erroneously, that he was poisoned by less than one twentieth of what he called, "Irish peasant blood."

From his earliest youth, Adam had made no attempt to gain his father's favor and, in fact, took a certain amount of pleasure in adopting the attitudes or behaviors that he knew incensed his father when he was in his company. Their conversations were stilted, artificial, and constructed solely to fill embarrassing gaps of silent space when they were in each other's company. It was very apparent to both that when they separated, each breathed a sigh of relief.

Patrick's concern for his children was focused primarily if not solely on his daughter, Ellen. He was most concerned about her living in Dublin, the capital of the Republic and a hotbed of nationalist politics. He was well aware that she was associating socially with young men who were politically involved, boys who could be dangerous for a number of reasons.

This was the subject of frequent conversations between the two. Patrick was concerned about the risk from not only the Nationalist interests who might try to do something, but also from people who saw his children as potential ransom targets.

The Desmond name was quite well known in both the north and south of Ireland due to the family's wealth. He had his security people watching Ellen, which was a source of great irritation to her. She never missed an opportunity to complain to her father and request that he call off the wolves, as she put it. For his part, he would never forgive himself if he relaxed the security and then something happened.

Patrick sometimes pondered how he would react if someone kidnapped Adam and demanded an exorbitant sum for his release. He could not quite envision himself parting with his worldly possessions to regain possession of a son that in his most charitable moment he looked upon as an embarrassment. Hopefully he would not be put to the test, because he would be pilloried in the public eye if he did nothing to retrieve his offspring.

Ellen raised the security issue again, "I would just tell them to give me my space. I swear to God they drive me nuts. Every time I look up, there they are, peering around a lamp post some place." Patrick did not respond, hoping to let the issue pass.

After a pause, he said, "I hope you aren't running around telling everyone you're from Belfast."

Ellen smiled. "Dad, people know awfully quick that you're from Belfast and not Dublin. Also your advertising down there pretty well spreads the name around."

They both laughed. "I suppose that's true," Patrick added. "How do you hide your daughter when you are spending millions on advertising the name? So, just be careful."

Hillary returned just as dinner was being served and apologized profusely for being so late in getting together with Ellen and Adam. Surprising as it always was to Patrick, both Ellen and Adam appeared reasonably happy to see their mother. While she was certainly not one's typical mother, Patrick reasoned that she did serve in one sense as a role model for the two. She was very successful in business and definitely ran her own life. This appealed to both Ellen and Adam. As for the more spirited side of her personality, Patrick figured they were either unaware of it or just not interested. The four of them sat in the family room situated in the rear of the house while the house servants prepared dinner and served all of them drinks. Patrick always felt uncomfortable seeing Adam being served hard liquor. He had complained about it a number of times, but Hillary always overruled him. Patrick had the impression that he was watching an eight year old child drink rather than a young man about to graduate from college.

After everyone had relaxed with a drink or two, the conversation livened up and all of them were laughing as Ellen told one story after another about her experiences on dates or funny happenings at work. She thoroughly enjoyed Dublin with its theaters, restaurants, and numerous pubs. It was a far more sociable city than Belfast, and there was a lot more going on that appealed to a young woman fresh out of the University. Ellen was a theater buff and never missed a performance at the Abbey or the Gate and was a frequent visitor to the National Art Gallery on Merrion Square. The pubs on Baggot Street were a regular stop after work, particularly on Friday evenings when the entire crew from the Desmond office would go to Dooleys for a pint or two.

As they were having dinner, everyone appeared to enjoy themselves, even Adam. Patrick thought how nice it would be if they could do this more often. He knew that Hillary could not tolerate such family togetherness more than one or two evenings a month. He studied her as he, she and Ellen engaged in conversation. He concluded that she was truly a great actress who could turn it on and off to fit the occasion. It was a pity that it was all an act, but that didn't bother him anymore. It had bothered him years ago, but now he could watch her performance and feel nothing. He knew Hillary held no special motherly love towards her daughter and even less towards her son, but she certainly did not actually dislike either one of them. It was rather that she had other things to do than to spend all or even a substantial amount of her time with them. She also did not enjoy being motherly nice for long periods of time. She could fake it for an evening or, in an emergency, for a weekend, but that was about it.

Hillary finally announced that she was going to get some rest. Patrick knew she was not particularly tired as much as she was bored. She needed excitement to keep her going and there was none here with her two children and her boring, not-too-intelligent husband. After she left the room, the conversation continued in earnest and Ellen and Patrick stayed up well past midnight laughing and talking about events in their separate lives. Adam had parted company from the two shortly after his mother had left. He explained that he had a paper to turn in on Monday and wanted to get to work on it. Both wished him well and immediately went back to their conversation.

Patrick thoroughly enjoyed his time with Ellen. It was one of the very few things in his life that he continued to have an interest in. He had noticed that in the last few years most of the activities or past times that he had found entertaining or challenging in his younger years no longer had that sparkle or energizing effect on him. At the end of the evening when he was getting into his bed, he realized for the first time since picking up Adam and Ellen that he had never once thought about the problem of the mysterious cousin in the States. Maybe after a period of time he would just forget about it and it would go away. He hoped it would anyway.

When Patrick arose the following morning, which was Sunday, the house was empty. There was a note left on the breakfast table from Hillary to Ellen and Adam explaining that she had to run to the office and would not return until later in the day. She said that she would call them sometime during the week. The cook then informed Patrick that Ellen had gone to meet some of her Queen's College classmates and would be back shortly after noon before she had to catch a return trip to Dublin on the 2:00 train.

Patrick read the Belfast Independent editorial page and noted that the writer's political arguments and the citizen's commentary regarding the upcoming Assembly election were becoming very heated. The Unionists, those favoring ties with Great Britain, still held a majority of the Assembly seats, but their control had been gradually weakening over the last two elections in particular. This weakening of the party favoring close ties with Great Britain seemed to further destabilize the situation between those in favor of unification with the Republic in the south and those opposed. Patrick could not understand why anyone in Northern Ireland wanted unification with the Republic. He knew the Republic was not going to pick up the tab for the costly Northern Ireland social programs that Great Britain had been paying for in the past. The result of unification with the Republic would be catastrophic for the economy and the stability of the north and would bankrupt the south if they tried to pay the bill. The result would be chaos.

The best solution in Patrick's mind was an independent Northern Ireland with continued support from Great Britain until the new nation learned to live within its means. That could take many years since the country had grown quite comfortable living with the negative cash flow at the expense of Great Britain. Patrick did not know what the latest figures were on the portion of the North's budget going to social programs, but he estimated it to be between one fourth and one third of the total cost.

Patrick was well aware of the fact that the demographics of Northern Ireland were shifting in favor of the minority Catholic population and that within another ten or twenty years the Catholics would have numerical superiority among those of voting age. That could prove to be an interesting time if they tried to take too much advantage of their political power.

Patrick did not consider himself as much an Irishman as he considered himself a Protestant tied politically to the British government. He looked to Great Britain for solutions to the problems of Northern Ireland and considered the Irish government in Dublin to be intent on acting contrary to his best interests. He was aware of the history of the Desmond family as being Catholic and agrarian Irish right up to the time his great grandfather married into the Anglican Adams family and traded loyalty to the Nationalist cause for a life of comfort.

How the Desmonds lived their lives for generations before made little impression on Patrick after a lifetime spent absorbing the comforts and perks that came with the substantial Desmond Family wealth. On those few occasions when he did think about the changes in the Desmond Family lifestyle, from the tenant farmer days to the present, he would conclude that any other staunchly Irish Nationalist would have made the same political concessions his family had made in order to lead the good life. Anyone that said otherwise was a damn liar or had been drinking too much of their homegrown "poteen."

Patrick was startled out of a nap when Ellen entered the breakfast room.

"Wake up, Dad. You have to run me over to the train depot, and I don't have a lot of time."

She ran by his chair giving him a friendly jab on the shoulder. Not slowing down, she continued on her way.

"I still have to pack up a few things, but I can be ready in about five minutes."

Patrick took a drink of his tea, which was now cold, in an attempt to bring himself around. With the house so quiet, he had dozed off and must have gone into a deep slumber. He looked at his watch and figured he must have been asleep for at least an hour. He rubbed his eyes and responded to Ellen, who was now half way up the stairway heading for her room to get her things, "No problem, whenever."

He received no response, but when he brought the car around, Ellen was at the front door with her knapsack hanging off her shoulder, wearing her blue jeans and those overly thick-soled shoes that he thought were so ugly.

On the way to the airport, Ellen suggested he come down to Dublin and spend some time with her. He could stay in her apartment in Ballsbridge. It would give them a chance to get together, because her social calendar would not permit another weekend away from Dublin for at least another three to four months. There was no mention of Hillary not being there to see her daughter off, and she seemed in good spirits, so Patrick assumed that she was not offended by her mother's absence. As he dropped her off at the train depot, he agreed that he would try to get away for a few days and would call her after he checked his calendar.

As he pulled out of the drop off point, two men from the Desmond Security Department stepped out of one of the company vehicles and followed Ellen into the station. They must have been following him and he hadn't even noticed it. He would have to be more alert in the future.

As Patrick sat in his office at the Port Towers, behind the carved oak desk that had originally belonged to his grandfather, Patrick twisted the sterling silver letter opener in his hands as he rethought the events of the past few days. The only sound was the ticking of the eighteenth century pendulum grandfather clock that Patrick had inherited when he stepped into the shoes of the president of Desmond Enterprises. He often wondered where the clock had come from originally but only knew that it had not been in the Desmond family before his great grandfather married into the wealthy Adams family. His great grandfather barely owned the shirt on his back and maybe even that was leased.

In the quiet of the office, Patrick thought about the information that Carter had given to him. Unity was always looking for new ways to approach him for money and this could be their latest gimmick. As he twisted the opener, he rejected the thought that this was a ploy. He had heard too many rumors. Unity would not have come up with this story unless there was some truth to it. Just how much was truth and how much was created for his benefit he did not know. What to do about it; that was the question. He could not just sit passively and await Unity's next move. That would drive him nuts. He rapidly twisted the letter opener and finally, in frustration, placed it back in the pencil tray of his desk drawer. He pressed the intercom and told Martha to have his security chief, Frank Baumler, come to his office. Within minutes, Martha announced on the intercom, "Mr. Baumler is here to see you."

Patrick pressed the transmit button, "Send him in."

Frank Baumler, age fifty-two, a former member of the Royal Ulster Security Force in charge of Intelligence Operations and now the head of Desmond Enterprises Security Worldwide, came in the door carrying his note pad. Many in the office had commented that Baumler was one of those people who just looked like a cop. Square shoulders, slightly weathered complexion, firm jaw, and eyes that studied everyone and everything. He was not a large man, average in height and proportion, but he had the look of one who could take care of himself. Patrick admired Baumler's cool and thorough manner of handling touchy problems that occasionally arose for Desmond Enterprises. He had the utmost confidence in Frank and trusted him like a brother. In fact, Baumler was one of the very few people, other than Martha, that Patrick trusted.

Frank Baumler had been with Desmond Enterprises for fifteen years and knew more about the secret lives of every executive and sensitive employee of the company than they did themselves. He was fully aware that Patrick had been screwing Martha for about as many years as she had been with Desmond Enterprises and he was also routinely briefed on the latest sexual exploits of Hillary Fairchild Desmond. Frank was also smart enough not to, as he said, "dip his pecker in the company inkwell," even though he had entertained the thought on more than one occasion. If others wanted to make themselves vulnerable to whatever pressures a discarded lover might wish to lay on a top executive, that was their business. It was Frank's job to know about it and to see that the recipient of the pressure did not do something stupid to injure Desmond Enterprises or others in the company. He was very good at carrying out this responsibility and so far a number of potentially embarrassing situations had been defused.

"You rang, Chief?"

Baumler always called Patrick "Chief," having transferred the title from his immediate supervisor in the R.U.S.F. over to Patrick when he was hired at Desmond Enterprises. Patrick enjoyed the patronage. He didn't receive much support for his ego from other quarters. Most of the top company people knew that Hillary made the tough decisions and that Patrick's primary mission in the company was to sign letters containing instructions that really arose from her.

"Have a chair Frank."

Patrick had not fixed in his mind how much of what Unity had told him he would pass on to Baumler. He was nervous about spreading the story around and having others press the issue for their own reasons. His trust level in others in the company, as elsewhere, was not high.

"I dropped Ellen off at the train depot yesterday, and, as usual, she had a few gripes about being over-monitored. Can we loosen the net on her a bit without weakening protection?"

"Chief, we're trying to keep our distance without sacrificing protection for her. I'll talk to the boys and see what we can do. Remember, many people, good and bad, know who she is, and that applies in Belfast as well as in Dublin. It goes with the territory."

Patrick opened the desk drawer again and began twirling a letter opener in his hands. "

"God, this world is nuts. What the hell is wrong with people who would even think of harming somebody like Ellen? My God, haven't they got better things to do?"

"Chief, we've got some good men watching her."

"I know, Frank. I'm not criticizing you or your people. It's just this insane damn world we live in."

"Well, Chief. You know the INA sort of keeps an eye on her from time to time, and with them, you know, we do have some professional courtesies that still exist. If the opposition on any issue is barking up a tree that we know is not going to produce a lot of fruit for them and is causing us some grief, we just go to them and tell them, boys, knock this shit off or we'll start following your kids around town. If you want to know something about Ellen Desmond, call me, and most likely I will just tell you unless it involves her sex life. Sorry Chief, I shouldn't have said that, but you get the point. Now that frequently works. Not all the time, but about half the time. When it doesn't we take more drastic measures. Maybe we get the guy that follows them, and we give him a new face. We don't like to do that unless it is absolutely necessary, because then they feel that they have to retaliate like they did with Billy McCann two years ago. He hasn't been skiing in Austria ever since. Anyway, I don't think you have to worry about anything in particular at this point. We are keeping a close eye on her and we can pull people in at a moment's notice if we see trouble. As for loosening the watch, I will tell the boys to use the utmost discretion but not to go easy on the security aspect. Okay, Chief?"

Patrick nodded in agreement, "Yeah, do that."

After Baumler finished bringing Patrick up to date on what was happening with respect to company security, the two men sat in silence as Patrick thought over how to approach the subject that had caused him to bring Baumler to his office in the first place. As he sat in his leather chair, twirling the opener and studying the man sitting on the other side of the desk, he concluded that it would be better to discuss this now rather than later when it had really gone down the toilet.

"Frank, I have a bit of a problem that I want to discuss, but I must first caution you that it requires your utmost secrecy. I don't want anyone else to hear about this."

Baumler nodded, "Chief, you can count on it."

Patrick then relayed to Baumler the information that had been given to him by Tony Carter. When he explained the issue of the potential problem with the inheritance to his grandfather, Baumler raised an eyebrow. He was familiar with the fact that Patrick's business had been handed down over two or three generations and was the mainstay of the Desmond fortune. He was also aware that others, in the past, had made claims that they were long lost relatives entitled to a share in the Adam's legacy, but all of these were very easily disproved. Having this potential claim passed on by Unity gave it a certain amount of credibility that concerned him.

Patrick did not mention the fact that his own father had said there may have been some games played by Patrick's grandfather, because he did not want to bring that out unless it was absolutely necessary. When he finished, he laid the letter opener on his desk, looked up at Baumler, and asked, "What do you think?"

"Very interesting, Chief. A couple of things come to mind. Unity could be bullshitting you or there could be something to the story. I think you have to handle this as though it were true in order to take the necessary precautions to protect yourself."

Baumler paused while he put his thoughts in order, then continued, "For openers, I would question that they can proceed on such a claim this many years later."

Patrick shook his head and said, "I'm told by Unity that they can if there was fraud involved."

"Well, was there?" Baumler asked.

Patrick thought about what to say and then replied, "I don't know if there was or there wasn't. There were stories."

"Hmm, tell you what I think, Chief. Find out who this so called relative is and let's find out what we can about him. Maybe we can get him steered in a different direction. There are a hundred thousand Desmond families in all of Ireland that we might aim him at."

Patrick again shook his head, "No, I don't think that will work. Apparently the INA agent who is in contact with him is steering him directly to me. They are working overtime to turn this thing into a real ball of crap for me. I'm about to go to the Nationalist Office in Dublin and tell them I won't give to Unity anymore. Trouble is, then Unity would get this guy on my ass just to get even. Frank, this thing could be a real problem from what little I know about it."

"Chief, let's do this. Get the information on this guy and let us check him out. We should find a soft spot someplace. Maybe the guy has no interest in bothering you, or if he does, maybe he would take a token payoff to disappear. Better to know what you are up against than to be in the dark."

The two men continued discussing alternatives for another fifteen minutes and then Baumler had to leave for a staff meeting. Patrick thought over what he had said and concluded that Baumler's suggestion to learn what they could was a good one. Right now, he didn't even know the guy's name or where he lived. He thought Carter had said his name was Packer, but he wasn't even sure about that. He would have to get more information from Tony Carter and that could be difficult if Carter sensed what he was up to. He had Martha schedule a meeting for the following day in the club restaurant.

Patrick had a sleepless night as he thought over what Baumler had suggested. He tried to lay out what he would say to Carter and how he would say it in order to get more facts on this long lost cousin. When he arrived at his office in the morning, Martha told him he looked like hell. He didn't reply as he shuffled past her desk and went into his office. All morning long as he sat in silence at his desk, he continued deep in thought, fruitlessly trying to script his noon meeting. Hours later, when he left for the club, he still had not resolved what he was going to say to elicit the information he needed to pass on to Baumler.

CHAPTER 19

The following day at noon, Patrick nervously sat in the plush dining room accommodations of the Royal Ulster Golf Club awaiting the arrival of Tony Carter. Exactly on the hour, Tony Carter entered the dining room and was ushered to Mr. Desmond's table. The two shook hands to add to the appearance of a normal business lunch, and then Carter ordered a glass of wine while Patrick told the waiter to bring him a vodka tonic. The two chatted about minor items in the news and the latest sports scores. Neither was overly interested in any sporting activity, professional or otherwise, but they wanted their meeting to conform with what was taking place at virtually every other table in the room. After a time, Patrick lowered his voice and inquired as to whether or not Unity had heard anything in addition to what he had been told on the previous Friday.

Tony Carter put on a big smile to dissuade any observer from becoming aware of the nature of their conversation. He wiped his hands on his table napkin and simply said, "No."

Patrick thought to himself that he had to be careful about how to get the information on the problem in Georgia.

"I suppose with my luck, this guy's name is also Desmond, right?" Patrick asked.

Carter smiled and said, "No, remember, I think I told you it was Parker."

Carter purposely did not give Patrick the purported relative's full name, nor did he add any personal information about what type of work he was involved with, his family, or other data that could be of use to Patrick.

Patrick remembered that Carter had said something about an Irish Pub in Atlanta, but he had forgotten the name or was so stunned with what Carter had been saying that he had just not heard him say the name. Patrick figured that while he knew little about Parker he had enough information for Baumler to find him. There could only be so many Irish pubs in Atlanta, and they would just have to go through the Parkers in the city to find the one that frequented the place. How Baumler would do that was of no concern to Patrick. In the meantime, he decided to go easy on pressing Tony Carter for additional information.

Patrick thought to himself that he had to reinforce the reason for having called Carter to the meeting. "I just wanted to tell you that we boosted our contribution a bit to Unity. I thought you might like to know that."

Carter gave him a broad smile and said how pleased he was to hear that.

"Patrick, I'll pass that on to the boys in the office. That means a lot. We've been picking up some big bills on this deal in Georgia, and while we want to help you out, there are limits."

Patrick knew Unity wouldn't lift a finger for him unless there were dividends in the deal for them. Now that each of the two men had something to take away from the meeting, they spent the remainder of the lunch trying to avoid an argument.

As Patrick was folding up his dinner napkin and preparing to leave, Carter said, "There's your wife, and she's waving at you."

Patrick looked up to where Carter was indicating and saw Hillary standing in the entryway to the dining room wearing her tennis outfit. She was using her hands to say that she wanted to talk with him but was not dressed properly to enter the dining room. Patrick was tempted to feign that he did not know what she wanted, but knew that if he did, she would very likely just walk in regardless of the rules and embarrass the hell out of him. She had done that before when he, in fact, mistook her signals as telling him she was just leaving the club. In her loud voice on that occasion, she had made it clear to all within listening range that he was the cause of her having to violate the sanctity of the dining room. Patrick quickly penciled in his member number, signed the luncheon slip, and, in the company of Tony Carter, headed towards the lobby and his waiting wife.

As he came up to her, he asked, "What's the problem?"

With a look of disappointment on her face and holding her fist in a mock threatening manner, Hillary told him that Mary Sloan, her usual tennis partner, had not shown up, and she was not only out of a tennis match this afternoon but also without a ride back to the house.

"I don't know what the hell she was thinking. I told her I was going to have Benjamin drop me here and she could give me a ride back to the house after the match."

Patrick wondered what else Benjamin, their yard man, had done for her today. Before he could respond, Hillary looked at Tony Carter and said, "Well, don't we introduce people anymore?"

Patrick immediately introduced his wife to Carter who now became, warm, friendly Tony Carter with a pleasant grin on his face.

"Mrs. Desmond, it is a pleasure to meet you. I knew who you were because I've seen you from a distance when you were with your husband.

I'm sorry to hear about the match. That happens to me too often as well, and I know how it can irritate a person."

Patrick did not ever recall Carter mentioning that he played tennis, but maybe he did. The two had never talked at length about their personal lives.

With the bait laid out before her, Hillary promptly took the hook and responded, "If you had your gear, you could take Mary Sloan's place. I still have the court reserved for two and it's only one-thirty now. Tell you what, the pro can fix you up if you want to get a little exercise."

Carter paused only long enough to not appear too anxious and then responded, "I could do that. I'm not the greatest player around, but I can usually get the ball back as long as it comes across the net slowly. If you are willing to put up with that, I'm willing to give it a try."

Hillary was now beaming to see that she had her afternoon social calendar filled with this ruggedly handsome looking associate of her husband's. She was a bit curious as to who he was, but she would learn all of that after her husband departed.

Patrick was almost bored listening to the two of them as they bantered back and forth in a jocular manner getting to know one another. He finally excused himself, saying that he had to get back to the office for a meeting. As he was leaving, Tony Carter assured him, with an almost genuinely serious tone to his voice, that he would get his wife back safely to the house after the match.

Patrick only waved and said, "Good." He could care less if Carter drove her off the pier and went in with her. They were good company for each other as far as he was concerned, but he was not totally comfortable with the two of them together. It could prove to be a bad mix for him, with both of them having certain interests regarding his financial situation and neither of them giving a damn about him personally.

After two weeks of hearing nothing from Carter or anyone in Unity, Patrick decided to take a run down to Dublin on the train to get away from Hillary and Belfast. He told Martha his plans, and she let Baumler know so that he could take the appropriate security measures. Patrick had reluctantly agreed to this policy when Baumler came on board Desmond Enterprises, although he, like his daughter, had a great distaste for the thought that he needed an escort. Fortunately, Baumler assigned a security agent who appeared to mind his own business more than Patrick's. In actuality, the agent was very good at what he did, including not looking good at it.

Patrick had told Ellen that he would meet her at Bewley's on Grafton at five that afternoon, so he took the noon Dublin Express, which would put him into Connolly Station around three. That would give him plenty of time to get to Bewley's. As he purchased his ticket in the Belfast Station, he noticed his escort at the newspaper stand, reading the latest edition of the Dublin Times. Patrick figured that the fellow, who was single, was updating himself on the current entertainment scene at their destination.

Patrick did not have a great amount of confidence in Ted Somers. He didn't seem able to detect trouble or do anything about it once it did develop. He always appeared either half asleep or completely asleep and not interested at all in where Patrick was at the moment or what he was doing. Even though Patrick questioned the wisdom of Baumler's assignment of Somers, it could have been much worse. He could have had someone who was constantly looking over his shoulder, and that would drive him nuts.

When Patrick boarded the train there were very few people making the run to Dublin, so most of the seats were available. The seating on the train was in rows, with one row of two seats facing another row of two seats with a table in between. Patrick enjoyed having the entire table to himself and today seemed to be his lucky day. Patrick laid his briefcase and overnight bag on the empty seat alongside him and pulled out the Belfast Independent to catch up on the local news. As the train slowly accelerated out of the dank, sooty Belfast Station, Patrick noticed Somers apparently fast asleep a few rows up with his mouth open, eyes closed, and head resting back on the comfortable headrest. As the train moved south through the rolling hills, past the small farms and villages of Northern Ireland, and on into the Republic, Patrick became mesmerized by the rhythmic sound of the iron wheels of the train clicking on the rail ends, and he too was soon fast asleep.

Patrick enjoyed visiting Dublin because it seemed to have so much more character than Belfast. The old-style architecture had been maintained and not torn down and replaced by steel and glass as was so often the case in Belfast. The people were much friendlier as well, but that was understandable in view of the "Troubles" in Northern Ireland. The contrast between the two cities was most evident in their respective train stations. In Dublin there were no police yelling out, "Single file. You over there, get into single file!" There were no guard dogs sniffing the passengers, looking for drugs and explosives. Patrick was curious to know if that cold welcome to travelers in Belfast ever produced any results that justified the adverse impact it created. He doubted that it did. As he left the railroad station, he hailed a taxi to take him over to Bewley's for the meeting with his daughter.

As they drove up Talbot Street and onto O'Connell Street, he thought to himself about Hillary's long time refusal to visit Dublin. She always said, "There are so many Irish there," and then she would laugh.

Patrick had the taxi drop him off on O'Connell Street by the statue of Daniel O'Connell. He was a bit early for his meeting with Ellen and took the few minutes to browse in Ashton's Bookstore. He was carrying his small overnight bag and his briefcase, but they would not be too burdensome for the short walk across the Liffey to Bewley's. He found a newly published LLewelyn novel and took it over to the café area where he ordered a cup of tea and sat down to skim over the book. He became immersed in what he was reading, and glancing at this watch he saw that he was already late for his appointment with Ellen.

He paid for the book, picked up his two bags and hurried out of the store. As he crossed the O'Connell Bridge, he saw that he was already ten minutes late but remembered that Ellen was frequently late herself and would find it hard to complain.

As Patrick came through the open entryway of Bewley's, he spotted Ellen sitting at a table in the back of the dining area. After they had exchanged greetings, Patrick went to the food counter and soon returned to the table with his tea, teapot, and small cake. Ellen commented that she had trouble even finding a table with the crowd in the café. Patrick looked over the crowd of shoppers and business people who were having their late afternoon cup of tea and wondered what had happened to Somers who he had not seen since he left the train. Maybe he made a wrong turn on the walk from the Station? Anyway, he wasn't going to worry about where Somers might be now. He wanted to enjoy his time with his daughter.

"How's everything in the office?" Patrick asked.

Ellen chuckled, "About the same. I don't want to sound like a broken record, but as I've mentioned too many times, there are a couple of your staff in Dublin that could easily be replaced by people with brains."

Ellen was never one to mince words and Patrick had a good idea of who she was talking about. He had instructed the office manager in Dublin to hire the two people that Unity wanted hired, again in the shipping department. He assumed they had other "duties" in Dublin and needed a cover of sorts, although working for Desmond was barely a cover for anyone. The INA knew very well who ran Desmond Enterprises and what their political affiliations were, so anyone who worked in the Dublin office was suspected of being an agent for the North.

"Okay, then, how's your social life coming along?" Patrick asked.

"Actually very good Dad. I've been dating this fellow that I would like you to meet. I think you would like him."

"If you like him, then I'm sure I would

The two of them sat drinking their tea and discussing politics and other matters of interest until it was close to six when Ellen looked at her watch and suggested that they head over to her place. Patrick explained that he had a room at the Shelbourne but would meet her later for dinner. Ellen was disappointed to hear that he would not be staying at her apartment but agreed to meet at Nico's on Dame Street, just around the corner from the Temple Bar area. Patrick was not familiar with the restaurant, but agreed to meet his daughter at eight.

They parted at the entryway to Bewley's and Patrick began the hike over towards the Shelbourne. The sidewalks were packed with office workers who were all proceeding in a fast walk towards their bus stop so that they could get back to their homes for dinner. It had started to rain so Patrick paused to put on his rain coat that was packed on top of the items in his nap sack. He walked over to the edge of the sidewalk, next to an office building, set his bags down, and began putting on his rain coat. The sidewalks were so crowded that he was occasionally jostled by a passerby in the process but eventually got the coat on and buttoned.

Patrick reached down to pick up his bags but his briefcase was no longer there. He looked both ways, up and down the street but could not see the case anywhere. His heart began to beat very rapidly and a cold, clammy feeling came over him as he stood in the rain trying to get his thoughts together. He immediately thought of the notes. He had made notes on the information he received from Carter, which he now thought he never should have done, and they, together with some confidential Desmond Enterprise documents, were in the bag. He didn't care about the cellular and the tape recorder. Christ, he would have given those away if he could just have his briefcase with the other materials. He didn't know what to do or which way to go because he had no idea where the thief may have headed. The longer that he stood in the same spot looking over the heads of the crowd, the less likely it was that he would ever retrieve his bag and he knew it.

He could see the blue hat of a Gardai policeman who was standing in front of a financial office down the street, and he thought about asking him what he should do, but, on second thought, he figured that he had better call Baumler first. As he stood there in disbelief that he had been so stupid as to set his bags down in this crowd, he felt someone bump into him. Now incensed with what was happening to him, he spun around to chastise whoever had touched him, and he was astonished to see Ted Somers standing there, no rain coat and with his suit soaking wet, handing him his briefcase.

"I think you may have dropped this sir." With that Somers tipped the brim of his cap and melted away into the crowd.

At first Patrick was immensely relieved to have his briefcase back, and he swore that he would never be so careless again. He then wondered how in the hell Somers got a hold of the bag. Had he come up behind him and picked it up to teach him a lesson? That must have been it. The more Patrick thought about it, the more irritated he became. Where did the son of a bitch go now? I'll let him know that I don't need any God damn lessons. Now that Patrick was again in full possession of everything that he had when he left Belfast, he again proceeded in the direction of the Shelbourne Hotel, angry that his security detail saw fit to play games with him. He would let Baumler know about this.

As he began walking, he could hear an ambulance with its abrasively high pitched wavering siren making its way through the crowded streets and coming to a stop where the policeman was standing. As Patrick came up to the scene, the attendants in their white suits were loading a young fellow onto a stretcher and placing him in the ambulance. Patrick assumed that he had been struck by a vehicle because the roadway was slick from the rain, and the young man, who seemed to be unconscious, had a great amount of blood visible on his upper body. A large number of people had stopped to watch. Patrick asked an older man standing there smoking his pipe with the bowl down to avoid the rain what had happened.

"Seems like this kid had taken this guys case, and unfortunately the kid should have tried somebody that was not so quick. The guy caught him and he put that kid away faster than I have ever seen in my life. Taught him a lesson for sure. Guy got his case back and disappeared into the crowd. Guy didn't look like much, but, boy, he could kick some ass. Cop was looking for him but he was long gone."

"Interesting," Patrick said and went on his way. Maybe he would forget about chastising Somers after all. "Very interesting," he mumbled to himself a few more times as he made his way in the rain. As he rounded the corner on Merrion Street, it was a relief to see the awning covering the entryway to the Shelbourne Hotel only a short distance ahead. His arms were about to give out from having carried the two bags all the way from Bewley's. He should have taken a cab to the hotel as Somers must have done. Maybe next time he would do it the right way and never again would he set his bag down on a crowded street anywhere.

Dublin was relatively safe as far as cities go, but there was no sense in tempting some druggy to go for the easy one. Patrick thought about the incident with his bag and how it had been resolved.

"Interesting guy that Somers. Sure doesn't look the part like that fellow said. I'll have to let Baumler know this. Somers will have to report it anyway," Patrick thought.

The manager of the Shelbourne had recognized Patrick Desmond as he entered the lobby, and he immediately turned and nodded to the bellman who scurried over to take the key that was being handed to him.

"Good to see you at the Shelbourne, Mr. Desmond, Sir, Edmund here will see you to your room," the manager said.

The two disappeared into the elevator while Somers sat sipping his tea, watching the floor indicator lights on the control panel climb as the elevator rose up the shaft. The elevator stopped at the floor where both men had their rooms. Somers checked his watch to note the time. He had learned that Patrick had the appointment at eight for Nico's from the other agent, and he estimated Patrick's return ride down the elevator shaft would occur in approximately twenty-seven minutes. He was a minute off.

Patrick took a cab down to Nico's. It was still raining out, and it was a fairly long walk from the Shelbourne to the restaurant. When he arrived, Ellen was not yet there, so Patrick stopped at the bar to have a drink while he waited. The restaurant was beginning to fill up, and while he was having his pint of Murphy's, he saw Somers enter through the front door and take a table in the dining room. Shortly after Ellen came in and joined him at the bar, while her shadow proceeded into the dining room and joined Somers at his table.

"Dad, I have a friend coming to join us for dinner. I hope you don't mind."

Patrick did mind. He did not enjoy sharing the little time that he spent with his daughter with others, particularly people he didn't know.

"No problem. Who is it? I assume it must be some male friend of yours, right?"

"A friend of mine," Ellen said. "The fellow I mentioned to you at Bewley's. I've been dating him for a while. Nice guy from Dublin. Catholic, but he doesn't wear it on his arm. He's about as religious as you are." Ellen chuckled. "If you can forget that, you just might like him."

Patrick nodded, smiled, and said, "I'll try."

He thought to himself that this could be a long evening. Within a few minutes a handsome, well dressed, young man came into the bar section of the dining room and went up to Patrick, holding out his hand.

"Mr. Desmond, I assume? I'm Tom O'Rourke. I've heard so much about you from your daughter. She is your number one fan."

"Very charming fellow," Patrick mused as he shook the young man's hand. He had a firm grip and looked Patrick directly in the eye.

"No lack of confidence with this guy," thought Patrick, who admired a certain amount of self-esteem as long as it didn't go overboard. He would withhold judgment until later.

"Well, I've heard your name mentioned as well. If I might ask, what line of work are you involved in here in Dublin, Mr. O'Rourke?" Patrick asked.

"Computers, Mr. Desmond, but please, it's Tom. I get nervous if someone calls me Mr. O'Rourke."

"Interesting," Patrick commented, as he motioned to the waiter to get O'Rourke a drink. While he was ordering his drink, Patrick continued to study the young man who was now turning his attention towards Ellen.

"Did your daughter tell you that we are thinking about training for the Dublin Marathon?" Tom asked.

"So I hear," Patrick replied while shaking his head to indicate what he thought about the idea. O'Rourke and Ellen laughed. They received similar reactions from others whenever they mentioned the marathon.

In a very respectful tone of voice, Ellen replied, "Tom has run three marathons already, and he's going to help me get in condition for this one."

"That's just wonderful," Patrick replied with a bit of a smirk. "I hope you all have a wonderful time in the process. What do you say we have dinner?"

As they entered the dining room now crowded with diners, Patrick caught sight of two Desmond Security agents sitting at a table towards the center of the room. The Maitre D" was ushering them to a table right next to them. Patrick tapped the man on the shoulder and requested another table off to the side that appeared to be open. The Maitre D' gave Patrick a barely visible but condescending one eyebrow lift and replied, "Certainly, sir," placing heavy emphasis on the "sir."

As they passed the security men's table, Patrick noticed Somers was lighting his cigarette. The lighter he was using caught his attention because Baumler had shown him some of the equipment the agents at Desmond Security used in their work, and the small camera disguised as a lighter was one of the devices. Somers was taking O'Rourke's picture. Patrick glanced at O'Rourke who seemed to be looking directly at the lighter.

Patrick had the impression that his dinner guest knew what it was, but how that was possible escaped him because the lens was completely camouflaged. Patrick even had a hard time finding it after Baumler had told him it was a camera. The three proceeded to their newly assigned table, and O'Rourke took a seat on the far side where he was in direct line of sight with the two security men. He kept up his lively chatter with Ellen, but he would very occasionally and subtly let his eyes sweep over in the direction of the two men who appeared to be ignoring the recent arrivals.

Patrick's curiosity was mounting by the second concerning this young fellow's interest in his daughter. He seemed to be aware of what was happening when he was having his portrait taken by Somers, and he could only have known that if he was in a similar line of work. He would discuss this with Baumler as soon as he returned to Belfast.

In the meantime, he tried to control his questioning of O'Rourke to the level that he considered normal for the father of the young woman who he had befriended. Patrick did not consider his daughter to be naive in matters of the world, but she had just graduated from college and only recently entered the business world, so in many respects she had a lot to learn.

During the course of the dinner, O'Rourke explained to him that he worked for Interlink, a small company located in Rathmines. He explained that Interlink was a computer service provider for local corporations. He had only worked for them for a short time, just having completed his course of studies at University College Dublin. Patrick figured he must have been involved in something else, because he was obviously in his late twenties and did not appear to be the type that would have taken forever to finish college. He would have liked to know what else he had done in the past five to ten years, but he thought he'd better hold down on the questions.

Patrick gathered from the conversation that O'Rourke had just met Ellen within the past two months. It was a recent friendship, but one that the two of them, from all appearances, were enjoying. The three sat at the table talking about social activities in Dublin, current events of a non-political nature and the comings and goings of mutual friends. O'Rourke would periodically return the conversation to topics likely to be in Patrick's sphere of interest so that he did not feel excluded from the lively discussion.

Their dinners were excellent, and following an after-dinner drink Patrick commented that he had put in a long day and was ready to head back to the hotel. The other two decided to go over to the Temple Bar area that was around the corner from Nico's and listen to some music before going home. Tom O'Rourke thanked Patrick for the dinner and drinks and told him that if he needed any computer information or assistance to give him a call. O'Rourke then handed Patrick his business card, and the two young people left while Patrick took care of the bill.

He had one last drink at the bar while the manager had the doorman get him a cab to take him back to the Shelbourne. Patrick had noticed that when they all left the dining room, the two security people had already departed and were presumably waiting for their charges from some barely visible vantage point. Patrick found the entire security thing distasteful, but recalling the events of that afternoon, he took comfort in the fact that his bags were safely locked in his room.

The following morning he arose early, even before the first light of day, so that he could meet Ellen downstairs in the lobby of the hotel. When she came into the lobby, he could tell that she had stayed out a bit later than she probably should have. When she saw him, her face, nevertheless, lit up, a sight that always pleased him. He enjoyed an early breakfast in the hotel dining room with Ellen before she had to leave for work, and then, when she was gone, he took a leisurely stroll down Grafton Street visiting some of the stores in the area that handled Desmond Enterprise's products.

Desmonds handled a wide variety of products from stationary to clothing, and their products could usually be found in stores that carried mid-range priced inventory items. Desmond Enterprises also operated their own retail stores, but they were located in outlying areas not serviced by, or in competition with, the larger metropolitan retail establishments. He noticed that some of the displays for products with Desmond labels were not placed in the high traffic areas and he would have to see that the word was passed down to the regional sales manager to get the products out where the potential customers could see them.

After a while, Patrick checked the time and reluctantly concluded that he had better hurry back to the Shelbourne to gather up his bags and head for the Station. When he passed through the lobby, he again spotted Somers sitting off to the side reading the Irish Times. Somers paid no attention to him, and Patrick proceeded on into the elevator and up to his room where he packed up his things. The desk had his cab waiting for him when he reentered the lobby, and the manager wished him a good trip as he departed the hotel.

CHAPTER 20

Patrick was in his office by three o'clock and had Martha immediately send for the head of security. Within minutes, Frank Baumler was seated in front of his desk with his usual pad and pen at the ready. "What's on your mind, chief?" Baumler asked.

Patrick was not exactly sure where to start. "First of all, I don't have a great amount of information on this guy in the States, but his name is Parker. I don't know the first name. I didn't want to appear too inquisitive when I was trying to get this. I had the impression that Carter was wondering what I was up to the way it was. Anyway, he apparently lives in Atlanta, Georgia, and the INA or whoever it is that is involved is in contact with him at an Irish pub in the city. That is about all that I have on the guy, but there can't be too many Irish pubs there. Also, a word of warning, Carter mentioned that they have an ex-Stasi guy working the file over there to try and find out what this guy's intentions are. He has implied that if they don't like what they see, they may resolve the problem summarily, if you know what I mean."

Baumler had no doubt what he meant and made no reply other than to add to his notes. Baumler doubted that Unity would actually make a move against a foreign national on his own turf, because that was the best way to bring an entire government down on your organization. Even Unity knew that.

When Patrick finished relaying his conversation with Carter at the Club, he asked Baumler if that was enough for him to go on in order to locate this guy.

Baumler stopped writing and nodded as he replied, "I think we will be able to find him. It may take a bit longer, time wise, than if we had his full name and street address, but we'll get him. As for the Stasi, Unity took a number of them on board when their employer downsized, and they are a tough bunch. They are also very good but not always good enough. Now, let me lay this on you. Your little experience in Dublin, that was interesting. I'll bet you were surprised to get your bag back, right?"

Patrick began to speak, but Baumler interrupted, "Pardon me, chief, but let me tell you the whole story. Somers saw the guy snatch the bag, because Somers had been watching the guy trail you for some time. He knew he was up to something. When you pulled over to put on your raincoat, Somers figured the guy would then make his move, and he was right. So, Somers was basically abreast of the two of you when the snatch occurred so that the guy wouldn't have a real lead on him in the crowd after he made his move."

Baumler took a sip of tea from his cup and continued, "Somers was moving on the guy before he left your side and caught him about thirty feet from where you were standing when you were probably still putting on your coat. He hit him with his sap, you know, the leather pouch loaded with lead. This will usually put out an elephant, but not this guy. The guy was stunned, but he had enough left in him to turn on Somers who then nailed him in the crotch with his steel toed boot and sapped him again with an uppercut to the jaw as he bent over to see if his balls were still there. That made it messy, but it finally did the job with the guy going limp and Somers now sort of holding him up because he wanted to grab the case. As Somers grabbed for the case that was sort of slipping out of this guy's hand, the guy muttered something in German, which got Somer's attention and he ran his hand around the guy's belt line. Low and behold, guess what he found? He was carrying a mini Glock nine millimeter with a silencer in a quick release holster, which Somers stripped off him as he slipped down to the sidewalk. Somers hardly attracted anyone's attention as all of this took place in about four seconds. This guy was no deadbeat. We think he was Stazi. Sound familiar to you?"

Patrick was silent as he tried to digest everything he was hearing. He asked Baumler what he made of it.

"The only group that I know of in Ireland that is hiring the Stazi is Unity. I would think that birds of a feather would all flock to the same employer, don't you think? They wouldn't want to be fighting their former comrades in arms. I wouldn't think they would anyway. I would say that there is a high probability he was on a Unity job. Why, I don't know, although I have given it quite a bit of thought. The only reasons I can come up with are that they want to increase the pressure on you following your conversation the other day with Carter, or they want to know what else you might be doing in Dublin and your briefcase might have told them that. They are also now aware that your daughter is dating a guy with connections to One Ireland, as we just learned, and that must be making them wonder what is going on, especially when that is combined with your newly discovered stateside relative who is cavorting with the INA over there. It could be a combination of all of these factors that made Carter or somebody in Unity nervous. They are still putting an occasional watch on Ellen, so they are at least somewhat curious about her orientation. You have implied a number of times that Carter did not trust you. Maybe Carter ordered it. He knows you better than anyone else in Unity."

Patrick was digesting Baumler's comment that Ellen was dating a One Ireland guy. Obviously that was Tom O'Rourke. Patrick wondered what else Baumler knew about O'Rourke.

"True," Patrick responded. "But if the Stazi are so good, why didn't he know that Somers was around?"

Baumler's eyes lit up. "I'll tell you why, chief." Baumler leaned forward with his hands on the desk, speaking slowly and distinctly to emphasize what he was saying, "Because Somers is so damn good. He looks a bit like a flake, and you wouldn't think he could handle himself in a tough situation, but looks can be deceiving, and in his current line of employment that is an asset. I wouldn't want to tangle with that guy."

Patrick agreed with Baumler's assessment of his agent. His view of him had changed considerably, and he told Baumler to see to it that Somers received the proper commendation or a bonus or other recognition for his work on the Dublin trip. Patrick then went into the business of Tom O'Rourke, the newfound friend of his daughter. By now, he figured that Baumler knew a lot more about the young man than Patrick did.

"What is the story on this O'Rourke guy? I did notice that Somers took his picture, and what really caught my attention was that this O'Rourke also picked up on the fact that he was getting into print, and let me assure you that Somers did it very smoothly. I picked up on the lighter that you had just shown to me a couple of weeks ago. When I knew what it was, I checked to see O'Rourke"s relative position to the camera and saw that he was looking directly at it. He immediately turned his face away, but by then Somers had the pic, but it was very clear to me that O'Rourke knew perfectly well what was going on. He was just too late to avoid it. He said he works for Interlink in Dublin. Here's his card."

Baumler studied the card for a moment then placed it in his briefcase. He told Patrick that he would return the original after he copied it unless Patrick needed it right away.

"No problem. Take your time. I don't expect to have any use for the card. I only took it because, sure as hell, I would forget the kid"s name."

"Well," Baumler went on, "we've been interested in this guy for the past month or so, ever since he started showing up at Ellen's apartment. We have thought that he was sort of a P.R. guy for One Ireland. Nice looking, good personality, sharp dresser, the kind of guy the young girls go for. That could well be his job, to get younger people into the group, but I must say, your comment about him picking up on the camera gives me some concern that he may have other duties. We'll put a tail on him and find out what is going on. Regardless, I would not be overly concerned right now, because you have to look at this sort of thing logically."

Baumler jotted down something then said, "One Ireland is primarily a social group that brings young people together. Sure it has political connections with the INA and is financed by them, but it really is more of a social group than political. Also, the INA, as well as any of the other splinter groups, does not want to do something stupid to bring everyone down on them for little or no gain. This O'Rourke"s relationship with Ellen could be a mere coincidence and perfectly harmless. Ellen is very good company as you well know and he just may enjoy being around her. Let's take it a day at a time. We're keeping our eyes open."

What Baumler had to say about O'Rourke provided a certain amount of relief to Patrick but, by no means, total relief. At this point in time though, there was little he could do to extricate her from the present position. She would never go along with leaving Dublin, because she would not want to see the danger she could be in. He would need more supporting proof of what was transpiring before he could ever convince her to come back to Belfast.

The following day after leaving his office in the afternoon, Patrick decided to go over to the Club and have a drink. He wanted to avoid going back to the house, which led to drinking alone in his dark study and becoming depressed by the events of the past few weeks. As he stepped out of his car in the entryway, the parking attendant greeted him and took the keys just as Hillary and Carter were emerging from the Club. They were both wearing tennis clothing and from all appearances had just finished a match. At first they did not notice Patrick as he was walking towards them and appeared a bit startled when he spoke, "Well, if it isn't the Royal Ulster Tennis Team."

Both Hillary and Carter appeared momentarily flustered to see Patrick. Hillary finally said, "I thought you were staying in Dublin a few days. This is a surprise. How did the trip go and how is Ellen?

Patrick explained that she was fine, but he had the definite impression that he was now the cause of a rapid change of plans for the two of them. Carter had a somewhat embarrassed look about him and was not taking an active role in the conversation, even though Patrick asked a few polite questions about how his game was coming along.

After more light banter between the three of them, Carter glanced at his watch and said that he had to get back to the office but that he would be glad to drop Hillary off at her house if she needed a ride. The look on Hillary's face said, "You know damn well I don't have my car here."

Instead she replied with a mask of civility, "I would appreciate that, if you don't mind." Patrick didn't miss what was going on and was enjoying the double entendres that were passing between the two.

After more meaningless comments designed to fill embarrassing pauses in their conversation, the two departed and Patrick made his way into the club. He headed straight for the bar area that was located in the rear of the building. As he entered the room through the solid oak doors with the ornate brass door handles, he was struck, as always, with the wonderful view of the rolling, lush fairways and the greens of the golf course that he could see through the floor to ceiling windows extending the length of the back wall of the lounge. Patrick did not play golf, nor had he ever lifted a tennis racket, but he did enjoy the club for its excellent food and most of all for this lounge.

Women had not even been allowed in the lounge area until approximately ten years ago when social mores, particularly with respect to women's place in society, had made such dramatic changes. Regardless of the change in club rules, it was still a relatively rare occurrence for a woman to enter the lounge area unescorted, which was just fine with Patrick. Whenever the subject came up in discussions with a few of the other Club members that Patrick socialized with, he would only say, provided Hillary was not present, "I am out of the old school, and I prefer the former policy."

As Patrick was enjoying his tumbler of Benedictine, one of the lounge regulars came in and spotting Patrick sitting alone. He came over to where Patrick was sitting. The fellow was a club gadfly who made it his business to know every other club member's business, and while Patrick politely returned the greeting, he was dismayed to see the fellow park on the bar stool next to his. Patrick did not know the man's name and had no interest in learning what it was. The man had an annoying habit of clearing this throat in a particularly loud manner which grated on Patrick's nerves whenever he heard it. He wanted to turn towards the fellow and suggest that he find some other way to get everyone's attention without being quite so offensive, but his better judgment had thus far prevented him from doing so.

After the fellow ordered his drink from the bartender, he immediately directed his attention to Patrick who, unfortunately for him, was the only other person sitting at the bar.

Patrick could feel the man's eyes focused on him, obviously wanting to strike up a conversation, but Patrick pretended to be unaware that the fellow was even sitting there. Hopefully, if he appeared to be deep in thought, which he had been until the arrival of this social retard, the man might just let him alone. Just then, the fellow chose to exercise his distinctive characteristic directly into Patrick's left ear, which about blew him right out of his chair. It was the most direct hit that Patrick had been subjected to from this fellow and it could not go unanswered.

Patrick turned to the man, who was sitting on the very next bar stool facing him, and in a rather loud voice said, "If you don't mind, I would prefer it if you did not make that eruptive racket directly into my ear."

Patrick turned back to face straight ahead, hoping the fellow would get the message and leave to annoy someone else. Such was not to be as the man now began a profuse stream of apologies claiming to have a throat disorder that made it necessary to use such extreme measures to provide temporary relief. As the fellow began to realize that his medically related explanations were not carrying the day, his talk wandered down to how everyone needed to learn more patience and to develop understanding for people with disabilities.

Patrick, continuing to ignore the man, thought to himself, "You, sir, definitely have a disability."

Taking Patrick's continued ignoring of him as a bit of an affront, the fellow took on another tone of voice, sort of a pseudo-friendly tone that at first had Patrick fooled.

"I see your wife is becoming quite a tennis player." Pause. "She seems to be on the court almost every day picking up on her game."

The man had put just a little too much emphasis on the word "game," which clued Patrick into what was coming. The man then took a big swig of his gin and tonic before continuing his monologue.

"This guy she always plays with, he's not much on the court, but they seem to be having a good time out there."

That was a little jab that the man knew would put a burr in Patrick's saddle, and he glanced over at him to see if it took. Just to put a period at the end of the sentence, he let loose with another high pitched, extended throat clearing, but this time he had feigned politeness by turning ever so slightly in the other direction from Patrick and mumbled an apology directed at no one in particular. Patrick was continuing to ignore the man, but this only seemed to fuel the man's interest in ruining his afternoon.

"Say, do you know if this fellow that your wife is with, on the court these days, is a member of the club or not? I thought there were some rules about how often you could bring a guest into the club. It seems he's with her quite a bit."

"Jab, jab, jab, you little asshole," Patrick thought. He had just about had it with this guy. He turned to his tormenter and said, "Why don't you ask him the next time you see him at the club? That's a good idea, because you seem to be around here a lot more than I am, and if he isn't a member you should suggest to him that he take his racket and depart the premises."

Patrick was enjoying visions of Carter picking this dork up and hurling him into the club pool, which at this time of year was drained. His bar mate was now silent, trying to fathom whether Patrick had been serious or was putting him on.

"Well, I gotta go," said Patrick as he signed the bar tab and left, just as the fellow was letting forth with his signature sound that Patrick could still hear after he had passed through the thick, solid oak doors of the lounge.

As he waited for the parking attendant to bring around his car, he thought to himself, "What in the hell did I do to piss off the gods? This last couple of months has been something else. Maybe my luck will change for the better. Let's hope so."

A few mornings later, as he entered his office, Martha passed him a number of telephone messages that had come in that morning and made it a point to let him know that both Carter and Baumler wished to meet with him. He went into his office thinking that it would be best to meet with his head of security first in order to learn whatever information Baumler had obtained. He could always call Frank back if Carter had some hot items that should be followed up on. He buzzed Martha on the intercom and told her to have Baumler come to his office. Soon Frank was sitting in front of the desk with his usual notebook and pen.

While Patrick slowly turned the letter opener in his perspiring hands, he said, "Well, what do you have for me today, Frank? Good news, I trust."

Baumler smiled. "Could be, chief. We have located Mr. Parker, and we have some information on him. It seems as though he is a retired attorney. He lives alone. No kids. Good credit and apparently a responsible sort of guy. He's in his mid sixties, frequents an Irish pub by the name of Murphy's. My favorite beer, I might add. Anyway, he's in fairly tight with a guy by the name of Flanagan who plays in the club and teaches Gaelic at the local university. The club has a reputation of being a Nationalist hangout, and we can only assume that this guy Flanagan is of that stripe. That may be the guy that your friend, Carter, referred to when he said the INA were trying to lead this guy in a certain direction. They do seem to be pretty tight, because this Parker is in there most every Wednesday night when the other guy plays the fiddle in the Irish group there. They say he's pretty good at it for whatever that's worth."

Baumler quickly glanced at his notes. "We've done some checking on this Flanagan. He has an ex-wife and a couple of kids in Dublin. His credit sucks, and he's had quite a few jobs over the years. Our guys in Dublin say that he was never higher in the INA than a mid-level operative but that he was generally well regarded in the organization and apparently has worked his way up in the American organization and is now boss of the southeastern region for fund raising. Seems like his politics, and his music, come first, before family, success at work, and so on."

Baumler thought for a moment to make sure he was covering all aspects of his report on Quinn Parker. "Anyway, we've got a guy in Atlanta who is trying to keep an eye primarily on Parker to see where he's going with this thing but also on Flanagan when he has the time. If he has an opportunity, he will try and get close to Parker provided he can do that without disclosing his hand."

Baumler paused for a moment before continuing, "This guy Parker has a crowd following him around. I wonder if he's picking up on his popularity—Unity, INA and now us. I trust, chief, that you know how important it is that Carter not be aware that we have a guy over there. I would hate to have something happen to him, and Unity wouldn't hesitate for a second to take him out if they thought he was getting in the way of something."

Patrick assured him that he would be very careful not to disclose anything to Carter.

"Now for the rest of the story," Baumler glanced at his notes. "This guy O'Rourke, he's an interesting young man. He's not just a PR guy for One Ireland. Seems as though he has responsibilities of a higher nature. He is the INA's bag man for the drug business in Dublin, which is a very lucrative source for their financing. The INA is not in the drug business per se, but they tax those who are, and it is this guy's job to see that everyone involved pays their taxes. He heads up a team of younger INA musclemen who act as the collectors and enforcers when people don't wish to pay their fair share. Seems he was formerly very active up here as a demolitions expert but things got too warm for him here in the north, so they sent him south to cool off for a while. Unfortunately for him, the word on the street is that he is beginning to tax the wrong people. I don't know if you are aware of it or not, but Unity is also in the drug business. Not in the north, though, because that would not be politically correct. But they are involved in drug trafficking in the south, and it has been a very profitable enterprise for them.

Seems as though your boy has seen fit to put the bite on some of the mid and lower level Unity distributors for INA's 10%.

I don't know if he doesn't know who he is taxing or if he doesn't care, but that could be a big mistake."

Baumler tapped his pen on his notebook to emphasize what he was saying and waited for Patrick's questions.

"I don't like the sound of this. What about Ellen? Somebody might decide to hit this guy when she is with him. Neither one of these groups is very careful about collateral damage when they're after someone. What do we do?"

Baumler anticipated the question and had already been working on a solution.

"We have put a tap on your daughter's line and are also checking on other taps already there. We have followed one tap to a Unity communications center, and we have placed a tap on the guy that we thought was following your daughter. We have confirmed that he is a Unity agent, and we are now thinking that he was in fact watching O'Rourke. It just so happened that he was always out there when O'Rourke was in the vicinity. We have the latest in phone gear and even placed a mike in his car, so we are getting everything this guy says either over his phones or to anyone in his car, where he apparently feels the safest, judging by what we are getting. We are quite certain that Unity has not picked up on our surveillance and that most of their attention to intrusion is directed towards the INA or the Republic Police, the Gardai. Consequently, we are getting good information from the Unity agent who believes his line is secure. We figure if anything serious is going to happen, we will get some lead time on it from these taps. In the meantime, if you have any suggestions, we'll be glad to listen."

Patrick said nothing for a few moments, absorbing Baumler's comments.

"Well, I don't know what to do. If I told Ellen to leave Dublin, she would refuse to go, saying I was being overly protective. She wouldn't recognize a threat to her well being if it was parked right next to her. Frank, just do your best to keep abeam of what is going on down there. If you have any friends in the Gardai, you might see what they have, if you think that would not be too risky. I don't know. I shouldn't try to tell you how to do your business. I'll just have to leave it all in your hands. Keep me informed."

Baumler took that as his cue that the morning meeting was over and stood up to leave.

"Will do, chief. Have a good day." Patrick said nothing, just stared at the wall as Baumler left, closing the door behind him.

Patrick sat for some time collecting his thoughts regarding his forthcoming session with Carter. He was becoming more and more convinced as time passed that Carter was behind the attempted theft of his briefcase in Dublin, but he was not sure why he would have ordered such a move. Patrick knew the Unity agent did not trust him, and Baumler had a good point that Unity was likely nervous with all of the other events taking place. His trip to Dublin likely came at the wrong time, shortly after being told by Carter that he just might have a very serious financial problem coming up in the future.

Maybe Carter thought he was going to try dealing directly with the INA to see if he couldn't get the wolves called off. Not a bad idea, but Patrick had already thought of that and concluded that it would most likely not work. Patrick cautioned himself that he would have to be careful not to show his contempt for the Unity agent for not only the move against him in Dublin but also for the public insult of his open tryst with his wife. What the hell is wrong with trying to be a little discreet? As Patrick thought about it, it seemed as though all aspects of his personal and business life were being flushed down the toilet. Maybe if he cut down on his drinking and put more effort into protecting his interests, he could turn things around. He would have to give that a try, but right now with everything happening all at once, he needed a drink just to relax and think. When all of this was over, he told himself, he would quit.

CHAPTER 21

The rain was picking up and the wind was blowing in his face as Quinn came around the south side of the lake. He was the only one out today and that was understandable. It was a lousy day to be running, but now that he could see the finish point not too far ahead he seemed to ease into his stride and was almost enjoying it when he came to his usual finish line at the large oak tree. He turned off the country music playing on his Walkman and took off the headset while he did his cool down walk. There was no one around other than the geese and ducks that were paddling around on the surface of the water and occasionally going under to look for food. He would have preferred better weather but having the lake to himself made it worth the wind and the rain.

He took his time walking back to his car, thinking again about his planned trip to Ireland. As he had told Sean, he had about picked the libraries bone dry and now it was time to head to Dublin and get into the old church records and other documents that just hadn't been photocopied, at least by any sources in the States. Sean had given him a number of Irish related books mostly dealing with the Famine that had precipitated the mass emigration in the mid-1800s when Quinn's family and many other families had left Ireland. Quinn had read most of them and, based on their subject matter, concluded in the process that Sean had a political motivation behind the books he selected for him to read.

When they met at the club, Quinn said, "No one could read all those Famine books and come away without sort of a hangover with respect to the British."

"Well," Sean said, "that's what I've been trying to tell you. They're bastards."

"Now, Sean, I don't think you can lay the Famine on the present British government. That was going on well over two hundred years ago. Today's Irish problem, as you call it, is an entirely different matter."

Sean's face reddened and his speech went up half an octave, "How in the hell can you say that when you don't have a gnat's ass of interest in what goes on over there?"

Cooling down a bit and feeling he may have overreacted just a touch, Sean continued, this time with a trace of a smile, "I'll see that you get educated on what's going on over there if I have to start jogging around that damn lake with you."

Quinn thought for a moment. "Maybe we'll make a deal. I read a book, you jog for a week . . . no, make it two weeks. It takes me about that long to plow through some of those books."

Sean chuckled and said, "God, I'd have a heart attack, but we'll see. Who knows?"

CHAPTER 22

When they were at Quinn's house one afternoon, Quinn made his airline reservations and Sean went through the various hotel possibilities with him. Sean was quite familiar with those listed in the tour book and pointed out some of the pros and cons of each. This one had a loud bar, that one had bad service, this one was over-priced, and that one was not located in the areas of Dublin that Quinn would most likely be frequenting. Quinn finally selected one that was not too expensive and that was situated directly across from the National Library. Sean thought that was a good choice and made the call to set up the reservation.

Quinn listened as his friend worked the price down from seventy-five pounds a night to fifty.

"Staying a week should reduce that rate shouldn't it? . . . Yes, well, it may be much longer. . . . I don't know right now, so hold it for two weeks. What will that do to the rate? . . . I see, down to sixty pounds. Now, that includes breakfast, right? . . . Good . . . now, that is right at the end of the season, can't we do a bit better on the price? . . . Okay, I'll wait for the manager. . . . Yes, sir . . . yes, two weeks. What do you say about fifty a night? . . . Okay, two weeks. . . Okay. I can handle say fifty pounds a night provided I'm there for two weeks, and if not it will be sixty. Do I have that right? . . . Good. . . . Fine, put me down."

Sean handed the phone back to Quinn, who gave his Visa card number to the clerk and everything was set. The two talked about transportation and Sean said, "You don't want to drive in Dublin. Besides, if you do, I may be over there by then, and I can get a car. You can take the train to Cork, and if need be you can rent a car there. No problem. It's the off season and they'll be glad to give you a good price." Quinn was pleased to hear that because he was trying to hold the costs down.

Sean had seemed almost more interested than Quinn in his newly discovered challenge, and there were others that he had met in recent weeks who seemed to take notice of what he was doing. One evening, when he was at the Atlanta Library, looking at the materials in the Ireland section, a young English fellow struck up a conversation with him. He was also looking over some Irish records that involved Cork, for the purpose of tracing his own ancestor who had emigrated to England about the same time that Quinn's had. Quinn was aware that the Irish had fled in all directions, including many to England and other parts of the United Kingdom during the Famine years.

"Yes," the fellow said in a pronounced English accent, "they came from Clonakilty in 1851, and I don't think they ever went back. I am having problems though. There just aren't too many records available. You know, they burned all the records. How stupid that was."

Quinn was aware that most of the court house records were burned during the Civil War, and he agreed that it was a great loss, particularly to people like the two of them who were trying to put the pieces together. The English fellow asked him how he was coming along with his research, to which Quinn replied with a laugh, "Sometimes I make some progress and most of the time I don't, but I'm at the point now where I think I'll run over to Dublin and see what I can find in their records. I will hopefully be able to actually find some relatives over there. That's what I would like to do."

"Oh, interesting," replied the Englishman. "That is what I hope to do as well. I may be over there at the same time as you. When are you going over?"

Quinn had not made the reservation at the time of the conversation, but he had the general time frame in mind. "I am planning on the latter part of October or the very first part of November."

"What a coincidence. I may be there about the same time." The Englishman was almost more excited about the trip than Quinn. The two chatted for a few minutes and exchanged business cards.

As Quinn handed him his card, he said, "Now, it says I'm an attorney, but really I'm retired."

Examining the Englishman's card, Quinn said, "Now, let's see, Stanley Morris. Now that's a good Irish name."

"Sure is, Quinn. Hope to see you in Dublin." Morris gave a wave and was soon gone.

The following Wednesday evening, Quinn dropped in at the pub. Sean had said that he would be playing there that evening. It was still fairly early and the place had not started to fill up yet, even though Sean and the group were already playing. Quinn went up to the bar and ordered a pint, trying Murphy's this time as he had noticed a few of the regulars seemed to prefer it over Guinness. He thought he would give it a try.

The bartender took his order and said, "I see you're trying to change your luck, eh?"

Quinn smiled and replied, "I'll try anything to do that."

A number of the other patrons that were friends of Sean's came by to tell him they heard he was going over to Dublin and that he should be sure and visit such and such a club in Temple Bar, the entertainment center of Dublin. Sean had already clued him in that Temple Bar was an interesting part of Dublin for him to visit but that he might prefer the pubs down Baggot Street.

"Whatever," Quinn had replied, "I'm not exactly into the bar scene. A little beyond that, I would say."

Sean had just laughed and replied, "If you're Irish, you do the pub scene. It's part of the life over there."

When the bartender came over with his pint, Quinn went back to the section where the tables were and found that his usual spot was still available, so he grabbed it. Sean had seen him walking through the bar and acknowledged his presence with a momentary wave of his bow, which was immediately put back to work, gliding rapidly but smoothly along the strings of his fiddle. In another ten minutes or so, the set ended and Sean picked up a glass of Guinness and came over to the table.

"Well, how did you like that last number? Something new we've been working on."

"Sounded great, Sean, but I have to tell you, I have a problem telling quite a bit of this Irish music apart. I'm not exactly the local music critic. I'll do okay if you just don't get technical with me. That's over my head."

Both men laughed, and Sean lit up a cigarette while checking to see who all was standing at the bar. Seeing a friend here and there, Sean gave them a wave and a smile.

A couple of the guys came over to say hello and asked him how he was doing.

"Just fine, just fine," giving his stock answer to anyone that asked him. Turning to Quinn, he looked at him for a moment and then said, "Bet you're getting cranked about your trip, eh?"

"Sort of, Sean. I am, and I'm not. When I was younger, I was more into travel than I am now. The difference here is that I've never been over there, and I have heard about it all of my life, so that gins me up a bit. I just hate sitting on airplanes for a long time. Not my favorite sport."

Sean thought for a moment and said, "Understandable."

Quinn recalled his conversation with the English fellow in the Library. "I met an English guy who was studying his family history in the Atlanta Library a few days ago. Interesting guy. His family came from Clonakilty during or after the Famine, and he apparently now lives in London. I suppose there are Irish descendants all over the world and most likely quite a few in England, but I would have thought the friction with Great Britain would have cooled their interest in going in that direction."

Sean had set his glass down and was leaning forward with his arms on the table intently listening to what Quinn was saying.

"What is the guy doing over in this country, did he say?" Sean asked.

Sean had a serious look on his face, and his unusual interest in this matter was a bit of a surprise to Quinn.

"Well, he's working for a London company, I believe he said. I've got his card in my wallet, I think. Let's see." Quinn pulled out his wallet and searched among the various business cards, credit cards, and ID cards and finally came up with the right one.

"Here, here's his card. Stanley Morris, Cosmic Engineering, Ltd., whatever the hell that is."

Sean took the card and studied it for a moment.

"I have some friends that might know this fellow, do you mind if I copy down his info?"

"Hell no. I probably won't even see the guy again, although that reminds me, he said he just might be in Dublin when I am over there. You might meet him if we're all there at the same time. Nice guy. He was interested in going over for the same reason as I am, to check the records in the Library, provided he can get off work."

As Sean was writing down the information on the card, he couldn't resist saying it, "He'll most likely get off."

Quinn took the remark as evidence of Sean's corporate cynicism.

Sean copied every piece of information on the card and studied the back of it to see if there was anything written there. As he gave the card back to Quinn, he commented, "Interesting. You meet the most interesting people in libraries. That's why I stay out of them."

They both laughed. It was almost time for Sean to get back on stage. He butted out his cigarette and quickly drained the remaining beer in his glass, followed by a somewhat partially suppressed burp and a chuckle as he stood up to get back to work.

"Are you going to hang around or is it getting close to your bed time?" Sean asked.

Quinn smiled, looked at his watch and said, "Bedtime."

Sean laughed and said, "Okay, I'll talk to you tomorrow."

A few mornings later when Quinn was getting ready to leave his house for his usual morning run, the phone rang and it was Sean.

"Guess what old buddy. I've set it up with the U to take some time off. I can leave for Dublin the first week of November, so I will be able to show you around a bit over there. I had to get a replacement, but there were about ten qualified guys at the pub that were more than willing to stand in for me. One guy has a master's degree, and the head honcho found him acceptable. Acceptable, my ass. Anyway, old buddy, I will be there. God, I'm excited to be going back."

Quinn was a bit surprised by Sean's enthusiasm at returning to Ireland when he had just been over there. "Sean, I thought you were just there?"

Sean was surprised by the statement and said nothing for a moment.

"How did you know that?" Sean asked.

"Sean, your secretary told me that before we met for the first time in your office."

Sean laughed. "Well, I'll have to tell her to keep quiet about what I'm up to. I thought I had her squared away on that before. Yes, I was over there on a business trip, but just for a few days. This trip I will have some time to visit friends. It didn't even feel like I was over there on that last trip."

"Well, Sean, I'm glad to hear you'll be there when I am. You know where I'm staying, so let me know when you're in town, and also," Quinn paused to emphasize what he was saying, "don't let me interfere with your schedule while you're there. I am sure I'll get along quite well without your guidance and counseling."

Sean said, "Hey, I want to be there when you find out your ancestors all served time in the Kilmainham Jail."

He laughed and then on a more serious note assured Quinn that he would not be interfering and that he would enjoy showing him around. Then Sean said, "Sorry guy, I've got to go teach a class. Have a good one, and I'll talk with you later."

Quinn decided to run a different route this morning and drove over to the Chattahootchee River Trail just off Highway 285. It was a pretty run that went along the river bed, through groves of cottonwoods. It was like you were running through a pristine forest. The only problem was that others up in the Cobb County area also enjoyed the beauty of the place and liked to run there as well, but this late in the morning, Quinn figured he would have the trail pretty much to himself.

It was about ten in the morning by the time he began his run, setting his timer as he always did, although the time over his normal five mile run never varied over a minute. Today, he would run the distance based on his time, because he didn't know where the two and a half mile turn around point was on the trail.

Quinn was listening to a country western tune with a tempo that perfectly matched his running pace.

"God, if I could listen to this all the way, it would be a breeze," Quinn thought.

As he ran, he thought about all the things that he had to do to get ready for his trip, which was coming up quickly. He still hadn't received his passport and was beginning to worry about that. He had been told that if need be, he could always visit the Irish Consulate downtown, and they would arrange for him to use a birth certificate for entry if his passport didn't come in time. He might have to do that. Quinn had made up a list of things that he had to be sure and pack, and as each day passed the list had grown longer. Travelers checks, belly bag, camera, umbrella.

Everyone he talked with said, "Be sure and take an umbrella." He found one that was only about ten inches long, collapsed, and would fit into his briefcase. "Perfect," he thought.

More than one of his friends had asked him if he really was going to wear his white bucks over there.

"Of course, I don't have another pair of shoes." This usually received a raised eyebrow, but Quinn wanted to be comfortable on the trip, and if someone was offended by what he wore that was their problem. When he finished the run, he walked for a quarter mile or so to cool down, drinking in the refreshing fall air that Atlanta was beginning to enjoy now that summer was fast fading. This was Quinn's favorite time of year. Not too windy, fresh cool air, and not much rain. Perfect running conditions.

It was another fifteen minutes before Quinn was pulling into the drive way to his house.

"For God's sake, I left the damn garage door open. Somebody could have walked right into the house."

Quinn pulled his car into the garage and left the garage door up just in case. He didn't want to find that there was somebody still in the house and no way to quickly escape. He noticed the house door from the garage was ajar, and now he was beginning to think that he would not have left both doors unsecured. His heart was beginning to pound as he stopped to listen for any noise coming from the house. He heard nothing, just the clicking sound of the electric clock on the kitchen wall inside the door.

Quinn had a gun, but unfortunately it was upstairs in his bedroom. He looked around the garage and saw a broken ax handle leaning against a support beam next to where he was standing. Quinn picked it up, but finding it too unwieldy he exchanged it for a hammer from the tool box on his work bench. Still not hearing anything from inside the house and not being totally certain that he had not left both doors unattended, he decided to go in. He quietly opened the door, stepped inside, and again stopped to listen. Nothing, just that damned clock.

He walked as softly as he could across the kitchen floor and peered into the dining area and across into the living room. Nothing seemed to be amiss, and he noticed that his TV set and his mother's old silver set were in their proper places. This made him relax a bit, thinking that maybe he had just unconsciously left the doors open. He moved a bit faster now, entering the living area and then to the base of the stairs that led upstairs to his bedroom and office. He again stopped, listened, and hearing nothing he proceeded slowly up the stairs. He went directly to his office and walked in to find his papers strewn around the floor, drawers wide open, his pocket telephone directory seemed to be missing, and it was then that he saw his computer was nowhere to be seen.

"Where the hell's my computer, for God's sake? The sons of bitches stole my computer."

Quinn stomped into the other rooms on the second floor, now hoping to find the thief that had taken his brand new computer. He had the hammer raised as he pushed open doors, inspected closets, and checked under beds. He then thought about the basement and ran down checking every possible place where a person could have hidden when they heard him drive into the garage. No one was in the house except for himself. He ran back upstairs to see if anything else had been taken and was relieved to see that his camera was still sitting on his book shelf just to the side of his desk from where the computer was stolen. Even his gun was still in the drawer.

He then saw that his wallet was gone and this caused him more concern than the computer. At least he had recorded all of his computer data on floppy disks so that he could easily reinstall that in another computer, but the wallet, the credit cards, his driver's license, all that crap that he would need for his trip. The more he thought about it, the angrier he became. He only had about ten bucks in the wallet, so they must have been after the credit cards. It must have been some punk kids. He had thought about a security system in the past. This did it. He would have one installed immediately.

CHAPTER 23

The following evening at the pub, Sean joined Quinn at the table during the break and told him that he had talked with some friends in Dublin who wanted Sean to play in their band when he was over there.

"They have a gig in Temple Bar at a small pub. It should be a good time. Anyway, I'll have my Guinness paid for. What's new with you?

Quinn told him about the theft of his wallet and computer from his house.

"The worst part is the wallet. I've been on the phone ever since it happened. Thank God they didn't get my passport, which I just received in the mail today. That's about the only ID that they didn't take. That would have really screwed me up. The credit cards are bad enough, but they are Fed Exing me new ones that I should have right away, at least I hope so."

Sean listened attentively as Quinn explained how he had found the house unlocked and open when he returned from running. Sean asked a number of questions until he had to go play with the band, but as soon as he returned at the next break, he took up where he had left off.

"What did you have on the computer?" Sean asked.

Quinn explained that there was just material from his family history project and some business letters, but it was no problem because he had it all on disk and the insurance company was covering the computer loss.

"It's just inconvenient, but ever since I bought that computer the newer ones have double the hard drive space and are almost twice as fast. Having it stolen was almost a good deal. It's replacing the stuff from my wallet that is the problem."

Sean kept asking questions and focused in on exactly what Quinn had found disturbed in his house upon his return.

"So, the only drawers that were still open were your desk drawers in your office, is that right?"

"That was it, Sean. Everything on or in my desk was thrown around the room as if that was where I kept all of my cash and gems. Dresser drawers weren't even opened, nor were the drawers in cabinets downstairs. They missed the gun in the bedroom dresser. I don't suppose they figured they had much time, and they only looked where guys usually keep things, in their desk drawers. They must have known about how long I would be gone, and they didn't want to be there when I came back."

Sean nodded as he took in what Quinn was saying.

"Yeah, they must have picked up on your schedule and hit the house while you were gone. Not the work of street punks. They aren't that thorough."

Quinn looked puzzled. "What do you mean? I figure it was some kids. Who the hell else would have any interest in what I have in my desk? Besides, they took the wallet."

Sean laughed. "Wallet, shmallet. I'll bet they didn't even try to make a buy on your cards. They didn't, did they?" Sean looked to Quinn for his answer.

Quinn thought for a moment and said, "I never asked the credit card companies. I called them as soon as I saw what had happened and figured that I got to them before anyone would get to a store to try to use them. But you bring up a good point. I'll call them tomorrow and ask if anyone did try to charge on them. The new ones all have new numbers, of course. Yeah, I'll let you know what they say."

Sean's comments about the thieves not being street punks concerned him, because he could not figure out who else would have done it. To be on the safe side, Quinn decided that he would have the locks changed the next day and call a security company to put in a system. He was also going to ask about any attempted charges on the cards. Quinn thought to himself that it was interesting that Sean should point that out. Quinn just didn't think in those terms, but apparently Sean did.

The next afternoon, Quinn dropped by Sean's office, but the receptionist told him that he was still teaching his class and would not be back for about thirty minutes. She knew who Quinn was from previous visits to the office and said, "If you would like to wait, you can have a chair here or wait in Sean's office."

Quinn had a book he was reading in his brief case and thought the office would be a better place to wait and he could read there without her typewriter clicking away at his side. "I'll go down to his office. Thanks. Oh, say tell him I'm there in case he decides to leave the building." The secretary said she would and Quinn walked down the hallway and into Sean's office. The place was in its usual state of disarray but with the addition of a few of Sean's personal belongings that were thrown on his desk while he was teaching his class. His briar pipe was sitting on the desk and when Quinn picked it up, it was still a bit warm to the touch which told him that Sean had left not too long ago.

Quinn moved some books off of the only other chair in the room and sat down, pulling his own book out of the briefcase that he carried with him. As he was settling into the chair, he took note of the items on Sean's desk. There were some bills and letters there that Sean had apparently been reading before he left for class. One letter on the top of the stack had an eagle logo on the letterhead and appeared to be written in Gaelic. Quinn thought that it looked a bit familiar and recalled seeing it some time ago when he pulled up the Nationalist Party home page on the Internet. Obviously some political correspondence for Sean.

Quinn sat back in the chair and got into the book he was reading which was one that Sean had given him. It was a fictionalized account of the Famine. Sean had said that it might be depressing to read, but Quinn had not found it to be so. He read it more as a history than for its gruesome portrayal of the terrible plight of the Irish people in the mid nineteenth century. As he read the book, he tried to picture how his family and, in particular, how his grandfather was faring in the dark days of the late 1840s. Some of the Irish made it through those hard years because they had some money or food to survive on, but the vast majority was reduced to starvation and eviction. The sad part was that there was ample food in Ireland at the time to feed the entire nation a few times over, but it was being exported to England for their use or for reshipment to Europe that was also suffering a food shortage.

Sean had told Quinn that it was historical fact that the English were intentionally committing genocide on the Irish Catholics but Quinn had a hard time believing that a country as civilized as Great Britain would stoop to that. He didn't argue the issue with Sean as he knew that was his hot button and he didn't want to light the fire. Quinn did have to admit that the history books that he had read, not all of which came from Sean, were very accusatory with respect to the English treatment of the Irish during the Famine years.

About a half an hour later, Quinn heard Sean's voice down the hall talking with the secretary and then his footsteps in the hallway as he approached the office. "Well, what do we have here", he said as he flung his class book and notes on the floor next to his chair. "Come over to look at some of our young, nubile, female students, I suppose. Eh."

"Not quite, Sean. Maybe a few years ago that was the case, but now I'm into books, family history, the market, the boring crap. Actually, I had to get out of my house for a while as the security people are putting in my system and I don't like to listen to drills going. Reminds me of the dentist's office. Anyway, I have to be back there at 3:00 so they can give me my training course. Don't want the cops to be arresting me for trying to get into my own house. One other thing, I did call the credit card companies and you were right. No attempts to use the cards. Maybe they saw that I returned right away and that put the 'kabash' on their plans for the cards. I don't know. Anyway, thought you might find that interesting in view of the fact you brought it up."

"Yes", Sean said, "it is interesting. By the way, did you call the cops? You never mentioned that."

"Gees, Sean, you know, I never thought to call them until the next day. I did call them the next morning when I was about to call my insurance company. I figured the insurance company would ask me that and, of course, they did. Anyway, the cops could have cared less, but they did say that they hadn't had any other calls in the neighborhood that day and then the guy said, he couldn't recall when they had a problem there. 'Nice safe neighborhood,' he said. I thought, 'my ass.'"

Sean was about to say something, but then he noticed the letter with the eagle symbol sitting open on his desk and he picked it up to put it in his desk drawer. Quinn was watching him and Sean made a comment that he would have to keep his desk a bit neater in the future. Quinn said, "What, and ruin your reputation?" Quinn then told Sean that he had pulled up the Nationalist Party home page on the Internet and noticed the eagle on that letter that he had put in the drawer. "Same one, right?"

Sean seemed a bit embarrassed but then pulled the letter back out of the drawer, looked at the logo and said, "yes, the Party symbol for strength and vigilance. Glad to hear you pulled it up. Maybe we can get you to join when you are in Dublin. We need the help of our Irish American cousins. There are forty million of you over here and you could determine our future. You know how many Irish there are on that island? You must by now, you've read enough books."

"Of course," Quinn said. "Three and a half in the Republic and one and a half in the North. How's that?"

Sean said, "pretty good. Now if we can avoid an economic downturn and not give our young people away to other countries, we can boost that number. The birth rate is better in the south than in the north you know."

"I know that," Quinn said, "and I also know that is what you people are counting on. Hoping the demographics will solve the unification problem."

"God, you could pass the test right now," Sean said with a laugh which required an adjustment of his glasses.

Whoa," Quinn said, looking at his watch. "I've got to get back to my house for my genuine security system training briefing. If you want, you can join me over there. I'm sure it' ll be interesting."

"No," Sean said, "I'm not quite that bored. Say, I've got an idea though. Did you ever see the movie 'Michael Collins'?"

"Can't say as I have," said Quinn.

"It's on tonight at the Peachtree Plaza. Let's take it in. Give you an Irish history lesson along with your popcorn. What do you say?"

Quinn agreed and the two decided to meet at the pub at six, get something to eat and then take in the movie. Quinn quickly picked up his things and headed for his house noting that he would be late if he didn't get a move on. "Later," he said to Sean as he closed the office door and headed down the hall to the exit.

Later, as they were sitting in the pub getting a bite to eat, Quinn said, "well, Sean, I suppose you are looking forward to seeing your kids again. Won't be long now."

Sean smiled and said, "just talked to them shortly before you came into the office this afternoon. They were just going to bed. Time change you know. Anyway, yes. I am looking forward to seeing them... and they, me. I hope so anyway. I'm going to look around Dublin when I'm back there and see if I can't pick up a teaching job that I can afford to hold. That and playing in a band somewhere just might pull in enough to let me afford to stay there. You know, it's not cheap living in Dublin. Rentals are higher than they are here and so's everything else. If I can't net enough to be able to send money to Annie, then I can't stay. That's all there is to it."

Quinn just nodded and made no comment. He probably should not have brought up the issue of Sean's kids as every time he did, it seemed to put a downer on his friend's spirits. It clearly bothered him that he hardly ever saw them except when he was on his rare trips over to Ireland. Quinn changed the subject and asked him if he had seen "this movie, 'Michael Collins', before."

"Of course," Sean said. "What good Irishman hasn't seen it at least twice, maybe three times. Sort of a cult movie for us Republicans. You'll find it interesting. Much of the plot actually takes place down in Cork, in fact not far from Kinsale. He was shot to death within about fifty miles of Kinsale and was born not far from there too. Clonakilty, in West Cork."

Quinn smiled and said, "I know, Sean. He was shot to death in 1922, I believe."

"Eh, wow. Very good," Sean exclaimed. "My efforts are paying off!"

"One thing that bothers me, Sean. Popular belief has it that the Republicans were the ones behind his shooting and yet, you apparently look up to him as an Irish patriot. Am I missing something?"

"We aren't all perfect, Quinn. Let's say that sometimes history changes ones perspective. Maybe that is what happened in the case of Michael Collins. There was a tremendous split in the party back then. Many thought that the deal Collins arranged for Ireland to be divided, North and South, was a sellout, but maybe, on the other hand, it was the best deal he could get for Ireland at the time. Going for a split country and getting it was probably better than trying to get the whole pie and ending up with nothing. I don't know but, in my opinion, his heart was in the right place. There is still a lot of animosity towards him even today, especially in West Cork which has always been the center of Irish nationalism."

Quinn found the movie very interesting, particularly in view of his extensive reading of Irish history and his association with Sean's Nationalist views. The two men returned to the pub for a glass of beer and spent another hour or more rehashing events depicted in the movie. "If you get down to Cork, Quinn, stay at the Imperial in Cork City. That's where he stayed the last night of his life. Nice hotel too." Sean paused. "A real pity that they killed him. That it was." Quinn could tell that Sean was genuinely affected by the movie even though this was at least the third or fourth time he had seen it.

The next morning, Quinn drove downtown to the Library as he wanted to review the microfilm on the Minnesota Census for 1860 to make sure that he had all of the names of the other Irishmen living in close proximity to his Grandfather that may have made the trip across the ocean at the same time as his grandfather emigrated. While he was at the library, a young fellow by the name of Peter Baker approached him and with an Irish accent said he had overheard Quinn mentioning to one of the patrons that he was researching the Desmond name.

"That is a name I'm looking into also." Baker introduced himself, and told Quinn he was now living in Londonderry. The two discussed their areas of particular interest with Baker explaining that his Desmonds had originally come from Clonakilty.

Quinn, by this time, had met a number of genealogists who would freely inquire of complete strangers in the research room as to their particular area of study so he did not find this encounter to be unusual. The two chatted a bit more and then Quinn went about his review of the Census microfilm. Baker left the library a short time later and Quinn soon forgot about the conversation.

Later that afternoon while he was still at the library, Quinn called Sean to see if he had his airline reservations squared away as he was hoping to take the same flight over to Ireland as Quinn. When he got him on the line, Sean told him that he had just talked with the airline, moments before and he said, "I've got a resie and I'm sitting across the aisle from where you're at, for whatever that's worth. I didn't know if I was going to get on that flight at this late date, but it must be my lucky day. Annie and the kids are meeting me at the airport and I'm going to stay over there while I'm in Dublin. We'll drop you off at the Rockwell if we can get us and our gear into her car. I can use her car while we're in Dublin so we'll have some transport to run around in. You won't need any wheels staying at the Rockwell, so don't bother renting a car."

Quinn had heard about driving in Ireland and had no intention of doing so. He had heard they "drove on the wrong side of the road," and had what they called "roundabouts" that were guaranteed to take care of at least one fender if you didn't know what you were doing. He would leave the driving to someone else, not himself. Besides, he had been told the trains were excellent and, if need be, he could take the train to Cork and then take a bus or if he absolutely had to, he could rent a car from there.

The two were talking about their trip that was leaving in less than a week when Quinn mentioned that he had met another fellow at the library researching another Desmond family. Sean was quiet on the other end of the line and finally Quinn asked, "are you there old buddy?"

After a pause, Sean answered, "Yes, I was just thinking. Who was this guy? You say he was Irish, or sounded like he was?"

Quinn said, "yes. His family apparently lived in West Cork, but he was living at the present time in Londonderry, in the North. Said he was here on business but didn't say who he worked for or anything. Pleasant guy."

Sean asked a number of questions. "What did the guy look like?... How old was this guy?...What was he wearing?...Did he have a briefcase or papers with him?" and so forth. Quinn answered all of his questions, describing Baker as in his mid thirties or so, about six feet tall, sandy hair, sort of an athletic build, an intelligent appearing guy.

After a while Quinn said, "Look, Sean, this goes on all the time. He was just some guy checking out his family tree, just like I'm doing. The library is full of these people. You ought to come down there sometime and take a look. I didn't know genealogy was this popular. Why all the questions?"

Sean was quiet for a moment and then answered. "Well, Quinn, you never know what is going on. There are things happening over in Ireland and you should probably be a little bit careful."

This was a real surprise. Quinn had heard only good things about the country and the people. What was there to be careful about. There were problems in the north, but he wasn't intending to go up there and Sean knew that. "Sean, what the hell are you talking about? Little old ladies from Boston go over there all the time. I've never heard of anyone having trouble in the Republic,or even the North for that matter."

Sean again paused and then said, "This is different."

That got Quinn's attention in a hurry. "Hey, Sean. What the hell is different about my going over there?"

Sean paused and said, "I'll talk to you tonight when I'm at home where I've got some privacy. OK. I've got to get going now. I've got a meeting to attend. Talk to you later."

Quinn was puzzled by the telephone call. He went over the events of the past year and could come up with nothing that caused him concern. There was the break in but after all, he lived in Atlanta. Ireland was a hell of a lot safer than Atlanta. He would give Sean a call later and find out what in the hell he was talking about.

Quinn called Sean later in the evening, a number of times, but never got an answer. Quinn figured that his friend must have gone over to the pub and run into some of his Irish friends. He would call him at the University in the morning. The following morning, he called his office and the receptionist told him that Sean had not come in yet, but that she would have him call Quinn when he showed up. The receptionist said that sometimes he went straight to class but usually came to his office afterwards.

When Quinn called later, the receptionist said that Sean had not shown up for his class which was a first. She had been trying to call him at his home but there was no answer. Quinn was now beginning to be concerned because he would have heard from Sean by now even if they had no plans to communicate. Sean frequently called him in the morning to comment on something on the news or to meet him for lunch or whatever. Quinn went running and figured that if there was no further word when he returned, he would go looking for him. When he came back to the house, there were no messages on his answering machine and the receptionist said that Sean had still not called.

It was almost lunchtime and Quinn figured that the pub would be open and someone there would know where Sean had taken off to. He jumped into his car and drove over to the pub, in time to see one of Sean's Irish friends enter the bar. When Quinn walked into the pub, there were a number of Sean's friends gathered together at the bar, but no one was talking and this was very unusual for this normally gregarious group. Quinn had gotten to know a few of them and he walked up to the one that he knew the best and asked him if he knew where Sean was.

The fellow looked at him with a stunned look on his face, "Haven't you heard?"

Quinn said, "No, what's going on? I've been looking for him since last night."

"Well," the fellow said, "I have some terribly bad news. Sean is dead. He was gunned down last night as he was walking to his car. Right out in front of the Pub. Never had a chance. Car came up, apparently they had been watching the front of the Pub, waiting for him, or whoever, to come out and they shot him a number of times and pulled out of the parking lot."

CHAPTER 24

As Patrick sat in his office, twirling the letter opener in his perspiring hands, he thought about his forthcoming discussion with Carter. For once, he felt he had the upper hand going into a meeting with his nemesis and he cautioned himself that he had to be careful and not screw it up.

Patrick was sure that he knew why Carter was being so open about his flirtation with the wife of the President of Desmond Enterprises in front of virtually everyone. It was Carter's chance to get back at the upper-crust, the cabin class, the ones that sped by him, going to their private schools when he was a street rat in the slums of Belfast. Carter was most likely one of those kids that hurled rocks at them in their sleek, black limousines then but, now that he was older, he had discovered there were more effective ways to bring them pain with embarrassment and ridicule than with a rock and sling.

Well, thought Patrick. Two can play the pain game. I'll just bait that hook and when I think it's way down that bastard's throat, I'll give it a sharp pull and we'll hang that son of a bitch out to dry. As Patrick let his imagination soar, envisioning the various possibilities of what could happen to Carter, his thoughts reverted to the real world and he brought himself back to his original purpose, to decide on what he was going to discuss with the man and how he was going to go about it.

First of all, Patrick cautioned himself, he did not want to let Carter even suspect that someone was in the States checking out this Parker fellow. He must be very careful and not intermix what Baumler had told him with what Carter had. That could be fatal. Secondly, the same went for the information regarding the people and groups in Dublin. It would be best to let Carter do as much of the talking as possible.

Patrick laid out two goals for their conversation. First to try to learn what he could regarding what was going on in Atlanta and secondly to try and ferret out what the slime ball and his wife were up to, if anything. Patrick was nervous about the fact that the two of them were in communication. That did nothing but bode ill for him, knowing the propensity of each of them to consider him totally expendable.

Patrick had arranged to meet Carter down by the fish market near the statue of King William III, the victor of the Battle of the Boyne and as he parked his car, taking in the odor of the place, he laughed to himself, thinking that the venue of the meeting was so appropriate under the circumstances. When he approached the Statue, he saw Carter talking to some of the vendors down by the stalls and by the time Patrick came up to the square, Carter had seen him and was coming over to where he was now standing. Carter had the semblance of a smile on his face which Patrick immediately noticed because it was so unusual. Patrick figured the lout was overcome by feelings of indebtedness towards him for letting him screw his wife. Carter would not be so grateful when this was all over, Patrick would do his best to see to that.

Patrick ignored his disdain for the man and opened the conversation. "Well, do you have any good news for me today?"

"Not really, Patrick. Apparently your relative in the States is making plans to come over here in the not too distant future and his INA buddy is going to either come over with him or meet him over here. That is the word coming from Atlanta. If you want us to take care of the problem right now, we'll be happy to accommodate you. We certainly owe you that."

Back to his old tricks, thought Patrick. He wants my name on the hit. No way. I'm not carrying that load. Trying to steady his voice, Patrick responded. "I would hope that we could resolve this in some amicable fashion if it actually becomes a problem which I don't think it will. Let's just see what happens." Patrick wanted to impress Carter, if he could, with the fact that all of this didn't really bother him as much as Carter hoped it did. Unfortunately, Patrick could feel the perspiration again building up on his upper lip and as soon as Carter looked away for a moment towards the fishing boats, Patrick took the opportunity to wipe off the visible evidence of his nervousness.

Carter had nothing of any significance to add to the matter in the States other than what he had already said and after some small talk about the fact they were lucking out not having any rain and a comment about all the shoppers in the vendor's stalls, he turned the conversation towards Patrick's trip to Dublin. "How did your trip go? I hope you had time to spend with your daughter."

You jack ass, thought Patrick. "Yes, we had a good time. She's doing fine at her job and likes Dublin quite a bit." Patrick was well aware that Carter knew everything that had occurred in Dublin and it was amusing to see Carter's facial expressions as he went on describing the trip, omitting any reference to the incident when he had left Bewley's café. Patrick figured that Carter must be dying of curiosity to know who the fellow was that clobbered his guy and returned the briefcase. For all Carter knows, it could have been a total stranger who just happened upon the scene and recovered the case, but the fact that the Glock was no where to be found when the agent went to the hospital would definitely raise questions in Carter's mind. Somers had stripped the Glock from the Unity agent very discreetly as there was no mention in the newspapers of the gun which indicated that none of the bystanders, or the police, were aware it had been taken. The two talked for a few more minutes and then Patrick announced that he had to get back to the office. Carter gave him another big smile and said he would keep him informed. Enough to gag a maggot, thought Patrick as he turned to walk away without responding.

As Patrick walked back to his car, he laughed to himself knowing that Carter was dying to know what had really taken place in Dublin. That was the only reason Carter had requested the meeting because he had no other information of any consequence to pass on to Patrick that he hadn't already told him. Nevertheless, Patrick told himself that he would have to be very careful about how he handled a situation that seemed to be getting more complicated as time passed. He had a lot of confidence in Baumler, but throughout his life he had gotten into trouble turning problems over to others to solve. This one, he was going to get some help on, but he was going to stay on top of it himself or he would end up with a tin cup in a food line some place. Patrick didn't think he would handle that very well.

The following week was an enjoyable one for Patrick as Hillary was going on one of her frequent shopping trips to London and to visit her old college friends from Ruthridge.

"Yes, I'm looking forward to seeing Jane and Madge. I'll be sure and say hello to them for you, Patrick." Just one more jab.

God, he couldn't stand either one, with their pompous and condescending attitudes and he knew she threw their names out at him just to piss him off. Patrick replied, "That's just wonderful, my dear. Be sure and give them my love."

Hillary said, with a barely detectable tone of sarcasm, "Oh, I will Patrick. How nice of you to say that."

Hillary had Robert, the houseman, drive her to the airport for the flight to London and after she left the house, Patrick gave out a sigh of relief and had the cook warm up some tea. He went into the library and mapped out his week, knowing that she would be gone at least that long. The thought entered his mind that possibly Carter had managed to arrange a leave of absence for the same period of time. Patrick hoped that he had so that Carter would have the opportunity to spend a week being snubbed and insulted by some of Hillary's friends. That group could give that Belfast street rat a new outlook on life. Maybe I could even get to like the guy if he went through their training program. I can hear them now. I say Mr. Carter, what school did you attend, alley rat one or alley rat two. Patrick laughed at the thought. No, they wouldn't be quite so up front. They would do it in little snippets. Small bites of his ass so that by the time he came home it would be all gone and he wouldn't be sure what had happened to it. They were masters at that. God, what ass holes they were. Oh well, Patrick thought, time for more pleasant thoughts.

Patrick took another sip of his tea and looked around the library at the fine wood work, the beautiful eighteenth century furniture that had been in the room forever as far as Patrick knew. The upper portions of the windows in the room were decorated with stained glass panels which brought out different colors in the wood furnishings inside the room depending upon the location of the sun during the days. Patrick wondered as he looked up at the stained glass if the original builder sought to achieve that result or if it was by mere accident. In any event, it added to the beauty of the room which was Patrick's favorite in the old home.

Patrick had found the rest of the house, for the most part, drafty and cold which was one of the reasons that he sought refuge in the library. That was the only room in the house that did not have a fireplace and was not subjected to the cold winds of Northern Ireland that seemed to sneak in under doors and window ledges, not to mention down the shafts of chimneys. Furthermore, the placement of the library windows was such that the room was favored by the sun throughout most of the day, provided it was not clouded over.

Patrick would have preferred a more modern home, but he would then have been violating a sacred trust if he did not live in and maintain the home that had been in the family since his great grandfather's time. As his eyes continued roaming around the room, taking in the various features that he was so familiar with, he found himself staring at the old books on the shelves. As he did so, he remembered what he had thought of some weeks before. He stepped out into the hallway and called to the cook to have Robert come into the library when he returned from the airport.

Shortly afterwards, there was a knock at the library door and the houseman, entered the room. "You wished to see me, Sir?"

"Yes," Patrick replied. "I was thinking, Robert, that these books and shelves have probably not been cleaned in over a hundred years. What do you think?"

The houseman studied the old leather bindings on the books and the oak shelves that were installed most likely when the house was built and nodded in agreement with a bit of a smile on his face. "Mr. Desmond, I have been here going on fifty years and to my knowledge, the books have never been removed from the shelves, unless you, of course, may have removed some of them to read." Patrick knew that Robert was a wise houseman and added the last comment knowing full well that Patrick seldom read anything, other than the evening issue of the Belfast Independent or the London Times.

"Very well, Robert. Then let's get at it." Patrick had Robert get the necessary equipment together for the task at hand, dust rags, cleaning spray and a step stool to reach the higher shelves. "We have to be careful not to damage the books with the spray, Robert, so just apply it to the rag and not directly on the book."

On tasks like this which were simple, Patrick was at his best and was quite capable of micro managing the activities of those under his direction. It was the more complex tasks that were a problem for him. The two began at one end of the library wall and began working their way around the room. It was obvious after a while as they removed the books, wiped them off and then cleaned off the shelves that no one had been at this task in many years, if ever. Some of the books tended to stick to the shelves, or each other, for whatever reason and the two men had to use considerable care in removing the books so as not to damage the bindings. Consequently, it was slow going but their progress was markedly visible as the bindings of the books that had been cleaned had a luster to them that delineated the ones cleaned from those not yet touched.

Occasionally the two men would come across a scrap of paper hidden between the books, in the books or behind the books, next to the shelf wall, and they would closely examine these various bits of antiquity to see what hidden treasures they contained. Some of them were notes written by long departed relatives concerning household matters or were receipts for purchases of one sort or another. In any event, they were interesting but of no major consequence to anyone. Nevertheless as each new find was discovered it was passed from one to the other and carefully examined. All of these were preserved as age alone had given them value if nothing else had. Patrick instructed Robert to set them aside in a box which would be kept in the book case for future inspection.

Patrick, himself, was even doubtful as to who or why anyone would reexamine the various slips of paper but someone, at some future date, could possibly find them to be of interest. Possibly they might want to know the cost of an ink pen a hundred years ago as was recorded on one of the slips. Or, maybe they would actually find the old ink pen somewhere in the house and wonder when it was purchased. The receipt would tell them that and everyone would thank Patrick for his foresight. Whatever. Patrick gave Robert careful instructions on exactly how the container for the old slips of paper should be prepared, its color and size as though all of this was way over the head of the houseman who was, dutifully, making careful notes as he was being guided through this difficult task. The two finished the first day with about one third of the task accomplished. Patrick noted that they had been at the job for over nine hours and with careful calculation, viewing both his watch and the shelf space that had been cleaned, he audibly estimated, for Robert's benefit, that the job would take over two more days to accomplish.

"Yes, Sir, did you wish to continue in the morning, Sir, and if so, at what hour?" Patrick could tell by the tonal variation of Robert's voice that he would be able to manage if the task were put off for a day or two.

"We will continue the job the day after tomorrow, my good man." Patrick meant that as a compliment as he appreciated Robert's work as a very able and obedient houseman. As he waited for some form of acknowledgment, he thought to himself, we all have our positions in life and it takes a certain amount of skill to carry them off gracefully. Robert has that skill.

"Yes, sir, I will report to the library at nine unless you wish me to be there earlier."

"No, Robert. That will be quite fine." The two parted with Robert taking the cleaning utensils with him as he quietly closed the library door behind him.

Patrick sat in the chair surveying the day's accomplishments with a certain amount of pride. Amazing, he thought to himself as a feeling of exhilaration surged through his body. I feel that I've accomplished more doing this than I feel after a week in the office. As he thought more about it, the thought began to depress him because he had learned over time not to think about how little he actually did for Desmond Enterprises and, here he was, being the whipping boy, again, for his own guilt. Desmond Enterprises needed an occasional hard decision or two and Hillary provided that with ease. The rest of the time, the company operated sort of on autopilot with the various top and mid level executives following long established company policies to keep the profits rolling in.

When he first took over as President of Desmond Enterprises, Patrick used to keep his office door open so that employees walking past the executive wing could see their own President hard at work for the company. After the first week, when he had familiarized himself with the rules and procedures laid down by his father and predecessors before him, he found that he had little to do. The phone seldom rang, his secretary, the aged Mrs. Whitley looked like she was asleep at her desk and employees walking in the hallway, now knowing that his door was open, were always craning their necks to see what major happenings were taking place in the President's office. After he had locked eyeballs with administration clerks, cleaning staff and an occasional embarrassed executive, he decided it would be better to close the door and, at least, relax even if there was nothing to do.

The years immediately following his taking over the Presidency of Desmond Enterprises, which coincided, not by chance, with the death of his father, Dennis Desmond, were years of learning for Patrick. What he learned in those years was not quite what he had in mind the first day he sat behind the large oak desk and adjusted the height of his heavily padded leather chair so that he didn't look like he was peeking over the top of the desk. During those first years, Patrick learned the skills of one who has too little to do such as never to walk out of his office without carrying a sheaf of important looking papers and always, always have a frown on his face as though the responsibilities of office were almost overwhelming. Not quite overwhelming but almost.

Patrick had apparently accomplished the learning process quite well because lower level executives, when brought to his Presidential suite were invariably frozen with fright to be in the presence of the person who sat at the helm of Desmond Enterprises driving the corporate ship through the shark infested and storm tossed seas of commerce. What they did not know was that he had spent endless hours reviewing exactly how he would handle himself and what he would say when he was introduced to these corporate fledglings. Every motion of his body, every movement of his facial muscles and every word he spoke, was the result of forethought, meant to convey the image of one, overburdened, but yet in control. Those closest to him in the corporate structure, who regularly bypassed him when major decision time came about, knew him for what he was but yet never betrayed him to the lower staff. He served his purpose quite well. Sometimes a figurehead could be more important than the real thing and as a figurehead, Patrick did a fairly good job.

He and Hillary had been married shortly before he took over as President of Desmond Enterprises. It was a marriage arranged at the bank between Dennis Desmond and Sir Charles Fairchild. Sir Charles wished to tie his substantial holdings in with a recognized mercantile firm with global connections and Desmond Enterprises offered him that opportunity. He had the Desmond family investigated with particular emphasis on young Patrick who was being groomed to take over the family business on the retirement or death of his father, Dennis. While Sir Charles did not receive glowing reports on the young man's scholastic achievements nor anything of interest regarding his business skills, he did not come up with anything bad about him either.

Sir Charles was not overly concerned about Patrick's business prowess as he was well aware that Hillary had business skills to spare. She had been calling the shots at Fairchild Investments since she graduated from Ruthridge and the profit and loss statements during her tenure were solid evidence of her abilities. Sir Charles told his friends at the Hunt Club that Hillary had balls of solid steel when it came to making the difficult business moves. She had no great interest in getting married but Sir Charles suggested to her that it would be good for their company were she to marry someone with business connections that would mix well with Fairchild. After Sir Charles had checked Patrick out, he told Hillary, "I have just the right person picked out for you and I am sure you will be very happy."

Hillary had her own views on marriage but they were quite different from those held by most people, including her own father. She was willing to marry, but only because it was the accepted status in society and gave one a certain amount of respectability. Other than that, she considered it a nuisance and knew that regardless of whom she married, she would never be faithful. When she had the conversation with her father, she was quite willing to go along with his wishes, provided the chosen one was not a complete dolt that would embarrass her among her friends at the club and in London society.

When she learned that Patrick was an Irishman, she almost put a damper on the entire arrangement because she considered all of the Irish to be a little too uncivilized for her tastes. Sir Charles expounded on the fine blood line of the Desmond family and the fact that they had intermarried with the Adams line and "we all know what a fine family that is." After Sir Charles went over some of the financial data on Desmond Enterprises and Desmond holdings, Hillary became more amenable to the thought of tying the knot with Patrick.

Up to that point in time, Patrick was oblivious of the plans that were being brought to fruition behind his back. His father Dennis and Sir Charles arranged for a visit of him and his daughter to Northern Ireland and a social event at the Royal Ulster Golf Club, hosted by Dennis. Patrick would be prevailed upon to escort Hillary to the event and then to show her around Belfast. Sir Charles advised his daughter that, "the rest is up to you." Hillary had only laughed and said, "Don't worry, Daddy, you can order the invitations now."

When the appointed day arrived for Sir Charles and his daughter to land at the Belfast Airport, Patrick was standing in the terminal with his father anticipating a ruined weekend hauling somebody's fat daughter around Belfast. When Sir Charles stepped out of his private jet, Patrick did not see him because he had his eyes focused on the young woman who was at his side. His father leaned over and said, "See what I mean." Patrick was impressed by what he saw and when Hillary turned on the charm, as she was quite capable of doing, it was like leading a lamb to the slaughter. He spent the next four days constantly at her side, taking her to dinner, to the theater, to discos, the games, whatever was happening in Belfast. She was a hit with his friends, as well, who found her confidence an appealing match for her charm. Her after hours skills exceeded even her almost limitless social talents and Patrick joked at the time, "I don't know if I'll be able to keep up with you." He would find out in the years to come that he could not.

It was six months to the day after he met Hillary that the two of them were married at St. James' Anglican Cathedral in Belfast. It was the social event of the year for Belfast society and every Protestant listed in the social register was present for the occasion as well as a few Catholics who had business ties with either the Fairchilds or Desmond Enterprises. The social gathering following the church ceremony was held at the Royal Ulster Golf Club which had closed all facilities to accommodate the Desmond Fairchild Wedding Reception.

Hundreds of guests flocked to the Club including the British Consul to Northern Ireland, Anglican Archbishop Remington and numerous other luminaries from the British and Northern Irish business and governmental communities. Patrick was overwhelmed by the flood of dignitaries and people that he had never met who were congratulating both he and his new wife, Hillary, who was standing beside him in the reception line. They kept coming in an endless line of humanity and after two hours of greeting people, he had clearly had enough of trying to appear that he was enjoying the festivities and saying over and over again, "How nice to meet you. Oh, yes. This is truly a beautiful day."

Patrick noticed that Hillary was holding up much better than he was. She was standing tall and straight in her wedding dress with a smile that seemed fixed upon her face as she aimed it from the person she had just met to the next person in line. She didn't seem to tire and he noticed that her greeting to each new person presented had not lost any of its enthusiasm, even after two hours of standing there, meeting and greeting everyone as though they were old friends. In time, the Reception Director who was in control of the event closed down the reception line and the party moved on into the dining room in anticipation of the Wedding dinner and the toasts. As Patrick moved through the crowd towards the dining room with his new wife on his arm, she still had the radiant smile as she nodded to acquaintances and strangers alike. As she continued nodding and waving with an almost regal air, she glanced up at Patrick and without breaking stride or her ironed on smile, in a low voice said, "Let's get a fucking drink".

In the dining room, they stood for a few moments at the head table as the flashes of the cameras blazed away on the obviously happy couple. Patrick had not acknowledged her request for a drink and again while the cameras were flashing, she looked up at him, beaming radiant in her designer wedding gown and, speaking through her frozen smile, said, "Patrick, my dear. Get me a God damn drink now and make it Absolute on the rocks." She paused and seeing no immediate response said, "Now, Patrick." Anyone watching would have thought she was telling him how happy she was to be his wife as her sparkling smile and appearance radiated joy and happiness. Patrick had never seen this side of his new wife before. He knew she could turn it on at social events when it was to her advantage to do so, but her ability to present a warm, sweet image over such an extended period of time which was totally at odds with her real self was a bit disturbing to her new husband. As he made his way over to the bar and everyone stepped aside to let him in to order a drink, he wondered just what he had gotten himself into. It was the first time that he had questioned his decision to marry this young woman but it would not be his last.

The reception lasted into the wee hours of the morning but by that time, the crowd had been whittled down, mainly, to the close friends of the bride and groom. The band played on and the drinks continued to flow so that now, not only were a number of the guests becoming inebriated, but so were the bride and groom. The band had played all waltz and classical music throughout the day but now they were into the harder material, the rock music, and all of the young people were cutting loose on the dance floor. Hillary had changed into her mini skirt and was putting on quite a show dancing with every fine looking young man she could pull out of the crowd. At first, Patrick took it in good spirits, but as the evening wore on and Hillary had focused her attentions on one particularly healthy appearing young fellow, it was all starting to wear a bit thin for the groom. He sat glumly at a back table with a few of his old school chums and watched as his new bride cavorted on the dance floor. The young man, she was then dancing with, was attending the reception as one of a number of friends of the Fairchilds and as Hillary told him when they were pressed firmly together on the dance floor, "You don't have to worry about having a good time here." She looked him in the eye and with a slight pelvic thrust, added, "Enjoy." After that, and a few more drinks, the young fellow threw discretion aside and was all over the flushed and ready bride.

Finally, when Hillary made a trip to the ladies room during a break, some of Patrick's friends, ushered the over enthusiastic guest over to a side door where they had a few words with him and he left the party without returning even to pick up his dinner jacket which was thrown over the chair next to the brides at the head table. When Hillary returned, she scoured the room, looking for her man of the moment but not finding him, she moved around the room seeing what else she could pick up. By this time, Patrick's friends had passed the word to all those with a liking for adventure, not to embarrass their companion. After a while, Hillary gave up her quest and told Patrick that it was time to go. She was finally shutting down and if he wanted anything, "You'd better come and get it now because I'm hitting the sack." The way she said it made him stop and stare at her because she had never spoken so casually about sex before.

The entire day had been a bit of an eye opener for Patrick with respect to his new wife. He was just beginning to question if she had been acting out a play for the past six months, and now that they were married, she could be her real self and let her hair down. He hoped that was not the case, because he did not like what he was seeing in her. Her new found arrogance and crudeness turned him off and furthermore, it made him nervous. He didn't like to be challenged or insulted by a woman and she had managed to do both a number of times on the first day of his married life. He hoped that her change in attitude was due to the stress of the day and not something permanent. He, hopefully, attributed it to the long day and the pressure that she must have been under, with the marriage ceremony, the reception line, toasts and dancing until the early hours of the morning.

They spent their first night of married life at the Desmond home, Park Ridge, which afforded them as much, if not more, privacy than any place else they could have stayed. Patrick had worried about suggesting Park Ridge for their wedding night, but when he mentioned it to Hillary, she made it quite clear to him that she didn't care where the hell they stayed, "As long as it's quiet. I like to sleep without somebody waking me up, making a bunch of racket somewhere." Patrick was pleased that she was willing to stay at Park Ridge, but as he thought about it later, he wished she had put it some other way. When he awoke the morning after the wedding, he reached his arm over to caress his new wife, but, to his surprise, she was not there. He felt the bed on the side where she had been sleeping and it was cold to the touch which told him that she had been up for some time. He leaped out of the bed thinking that possibly she was feeling ill from the prior day's activities and searched the upstairs rooms looking for her before he caught a glimpse of her through an upstairs window, sitting out on the patio having a cup of tea and reading a newspaper. Relieved that she was apparently alright, he put on his robe and joined her after telling the cook to send out his usual breakfast fare.

"Well we're up early aren't we."

She just looked up at him and merely shook her head. "I always get up early so you may as well get used to it. I wanted to get a buy order in on Westerly Petroleum because they have discovered a new field in the gulf and it's a whopper."

Patrick looked at her and wondered how anyone could get interested in an oil field or stocks at this time of the day after drinking and dancing all night long. "Interesting. How in the hell did you know that?"

"Well, while you were talking with those Casper milk toast idiots at the reception, I was scratching that fat Willerby's ass over by the punch bowl and he is the president of Westerly. I did everything but blow him, and finally he got the message that I might if he just gave me a teeny weeny... that was what I said to him...a teeny, weeny tip on what was happening in oil land. I think it was the weeny part that made him think. So, we'll see what happens to Westerly. I just put the buy in. He said the announcement should be out about noon." Patrick's hand shook a bit as he lifted up his tea cup and Hillary noticed it. "Drink a little too much yesterday, Desmond."

Actually he felt quite fine, it was that he was annoyed at her foul mouthed repetition of her conversation with Willerby. "No, I feel just fine."

Hillary finished her breakfast, got dressed and headed over to the Belfast Fairchild Investments office just as though it was another work day. Patrick had signed out of the office for the entire week and as her Rolls passed down the driveway of Park Ridge, he watched it disappear into the east bound lane heading for Belfast. "I'll be a son of a bitch," he said as he shook his head in disbelief. "What in the hell have I gotten myself into."

In the coming months, the relationship between the two took on a routine with both parties adjusting to their own form of married life. Hillary was focused on her Fairchild Investment concerns with a growing interest in what was happening at Desmond Enterprises. In time, she was actively involved in decisions affecting that corporation as well, which Patrick did not mind, as his interest in the company was superficial at best and only directed to how much money the company was making at any given time. His concern for the company did not get down to the level of anticipating and preventing problems. As a matter of fact, ever since his father had left the business basically in his hands due to failing health, the corporate profits had been on a steady downturn. As Hillary became more and more involved in management and top level executives of Desmond Enterprises began turning to her for major decisions, the profits began to turn around and get back into the black.

One of Patrick's purposes in getting married was to have children. He had always looked upon that as one of his obligations in life ever since he attended Unity Boys Camp and they had hammered the argument home to him and the other Protestant boys that if they didn't have a lot of children, the Pope would be the mayor of Belfast. After a number of years, when he matured a bit more, he realized that the Pope had no interest in becoming the mayor of Belfast, but the notion of having children did stick and it wasn't more than a week since the wedding that he suggested to Hillary that they begin a family immediately.

Hillary looked at him as though he had lost his senses but after many more weeks and months of suggesting, arguing and pleading, she finally agreed, provided he find someone else to take care of the kids. She had no interest in, as she said, "Wheeling babbling, drooling brats down the street with all of the other fat ladies." What had sealed the bargain as far as Hillary was concerned was Patrick's agreement not to interfere with the way she led her life in exchange for her agreement to have two, and not more than two, children. When she finally did become pregnant, she was unbearable to say the least. If she told Patrick once, she told him a thousand times, "Here goes my God damn figure."

Patrick , watching the pregnancy take place, felt renewed affection for his wife. Something he had not felt since before they were married. He had high hopes as the pregnancy progressed that she would take on more of a family role now that she was about to have a child, but that was wishful thinking on his part. At the hospital just prior to birth, when Patrick had suggested that he take a video of the actual birth, she told him, "You take a video of me then and I'll shove that video camera right up your ass." At the time, there were a number of people in the room who were visibly embarrassed at her outburst, but Patrick, seething inside, just chuckled as though to pass it off as a little joke. By that time, he had come to realize that she would never change and he would just have to accept that fact.

True to her word, after the baby was born, Hillary had no interest in being around the infant. One of the maids was immediately assigned the task of taking care of the child full time which permitted Hillary to be up and about and back in her office at Desmond by the end of the week. They named the child Ellen after Patrick's mother, Ellen Regan Desmond. Pursuant to her agreement with Patrick to have two children, Hillary presented herself to Patrick ninety days after giving birth to Ellen and said, "Let's get rolling on the other one right now. I want to get this messy business over with soon so I can get back to work." Nine months later, Adam was born and five days later, Hillary was back at work for good. Another maid was assigned to take care of Adam and within a month, Dennis Desmond, Patrick's father passed away after a long illness. Patrick Desmond was now solely in charge of Desmond Enterprises, at least superficially. By that time, Hillary was calling all of the important shots for Desmond Enterprises.

After a time, Patrick began getting comments from people around him regarding Hillary's social life. They were small, almost innocent comments regarding the fact that she was seen at a dinner or in a restaurant with some man, "I'm sure it was on Desmond business. She sure has a business head." At first he ignored the remarks, primarily because he just did not believe that his wife could be carrying on with another man. After all, she was married and came from a very fine English family, the Fairchilds of London. As the remarks continued and increased in frequency, Patrick suspected that she may not have taken her wedding vows as seriously as he was hoping she had. He began putting all of the evidence together and when combined with her lack of contact with him on the marital couch, he started to realize that his marriage was seriously flawed. He had Frank Baumler, his security man at Desmond Enterprises, do some discreet checking on his socially active wife and he was soon presented with a report on Hillary Fairchild Desmond.

With Baumler seated in front of Patrick's desk at Desmond Enterprises, he told him, "Give it to me straight Frank, although I know you would anyway." As he waited for his head of security to open his notebook and pull the ball point pen out of his shirt pocket, Patrick nervously twisted the letter opener in the moist palms of his hands. While Frank was looking down at his notes, getting ready to speak, Patrick took the opportunity to wipe the telltale moisture from his upper lip while pretending to rub his chin.

Frank Baumler looked up at Patrick and said, "Chief, I don't want to seem disrespectful, but it's sort of a good news, bad news report. I'm serious about this because if it was the other way around, quite frankly, your marriage would be in much more serious trouble than it is." Baumler thought about what he had said and added, "although it is obviously in serious trouble, as you will see."

Patrick nodded, not understanding what he was getting at. "Go ahead, Frank. Let's have it."

"Well, Chief, the good news is that your wife does not have one, steady fellow that she seems to be tied up with. The bad news is that there are a number of guys that she spends time with in places that we can only assume she is engaging in...ah... inappropriate relationships, like hotels, motels, that sort of thing." Baumler paused and went on, "to put it in the vernacular, she is obviously screwing around but she does not seem to be tied into any one guy, for whatever that is worth."

Patrick asked a number of questions to remove any doubt from his own mind that what Baumler was concluding regarding his wife was accurate and after hearing further supporting data, agreed that it was. Baumler did add that she seemed to be handling her other relationships somewhat discreetly, "For whatever that is worth."

Patrick wiped the perspiration from his upper lip and spun the letter opener in his hand until it slipped out of his moist hands and fell to the floor with a loud clatter. Baumler stood up to go around the desk and retrieve the opener, but Patrick waved him back in his seat and said, "Well, what the hell do I do about this?"

Baumler was silent for a moment, not being sure if Patrick wanted his suggestions or if he was just talking out loud.

Patrick looked up at him and said, "What do you think Frank?"

Baumler shook his head and said, "There's only one thing you can do and that is to tell her to knock it off, that word of her carrying on is getting around town and it's embarrassing, among other things."

Patrick thought for a while and then thanked Baumler for his report, requesting that he make sure word of his findings did not get out to any of the other staff at Desmond. When Frank left the office, Patrick sat and thought about what he had said for a long time. He had known that his marriage was in deep trouble, almost from the start, but he had been kidding himself into thinking that, in time, it would improve. Well, obviously it wasn't improving.

It was two days before he saw Hillary in the house and when he told her he wanted to talk with her, she at first told him she had to leave right away as there was a meeting at the Fairchild office and she had to be there. He said, "No, Hillary, I've got to talk to you right now." That was the most determined she had ever seen him act and it momentarily brought her to a standstill.

"Well, out with it then, I've got to get going." The two went into the library which was the most private area in the house and he told her straight out what Baumler had reported to him and also the comments that he had been receiving from various people over the past number of months.

When he had finished, she looked at him and said, "So," with a quizzical look on her face as though to say, what's important about that. Couldn't that have waited until later. Her response stymied him and he didn't know what to say. There was no contrition evident in her voice or in her demeanor. She acted as though her behavior was the most natural thing in the world for one who was a wife and mother of two children. "I thought we went through this a few times before."

Finally Patrick found his tongue and wiping the perspiration from his lip, he went on, "Doesn't your marriage mean anything to you at all?"

She continued looking at him as though he was the dolt in the conversation. "Of course it does, Patrick, but don't you remember our agreement. I live my life the way I choose and you lead your's the way you choose. You agreed to that. Now I have to go to the office. Your own guy told you I was being discreet, so don't bother me with this crap again. I find it irritating." With that, she picked up her briefcase and pranced out the door and into her Rolls for the drive into Belfast.

It was not too long after this conversation with his wife that Patrick's secretary, Mrs. Whitley finally put in for her retirement. She had been with Desmond Enterprises for fifty-one years and was originally hired at the time that Patrick's grandfather, William Desmond, was the President of the company. Mrs. Whitley suggested to Patrick that she would be glad to find a suitable replacement, but Patrick now had some ideas of his own as to what he was looking for. He told Mrs. Whitley that he would take care of that and not to bother herself. Rather, she was to enjoy her remaining days with the company and he would try to find two or three experienced secretaries to take over her workload. Mrs. Whitley, laughed, blushed and said, "Oh, Mr. Desmond, you are too kind. One with some brains would handle the job quite well." He laughed with her but thought to himself. That's not exactly what I'm looking for. Patrick knew that the job did not require a great deal of work. He only needed someone with some common sense that could handle the phone and not get his appointments screwed up. It seemed to him that someone young and attractive could handle that just as well as an older, more experienced secretary. He would see what he could do about that.

Patrick had noticed one of the younger women that was recently hired as an administrative clerk who appeared to have the necessary qualities. Not only that, but she had an intelligent look about her and handled herself very well when she was in the company of other staff personnel. She was not a chatterbox, was always neatly dressed and had a certain confident air about her that he found particularly appealing. One day as he was walking through the executive hallway, he came upon her approaching him from the opposite direction. She was not looking at him, but seemed to have her mind on her task of the moment. As he came up to her, he stopped and asked her if she was new with the company.

She looked at him, smiled and with an air of confidence he found appealing, said, "Mr. Desmond, yes. I joined the company just last month as a staff clerk. I enjoy it very much, Sir."

He was pleased that she knew who he was, but assumed he had been pointed out to her by one of her co-workers. "Have you had any secretarial experience at all?"

The young woman paused, a bit surprised by his question, but again answered in a straight forward manner, "Yes, some. I did secretarial work in a small office in the city center for two years. Some typing, but mostly computer work."

Patrick smiled and said, "Interesting. Come by my office in the next day or so. I have a position you may be interested in. By the way, what is your name?" She told him her name was Martha Blair and she would be only too interested in discussing another position. They parted and both went their separate ways. As Patrick returned to his office, Mrs. Whitley was sitting at her desk preparing some mailings that were to be sent out to corporate customers. She said nothing to him as he went into his office which was not totally unusual, but he wondered if she had caught a glimpse of him talking to Martha Blair. If she had, he wondered if she had picked up on what he was up to. Mrs. Whitley had known him ever since he was a small boy and Patrick occasionally felt that she could read his mind.

The following day as he was sitting in his office, Mrs. Whitley buzzed him on the intercom and informed him in a very formal tone of voice that a Miss Blair was requesting to see him. Patrick told her to send her in and shortly thereafter, Mrs. Whitley opened his office door, and Martha Blair was brought in. She was dressed in a two piece suit that closely followed the contours of her very fine figure which Patrick was studying as she entered his office. He told her to have a chair and then he asked her a number of questions concerning her education, prior work experience and employment interests.

Patrick was concerned particularly about any intentions she may have about moving on to other jobs elsewhere or going back to school. He knew he was not following normal company policy by what he was doing when there was a personnel office right down the hall that would customarily handle such matters. Handling his own interviews for a secretarial position would attract the attention of others in the company and he didn't want to hire someone only to have them leave after being there a short time for an opportunity elsewhere. He wanted to make sure that Miss Blair had every intention of being around for a while.

They spoke for close to an hour and in that time, Patrick found her to be a very intelligent, young woman with not only physical charms, but also a warm, confident personality that he found very arousing. He could tell that she was likewise enjoying his company which was more than he could say for what he could perceive of Hillary's reaction to him in their conversations. He offered her the secretarial position, saying that it was going to be vacated by Mrs. Whitley the following week, and she immediately accepted.

"Now, can I call you Martha?"

"Please do, Mr. Desmond."

"OK, Martha, now don't mention this to anyone because I am skirting company policy by not running this through Personnel. I just happened to notice how you handled yourself around here and I was impressed." He paused and added, "I thought the two of us would work together quite well."

Martha looked at him and smiled as she said, "Mr. Desmond, I won't breath a word about it."

He thought to himself that there was something about the way she looked at him when he told her they would work together well that gave him a considerable amount of pleasure. God, she was attractive. Some women have that perfect mix of physical features and an indefinable aura that captures the attention of men. Martha Blair had those qualities and as they talked, Patrick was congratulating himself on his find.

The following day, he spoke with the woman handling personnel assignments and told her that Miss Blair had been personally recommended to him by a business associate and that he had already interviewed her as the replacement for Mrs. Whitley. The Director of Personnel eyed him coldly as it became clear to her that Patrick had totally ignored her office in his selection process and that she was being deprived of the opportunity to wave this plum of an assignment around the Desmond corporate offices, dangling it in the faces of numerous hungry applicants who would have given anything to be the President's secretary.

The Personnel Director assured him that the necessary paperwork would be processed to effect the transfer of Miss Blair to Executive Offices and then asked him if Mrs. Whitley was going to be involved in any training or familiarization process. Patrick had not even thought about that as it was not his major concern. He was taken back a bit but recovered quickly and assured the Director that he was on his way to speak to Mrs. Whitley that very moment. When he returned to his office, he called Mrs. Whitley in and told her the same story that Miss Blair had been recommended by a business associate and would she be so kind as to train her in as her replacement.

Patrick could detect that Mrs. Whitley was a bit bothered by the fact that she was being replaced by a person so young and with such limited experience but Patrick assured her that if she did not work out, he would have an adequate excuse to replace her, but that he was obligated "by certain connections" to, at least, give her a chance. He gave her his best, what else could I do look, but he had the impression it was not selling.

Later that day when he came out of his office, Martha Blair was seated at a chair next to Mrs. Whitley's and she was showing her the various files and the tasks that were associated with them. As he walked past, he looked down and said, "Hello, Miss Blair, good to see that you are learning from the expert." He stopped for a few minutes and explained to his new secretary that Mrs. Whitley had been with the company since his grandfather's time and knew more about how everything worked than anyone else in the company, including himself. This seemed to put everything back on track with respect to his outgoing secretary as her facial expression changed immediately as she said to the new girl, within hearing of Patrick, "You'll like Mr. Desmond a lot. He is the nicest person." Patrick hoped Mrs. Whitley was right, that Martha Blair would like him a lot.

Patrick's new secretary had been employed as his secretary for a little over a month during which time, Patrick had been pleasantly surprised to discover that his selection of a secretary had been excellent. Her work was flawless and if he delivered a tape filled with dictation, it was completed in half the time that he was used to with Mrs. Whitley. Not only that, but she had a unique way about her that he found unbelievably sensuous.

Martha hardly spoke but there was no sign of shyness. She had a confident bearing that accentuated her femininity and while her manner of dress was very appropriate and business like, her suits and dresses managed to display her natural attributes to their fullest. At times, when his office door was open, Patrick found himself almost in a trance as he watched her typing at her desk. If he had important work to do, or something that he wanted to concentrate on, he had to shut the door to get her off of his mind. In time he knew he was going to make a move on her. He had to. He and Hillary no longer shared any form of intimacy and he had no intention of contacting a professional purveyor of such services as that did not interest him and it was also a bit risky for a number of reasons.

The opportunity finally presented itself when he accompanied her to a noontime dinner for corporate presidents and their secretaries. While the drive over to the site of the occasion afforded him some opportunity to establish a less formal rapport with Martha, the dinner itself involved a series of speeches and no opportunity for the two of them to talk. On the way back to the office, Patrick suggested they stop at a small club on the outskirts of Belfast and have a drink. Martha was agreeable so he drove in the direction of the bar. Patrick had a problem trying to read what was really going on in his secretary's head. She spoke very little and consequently, he wasn't sure if he was on solid ground in making a move on her or not.

As they sat in the lounge enjoying a drink, he worked the conversation around to her private life and how she spent her time outside of the office. She told him that she had only recently moved to Belfast from the country and so far did not have too many acquaintances in the city. He was pleased to hear that as he was concerned that she may have been involved with some fellow or, for that matter, about to be married to someone.

They continued to talk while having another drink and, in time, she began to loosen up a bit more and the two began to relax and enjoy one another's company. The time passed quickly and when Patrick checked his watch it was already after three. "No sense in going back to the office now, let's have another one and make this an enjoyable day." Martha looked at him and smiled, showing him her perfect teeth. She had absolutely clear complexion and beautiful eyes that he found extremely attractive. After another drink or two, Patrick began telling her about his own family situation and finding that she was receptive to listening to his personal problems, he unburdened himself to her of his floundering marital situation.

Patrick let her know that what he was telling her he had told to no one else as it was embarrassing to him and with that she placed her hand on his arm and told him that whatever he told her would never go elsewhere. He took her hand and thanked her for that as he leaned over and kissed her lightly on the lips. As he leaned back, she smiled and squeezed his hand which Patrick took as a positive sign that he had not over reached himself. They continued talking while they ordered another drink and as the late afternoon sun was setting, they made their way out to Patrick's car and headed in the direction of Martha's apartment on the east side of Belfast. When he parked outside of her apartment, she invited him in and that evening they shared not only their most private secrets with one another, but everything else as well.

Martha was, in a sense, a life saver for Patrick from a marriage that provided him no satisfaction whatsoever. She had come into his life at the right time, just when he was about at his wits end with Hillary. He was too well known in the Belfast area to be out chasing whores in the pubs and bars and he had never cared for that anyway. Martha was intelligent, beautiful and had the one extra attribute that Patrick had come to miss so much while he was married to Hillary, she was quiet. They had a great relationship and Patrick took good care of her so that she was happy with the way things were and was not pressing him for a more formal involvement. He bought her a home in a nice area of Belfast, provided her with a car and made sure that she had adequate funds to live comfortably.

In the meantime she continued to function as an excellent secretary and Patrick marveled at the fact that she could separate her two functions in his life with such ease. It was as though she were in fact two different persons. At work, she was the efficient, quiet, competent secretary. At her home, with him, she was the warm, loving, intelligent companion that he so enjoyed. As the years passed, this relationship only grew and in time, not only Hillary was aware of his involvement with his secretary, so were all of the other employees at Desmond Enterprises. Nevertheless, the two people continued to exercise the maximum amount of discretion and Patrick was very careful not to demonstrate favoritism in the office although those occasions seldom were presented because Martha worked only for him. Martha, for her part, never flaunted the special status that she had achieved and the other employees, once they were used to the fact, no longer considered it a worthy topic of discussion.

CHAPTER 25

Quinn was in shock as he stood in the pub talking to Sean's friends and learning that he had been killed. He was at first speechless but finally asked, "Why did they do that? Was he robbed or what?"

"No robbery. They just killed him."

Quinn said, "Well, that just doesn't make sense. Who the hell would have done that?"

The fellow he had been talking with gave Quinn a strange look and only said, "Who knows. Maybe politics."

That must have been it, Quinn thought. If it had been hoodlums looking for an easy buck, they would have taken his wallet or watch or something and apparently that didn't happen. He must have been killed for what he was doing politically. Quinn stood, silent for a long time, as he tried to absorb what he had been told. "Has anyone contacted his family over in Ireland?"

"Yes, Robbins did early this morning. Called his ex-wife and told her. She was quite broken up, I guess."

Quinn asked about what funeral arrangements there were and who was handling them. Sean's old friends from the Pub were taking care of that and were accepting donations for the cost so Quinn wrote a check and gave it to the fellows. After a while, he told some of Sean's closest friends to call him if there was anything that he could do. As he drove home, he thought that he would give Anne a call, but not right away. He would wait a few days or maybe he should wait until he was in Ireland the following week. That way, he could pay her a visit. He was glad Sean had given him her number as he wasn't even sure what last name she was using, but then Sean's friends would know.

Later in the day, Sean's friend, Joe Robbins, called and said that they were going to try and send Sean's body back to Ireland as that would be what he would have wanted, but it was an expensive proposition and, he wanted to know, could Quinn help out a bit more on that expense. Quinn said he would be glad to contribute and to let him know what his share was. While he was talking with Robbins, he wrote down Anne's address, telephone number and the name she was going by in Dublin so that he would be able to locate her when he was there.

Before they shipped the body back to Ireland, there was a wake in the Pub for him with his casket up on the stage draped over with the flag of Ireland's colors, green, white and orange. The Pub was closed to the public and it was a somber occasion, but the bar was open and toasts to Sean were being given by his closest friends. After a while, the other members of the band formed up behind the casket and played some of the tunes that Sean liked the best. After that, those present assembled around the casket and sang the Irish National Anthem which was a very moving scene for everyone, including Quinn.

> ...soldiers are we, whose lives are pledged to Ireland.
> some have come from a land beyond the wave,
> sworn to be free, no more our ancient sireland
> shall shelter the despot or the slave.
> Tonight we man the bear-n baogail, in Erin's cause
> come woe or weal;
> mid cannon's roar and rifle's peal, we'll chant a
> Soldier's Song.

Sean was dearly loved in the Atlanta Irish community and it was evident in the faces of his friends all gathered together to give their final farewell to an old friend. After the wake and while everyone was still there, the casket was taken through the Pub and out into the waiting hearse for transport back to Ireland. As the casket was carried through the pub by as many as could be fit into the task, everyone came up and touched their hand to the wooden, flag draped, coffin to say goodbye to their friend, including Quinn. As the hearse drove away, down the dark street, Quinn headed for his car and home. It had been a bad day for him and he was glad to see it come to an end.

For the next two nights, Quinn had a hard time getting to sleep and kept waking up, thinking at first that Sean's death must have been a dream. He would then realize it was not a dream and would spend another fifteen minutes to a half hour trying to get back to sleep. After the second night of this, having been restless all night long, at the first sign of light, he arose and put on his running gear. Maybe he could run out of his morose frame of mind and get back to the business at hand. Sean was dead and apparently there was little that could be done about that. Quinn headed over to the lakes and did his stretching exercises next to his favorite old oak tree by the side of the lake where he did them every morning.

As he was leaning against the tree, motionless, stretching out his Achilles, he glanced over at the running path and saw one, lone, runner jogging along the lake trail. He was thinking what a shame it was that more runners were not out because it was such a beautiful morning. No wind and with the sky just beginning to brighten up. The sun had not yet come up high enough to bring its warming rays down onto the path and that wouldn't happen for another hour or so which was fine with Quinn. He didn't like to run with the sun in his eyes.

As he watched the solitary runner come closer to his position, he began to watch his stride and how he was handling his run. It was sort of a routine appraisal that he went through when he saw another runner. The man's stride and speed seemed familiar to Quinn and when he looked closer, he saw that it was the same blond fellow that he had seen at the Pub and that he had seen the one morning when it was just beginning to lighten up. Quinn finished his stretching and walked over to the path so that he was almost on the path when the runner went by him. The fellow had not seen Quinn approach and when he did, he quickly looked away, over towards the lake. Neither spoke to one another as they passed with Quinn now beginning his run in the opposite direction, of the other fellow, around the lake. He thought they might meet again on the other side and he would take another look and make sure it was the same fellow from the Pub. Quinn thought he had acted strangely that night and also this morning, obviously turning away from Quinn. Maybe it was just to avoid having to greet him as that was the way some guys were out here on the running path. Quinn ran the circuit of the lake and back to the tree but never saw the blond fellow again. By the time he had driven back to his house, he had forgotten about the incident.

Quinn had been trying to contact Robbins to find out if anything further was known about how or why Sean had been killed, but he hadn't been able to contact him. Robbins was apparently busy notifying Sean's friends in Ireland and probably trying to make arrangements for shipping Sean's personal items back to Ireland. Quinn had notified the Receptionist at the University the very next day after he had heard the bad news and she took it very hard but said that she would see that the administration arranged to have all of the death benefits paid to his beneficiaries.

Quinn left her his number if she needed any additional information and requested that the school let him know as to the distribution of benefits so that he could pass that on to Sean's family when he was in Dublin. The school administrators office called him shortly thereafter and said they were delivering him a form that had to be signed by the guardian of Sean's children and "would he please see that it was completed and returned so that the benefits could be paid promptly." He said he would take care of that.

With those papers in hand when he went to Ireland, it would be imperative that he visit with Sean's wife, Anne. Up to that point, he had thought he should see her, but he was a bit nervous about the "ex-wife" effect. Sean had said that he got along well with Anne, but Quinn had always assumed, that was Sean's impression. He was not sure that was also his ex-wife, Anne's, impression. Now he had a definite reason to meet with her and he could pass on his condolences to her and the two boys when he brought the papers to be signed.

A few days before Quinn was to leave for Ireland, he finally got ahold of Joe Robbins and arranged to meet him for lunch in Peachtree Square. When Quinn walked in the Fig Tree Restaurant, Joe had already arrived and was sitting at a booth in the back.

As Quinn slid into the booth, Robbins commented, "This has been a bitch of a week. I talked with Anne on the phone and I thought she was going to lose it. I really think the two of them were going to get back together and, for Sean, the center of the world was the two boys. They're now old enough, as well, to know what they've lost, so it was as hard on them almost as on Anne." Quinn commented that he would be seeing her when he was in Dublin and Joe told him to be sure and say hello to her for him.

Quinn then asked him, "Joe, did anybody see this happen and do they have any idea who in the hell did it?"

"Well, there were a couple of witnesses. May have been more but they may not wish to step forward, you know. But, the ones that did only said that it was dark out. They weren't even sure of the make of the car but there seemed to be about three men in the car. They all appeared to be white guys and the one that did the shooting was a blond guy. They could see him, because he sort of stuck himself out of the passenger door to do the job. It was definitely a hit for political reasons. The cops have been in the Pub quite a bit asking questions but, as you have probably figured out, some of the boys have to be a bit careful themselves so hardly anyone has been in there since it happened. They don't want the cops to be asking them anything."

Quinn was not surprised at that. He figured many of the Irish patrons of the Pub were actively involved in one way or another with the INA. He always assumed that it was primarily for fund raising but now that he thought about it, maybe it was a lot more than that. He had occasionally seen articles in the newspapers about Irishmen being arrested for transporting weapons from the United States to Ireland for both sides of the conflict. Maybe that was what Sean had been involved with. Quinn was curious, but he knew that was well outside of his job description and furthermore, he figured it was best if he did not know the answer. Quinn and Robbins talked for some time about the logistics of getting Sean's personal items back to the family and closing out his various credit and bank accounts. Robbins said he had gone through Sean's papers and they were a mess which was absolutely no surprise to Quinn having observed his office and his personal habits.

Quinn offered to help Joe with some of the matters that possibly involved legalities which was a relief to Robbins as he had already been called by a few of the overdue credit accounts who were trying to convince Joe that Sean's friends now had the obligation to pay the bills. "Let me take care of those jerks. Don't tell them I'm an attorney, just say that I'm Sean's friend handling that business."

That was a relief to Robbins as these people were calling him at all hours of the day and night. After the two men had resolved how to handle Sean's personal matters, Robbins began asking Quinn questions about his dealings with Sean. Quinn explained that their initial contact came about as a result of a translation job that Sean had done for him on Quinn's old family letters and then Sean became interested in Quinn's research on his family tree.

"Not something I would have gotten into, someone else's family history, but Sean did. Anyway, that was about it but we became friends and, of course, talked about everything after that. You know how he is." Quinn caught himself, "...or was."

Robbins pressed on. "Did you ever talk about Sean's work here in the States?"

Quinn looked at Robbins for a moment. "I take it you mean other than what he was doing at the University?"

Robbins smiled, "Yes. Other than that."

Quinn said, "Not really. I knew he was active in Irish politics and he was always indoctrinating me in Republican views but he never mentioned exactly what he was doing and, frankly, I never asked." Robbins just looked at Quinn and nodded as though he was trying to tell whether Quinn was being fully truthful.

There was a break in the conversation while the two men had their sandwiches and soup. While Quinn was eating, he thought over what

Robbins had told him about the shooting and it triggered his memory about his encounters on the running path. "You know, you mentioned a blond guy did the shooting. There are literally no blond guys that are regular in the Pub and if one does happen to stroll in, he sticks out like a sore thumb because, it seems, all the Irish have black hair. Dark, black hair unless they're like me and now either it's gone or it's gray. Anyway, One night..." Quinn told Robbins about the incident in the club where the blond fellow was staring at Sean and occasionally at him and it had bothered him a bit, at least to the point where he remembered it. "Well, one morning I saw this same guy running on the path and just the other day, I saw him there again.

Apparently the guy is a runner. Anyway, I had the impression that he recognized me and tried to turn away so that I would not, maybe, recognize him. I don't know, but it was sort of an unnatural movement like he wanted to avoid me. Now that was just two days ago."

Robbins eyes lit up and he became very interested in what Quinn was saying. "Did the guy look Slavic or German by any chance?"

Quinn thought about that for a minute and said that he did have what Quinn would call a European sort of look about him. Blond, light skinned, somewhat ruddy complexion that you see on some European people. "That is about as close as I could call it. I would not say that he had an American or Australian look about him, if you know what I mean."

"Interesting," commented Robbins. Quinn could tell by the look on Robbins face that he had an idea as to who the person was.

"If you see this fellow again, let me know immediately if you would. Also, I would be a bit careful if you do see him."

"Whoa. Wait a minute," Quinn said. "Why in the hell should I be careful? That's the same thing that Sean said to me the other day. What's that about?"

Robbins smiled at Quinn and said, "Don't be naïve, Quinn. Sean wasn't killed because somebody didn't like what he was wearing. There's a war going on and Sean was one of the soldiers. Now don't tell me that you hadn't figured that out in the year you associated with him at the Pub."

"Well, true." Quinn said, "I did have an idea that Sean was into something that may have been politically sensitive, but I purposely kept out of it. I didn't ask about it and I still don't want to know about it."

Robbins said, "but maybe they don't know that. Maybe they think you do have some sort of role to play. I'm not trying to scare you, I'm just trying to make you aware that they saw fit to take Sean out and you were one of his most frequent associates. You should exercise a certain amount of caution just for that reason if for no other.

Quinn thought for a moment. "I never thought about that."

Robbins went on, "You know, Quinn, why not consider working with us a bit? We can always use help in one form or another."

Quinn had resolved long ago not to get mixed up in Irish politics. Sean had pressed the issue ad infinitum and Quinn had successfully avoided his arguments with his usual come back of, "We handled our problem with the British about two hundred years ago and I have no interest in taking on someone else's fight."

The two argued back and forth for another fifteen minutes without coming to an agreement when Robbins announced that he had to get back to his job at the Pub where he worked part time as a bartender. As they were about to leave, Robbins said, "Remember, if you see the blond guy again, let me know. From what you say, I think he's the one. Word had it that there was a German guy sent over to do us some damage."

Quinn said nothing, just shook his head in disbelief and picked up the tab for the lunch. After he paid the bill, the two men left the restaurant. After they parted company, Quinn headed for his car and home, a lot more concerned about his well being than he had been before this luncheon meeting with Robbins.

Quinn thought about his discussion with Robbins and the issue of his becoming politically involved with the Nationalist cause. He was not as uninterested in the situation as he led Robbins to believe. He agreed with much of what Sean and Robbins were saying. Quinn was very sympathetic with respect to the Nationalist view of Northern Ireland and if he had to take sides, he would clearly have favored the Republicans. He thought that what the English had done to the Irish for so long a period of time deserved retribution and a return of Northern Ireland to the Republic was long overdue.

Quinn favored a return of control to the Republic, but not immediately. Demographics would eventually solve the problem with a growing Catholic population and that change in the numbers would have to occur before a change in government took place. Since Quinn's learning that it was a pro-British element that had taken Sean's life, He had even stronger feelings for the Nationalist cause, but not yet to the extent that he would become actively involved in something that he felt was someone else's business. For now he would stay out of it.

On the day Quinn was to leave for Dublin, Joe Robbins called him early in the morning. "Hope I didn't wake you up, Quinn."

"No problem, Joe, been up for hours," Quinn replied as he sat up on the bed and stretched. "What's on your mind?"

Robbins told Quinn that a fellow by the name of Noel Galvin would be calling him at the Rockwell Hotel in Dublin and he would give him some help on his research at the National Library and at the Archives. "Sean apparently had arranged this some time ago and Galvin knows his way around that business."

After he hung up the telephone, Quinn wondered how Robbins had known about the fellow that Sean mentioned he would get to assist him in Dublin. Sean obviously mentioned that to Robbins before. No matter, he wanted all the help he could get and he would be glad to have this Noel Galvin give him a hand.

Quinn left for the airport at five in the afternoon to give himself plenty of time to check in and get to the gate for the seven-thirty evening flight to Dublin. After a tram ride to the E concourse, He made his way over to the departure gate where he found a somewhat quiet place to sit and read. In time, they called his row number and after showing his boarding pass and passport, Quinn boarded the Boeing 767 and made himself as comfortable as he could for the long trip to Dublin.

As the Boeing 767 descended through the clouds on it's approach to Dublin, Quinn began to pick up glimpses of the land through the cloud decks. All that he could see were fields sectioned off by what appeared to be stone fences forming a virtual grid over the land. He was immediately struck by the deep green color. He had flown over farm lands in the Midwest many times on his trips to Minnesota, but this really was the emerald isle as so many called it. In time the aircraft was on its final approach to the Dublin Airport, passing over what appeared to be an island or peninsula with sailboats anchored in the bay. It was a pretty site and Quinn made a note to look on a map and find out what it was.

Quinn passed through customs and went to the baggage area to retrieve his bag. As he stood with all of the other passengers, waiting at the carousel for his bag to come from the airplane, he looked over the people that he had made the trip with. They seemed to be about an even mix of Irish and Americans coming to Dublin. A number of people were standing about the baggage area holding up signs with names on them apparently to pick up arriving passengers.

Quinn was not expecting anyone to greet him at the airport and was very surprised to see a young man holding up a sign with "Quinn Parker" written across it. He had noticed the young man on the way towards the baggage area because he had been talking with the fellow that Quinn had noticed in the Atlanta Terminal prior to departure. Quinn walked over to the fellow carrying the sign and asked if he was looking for him or if there was another Quinn Parker on the plane.

The young man introduced himself as Noel Galvin and Quinn immediately recalled the name that Robbins had mentioned. The two men shook hands and Galvin discarded his sign while he explained that Sean had discussed Quinn with him a number of times and then Robbins had told him when Quinn would be arriving in Dublin.

"Anyway, welcome to Dublin. I will drive you over to your hotel. I believe Sean or Robbins said you were staying at the Rockwell. Very nice and well situated to the Library."

While Galvin spoke, Quinn studied the young fellow. He figured that he was in his early thirties. A bit younger than Sean, but with the same distinct Dublin accent. He seemed very alert with a sort of scholarly look about him which was along the lines of what Quinn expected he would look like if he, in fact, ever did meet him. He was dressed rather casually, sweater under a jacket and slacks that had been around a bit. Very much in accord with how the other locals seemed to be attired. When Quinn spotted his bag coming onto the moving conveyor line, Galvin ran over and picked it up before Quinn could get to it. Quinn felt a bit guilty about imposing on this fellow and told him so.

"I really don't want you to put yourself out for me while I'm here in Dublin. I hope Sean told you, I'm not in any position to be paying you guys for everything you've done for me. I wish I could but I just can't."

Galvin laughed, picked up Quinn's bag and said, "Sean explained all of that. Forget about it. You were a friend of Sean's and you're a friend of ours." As the two headed out of the terminal towards the parking lot, he continued talking, "Sean would have done this and, in a sense, I am doing this for Sean. Maybe a bit of therapy, eh. Anyway I happen to have the time available right now and I enjoy doing research on most anything in the National Library. I suppose you could say it is a sort of a hobby of mine, but actually it goes beyond that. More of a panacea. You are doing me a favor. I'll also be working on my own projects while I'm in the library so don't feel like you're putting me out. Not at all."

Quinn expressed his appreciation while he unfolded his umbrella to hold over the two of them as they made their way to the car. It was not raining very hard, but just enough to get a person wet if they were out in it long enough.

"Oh yes," Galvin quipped, "I hoped Sean told you about our weather, but I see you had your umbrella at the ready so he must have."

"He did, Noel, but he told me that it might be fairly cool and I don't find this too bad."

"Well, he probably told you we are benefitted by the Gulf Stream so it never does get very cold up here, at least not what you would expect from a place fifty some degrees north latitude. Moscow is about the same but here it seldom gets below ten degrees Celsius, or around forty degrees Fahrenheit. It's the wind and the rain that make it a bit uncomfortable and for the locals, it's the short winter days, the clouds, rain and wind that sometimes drives them a bit batty. Shouldn't be too much of a problem for you though on your trip. By the way how long are you planning on staying?"

Quinn thought for a moment. He had an open return and really didn't know how much time to plan for his stay in Ireland. "It all depends on what I run into. If it dead ends or I don't find what I'm looking for, then I'll probably become the common tourist, take in the sights and go home. I don't know. We'll see."

Galvin was silent for a few minutes as he concentrated on the traffic and maneuvered the car out of the terminal area and onto the N1 roadway for the drive into Dublin. "The airport is on the north side of the city, so it's a bit of a drive into the City Center but I'll try to be the tour guide on the way,...but I'm not very good at that sort of thing."

Galvin asked Quinn a number of questions about how he intended to pursue his research in the National Library. Quinn told him that he was not sure as he would have to see what was available and then lay out some course of action. Galvin suggested a plan that Quinn could follow and in doing so revealed that he was fairly familiar with Quinn's family tree. "Sean kept me up to date on what you were coming up with so that I could give you a hand when you were here. We also discussed checking some things out before you arrived so that we could give you a running start. I have done some of that in my spare time, but not as much as I would have liked. Anyway, we can discuss that in the Library."

As they drove into the outskirts of the City, the traffic increased and Galvin named the thoroughfares that they were proceeding on and how they lay in reference to the City Center. "Here we refer to Downtown Dublin as the City Center so if you hear that term you will know what it means. We are on the north side of the City Center now and I'm going to take some side streets to get over onto O'Connell Street which we will take to the south to cross the Liffey River and get down by the Rockwell. This is Parnell Square we are coming to and if you've read your history, you know that Charles Parnell was one of the early Irish Nationalists pushing 'Home Rule' and the guy had quite a following until he was found in the wrong bedroom."

Galvin had to swerve the car to avoid striking a pedestrian trying to make his way across the congested street without waiting for the light to change. "Crazy bastard..."

"Anyway, back to Parnell. Now, after all the dust settled on his extra curricular activities, they named this park after him, Parnell square. Over there's the Gate Theater you might want to visit. Live theater with an excellent reputation. This is O'Connell Street we are coming up to. Named after Daniel O'Connell who is recognized as a great patriot. Not a revolutionary, in fact he is considered a pacifist. In Ireland, we have learned the hard way that pacifism is not the answer."

Quinn thought to himself, well the lectures are starting again. He made no response to Galvin's comments regarding O'Connell, rather only remarked that the traffic was heavy for this time of day. Galvin ignored his response and pointed out the Post Office building on their right side.

"That's the GPO, the Post Office, where you can still see the bullet holes from the 1916 Rising. Brave men gave their all there and were brutally treated by the English for their love of Ireland."

Quinn was familiar with the history of the Easter Monday Rising and said, "Not England's finest hour. Terrible how they treated those men, but it was in what the English did to them that gave meaning and eventual victory to their sacrifice."

Galvin looked over at Quinn with a somewhat surprised look on his face. "Well, you do know your history. Sean said that he had been working on you to realize your real roots. Maybe you are coming along." Galvin smiled as he said that so as not to offend his guest.

As they drove on to the Rockwell Hotel, Galvin pointed out O'Connell's statue, the Liffey, the Irish Times Building, Bewley's and Trinity University. Quinn was following with great interest the location of places that he had been reading about for the past year. Their route of travel took them along Nassau Street with Trinity University on the left side and shops on the right. As he caught sight of the campus buildings of the renowned university, he told himself that he would tour the campus at the first break in his research schedule. In time, they pulled up in front of the Rockwell and after retrieving his bags, Quinn thanked Galvin profusely for the ride and his commentary on the city. Galvin pointed out the National Library Building directly across the street and the two agreed to meet in the Research Room the following day at ten.

The next morning Quinn was filling out the necessary paperwork to get his Researchers Pass when he spotted Noel Galvin entering the lobby carrying his briefcase. Quinn motioned to him and as the two men talked, Quinn completed the paperwork, passed it to the attendant and received his pass. After he had done that, Noel pulled out his notebook and laid out what he suggested would be a good way for Quinn to proceed.

"You have good information on the Townland that your Grandfather came from, Ballinacurra I believe is what I have. Assuming that is correct, we should get the Catholic Parish records for that Townland and proceed from there. Assuming your family is there, we are then on our way. Records after the 1840's and 50's only improve, so let's hope we find them on those early ones."

Quinn realized that the Church records were the key document and he found this a bit disheartening. "We may have a problem there. I looked for those records in the Mormon Library in Utah and they didn't have them. That may mean something as the Mormons had virtually all of the other Irish records that I looked up. I came to Dublin in hopes the National Library might have them."

Galvin only shrugged and said, "Many of the Parishes didn't turn their records over to anyone and the Mormons probably copied their records up years ago. Let's hope the Parish gave them up since the Mormons were here. If not, there is always a visit to the local parish. You may want to do that anyway as they will have the originals of some records that you may want, such as birth certificates and that sort of thing."

Quinn followed Galvin into the Records room and watched as he removed a reference book of Parish records from the book rack. He then looked up the Parishes that were located in the Cork and Ross Diocese which encompassed the southwestern portion of County Cork, including the village of Kinsale. Galvin rather quickly located the Catholic Parishes that were in the immediate vicinity of Ballinacurra and noted them on his work pad. One of the parishes was named for the village Kinsale and the other was named Inishannon. The Townland of Ballinacurra more or less straddled both Parish boundaries. He then selected another volume from the book rack looking up the Parish names that he had recorded. Under the Parish name were lists of numbers which he recorded on his work pad and also entered the same numbers on call slips that he had brought with him. When all of the information was properly recorded, including his Library pass number, he took the call slips to the front desk and gave them to the clerk. He motioned to Quinn to follow him back to the microfilm reader where he had left his briefcase, pulled up a chair for Quinn and one for himself. "Now all we have to do is wait for the staff to bring us the films and we can start going blind trying to read these things. Many of the records you probably saw in Salt Lake were typed. These aren't. None of them."

Quinn promptly informed him that most of what he saw in Salt Lake was not typed either so maybe they were copies of the original Irish films which had been made up in the early 1950s. "Let's hope that we come up with something before our eyes give out. But listen, Noel, you don't have to tie yourself up with me. I watched how you went about that and I can work on this if you want to do some of your own research."

Noel shook his head. "Let's not go through this again. I told Sean I would help you and I will. Also, I find this interesting."

Quinn questioned how Galvin had come up with much of the detail on his family that he apparently knew before Quinn arrived in Dublin. Quinn did not recall ever laying out all of the specifics to Sean, Robbins or anyone in that group but maybe he had given some of the more detailed facts to Sean and he just didn't recall.

After another ten minutes of waiting, a clerk came up to the numbered microfilm reader with the films that Galvin had ordered. Noel deftly inserted the film into the sprockets, turned on the reader light, adjusted the focus and began spooling up to the first entries. He had to spool about half way through the tape before he came to the Parish of Kinsale which had both birth records and marriage records from the early 1800s. Before beginning the search of the data recorded on the film, Galvin turned to Quinn and said, "Let's make sure we know what we are looking for before we get into this thing. Now what do you know about your Desmond family in the Ballinacurra area? I have my own facts, but I want to hear what you have first."

Quinn thought for a moment to review exactly what he did have and said, "My grandfather, Jeremiah Desmond, I assume was born in the area. He had two brothers, both younger than him. Michael and then William, the youngest. Beyond that I know nothing."

Galvin shook his head. "This is not going to be easy. I know you have said the Tithe and Griffiths records showed few Desmonds in the area. I think you are about to see quite a few in these records. The Tithe and Griffiths records show the lessees of land but there are subtenants and maybe subtenants beneath those shown in the records that may complicate things. All those subtenants will be in the church records. We should note every record containing a Jeremiah, Michael or William Desmond that we find and then try to match them up when we are done. That includes listing parents in birth records, witnesses to marriages, sponsors at Baptisms, and so forth. Fortunately we know also that your grandfather was born around

1835, correct?"

Quinn wondered how in the hell Galvin knew that fact. "I believe that is correct but it may be off a year or two. I don't believe anyone actually had a birth certificate that I know of."

Galvin said, "OK, let's do it," as he scrolled to the first page of the Kinsale Birth Records. The two men peered eagerly at the entries which, again, varied in clarity from barely readable to excellent. All entries were hand written with great flourishes of the pen making some of the letters hard to decipher. After time spent learning the writers technique, Quinn was able to recognize the more difficult letters with ease. They came upon a number of Desmond entries, as a father, mother or sponsor for the Baptism of the child but none of them bore the surname Jeremiah or William. There were always five persons named in the birth records. The father, the mother listed under her maiden name, the child and the two sponsors. Galvin explained that the sponsors names were important to record as they were frequently relatives of the father or the mother.

Galvin looked over at Quinn with a smile on his face and said, "I must not be awake yet this morning. If you're grandfather was born around 1835 we should really start there and not back here at 1810. Now you say that his brothers Michael and William were younger. Do you know how much younger they were?"

Quinn thought for a moment, "I don't. I don't recall anything in the letters that would give a clue either. From the tone of the letters though, I would not think that they were very far removed in age.

Galvin said, "Fine". We'll start with 1834 to be safe." He scrolled through the film until he came to January, 1834 Birth entries. The two men found a greater concentration of Desmonds in these entries than were in the earliest ones making the search more difficult as they closely examined every Desmond named in the entries. Finally they found their first William, some Michaels and, soon, a number of Jeremiah Desmonds. Two of the four Jeremiah's were fathers which disqualified them and the one William was a sponsor which did not seem to equate with the assumptions regarding his birth date. There were two Jeremiah baptisms and Quinn wrote down the names of the parents of both, and the sponsors names as well. The further examination of the Kinsale Birth records which the two conducted up to 1850 produced pages of Jeremiahs, Williams and Michaels together with the names of sponsors and parents.

Quinn was a bit overwhelmed with the frequency of the names and was beginning to be a bit despondent with what appeared to be a hopeless search for a person who had a name in common with so many other people.

Galvin looked over at Quinn and noting the look on his face, laughed and said, "Relax my friend. We're doing fine. Let's take a look at the list and see what we have here."

Quinn passed him the pages of names and said, "We must have at least a hundred Williams, Michaels and the same number of Jeremiahs. This is going to be fun."

Galvin slowly read over the list of names, concentrating on the parents names and noting those that had given birth to a Jeremiah, Michael and a William. He then went over the list deleting those that had born a William before a Jeremiah. When he had finished, he had four Desmond couples who had given birth to a Jeremiah Desmond, then a Michael and later to a William Desmond. He then suggested that they go back through the tape and record the other children born to these four couples as that may be of value further on down the line.

Quinn was beginning to appreciate the assistance that he was getting from Sean's friend, especially when he noted the time and saw that it was almost five in the afternoon. The library on this day was open until nine in the evening but most days, it closed at five. Quinn suggested that they take a break and get a bite to eat as they had been at the task since morning. Galvin agreed and they buttoned up the microfilm reader, gathered up their papers and gave the films back to the front desk with instructions that they would be back shortly to pick them up again.

Galvin and Quinn walked down Kildare Street to Nassau where they located a small café across from Trinity University and each ordered a soup and sandwich. While they waited for their food to arrive, the two engaged in conversation.

Quinn was curious about Galvin's background and asked him. "What sort of work are you involved with when you aren't working with people like me?"

"I am teaching on a part time basis at U.C. Dublin, that's for University College Dublin, which is just to the south of where we are now. I teach History and Political Science two days a week. In fact, I can be in the Library tomorrow but not for the next two days, so you are going to be on your own. You have plenty of work to keep you busy there for a week or so anyway."

When they finished their snack, the two returned to the Library and continued their search through the Birth Records. They were now beginning at 1820, examining the Birth Records for all children and sponsors listed for the twenty-four couples that had given birth to a Jeremiah, a Michael and William Desmond, in that order, in the proper time frames. They again were accumulating many names and more children born to the target couples. The number of children of these couples ranged from three to ten.

Quinn commented on the fact that there was a tremendous decline in the number of Birth entries after 1846 which Galvin explained to him was due to the Famine. They had barely begun the second search when the Library Staff announced that the Library was closing. Quinn had no regrets as he was very tired from the trip as well as the little sleep he had the previous night getting used to the time change and the lengthy day spent in the Library. As they left the building, Galvin told him he would see him at the microfilm reader at ten when the Library opened.

The two parted company and Quinn walked back to the Rockwell, picked up the key to his room but before returning there, he first had a half pint of Guinness in the Hotel Pub. He then went up to his room and immediately into the bed. He flipped the television onto Sky News which he watched for not over five minutes before he fell sound asleep. Quinn slept soundly for at least nine hours and when he awoke, he felt refreshed and ready to take on another day in the Library. He had breakfast in the dining room, read the Irish Times, had another cup of tea, gathered up his notepad and headed for the Library.

Galvin was seated at the microfilm reader as Quinn pulled a chair up next to him to view the films. By the time the library closed on the second day at five, Quinn's notepad was filled with six more pages of names and they still had five years of Birth Records to go through before they completed the search of records relating to the four couples. As they picked up their papers preparing to leave, Quinn commented that this was taking quite a bit of time.

"Wouldn't it be a lot easier if we went to Land records or Estate and Will records first because we know that there were sizeable land transfers involved in this family tree? Seems to me we could find them by doing that."

Galvin nodded. We could go there but it wouldn't really save us that much time and we wouldn't really know what all was involved when we were examining those records. We would then have to reexamine them after we had the information we're picking up now. Furthermore, when we get to that point, we will be fairly sure of who all the players are, something we wouldn't know if we didn't do this. Another point is that those records may not be complete due to the destruction in the Civil War and last but not least, you want to know that you have the right Desmonds. Have you noticed how many Jeremiah Desmonds there are just in this small part of Ireland?"

Quinn laughed. "No joke. How the hell does anyone find someone in these records without knowing a fair amount about their life in Ireland?"

"Short answer to that one," Galvin replied. "They don't."

As they left the Library, Galvin reminded Quinn that he would be out of touch for two days teaching at U.C. Dublin but would meet him at opening time in the Library on Friday. Galvin told Quinn what he should do in the two days and how he could locate the necessary microfilm records to do his work. As he spoke, Quinn made notes so that he would not forget how to extract the proper films for his research. As a final instruction, Galvin told him that it was most important to make complete notes on everything that he was doing so that they didn't have to examine records more than once. Quinn assured him that he had learned that already from his research in the States.

After Galvin left, Quinn noted his watch and saw that he had the evening free in view of the fact that the Library would be closed. The Library was closed until nine tomorrow so he didn't want to do anything that kept him out too late as he would be putting in a full day then. Quinn went back to the Hotel and spoke with the Concierge about recommending a restaurant. The Concierge made a reservation for Quinn at an Italian restaurant within close walking distance of the Rockwell and after cleaning up in his room, Quinn took in an early dinner.

When he headed back to his Hotel, the streets were still fairly busy with traffic and pedestrians which was fine with Quinn as he had never enjoyed being out and about in a strange city at night. He knew Dublin was relatively safe, but his experience in the States had imbedded a wary attitude regarding dark city streets, with no one in sight. It was a four block walk back to the Rockwell and a light rain was falling but Quinn had his umbrella out so that was not a problem. When he came down Nassau Street to cross over to Kildare he stepped off the curb without thinking that the Irish drove on the "wrong" side of the street. He narrowly missed getting hit by a car and scolded himself for not being more careful about what he was doing. He was used to looking one way for traffic in the States, but it was the opposite here. He would be more careful next time.

Quinn returned to the Rockwell, but tonight he had a pint of Guinness in the Pub instead of a half while he enjoyed a conversation with a couple of Irish government employees who were in Dublin for a conference. When Quinn told them about his near miss with the car, they said that was a fairly common occurrence with the tourists and the city of Dublin had recently painted arrows on the street crossing points to warn tourists to look in that direction for oncoming traffic. "Good idea," commented Quinn. As he finished his pint, Quinn said goodnight to the two men and soon was sound asleep in his room with the television blaring and Sky News giving the days events around the world. He would wake up around three in the morning and finally turn it off before going back to sleep.

For the next two days, Quinn was at the microfilm reader until the five o'clock closing hour. He had about filled up his note pad with information at the end of the second day. He followed Galvin's instructions and copied the birth and marriage information for the target names from both Kinsale and the adjoining Parish, Inishannon. With the marriage records, he had to begin with 1810 so as to be reasonably sure that he was including the couple that had given birth to Jeremiah Desmond in the 1835 time frame. It would be unusual in the 1800s for a couple to have children when they were beyond the age of forty, although it certainly did happen. The names were all so similar that they were beginning to form one huge confusing mass of Jeremiah, Michael and William Desmonds together with hundreds of other names of sponsors or witnesses at marriages.

When he had completed his review, he hoped that Galvin could make some sense out of the voluminous data the two of them had compiled. Quinn had his doubts, but he did have confidence in Galvin and found his patient analysis of data to be reassuring. In Quinn's mind, after a summary review of the data he had collected, there were at least twenty Desmond families that qualified as the family of his grandfather, Jeremiah Desmond. Which one it was, if any, he would have to leave up to Galvin.

At the end of the second day, Quinn was packing up his papers when someone came up to him and said, "Well, how's the research on the Desmond Family coming along?" At first Quinn did not recognize the fellow but when he held out his hand, the fellow said, "Peter Baker. We met in Atlanta at the library." Then it came back to Quinn that this was the fellow that he spoke with in the Atlanta Genealogy section and he was looking up a Desmond line as well. Quinn shook hands with Baker and continued to put his things away as he told him that he had been working in the library since arriving and was coming up with too many names that fit the bill rather than not enough. Baker told him that he had been in the Library the previous week and was having a similar experience. Quinn recalled that he was searching for the Desmonds in the Bantry area and not in Kinsale.

Baker asked him, "Have you got the Townland located yet? That is the hardest part."

Quinn replied, "I think I've got the Townland, but I haven't found the exact family just yet. The problem right now is too many possibles and I have to narrow them down."

Baker wished him well and told him that he would be in the Library for the next few days and he would be glad to assist him if he needed any help. Quinn assured him that he had all the help he needed right now with Noel Galvin and when he said that, Baker perked up. "Oh. Is he local?" When told he was, Baker went on. "Well, that's great. How did you ever luck out to find this guy?"

"Friend of a friend from the States. He's been a real help and if it weren't for him, I don't know how I would have come this far. He's not here today, but he's coming back tomorrow. Just in time to rescue me from a real pile of confusing information."

Baker told Quinn that he just stopped in to pick up a book but would be glad to pop for a beer if Quinn had the time. Quinn passed on the offer as he was tired and he just wanted to get back to the Hotel, have a good meal and hit the rack. Maybe sometime over the weekend if that fit in with Baker's plans. Baker assured him it would and they agreed that they would see each other in the Library sometime Saturday.

The next morning when Quinn arrived at the Library, Galvin was again already there. Quinn asked him how he got in ahead of him when he, Quinn, had been standing at the entryway, first in line, waiting for the place to open.

"You have to know the right people, Quinn. Actually, one of the staff here in the Resource Room is an associate of mine in the 'One Ireland' group. By the way, he mentioned to me that you ran into someone you knew here in the library last night. Who was that?"

"No one you know. A fellow Irishman that I ran into in the library in Atlanta. He was working on his Desmond Family line which was what caught his attention when we were both in the library at the same time. Lives in Londonderry now, or did then, but his family apparently came from the Bantry or Clonakilty area. I get these people confused. You'll probably see him here again because he must be in Dublin on business of some sort. Seemed like a pleasant fellow."

Galvin just nodded and said, "Interesting, well, let's get back to business. Let's find a table off to the side where we can go over all of the notes we've accumulated without bothering anyone." The two found a desk well away from other researchers and spread out the voluminous notes that they had accumulated over the past week with the hundreds of names, dates and events. "Now comes the fun part," Noel said. "What we are going to try to do is to determine the most probable Desmond Family or Families that you are related to. We have your other Minnesota Irish names, Farrell and O'Leary to work with and we have plenty of those in the records in conjunction with Desmond names, either in a Baptism or a Marriage."

Galvin spoke as he thought his way through the process, reading the notes and making his own notes in summary. When he had finished going through the hundreds of notes made previously by the two of them and those made by Quinn, he said, "We have a number of possibilities here. Twenty eight families in both Parishes, Kinsale and Inishannon, have named sons in the appropriate order and birth years. Of those, seven couples had marriage witnesses with the names O'Leary or Farrell. We know that your grandfather married a Farrell after he emigrated, but they also were said to live in close proximity to one another in Ireland, so we will include them in our analysis. So, we are down to seven possibles. Now none of those seven are in the Tithe and Griffith records which you have already found."

Galvin spoke to Quinn slowly explaining what it was that he was looking for in the records. "There is some significance in the fact that Jeremiah is a name found in the Tithe and Griffith records, but we know that our Jeremiah, Michael and William were too young to be listed. However, and this is of some significance, the first born male in the family usually was given the patriarch's name and that is carried down through the generations, so the listing in the tax records is worthy of investigation. Let us assume that Jeremiah Desmond in the tax records is the Grandparent of your grandfather."

Galvin paused as he organized his thoughts. "One of these seven names could be the son of the one in the tax rolls. It was customary in those days to name a son after the father but not the first born son as he was named after the grandfather. Now, looking at the seven possible fathers that we have listed, there is only one where the first born son is named Jeremiah and that father's name is Thomas Desmond, married to Catherine O'Brien. His wife's name is very significant because your grandfather, Jeremiah, named his only daughter Catherine and it was customary, then, to name the first born daughter after the paternal grandmother, in this case Catherine O'Brien. I think we have the right one."

Quinn was very thankful to have Galvin's assistance in this search because he questioned that he would have been able to work his way through this maze. Quinn commented, "Very interesting. If this is the right one, what I find even more interesting is that Thomas Desmond had three sons that we have found in the birth records. Also, I see that Michael was born one year after Jeremiah and a year later, William was born. So they were all close in age."

Galvin spoke up. "Also, in all of those birth records, you will note that the Townland of the parents is shown as Ballinacurra so the family resided there at least when the three sons were born. Furthermore, on the marriage record of Thomas to Catherine, his residence is shown as Ballinacurra and hers is Dromcara, which, as I see on the Ordnance Survey map is within walking distance. Makes sense. Well, we are off and running. Now what we do is check death records which we hopefully will find in gravestone inscriptions and then off to the Archives for the Estate records and the 1901 and 1911 Census records. That ought to bring us fairly well up to date on the Thomas Desmond Clan." Galvin slapped Quinn on the back and said, "I think we're on the right track, my friend."

Quinn sat back in his chair, nodded in agreement and said, "I hope so. We need more support to be sure, but it looks like we may well have the right family. We'll know pretty quick if we do. Must say, this is interesting."

CHAPTER 26

Wen Patrick awoke, it was still a bit dark out and he thought at first that he would enjoy the warm comfort of his bed but after a while, not being able to get back to sleep, he decided he would get up. He looked at his watch and noted that it was going on seven and he could faintly hear noises coming from the kitchen area so he knew that the cook was preparing breakfast. This week, Hillary was again in London, Ellen was in Dublin and Adam was at Royal Crest. Patrick ate most of his meals out or over at Martha's but that did not mean the cook had nothing to do. She did the cooking for the house staff which included the houseman, the maid, the chauffeur, gardener, the yard boy and herself. Of all the people on the staff, the chauffeur was the one whose presence Patrick occasionally questioned, but Hillary refused to let him go because he would frequently be called upon to drive her someplace that she did not want to drive, or to the airport for drop off or pickup. Furthermore, he kept Hillary's Rolls spotlessly clean and waxed which she enjoyed very much. Patrick was also of the opinion that he provided other services for Hillary as well, which, he believed, was the primary reason that Hillary wanted him around.

On this particular morning when Patrick came down for breakfast, he picked up the latest edition of the Belfast Independent which the houseman had strategically placed on the breakfast table for his employer's perusal. He noted that there had been another bomb explosion in a pub in Belfast killing four Protestants, with the Irish Nationalist Army taking credit for the operation. The INA claimed that it was in retaliation for the killing of a Catholic taxi cab driver the previous week, which had been done in retaliation for something else the Catholics had done.

Patrick shook his head in disgust as he read through the article but his disgust was aimed not at the senseless brutality involved but the fact that the Papists had apparently gotten away. The Provos, Unity's militant arm, would undoubtedly affect their revenge within the coming week or two. As he was reading the paper and having his breakfast, the houseman stepped into the room and asked him if there was anything special that he wanted done today. Patrick thought for a moment, looked out through the patio doors and saw that it was a rather glum looking day with a light rain beginning to fall. He looked back at Robert and said, "Let's finish the shelf cleaning project. I had almost forgotten about that."

Robert's face did not change expression as he replied, "Yes, sir. I will get at that right away." He paused for a moment, uncertain as to whether or not his employer was again going to participate in the cleaning but Patrick resolved the confusion. "You go ahead and I'll be in there shortly."

"Yes, sir, Mr. Desmond. May I suggest, sir, that if you wish, I can certainly take care of this myself if you would prefer to do something else."

"No, Robert. Actually I enjoy the change of pace from the routine at the office. Thank you anyway. I will be in there when I finish breakfast."

"Very well, sir, I will get everything together." Robert didn't enjoy being so closely supervised by Patrick, but it happened only very occasionally so it was something that he had learned to deal with. He did not dislike his employer, in fact he rather liked working for Patrick Desmond. Mrs. Desmond was another matter. She was the tough one that tolerated no mistakes. Patrick was much more easy going and rather oblivious to what the staff were up to. On occasion, one or more of the staff would take an afternoon off provided they thought the coast was clear or they would not report for work at the appointed time if they thought Patrick would not pick up on their delinquency. They wouldn't try anything like that if Hillary was on the property.

In recent years, the staff had also begun to realize that Adam was one to reckon with as well. He had always been a bit of an effeminate, spoiled brat, but now that he was assuming manhood, or the equivalent, he was becoming an overbearing, arrogant little snob. Ellen, on the other hand, was always the favorite of the staff. She was like her father, only much more alert and organized. She had become aware on a number of occasions that various members of the staff were cutting corners on their duty day but, she concluded, as long as they did not overly abuse the program, she would keep it to herself.

By the time Patrick entered the library, Robert had the necessary equipment waiting for him. He was busy removing books, wiping them off, and then cleaning the shelf they had been removed from before replacing them. Patrick again began on the other side of the room and the two men worked together in silence with each one thinking his own separate thoughts. Patrick's thoughts revolved around whether or not Carter had learned anything new, assuming, of course, that he was not in London with Hillary. He chuckled to himself at the thought. Her crowd of wind bag friends would pick him apart with little snipping comments like a school of Parana fish chumming on a side of beef. The vision caused him to laugh out loud and Robert looked over at him to see if there was something he needed. Patrick waved him off and said he had just been thinking about something at the office that he had found rather humorous. Robert smiled and went about his work.

The two men worked most of the morning, had a brief lunch and were back at the task for another two hours when Robert said, "Mr. Desmond, there are some papers on the inside of the cover on this book and you may wish to look at them." Patrick set down his cleaning rag and the book that he was working on and took the papers from Robert. There were two pages of what appeared to be a very old letter from an attorney's office in the United States. The papers looked interesting so Patrick sat down at the desk in the library and began reading them. The letter was from an attorney in Chicago, Illinois, and it was addressed to his grandfather, William Desmond, Kinsale, County Cork, Ireland and was dated January 15, 1880. The letter was apparently in response to an inquiry directed to the attorney from his grandfather and without the letter of request, Patrick was not able to discern exactly what the inquiry was. He could only surmise what the original request was from the attorney's response.

The letter read as follows: "In response to your's of September 3, 1879, I have either conducted a search on my own or had others, under my direction, search public records in the states of Wisconsin, Illinois and Minnesota for death notices of a Jeremiah Desmond, unmarried, between the ages of forty and fifty-five and our search has produced the following." There was then a list of six persons, named Jeremiah Desmond with their dates and residence of death listed. All of the deaths occurred in the years 1879 and 1880. One of the names had a large circle drawn around it in ink and that was for Jeremiah Desmond who resided in the City of Columbus, County of Columbia, State of Wisconsin and who died on February 20, 1879 at the age of forty-five. His birth date was shown as ca. 1834. Place of Birth: Ireland. At the bottom of the letter, below the signature and following the abbreviation, "Encl.", it went on to say, "Our statement for services rendered is attached."

There were no death certificates or statement attached and Patrick told Robert to bring the book over that he found the papers in but there was nothing further to be found in the book. Patrick then conducted a search of the other books in the immediate vicinity of where Robert had found the book that contained the letter, but the books were empty of any other documents. As he was searching for additional papers, Patrick thought he should downplay his interest in the letters so he said, "These old papers are interesting. I guess I get a little carried away with their age." He then went back to the desk and placed the letter in the desk drawer for further examination when he had some privacy. He did not want to add to Robert's curiosity concerning the letter's contents so added, "Interesting, but a bit out of date. I'll see that this gets in the box. Have you made that up yet Robert?"

"Yes, sir. I have it in the work room. It just needs another coat or two of varnish and it will be sitting on the shelf about the time we finish this cleaning job."

"That's fine, Robert. These old papers that we're coming across may have some relevance to somebody or something in the future or if not, they're just interesting to look at because of their age." Patrick then went on with his cleaning as though the letters were no longer of any interest to him. While he said nothing about the letters, his mind was racing trying to put together what his grandfather was inquiring about. Possibly he was searching for his brother in the States and had heard or suspected that he had passed away and wanted to verify the fact. The Jeremiah Desmond that was circled on the paper was most likely his brother. His grandfather undoubtedly knew where his brother lived in the States and tied the death notice to his brother that way.

Patrick had heard the stories that were mumbled around the Desmond household by his parents and, on occasion, by overhearing servants when he was a young man to the effect that there was something tainted about the way the estate was passed down through the generations. He had never made any inquiry himself and his attorneys had never mentioned any problem, so if there was something that had been done in prior generations, it had weathered the test of time and was no longer of interest to anyone. He had no interest in investigating the matter himself because he had the feeling that it would be better to let the sleeping dog lie. If he investigated, he might be creating a problem that would have just died a natural death on its own.

As he continued removing and wiping off the books, he remembered that the letter said all of the people on the list were unmarried. That would seem to mean that the Desmond that Carter was so concerned about was barking up the wrong tree. If the one in the letter was unmarried, he had no children and the Desmond in Atlanta was not one of his descendants. It was obvious from the letter that there was no shortage of Jeremiah Desmonds in the States back in the 1800s. It would be easy for someone researching their family tree to become confused as to which one was their actual ancestor. The more Patrick thought about it, the better he felt as he was becoming convinced that he had found some hard evidence to short circuit any claims of this creep in the States that was trying to get into the Desmond family fortune. It wasn't going to happen on Patrick's watch. He began to whistle as he continued the cleaning project and by dinner time, the job was completed and the library had a new, shiny look about it.

Patrick tried to contact Carter while Hillary was still in London but was unable to get ahold of him. Carter's secretary would only say that Mr. Carter was out of town on business which more or less confirmed Patrick's suspicions that Carter was in London with Hillary. Serves him right Patrick thought. Patrick left word with Carter's secretary to have him call when he returned. Over the weekend, Patrick called Ellen at her apartment in Dublin but no one answered so he left a message on the answering machine, telling her to call him back when she returned.

When Ellen returned the call, she went right to the point. "No sense in trying to keep it a secret. I'm sure there will be a report on your desk by Monday on this anyway. One of the disadvantages of being followed around at all times. I spent the weekend with Tom O'Rourke. I may as well tell you, we are considering sharing an apartment together. I hope you aren't disappointed, Dad, he is a very nice fellow."

Patrick did not know what to say when Ellen gave him this news. It was about the last thing he wanted to hear from his daughter. He could not tell her what he knew about O'Rourke because she would think it was some sort of trick to get her to come back to Belfast. All he could think of to say was, "We can talk about this later. I'll have to give it some thought."

Ellen said, "Very well" and went on to give her father her opinion of the management in the Dublin office of Desmond Enterprises. She was very unimpressed with how it was being run and suggested to her father that she be given more responsibility so that she could take some steps to clean up the operation. "What we need right now is a quality control section with some clout and I would be glad to take the job. Most of the people in the office already think I'm a jerk so what have I got to lose. What do you say?"

Patrick didn't want to ruffle the feathers of the Dublin office staff. "Ellen, let me talk with Hillary about this. She'll be back on Monday and let's see what she has to say. You've only been with the company for a little over a year and it might not hurt to give you a little more time before we move you on up. Think about it. We can talk more next week." His daughter was silent on the other end of the line which told Patrick that she was not happy with his suggestion.

The following day when Patrick was in his office, Martha rang him on the intercom and announced that Frank Baumler would like to meet with him for a few minutes if he was available. Patrick told her to send him in and soon Baumler was sitting down, pen in hand, holding his notebook and waiting for Martha to finish pouring tea for the two of them. When she had left and the door was closed, Baumler waited until Patrick nodded, indicating that Baumler could proceed with whatever it was that had brought him there. "A couple of matters, Chief, that I am sure you would be interested to know. First of all, your daughter is now living in an apartment in the Ballsbridge section of Dublin with one Thomas O'Rourke, as you know, employed by Interlink and very active with 'One Ireland' and last, but not least, rather high up for his age with the INA. Not a good situation, particularly when we are picking up increased activity from Unity directed at this guy. I am told that O'Rourke is stepping on the wrong toes with his tax collection operation involving the Dublin drug dealers. I am also told by some pretty reliable people that Unity, in the last few months has become a major supplier of high grade heroin for the Dublin market."

Frank continued, "Anyway, Unity has assigned more men on O'Rourke and we are having to back off a bit so that we don't bump into them. Unity knows we are in the picture and, of course, O'Rourke must, as well, because I assume that your daughter told him that she was being tailed by Desmond staff. I know you told her not to, but you know how kids are about this. They all think it's a big joke. Well, anyway, it's not a big joke anymore, Chief, because I don't know what the increased activity on O'Rourke means but I have some other information that may explain. I will get to that in a minute. What I'm getting at is maybe they're thinking about sending him another message to lay off of Unity drug dealers. I'm sure they've told him that in one way or another already and apparently he has ignored them. Anyway, that is the current status of that situation and I would suggest that you somehow derail this relationship between your daughter and O'Rourke or send her on a round the world cruise or anything to get her out of the vicinity of Mr. O'Rourke."

Patrick was visibly shaken by what Baumler was telling him. A drop of perspiration rolled off his upper lip and onto his chin which he wiped off with his handkerchief while he tried to figure out what to do about Ellen's living arrangement in Dublin. "If they tried to take O'Rourke out, do you have any idea how they would do that?"

Baumler thought for a moment and replied. On a job in the Republic, they would most likely want to do it as cleanly as possible. No collateral damage. They'd try to make it look like an accident. They don't want to upset the Gardai any more than they absolutely have to. That's my hunch anyway. They have taken people out in the Republic before, obviously, and have never been messy about it. No explosives. Nothing like that."

As he thought about it, Patrick figured that Carter must be aware of what was happening down there. Maybe he could somehow let Hillary know what was going on and she could handle Carter. No, that would be too risky. Then Carter would be aware that Patrick was getting some high grade intelligence information on Unity and that could present other problems. While Patrick sat mulling over the various implications of Baumler's report, Frank went over to the cabinet, heated up more tea and brought two cups back to Patrick's desk.

After a pause, while both men sipped their tea in silence, Baumler continued. "Now Chief, the other info I have on the O'Rourke business. I'm not totally sure on how to take this but I will tell you what I know. I get information from any source I can. I'm not particular about that. You know what I mean, right."

Patrick nodded. He knew that Frank Baumler, while loyal to Desmond Enterprises, was basically apolitical. He was not a fan of Unity, Great Britain or the INA. In fact, he harbored a certain amount of dislike for all three. He had virtually no opinion with respect to the Republic any more than he had an opinion with respect to Sweden. Consequently, he maintained lines of communication with people in positions of responsibility who could tell him things that he would want to know. He bargained for this information, sometimes trading information that they would want but he had to be very careful when he did that so as not to make himself any more of a target than he already was. Whenever he started off a conversation by telling Patrick that he received information from "any source I can"; that told Patrick that it was coming, most likely, from either the INA or Unity. Patrick sat eagerly waiting for Baumler to continue. This time it was from Unity.

"I am told by a cop I used to work with who is now with Unity that, as he put it, they are sending some blonds to Dublin and the way he said it told me that he was saying something is going to happen."

Patrick sat up in his chair. "What do you mean, some blonds?"

"I'm sure he meant the Stazi. They refer to the Stazi as the blonds. There is no love lost between Unity's security people and the Stazi."

"Well, what does that mean to you, Frank?"

"It means to me that I would get Ellen away from this O'Rourke one way or another."

Patrick sat back in his chair, let out a long breath and just said, "Jesus Christ, how the hell am I going to do that?"

"I don't know, Chief."

Frank picked up his notepad and placed the teacup back on the serving stand. As he did so, he looked over at Patrick. "That's all I have today Chief, unless you have any questions."

Patrick looked deep in thought and after a while said, "No, not right now. I could use some good ideas on this O'Rourke business."

"I'll keep you closely advised with whatever I hear Chief. I have my best men watching that situation and if the kettle begins to boil, we just may go in there and snatch her out of the way if it's alright with you."

"By all means, Frank. Don't hesitate a second if things get tense. Get her back here and I'll somehow get her to understand. You may have to keep her someplace in the Republic if she refuses to come back here without him. You have my permission to do whatever you think is required. Just keep me informed. If that happens, I can be down there in just a few hours."

"Well, Chief, if there is nothing else, I'll get back to work." Patrick was deep in thought and didn't notice Baumler leave the room.

CHAPTER 27

Frank Baumler's office was not plush. There was an old wooden desk that had served various purposes and people at Desmond Enterprises over the years. Frank found it in a storeroom and thought it would be just fine for his office. The office was small but large enough to handle the desk, a metal filing cabinet that had seen better days and a tattered simulated leather couch where the occasional visitor to the office could sit. A single fluorescent light provided the only illumination for the room that had no windows to the outside. Frank's desk was usually tidy with only a telephone, calendar, and notepad visible. Today, there was an additional item, a three page report which Frank was reading as the other person in the room sat on the couch nervously strumming his fingers on his briefcase. "So, you actually met this Quinn Parker?" Frank Baumler looked up at his agent, Stan Morris, waiting for his comment.

"Yes. Seemed like an ordinary guy working on his family history. Nothing noteworthy about him. He is a retired lawyer, decent reputation, good credit rating, lives alone in Atlanta. Was married at one time. I didn't have much time to talk with him so you have to keep that in mind. I didn't want to be too nosey. Were I to say whether or not he would be a problem for Desmond Enterprises in the future, I would say he would not. He did not seem to me to be the type, you know... looking for an easy buck."

Frank thought for a moment. Though he had never met or even seen Quinn Parker, for some reason, that was his take on the fellow also. On the other hand, they could both be very wrong in their estimate of the man. "Interesting. So you were there when they got Flanagan. How did that happen?"

Morris smiled as he said, "I'd like to tell you it was due to my outstanding foresight, but really it was largely by chance. I had been concentrating my surveillance on Parker as you instructed and using any free time to see what Flanagan was up to. From what I observed about Flanagan in the Pub in Atlanta, he seemed to conduct a fair amount of what, I assume, was INA business from there. Anyway, on the night when they got him, I had been working on Parker most of the day and when I saw the lights go out in his house, I figured he was in for the night so, even though it was a bit late, I drove back to Murphy's just at about closing time. It was too late to go in the Pub so, for the hell of it, I parked off to the side of the parking lot to watch the door just to see who Flanagan might come out with. No reason in particular for doing that. I just thought it might prove to be interesting. Anyway, after most of the patrons had left, the help starting coming out and eventually Flanagan walked out, alone, and started across the drive in front of the club over to the parking lot."

Morris described how the shooting went down. "It was just then that this car pulls out from a parking spot, not far from me with three guys in it. One driving and two firing at Flanagan. From what I could see, they both nailed him and they were using silencers so it didn't make a lot of racket. This was no amateur job. I had a good look at two of the three because there was a lamp in the parking lot and it shown in the car as they went right by me. I recognized the blond headed fellow right away from your photo album as Werner Hoffman and one of the other guys. I don't know his name, but I know he's in your book too, a soldier for Unity. The other guy who was driving, I didn't get a real good look at him. I took down their license number and had it traced by our Company man in Atlanta. It came up stolen. I left the parking lot just as soon as I thought it was safe to do so. I didn't want to follow the three guys because I didn't think that would be smart and I didn't think it involved anything we were working on. Just another Provo INA scrabble. That completed my assignment as I understood it and I came back at the first opportunity."

Frank nodded. "I agree. I assume that from what you have in your report that Parker wouldn't find it unusual to run into you again, right?"

"That's my read."

"Good, you're going back to Dublin in the next day or so to bump into Parker again and to try and figure out what progress he has made and what he intends to do with it, so take a day or two off and come back. We'll talk about your visit to Dublin."

As Baumler thought about the shooting in Atlanta, he concluded that if Unity was so worried about the Parker matter that they had to take out Flanagan, they would certainly consider taking out Parker. They probably hadn't done it yet because he was an American. Now that Parker was in Dublin, maybe they could pass it off as a robbery-killing by a druggy that only coincidentally involved an American.

Baumler also figured that the INA certainly knew everything that he knew about the matter and must have concluded that Parker was at risk. They would not want to lose their "golden goose," so they must be trying to take care of him without being too obvious about it. Maybe that was why he had not read anything in the papers as of yet about an American tourist having been knocked off in Dublin. He reached for the phone and buzzed Patrick's Secretary, Martha Blair, and told her to set up a meeting with her boss so that he could brief him on "current events."

Patrick pushed open the solid oak doors that opened into the lounge area of the Royal Ulster Golf Club and breathed a sigh of relief to see that no one else was there, other than the bartender. He wanted to be alone and get his thoughts together. Furthermore, he needed a drink. He told himself he should slow down a bit but the pressures in his life had been building and a good belt was the only thing that he had found that brought him some relief. Patrick sat down on the bar stool and the bartender brought over his drink, Absolute with a touch of tonic. Sipping his drink, Patrick thought over what Baumler had told him this morning. Apparently his long lost cousin was down in Dublin this very moment, poring over old records in the hopes of dethroning Patrick from his plush lifestyle. At least that was the black vision that Patrick had been thinking about ever since Baumler's briefing.

All of the little snippets of dimly remembered facts regarding the inheritance of the Adams Estate had been coming back in bits and pieces over the past few months. Particularly since Robert had discovered the letter from the American attorney in one of the old library books. At first Patrick thought the letter helped him, but as time passed, he began to see it in a different light. Patrick had assembled as many small bits of information from his past that he could recall and they all pointed in one direction; there was something wrong with the way the property was transferred. He did not know how it was done, but as every day passed, he was becoming more convinced that his tenure at the old Desmond homestead of Park Ridge might be coming to an end.

Patrick was torn between wanting to hire someone to check the records and find out if in fact he had a problem or to just ignore it and hope it went away. If he hired someone and they discovered a problem that this Parker wouldn't find, he would just be creating an opportunity for blackmail. Besides, Unity was checking it out and they were at least implying that it looked like he did have a problem. But then, maybe they were lying to him in order to control him. With that thought, he drained the last drop of vodka from the glass and slid it across the bar. "Fill it up, Kenny, and easier on the Tonic. I've had a hard day."

Carter had asked him if he wanted to have this Parker fellow taken out. Patrick did not want to lower himself to being involved in an outright murder but lately, the thought of Parker no longer being around was becoming more and more attractive. God, he thought, what in the hell am I coming to. He swore that he would never agree to do that but as he thought about it, he realized that he had not told Carter not to do it. Did that make him some sort of accomplice. Maybe he should go down to Dublin, find this guy, Parker, and pay him off, or whatever, to get the hell out of his life. The conflicting thoughts had been coming from all directions and they were driving him crazy. He had lost weight and Hillary had commented on it. In her insulting manner, she had said that it "sure as hell wasn't from overwork."

Patrick had two more drinks and as they took their effect, he began to relax a bit and think more clearly. He had always told himself that some of his best decisions came after a few drinks. As he sat at the bar, he decided that the best course of action was to do nothing and see what happened. After all, he could always get a job at the Post Office. He chuckled at the thought as he drained his drink. The bartender asked him if he wanted a refill, but Patrick declined the offer and mumbled something about having had enough for now.

As Patrick stood waiting for the valet to bring up his car, he saw Tony Carter's car enter the Club gate and head into the parking area. He pulled up in front of Patrick, left the car for the attendant and gave Patrick a hearty hello as he approached. Carter had a big smile on his face and held out his hand to shake Patrick's, explaining to him at the same time that he was meeting Hillary for a round of tennis. He looked at his watch and commented that he was at least a half hour early so why didn't the two of them have a drink as long as they were both there.

Patrick commented that a good drink couldn't hurt Carter's game, so why not. Patrick was always much more glib and capable of dealing with Carter after he had a few. The two men made small talk as they walked back to the lounge and after they were seated and had ordered a drink, Patrick began asking Carter questions. He first warned himself that he had to be careful not to give anything away that Baumler had told him. Patrick assumed that Carter was aware of everything that had happened in Atlanta and that Quinn Parker was now in Dublin, so he thought he would test him to see if he was being as forthright with him as he claimed to be.

"Anything new, Tony?"

"Everything's new. What are you wondering about?"

God, here we go again. "You know, the Atlanta guy?"

"Oh, that business. Patrick, Patrick," Carter went into his condescending mode. "We are watching this thing like a hawk. You mean your cousin. He's in Dublin, as we speak, and he is climbing his way up through the records. I would assume you will be meeting him in the not too distant future." Carter enjoyed this and it showed. "Our attorneys tell us that you may have a problem, but they haven't told me yet what it is. They like to drag these things out so that they can pad the bill, you know."

As Carter talked on, Patrick could feel the perspiration building. He was too deeply engrossed in what Carter was saying to try to conceal it so he just took his hand and wiped it across his mouth. Patrick knew Carter would stretch this out as long as he could to watch Patrick squirm. Again, the big question. "Do you want us to take him out?" He knew if he ever agreed, Unity would own him for the rest of his life. But, what to do. Who was his greater enemy, Unity or this Parker fellow that he had never met. He had to play it cool, or at least as cool as he could. "I'm not worried about this guy. If something is wrong with the title to the property, I'm sure we can work things out. Just keep me up to date. How's your tennis game coming along?" When Patrick got that out as nonchalantly as he could without his voice trembling, he was rather proud of himself because he could see that it set Carter back a bit.

"Games coming along. Sure, we'll let you know what's going on. Hey, there's Hillary at the door."

Patrick walked out of the lounge area with Carter and mustered up a polite greeting for his wife who was quite occupied saying hello to Carter. It was obvious that they hadn't been together in an intimate manner since the previous day. As Patrick drove back to the office, he thought to himself, "enough of this bullshit. I'm hanging by a string waiting for someone to come by and snip it. I've got to do something to save my own ass because it seems everyone else is taking good care of theirs."

When he returned to the office, he was reading through his mail when Martha buzzed him on the intercom. "Do you have a few minutes?" When she came into the office, she closed the door and sat in the chair facing Patrick.

Patrick was having a bad day and he was hoping that this was not another problem in the making.

Martha looked at Patrick and saw clear evidence that whatever the pressures of recent months were, they were taking their toll. He had dark areas under his eyes, more lines on his face and he was obviously losing weight. His suit no longer fit him properly and she was going to have to get him to a tailor so that people did not begin commenting on his appearance.

Patrick felt uncomfortable with her just looking at him. "Ok, what's up?"

"Something you ought to know about. Hillary has assigned Adam to the shipping department here at Desmond. I believe that Tony Carter has put her up to this as that department is virtually in the hands of Unity people except for the management which has always been appointed by Desmond staff. His job title is Superintendent of Shipping. Patrick, that job is way over his head. Sorry to say that but management staff are beside themselves over this. I thought you ought to be aware."

"Jesus Christ. She didn't even mention it to me. Adam is totally unqualified for that job and she knows it. You're right, Carter is behind this. He would like nothing better than for Adam to take over the company. When does this take effect?"

"He's been working there part time for the past few weeks, or at least he's on the property. I notice that his name is on the employee roster as a full timer starting the Monday after he graduates."

Patrick shook his head. "I had no idea. What do you think I should do about this?"

Martha frowned as she spoke, "You know what I think, Patrick. You have to tell them to go to hell or they are going to totally ruin your life. I would get a broom and clean out that department of all Unity people. What the hell, you contribute more to them than any other company and they are still giving you crap. Sorry, Patrick, I should keep my mouth shut. You know all this."

"No, Martha. That's OK. You're right but at this moment I have other things on my mind and I don't want to get into any additional hassles right now.

"OK, Patrick. I thought you ought to know."

When Frank Baumler first heard that Adam Desmond was being assigned as the superintendent of the Shipping Department for Desmond Enterprises, he had laughed but then after sober reflection, he took on a different attitude. He could see the hand of Tony Carter behind the appointment well before Patrick told him that Carter had been a key player in the decision.

Hillary had admitted to Patrick when her tongue was well oiled with booze that Carter had at first suggested and then let it be known that Unity thought it would be best to give Adam a position of some responsibility and the Shipping Department would be a good choice. Carter let her know that this was not just some whim on his behalf. He exerted considerable pressure on her with respect to upcoming union negotiations to see that the assignment was made. As she told Patrick, she realized that it was a job that exceeded Adam's "apparent talents, but he just might grow with the responsibility."

Patrick had laughed aloud when she said that and after a bit, even Hillary began to laugh. It was the only time in years that the two of them had a good laugh together. It was short lived though as Hillary got control of herself and began berating Patrick for not spending more of his time with Adam. Patrick did not respond as any time spent with Adam was time wasted as far as he was concerned. Patrick did not mind wasting time as that was something he did with regularity, but he preferred wasting it in other ways.

In the first few weeks after Adam had begun working full time as the Superintendent of the Shipping Department, Patrick observed his demeanor to run the gamut from unlimited confidence to the depths of depression, with the latter state taking on a certain permanence. In the first days on the job, Adam's normal arrogant behavior assumed new heights of insolence towards those under him in the pecking order, with the exception of the Unity staff in Shipping. When he was at Park Ridge, the staff found new and novel ways to avoid being present when he was there. Patrick observed that sick days for the kitchen staff were skyrocketing. Robert, the Houseman, found it necessary to absent himself from the home for extended periods at about the same time that Adam normally returned from a day's work at Desmond Enterprises.

Just when Patrick had resolved that he had to do something about his son or he would lose his entire house staff, Adam seemed to change, slowly but surely. He stopped carrying his brand new brass handled cane and something happened to his bowler because Patrick hadn't seen him wearing it for days. Possibly Adam realized that the staff was laughing at him because they found it a bit comical. Adam also stopped ordering whatever house staff member was present to fetch him this or that when it was virtually within reach of the young man. He no longer came in the home immediately ordering tea to be delivered to his room. Unfortunately, he passed through what was an almost normal state of human behavior at lightning speed and went into a downward spiral of depression.

Adam no longer worked late in his department. He was back at Park Ridge every day even sooner than Patrick, which was difficult to do. He would retire to his room and not be seen until the following morning when he would silently steal out of the house and depart for his office. After days of this behavior, Patrick called Baumler into his office to discuss the matter and see if he had any ideas as to what was going on to put his son through this roller coaster of mood swings.

Frank Baumler came into the office, closed the door and sat down. As usual, he had his pen and notepad at the ready. "What can I do for you

Chief?"

Patrick laid out his observations regarding his son's behavior over the past few weeks since he had begun working in Shipping. "This is not at all normal, Frank. Something is going on. Adam, between you and me, has always been different, even strange, but the last few weeks have been bizarre to say the least. What do you think? Have you talked with him at all or had an opportunity to see what I'm talking about?"

"Chief, I agree. I noticed it too. I didn't bring it up before because he's your son and that makes it a little difficult to deal with. I understand that he went into that department with the thought in mind that he was going to be the manager there. Since then, he's been pounded into a corner by those Unity guys and basically told to stay out of the way. He's having a real life experience down there. I think that's his problem."

"Frank, what do we do about this? Hillary insists on keeping him there."

Frank Baumler didn't want to offend his boss by telling him that his only son had a long ways to go to hold a job five levels below the position he was presently in. He said he would call Adam into his office for a very private chat and see if he could plant the seed for Adam to request a transfer.

After Baumler had left Patrick's office, Martha put a call through from Ellen in Dublin. She explained that she just wanted to say hello and that everything in the office was "absolutely perfect. Well, not quite, but that can wait." Ellen asked about Adam and how he was doing with his new job. Ellen added that "This may be a bit of a challenge for him, don't you think Dad?"

Patrick thought to himself how perceptive his daughter was. "We're watching it, Ellen and if problems develop, we'll pull him out regardless of what your mother wants."

Ellen then laughed and said, "Good luck on that one, Dad."

A few days later, Frank Baumler put in a call to the Shipping Department to speak with Adam. After some delay, Adam picked up the phone and with a somewhat anxious voice said, "Hello, Adam Desmond here." Baumler thought he sounds like a ten year old kid getting a call from a girl, but as he thought about it, he figured Adam probably received zero calls in his normal work day. After all, who in the company would have called him for anything? The word was out that he had all he could do to find his office, much less solve a problem of some sort.

"Adam, Frank Baumler here. I was wondering if we could have a chat. Baumler was not sure what he would say to Adam but maybe he could help solve a problem that was the topic of conversation around every water cooler in the company.

Adam's voice had a definite tremor to it. "Well,..ah... I'm... rather busy right now... maybe some other time."

"Sorry, Adam, this is something that we have to deal with right now. Nothing to worry yourself about, but a square that I have to fill in my annual report. Part of your job as Superintendent of the Shipping Department, you know. So if you could make it over here in the next fifteen minutes, that would be fine."

Adam was silent on the other end of the line and then said, "Ah... well... yes. I'll be there... ah… shortly." Click.

When Adam walked into his office, Frank Baumler was shocked at his appearance. He had lost weight. His eyes were sunken back in his head, he had constant tremors in his hands and he couldn't stop fidgeting as he sat on the couch in Baumler's office, obviously hoping this meeting would be short lived. Baumler decided that it would be short lived. He was going to get right to the point and not pussyfoot around.

"Adam, you look like hell. What the hell is the problem? What's going on in Shipping?"

Adam stood up and started heading for the door. Baumler scrambled around his desk, grabbed the young man's arm and set him back down on the couch. He knew he was treading on thin ice by manhandling the President's son, but he saw no other choice. "No you don't ,Adam. You're not running out on this one. I want some answers. I think I know what they are, but I want to hear it from you."

Adam was shaking as he sat on the couch. "If I tell you what I know, they'll kill me."

"Who'll kill you?"

"The Unity guys. You know they run the Department. I just sign papers. You know it and everybody knows it. That's why they wanted me there in the first place. At first I thought it was going to be a real job. I really tried to do what I thought I was supposed to do but they put the pressure on. Slow at first and then more and more." Adam was shaking and now sobbing as he spilled out the story of his employment in the Company.

Baumler felt sorry for the kid. He had been sent like a lamb to be slaughtered by this bunch of bastards. Baumler felt anger rising in him that Patrick, the kid's own father, had not stopped the assignment. He had thrown his own son to the wolves. True, Adam was a weakling. A sniveling, arrogant, spoiled little weakling, but there were other ways to deal with a kid like that without destroying the small portion of him that was worth saving. Baumler said, "Go on, kid, spit it out. Let me help you. I'll clean that pack of rats out of there, but I need your help to do it."

Adam relaxed a bit as his confidence that Baumler would really help him grew. "I'm not a dumb kid like most people in this company think. I know what they think. I could see it in their eyes. I think that's why I acted the way I did when I first came here. Screw `em. I didn't need them. Anyway, when I took over the job, I made it a point to learn how the Department operated. Right away, Kelsey and the other Unity guys told me to relax, go read a dirty magazine or whatever. They would handle everything. I didn't go along with that. I ignored them and continued asking questions, going through the paperwork on shipments, asking why this one was late, where's the paperwork on that one that just came in, and so forth. As time went on, my relationship with these guys deteriorated. They wouldn't answer my questions. They ignored my requests for documents. Finally I called the foremen in and we had a little talk. I told them I was going to do the job the way it was supposed to be done. That is the first time Kelsey told me that my job was to sit in the office and shut up. He said if I bitched to anyone, I would wake up in the bay, or not at all. He slapped me around that day just to show that he meant what he said. Then he was real nice. He said, 'you be a good kid and we'll all get along.' He said, and I'll never forget it, he said, 'you run along and be a nice kid now.'"

Adam was now throwing the words out. It was like a kettle boiling over. He had been holding all of this in for so long apparently not capable of trusting anyone that would or could really help him. "That day I did go back to my office. I didn't know what to do. My old man wouldn't help me. I knew that. Unity has a lot of influence in the company and they sort of control my old man. I thought about leaving Desmond but that didn't last long because Kelsey came in the next morning and told me not to get any ideas about resigning. He said the men all liked me there. That's what he said, and it wouldn't be real good if I left. The meaning was fairly clear to me what he meant. Anyway, since then I made up my mind that I would see what they were up to in the Department."

Adam seemed much more relaxed now that he was getting all of this off of his chest. "All the shipments seemed to be in order from what I could see. I would wander around the Department. Not ask any questions, just look. I started to understand how things worked. Shipments came in with goods packed in the containers. The containers went to the steam cleaning rooms to remove seal traces and were sent back to SeaTrack for reshipment to Asia. Either loaded with exports or empty as most of them were. I began to count the containers because it was easier to do that than to be seen going through paperwork in the office. Kelsey didn't like me checking the paperwork. Container inventory sheets were kept in the office on a clip board that was visible to anyone. I began to notice that more containers were sent on a ship than were called for at the port, say Bangkok. I wondered why they did this, but figured that they might be for extra loads that were ordered while the ship was en route. In time, I figured that is why some of the empties were sent but then I began to notice that not all the empties came back with the ship. Twenty-five containers would go and twenty-three would come back. About two weeks after the main load of containers came back for cleaning, the other two would show up on a truck, from where, I don't know. I began coming back to the office late at night. Sometimes two o'clock in the morning. To find out where the containers had been or what was their load, but I could never find it. I would find the shipping documents on the twenty-three containers, but no mention of the other two that had obviously been imported because they had seal marks on them that had to be cleaned off . I then realized they must be doing something with the paperwork to get twenty-five loaded containers into the country instead of the twenty three that left the port, but I don't know what it is."

"Jesus Christ, Adam. Unity is hauling shit into the country on those extra containers and we can just about guess what it is. You keep a low profile. No more night work. We've got our auditors in there and they can check all the things they want to check. Stay out of their way. Don't talk to them or it may get you in trouble. Be patient, we'll get those sons a bitches out of there and I'll see that you get the job back. I'm proud of you, son. I'll confess, I was one of those that didn't think you knew what you were doing. I apologize. We all make mistakes when it comes to judging other people. Watch yourself and don't tell this to anyone else, even your father. When you walk back into your office, look harassed. Make those guys think you are getting crap from all sides. If you want to talk to me, call me at home." Baumler scribbled a phone number on a note pad and gave it to Adam. "I won't be calling you in your office. I'll get a message to you through Martha Blair if I want to talk with you. They'll think it's from your old man. Don't worry, you can trust Martha to keep her mouth shut, and also, Adam, you can trust me to keep my mouth shut. This is going no where. Not upstairs or anywhere. Good luck."

Adam stood up, greatly relieved now that he had told his story to someone. He walked up to Baumler's desk, now with a smile on his face, to shake hands with him. Frank stood, shook his hand and as Adam turned to leave, Frank said, "Take that smile off your face. It doesn't look good coming out of my office." When he had left, Baumler was moved by the experience. He thought to himself that the kid had a lot more guts than he ever gave him credit for. As he thought over his meeting with Adam, he wondered what he should tell Patrick. Patrick would be asking him if he had more meetings with his son. Baumler had always made it a point to level with Patrick on everything, but this was different. This business worried him. He did not have complete confidence that Patrick would manage to keep this to himself. He might blab it out to Hillary in the middle of a drunken argument or he may start asking Carter "well crafted" questions regarding containers. Frank Baumler had no doubt that Tony Carter was the craftier of the two. Loose lips sink ships was an old saying and in this case, Baumler thought, the sunken ship could be Adam Desmond.

CHAPTER 28

Q uinn met Galvin just as the two of them were entering the National Library. They exchanged greetings, showed the attendant their passes and were soon set up at a table in the research room. Galvin located a number of manuscripts containing gravestone inscriptions from both Kinsale and Inishannon. Some of the inscriptions contained more information than others including parent's names, place of birth, maiden name of spouse and other information of relevance to one studying family history. One of the Inishannon manuscripts for the Roman Catholic Church of St. Martin contained two entries of great interest. One for Catherine Desmond, wife of Thomas Desmond, and one for Michael Desmond. Catherine Desmond passed away in 1850 quite possibly from The Famine or one of the many diseases running rampant during The Famine. The inscription on the gravestone of Michael Desmond was most interesting.

"Michael Desmond of Ballinacurra, the son of Thomas and Catherine Desmond departed this earth on August 14, 1879. Here lies Michael, an Irish Patriot who loved his Country and died from an assassin's bullet believing in her cause. Erected by friends of Michael Desmond."

Galvin let out a low whistle. "Most interesting. It was at about this time that your grandfather William took over the land formerly owned by the Adams Family. Why didn't he bury his own brother and, also, take note that this brother Michael was apparently an Irish Nationalist. He must have been an outcast in the family and not representative of his family's beliefs or his own father would never have succeeded in marrying into the Adams Family. Very interesting. We'll have to get the newspaper articles that cover his shooting. The Cork papers would have that and we can get those right here in the Library. It is also interesting that Thomas Desmond and the other brother, William are not buried in the same cemetery. Nor have we come up with a William so far, buried anywhere. Let's finish off these other manuscripts for Kinsale and see if he is in there."

The two eagerly pored through the remaining Catholic Cemetery manuscripts of gravestone inscriptions, but there was no entry for a Thomas Desmond or William Desmond that would match their residence or approximate age. On a hunch, Galvin selected the Anglican Cemetery records and in the cemetery of St.Michael's Anglican Church, there was a grouping in one section of the cemetery of a number of Desmonds. Thomas Desmond of Ballinacurra passed away May 12, 1879. Margaret Adams Desmond died in 1875 and William Desmond, the son of Thomas Desmond died in 1915. "Well, most interesting", Galvin smiled as he said, "looks as though Thomas Desmond had a change of faith right at about the time he came into the Adams wealth. It is also interesting that his son William did the same, but not his son Michael who stayed a Catholic to the end. Must have been some bad blood among the family members there."

After Galvin returned the manuscripts to the front desk, he searched the newspaper reference books to find the microfiche numbers for the Cork newspapers and found a number of entries for The Cork Chronicle, The Cork Evening Post, The Southern Reporter and others. Galvin selected first the Evening Post, filled out the call slip, took it to the front desk and the two then waited at the microfiche reading table for delivery of the films. Soon Galvin was sliding the film between the two plates and adjusting the lens so as to locate the issue that would have been published immediately following August 14, 1879. The next publication date that he located was the fifteenth which the two men skimmed over, looking for an article on the shooting but none was found.

There was no publication on the microfiche until the nineteenth of August and as they perused the second page of the newspaper, Galvin said "gotcha" as he pointed to a short article covering the death of Michael Desmond. The heading was, "Cowardly Act Takes Life of Kinsale resident." The article went on to read, "Michael Desmond, the son of Thomas Desmond, recently deceased, was shot down in cold blood by the cowardly act of an unknown assassin outside of his home in Ballinacurra. There were no witnesses to the dastardly act and the killing was not discovered until the following morning. Michael Desmond, a known Fenian and activist with the Land League in County Cork, had many enemies, any one of whom could have taken his life. The Police are investigating. Michael's only surviving family member is a brother, William. Another brother is said to have emigrated to the States years ago. His whereabouts are unknown."

Galvin leaned back in his chair. "Most interesting. No sense in poring through the follow on issues of the paper, although you may wish to do that. It would probably be easier to get police records on the matter down in Cork and they would provide the eventual outcome. The newspapers may not."

Quinn agreed and asked, "What was the Land League?"

Galvin thought for a moment and said, "I'm not the local expert on all of the groups throughout the years, but I believe that in the late 1870s, there was another famine and many people were being evicted, particularly in County Cork. It got so bad that the small plot holders, subtenants, were banding together and fighting eviction. It actually got down to bloodshed. In fact, it was called The Land War. Charles Stewart Parnell was involved back then and was a spokesperson for the small tenants. So, this Michael could have been a casualty of The Land War or it may have been something else. The police records might provide more information on what was behind his death."

Galvin informed Quinn that he was not going to be around for the next few days as he had to go to Donegal on business. He suggested that Quinn visit the card catalogue room in the Library and see what he could come up with there. They had a variety of resources that were alphabetized on three by five cards and he would undoubtedly find relevant items to his search. The two made arrangements to meet back in the Library the following Tuesday at opening time. Galvin put his papers back in his briefcase, wished Quinn luck and left the Library to take care of business before his trip. Quinn continued to review follow on articles in the Cork Evening Post searching for more information on the death of Michael Desmond, but he found nothing.

When he took the films back up to the staff counter, Quinn was surprised to see Peter Baker talking with the clerk. Baker asked him how he was coming along. Quinn's first inclination was to pass on the good news that he was right on track with locating the Desmond Family but his better sense took over and he merely shrugged and told Baker, "It's a slow process. How're you doing?"

"Oh, a little here, a little there. You know how it goes. I just dropped in to see if they had a particular issue of the Galway paper for 1853. If you'll wait a minute while I check that, we can go over to the 'Duke' and have a pint. What do you say?"

Quinn thought, "Why not?" He needed a break anyway. "Sure."

Baker said he'd be just a minute and headed over to the reference section, scanned the newspaper directories and pulled out one of the books which he took over to a table. He quickly thumbed through the book, apparently found what he was looking for and made some notes. Soon the two were on their way to the Pub, located just a couple of blocks from the Library on Duke Street. As they walked over to the pub, Quinn asked Baker how long he was going to be in Dublin.

Baker laughed and said, "As long as I can convince my boss that I'm accomplishing something for him down here. I doubt I will be here over another week, if that. I get down every few months so what I don't accomplish in the Library on this trip, I'll continue next time. In the course of their conversation, Baker mentioned traveling to Dublin from Londonderry. Quinn thought about Galvin's question regarding how Baker referred to Londonderry. He recalled in his reading that there was a point of friction between the Catholics in the North and the Protestants as to the name of the City. The Catholics referred to it as Derry and the Protestants used Londonderry. It was strange that Baker used the Protestant reference rather than the Catholic. Quinn had assumed Baker was a Catholic with his family having come from Galway. He would have to discretely inquire on that point.

When they came to the Duke, they found that a good share of Dublin's office staff had beaten them to the good tables. The two men found a stand up and drink counter in the rear of the bar and while Quinn held down the fort, Baker went to the bar and retrieved two pints of Guinness.

"Well now, you have to tell me what you're finding out about your Desmonds. I'm still not convinced that we aren't working the same line." Baker took a drink from his glass while he waited for Quinn to respond.

Quinn could play this game too. His suspicions of Baker had only increased since he had pondered the "Londonderry" business. What he couldn't figure out was what incentive anyone would have to know what he was doing in the Library or what he was finding. "Well, as I said it has been an interesting trip, but what I have learned primarily is that there are hundreds of Desmonds in County Cork. If I had known that it was like looking for a needle in a haystack, I probably wouldn't have made the trip."

Baker stared at him for a moment trying to determine if he was getting the straight story from Quinn and then said, "Well, if you ever do locate your Desmonds here, if there are any, are you intending to look them up. I suppose that could be interesting unless they're the type that you wouldn't want to meet up with."

From everything Quinn knew so far, his Irish Desmonds were undoubtedly a hell of a lot better off than he was and it could well be the other way around, that they may have better things to do than to entertain their "barely getting by" stateside relative. "I really haven't thought about that. I would most likely give them a call and say hello. If they wanted to make more of a connection than that, I would probably be agreeable, but I would leave it to them."

The two men continued light conversation discussing the various live theaters in Dublin and the other attractions that Quinn should try to visit while he was there. They also discussed his travel plans while in Ireland, other than his possible trip to the North. Quinn said that he would like to get down to Cork and possibly visit the Kinsale area so that he could get a feel for where his ancestors may have lived.

Baker laughed when he said that and explained that Kinsale had changed "a whole hell of a lot since any of your ancestors lived there. It's a tourist haven now. At least the village itself is. Kinsale is right on the water and it is a haven for American and European tourists to visit and buy property down there. You will see about as many Americans in Kinsale as you will Irish. Very popular place so if you do decide to go down there, first make a reservation. There are some smaller hotels and also many B and B's which are quite nice. Also many good restaurants."

After another pint, Baker said that he had to call it a day. He had a number of reports to send in the next morning and he didn't want to make a night of it. He asked Quinn how many more days he was going to be working in the Library and when Quinn told him at least another two or three, Baker said he would look for him there.

Baker left the pub and Quinn saw a vacant barstool which he headed for, taking his pint with him. Now that he was alone, he surveyed the people in the bar as a matter of interest and presumed from what he saw that most of them were Irishmen. There were a few people that had the tourist look about them, but very few. The fellow sitting next to him turned to him and spoke in a heavy Irish brogue and asked him how his evening was going. They carried on a conversation for quite a while with Quinn telling the fellow about Atlanta and goings on in the States. As Quinn was finding out, the Irish were much more approachable than their counterparts in the States and far more likely to initiate a conversation with a complete stranger.

On the way back to his Hotel, he realized that this quality of the Irish tended to make him a bit nervous at first because if someone in the States came out of nowhere and began talking with you, that would put a person a bit on guard wondering, what does this guy want. He decided that he would have to learn to relax a bit more. As he walked back to his hotel thinking these thoughts, he took note of the fact that there were very few people out on the streets and little if any car traffic. That made him a bit uneasy, but he tried to remind himself that he was in Dublin and not in Atlanta, Chicago or Detroit. Nevertheless, he made it a point to check out his surroundings as he walked along the dark street.

Occasionally, just to be safe, he would check his backside with a quick glance and it was then that he thought he saw another person walking in his same direction about a block behind him. He couldn't see the person very clearly due to the lack of light but timed his next glance so as to put the person under or near the street lamp at the last corner he had passed. When he figured the timing was right, he quickly turned and saw a man that he was stunned to recognize as a man Quinn had seen at the airport and who he was sure was the one that had pulled him away from the car that had almost hit him.

At first, Quinn was gripped with fear and he felt his heart racing wondering what he should do, but then he thought if it is the same person, he obviously saved his life the other evening. He would not have done that and meant him harm tonight. Quinn thought about stopping and speaking with the man, but that might not be wise either. Furthermore, there remained some doubt as to whether or not this was in fact the same person he thought he had seen before. He decided to keep walking and occasionally check to see if they were maintaining the same distance. When he did, he saw to his relief that the man was making no attempt to shorten the distance between the two of them. As he relaxed a bit more, he wondered why he was being followed. For what purpose. If he was not a target for this guy, what was he?

Quinn finally realized that the man must be watching him either to know what he was doing or to protect him, but who would be interested in protecting a retired attorney from the U.S. living on limited funds who spent his time in libraries. That didn't make much sense. He thought for a minute that he should run back to this guy and tell him he was watching over the wrong guy. No, he wouldn't do that either. He would just be aware of the fact that for some reason or other, he was an item of interest for someone. That, more or less, confirmed his already growing suspicion that there was something definitely going on with his trip to Ireland that concerned somebody. He would have to try to figure out what it was and in the meantime, he concluded that he was going to have to be careful because whatever it was, it seemed to be rather serious.

When Quinn returned to the Rockwell, there was a telephone message from an Anne Flanagan. At first, when he looked at the name, he drew a blank but then he realized it had to be Sean's former wife. There was a telephone number on the message and in parenthesis, was written, "Dublin". Quinn looked at his watch and saw that it was a little after ten o'clock so he decided he would call her in the morning. He felt a bit guilty that he had not called her before this, having been in Dublin now for over a week. Time had gone by so quickly since he arrived in Ireland that he had also neglected to spend some time looking around the City and learning what there was to know about Dublin. He was fascinated by the architecture and the almost universally healthy appearance of the local populace. He had felt quite comfortable and at ease since arriving in the country which he attributed to the warmth and hospitality of the people. He did not want to spend time here and not learn as much as he could about the people and culture that contributed so heavily to his own background. They were an attractive people and everyone that he had spoken to since arriving in Dublin seemed intelligent and very polite. He thought maybe as time passes, I will find out that they have their problems just as we have ours.

The following morning, which was Saturday, he pulled out the papers that he had brought with him to Ireland for Anne's signature. He felt even guiltier for not having called her before as he thought that she undoubtedly needed the benefits that were being held up for her signature. He decided then and there that he would forego the Library today and, if necessary, take a taxi to her home, get her to sign the papers and then express deliver them back to the School. If he had some time left over, he would, at least, jump on one of those double decker tour buses that went around to the major tourist sites in Dublin. They allowed you to get off at one spot and catch the next double decker to the next point of interest. It was an inexpensive way to get a good look at Dublin.

Quinn dialed the number on the message slip and waited while the phone rang. He was about to hang up and try later when a feminine voice said, "Hello". When Anne had identified herself and Quinn explained who he was, he immediately apologized for not having called sooner, but that he had been working with Noel Galvin in the Library and had become immersed in paperwork. He then offered his condolences for Sean's death and told Anne that he had not known Sean for an overly long time, but had become close friends in the time that they had together. She was silent as he talked about Sean and when he had finished, she just said that she and the boys would miss Sean very much. Quinn then asked how she had known that he was at the Rockwell.

"Sean told me that you would be staying there when you came to Dublin, but I wasn't really sure when you were going to be here so I called Joe Robbins in Atlanta and he told me that you were already here. So, I guess you could say that I tracked you down."

"Well, however it came to pass, I'm glad that you did. I was about to call you anyway as I am getting a bit burned out looking at hard to read writing on microfilm." Quinn went on to explain to Anne that he had papers for her to sign that the school needed before they could disburse whatever benefits they had to Anne in care of her two children. Quinn did not explain that in view of the divorce, she was no longer entitled to any of the benefits attributable to Sean's death.

"Well, I appreciate that, Quinn, may I call you Quinn?" When assured that was preferable to anything else, she continued. "I can meet you anywhere you would like today because I'm not working and the boys are involved with a church youth group over the weekend. In fact, I'm free over the weekend if you need someone to show you around Dublin."

That was a pleasant surprise for Quinn. "That was exactly what I had in mind. I would really enjoy that. Tell me where you want to meet. I am available now or whenever you want to get together."

The two made plans to meet in the lobby of the Rockwell in exactly one hour. Quinn put the papers in his sport coat. Checked out what he was wearing to see that he looked presentable for Sean's wife. Buffed some of the dust out of his faded white bucks, took a quick shower, shaved and pulled a clean shirt out of his bag as the other one was beginning to show a bit of wear. Picking up his rain coat and umbrella, he made one final check of the room to make sure he had everything and then went down to the lobby to wait for Anne to arrive.

Promptly at the appointed time, an attractive young woman came into the lobby and glanced around before seeing Quinn and came directly over to him. Quinn guessed that she was in her mid to upper thirties, dark black hair, typical of younger Irish women, bright eyes, healthy complexion with that Irish glow, and as she walked towards him, he thought to himself that Sean had very good taste. When she came up to him, she held out her hand and introduced herself. Quinn had to ask her how she knew that it was him when there were a number of other men in the lobby that it could have been.

"Well, this is a bit embarrassing, but Sean had told me that you always, and he stressed *always*, wore the jacket with the leather elbow patches and faded white shoes. Now that is easy for somebody to spot. I hope you aren't offended."

"God no. That almost brings a tear to the eye. That is just like that rogue. Now, he should talk. Obviously you did not manage his wardrobe. Especially the selection of his ties, or should I say, tie. What a guy. I really enjoyed him, but let's find a café someplace where we can chat a bit and become better acquainted."

After they sat down in the restaurant, Quinn went through the papers with her, he explained what she was signing for and what benefits were involved. When the business of completing the benefit papers was concluded, Quinn put them in his coat pocket and said, "Now let's get down to business. You have to tell me about yourself and the boys. Sean talked about all of you so often that it was very obvious you were the most important people in his life."

Anne told Quinn about her job. She worked part time for RTE, which was a well known company in Ireland that was involved in radio and television. He may have seen the initials somewhere and if not, sooner or later he would. She was a secretary in the company and liked her job very much because it allowed her the flexibility to stay involved with her boys. "The boys are Kevin and Neil. They are eleven and nine respectively. Good boys. They attend St.Brendan's Catholic School in Dublin and are very active in sports. Kevin, I think, resembles me and Neil resembles his father quite a bit. Not only in his looks, but his mannerisms. They are both intelligent. Good students. Neil is a bit more artsy, just like his old man. Oh yes, both are involved with music which pleased their father a great deal but, I suppose you've noticed that most Irish people enjoy one form of music or another."

Quinn told Anne that was always his understanding, but that he had been locked up in the Library with Noel Galvin. Anne nodded and said that she had met Galvin a few times when he was with Sean.

Quinn and Anne walked over to Trinity University and went in the side entrance by the school library and onto the cobblestone commons area. Anne explained to Quinn that the University and the area they were standing in dated back to the time when the College was built in the latter half of the sixteenth century on land confiscated by the English from a Catholic monastery. She went on to say that virtually all of the Catholic religious sites were taken over and very few, if any, were ever given back. Anne looked up at Quinn and said, "I suppose you think that St. Patrick's Cathedral, that we'll go to, is a Catholic Church." She paused a moment and said, "Wrong. It used to be, way back when but today it is an Anglican Church. Still worth visiting though. Beautiful structure."

The two walked around the campus and went into the old Library building to take the Book of Kells tour. Quinn was amazed at the beautiful painted illustrations on the pages of the book, which records the four Gospels of the New Testament, were said to have been drawn around 800 A.D. They then toured the Long room with its finely crafted high wooden ceiling and stacks of ancient bound volumes with a few privileged researchers working at tables set up between the stacks. The tour of the University gave Quinn an even greater appreciation for the history and culture of the Irish people. The Celtic tradition was graphically displayed in the pages from the Book of Kells and the beautiful Long Room with its two hundred thousand volumes dating back hundreds of years presented solid evidence of Ireland's historic pursuit of scholarship. Anne pointed out the golden harp on exhibit in the Long Room that was said to have belonged to Brian Boru, the Irish hero who defeated the Danes in early times but she said, "I think this might not be quite that old, but it is very old, dating at least back to the fifteenth century and well worth viewing."

As they left Trinity University, Anne led Quinn to a bus stop near the front entrance to the University where they waited for the double decker tour bus to come by. When it finally pulled up and the doors opened, Quinn paid the tour fee of five pounds for each of them and they clambered aboard. It was a little chilly out but Anne said, "Let's go up on top and if we can sit right up front by the windscreen it won't be too bad. We can always come down if it is too cold."

When they climbed the narrow stairway and entered the top deck, they found that they were the only ones up there. Anne said, "This would never happen during tourist season. You picked the right time to come over but maybe a little bit earlier might have been a bit more comfortable weather wise. Anytime after about the middle of September avoids the heavy traffic. Anyway, I'm glad you came over, regardless of when. She looked over at him and gave him a bright smile. Sean spoke so highly of you and I wanted to meet you."

Quinn was enjoying his time with Anne. She was not only very attractive, she was a fun, intelligent person to be with. As they sat up on the deck of the bus, Anne would point to a building, a statue or some point of interest and explain its significance to Quinn. He looked over at her as she talked and he had a hard time listening. She was beautiful as she sat there with her deep black hair, eyes that he now saw were a bright green and with the cool wind that whirled about the two of them, her cheeks took on a reddish glow. Quinn had not been so attracted to a woman in quite a while and was finding the experience pleasurable.

After they had toured St.Patrick's, Quinn and Anne left the bus for good at St.Stephen's Green. They entered the park like setting through the gate at the end of Grafton Street. The afternoon sun had come out and when the wind died down, it was quite comfortable walking through the Green with its many trees and flowering plants, watching the ducks in the ponds and listening to Anne explain the history of the Green and the role that it played during the Civil War in 1916.

Both were silent for a minute or two and then Anne looked over at Quinn and asked him how he spent his time in Atlanta now that he was retired from his law practice. He wondered for a moment how she knew that he was retired from his practice, but figured that Sean had mentioned that. "Right now and for the past year or so, I have been busy with this Family History business. I also read quite a bit. I usually work out every day. I'm on my computer. I clean my house. I attend the theater every now and then and I get together with friends."

Anne waited a moment and then asked Quinn, "Do you have a lady friend in Atlanta?"

Quinn chuckled and said, "I was just about to ask you a very similar question. No, I don't. I was divorced a number of years ago and just haven't gotten around to that sort of thing. Now, how about you? What is your status here in Dublin?"

Now it was Anne's turn to laugh. "Oh, let's see. I have all sorts of guys calling me, wanting to marry me and take me away to some great place. No. It's not quite that way. When they see two growing boys that eat a lot of food, need clothes and other things, the guys usually end up running down the street, never to be seen again. It's not a bad life though. I look at it as having two men in the house that I am concerned with. They are enough to keep two of me busy all the time."

They both smiled as they pondered their separate situations. Quinn thought for a moment and said, "It doesn't sound like a bad life to me. Two good kids to raise. I suppose though that with the right person around, it could even be better. Who knows?"

The afternoon sun was passing behind some of the taller buildings and the air was getting a bit cool so Quinn suggested that they find a warm pub or restaurant where they could get comfortable. As they walked up Grafton Street, Anne said, "You mentioned that you liked attending the theater. We have an excellent selection of theaters in Dublin. If you would like, we could take one in, even this evening if you have the time."

Quinn looked over at her as they walked and said, "I would really like that. I don't enjoy attending the theater alone. Don't ask me why but I've always had a problem with that."

The two walked up Grafton to a music store where they could buy tickets for the Abbey Theater that Quinn wanted to visit while he was in Dublin. Anne insisted on buying her own ticket which Quinn consented to only if she allowed him to buy her dinner beforehand. After a while she agreed to that but only if she could pick the restaurant. "Juno and the Paycock" by Sean O'Casey was playing, as it frequently did, at the Abbey. Anne explained that the theme of the play dealt with the war between the Free Staters, who went along with the division of Ireland, and the Republicans, who wanted the north to be part of the nation, all of which took place during the early twenties. She told him that she thought he would probably find it quite interesting.

As they came out of the music store, Quinn looked at his watch and commented that they had about two and a half hours before the play began which gave them more than enough time to have dinner and walk over to the Abbey which was just across the Liffey. He suggested that if she would like, he would get his room key and she could use his room to freshen up or even rest up a bit while he waited in the Hotel Pub.

Anne thanked him and at first declined but then, on second thought she agreed and suggested that they split the time, thirty minutes each and she would wait in the lobby for him. Quinn laughed and said, "Great idea. I'll buff up my white bucks and clean up a bit." After they had gotten organized and had dinner at an Italian restaurant on Westmoreland Street, they walked across the Liffey River and over to the Abbey Theater. Quinn enjoyed the play and Anne did also except for the fact that she had seen it a number of times before. As they exited the Theater, Quinn suggested they stop and have a drink and he would then get a cab to take her back to her place. Anne said she could take a bus, but Quinn wouldn't hear of it.

They walked back to the Temple Bar area south of the Liffey, found a small bar that was fairly quiet for a Saturday evening and spent the next hour telling each other about their separate lives. Quinn had the bartender order a cab for them and within fifteen minutes, the taxi pulled up in front of the bar. Anne asked Quinn if he would like to tour the countryside around Dublin the next day and she didn't have to ask twice. They made arrangements for Anne to pick Quinn up in her car in front of the Hotel at eleven in the morning. As they walked out to the cab, Quinn paid the fare and thanked Anne for the very enjoyable day. He told her that it was the most entertaining day he had spent in quite a while. Anne looked up at him and said, "Quinn, it's been a long time since I've enjoyed someone's company like this. I'll see you in the morning."

Quinn stood in front of the bar watching the taxi as it left with its passenger, a bit mesmerized by the experience of the day. He went back into the bar to have a nightcap and to savor the moment. It had been a long time since he was attracted to a woman as much as he was to Anne. He finished his drink and went up to his room and that night, he had the best night's sleep since arriving in Dublin.

The following day, Anne picked Quinn up and they toured the historic site of Tara which lay to the north of Dublin approximately twenty-five miles. Anne explained that the ancient site consisted of high ground with no visible structures other than earthen formations which historians had defined as being significant to what had taken place there. The real significance of Tara, Anne said, was that it remained the symbolic focal point of Celtic culture with a history dating back to 200 A.D. It was obvious to Quinn that she considered it to be hallowed ground, sacred to the Irish and key to the Nation's past. Anne then drove the car down the east side of Dublin, through Dun Laoghaire and Bray and down to Powerscourt Gardens in County Wicklow. They spent some time there and then drove over to the Powerscourt Waterfall where they walked the grounds and viewed the waterfall which was giving a spectacular performance due to the recent heavy rains.

As the afternoon waned, Anne drove to Johny Fox's Pub on the outskirts of Dublin where they had dinner amid a treasure trove of Irish antiques and artifacts. A smoldering peat fire going in the fireplace at the Restaurant cast a warm glow over the two diners as they continued their conversation learning more about one another. Anne dropped Quinn off at the Rockwell around nine and after thanking her for a wonderful day, Quinn said he would like to spend some time with her during the week if she could fit that into her schedule. Anne gave Quinn a big smile and said that she would like that very much. She told him to call her Wednesday evening as she did not have to work the rest of the week but "remember, there are the boys that I have to take care of."

Quinn said, "I know. Maybe we could do something that involved them as well. Give it some thought and I will call you Wednesday." As she drove away, Quinn was a bit depressed at the thought that he would not see her until later in the week. He had given no thought to his Family History project since he met Anne on Saturday morning and he had already missed one day of research so he set his mind to getting on with his work in the Library so that he could be on speed by the time Galvin met him Tuesday morning.

When he went up to his room, he reviewed his notes from the last day in the Library. He decided that he could spend his time again reviewing the Cork newspapers to learn more about the murder of Michael Desmond or he could check out the card catalogue room that Galvin had mentioned. He would decide in the morning.

The next morning as Quinn sat in the Hotel dining room watching people hurrying down the street with umbrellas, trying to shelter themselves from the wind and rain, the scene tended to dampen his spirits a bit. This time of year was fairly pleasant in Atlanta and for a moment, Quinn missed his home and his running which he had gotten away from while he was in Dublin. He had brought his running gear with him, but could not imagine where anyone could jog in Dublin unless they drove to the outskirts. He had noticed the green at Trinity University and figured that would suffice but it involved a bit of a logistics problem of walking a considerable distance before and after his run in his running shorts and jacket. That would make him a bit of an anomaly surrounded by people dressed for work and Quinn was always a bit self conscious about that sort of thing.

When he entered the Library, he hung up his coat in the cloakroom, stuffed the collapsible umbrella in one of the pockets and went upstairs to the Research Room. He went immediately to the card catalogue section and began familiarizing himself with what was there. The card sections were divided into a number of categories which appeared to be of interest to Quinn. There were some land records, cards on wills and estates and books of references to individual's names together with a brief synopsis of the information referenced and the call number for retrieval by the staff. Out of curiosity Quinn first examined the name books to see if there was anything there on the Desmond line. There were a number of entries under Desmond, but none of the given names were familiar and the information noted did not seem relevant to what he was looking for. He did find a number of entries related to the Adams family but again, nothing that would seem to connect to his Desmond line.

He next went to the land records and again looked up the cards for the Desmonds and the Adams families. He soon saw that the cards related almost solely to large land holdings from the mid to earlier nineteenth century and not for the period of his interest, 1880 or thereabouts. The information was apparently restricted to historical interest items and was clearly not intended to be the repository of recorded land transactions into modern times. In checking his reference book, he noted that those records would most likely be found in the Valuation Office near St.Stephen's Green. He would suggest to Galvin that they look at those records next, but knowing Galvin's thirst for detail, he would want to go to the Archives first.

Quinn then went to the alphabetized cards, captioned "Estate Records," and pulled out the tray that would include the name Desmond. To his joy and amazement, there was an entry under Thomas Desmond with the simple entry "Will of Thomas Desmond, 1879." He wrote down the call number in his notes and also on a call slip which he took to the front desk. The staff member checked the call number with a reference book stored under the counter and informed Quinn that if the record was available, it would be in the Archives. Quinn was disheartened that it was not available in the Library but he was excited to know that there was a will by Thomas

Desmond in existence. Galvin had mentioned that the Archives had some of the Estate records and possibly the Archives had additional records, other than the will, that would relate to Thomas Desmond. Quinn noted the comments of the Staff member in his notebook and returned to the catalogue room to see what else he could find. He spent the next hour or so rummaging through the various card collections, following up on some dead ends that he discovered did not relate to his Desmond family and, noting that it was about lunch time, decided to take a break.

Finding that the weather had improved and he wouldn't need his umbrella, Quinn took the papers that Anne had signed over to the DHN Express Mail offices for rapid delivery to the University. They guaranteed two day delivery and normal airmail from Ireland to the States was something like ten days.

Taking a break from what was becoming somewhat monotonous research, Quinn went for a walk down Grafton Street and stopped at Bewley's where he had soup, sandwich and tea.

He spent the afternoon and part of the evening engaged in various pursuits in the Library, none of which were particularly rewarding. He had about worn out the Library as far as he was concerned and looked forward to getting together with Galvin in the morning and moving their efforts over to the Archives. The following morning, Quinn was there bright and early and this time he was ahead of Galvin. About ten minutes after the Library opened, Galvin finally walked in and came over to the desk where Quinn was seated reading an old volume of Irish History.

"Sorry I'm late. I had to stop by the school and send grades in to the Administration Office. Anyway, what did you come up with since we parted company?"

Quinn pushed the book aside and pulled out his notes. "I did find something of considerable interest." He then told Galvin about the reference to the Will of Thomas Desmond of Ballinacurra.

Galvin said he was not surprised that there is a will because he apparently owned quite a large parcel of land. "We should also find extensive land records if I'm not mistaken. I take it you didn't come up with anything else in the card file, newspapers or anything else right?"

Quinn felt a bit guilty having to admit that the only piece of solid information he had come up with was the card file entry on the Will that just about came up and hit him in the face. It was not the result of an in depth search of anything. He opened the file and "bang", there it was. "No, that was it, do you want to take a look at the records in there? Maybe you could find something that I couldn't, but I reviewed the name books, the land records and the estate files. There are other records in there that I didn't think applied to what we are looking for, map catalogue, architectural drawings and that sort of thing. Maybe later on but I didn't think they had any relevance now."

Galvin smiled, noting the look of disappointment on Quinn's face. "It's a slow process and sometimes you strike gold, but most of the time, you don't. The will is very important so at least you confirmed the existence of the record. I figured there would be a will but I wasn't so sure there was a record of one with all the destruction of public records that took place at the turn of the century, with the Rebellion and then the Civil War. Let's take a walk and go down to the Archives. It's about a fifteen minute walk from here so we'll get our exercise."

Quinn and Galvin walked south to St.Stephen's Green and then west a couple of blocks before they entered the National Archive Building. Galvin already had a pass to go up to the Research Room, but Quinn had to fill out the necessary papers and check out a storage bin for his coat. With this done, the two men boarded the elevator which took them up to the Research floor. It was not a particularly large room and Quinn commented to Galvin that "they couldn't have too many records stored in here."

Galvin said, "They don't. This is primarily a reference room and you use the call slips to pick up whatever you're looking for. Come on, and I'll show you how this works. Galvin showed Quinn how he could find more detail on the Tithe and Griffith records, when he had the time. There were working notes in the Archives drawn up by the enumerators who prepared the records in the eighteenth century. Galvin told Quinn that the notes would provide much more detailed information on the households than the bare statistical data in the directories that he had looked at so far. Galvin did not want to waste time with that now, as they had a tie in to the target family up to 1880, but Quinn might want to fill out the detail later on. "Let's take a look at the Will Books and hope that the one on Thomas Desmond is in there. Most of the Wills since the latter part of the 1850s should be in these books, but not all are."

Galvin found the reference to the Thomas Desmond Will that was filed in 1879 in County Cork and filled out the necessary call slip for retrieval. It was almost lunch time and when Galvin turned the slip in, the clerk at the desk advised him that it would not be available until after lunch which extended from noon until one o'clock. In the meantime, Galvin went back to the reference books and retrieved the information necessary to pull up the census reports for the 1901 and 1911 census data. That would be very useful in locating the descendants of William Desmond.

Having accomplished that task, the two browsed through card files and court records while they waited for the Will copy to arrive. Finally a clerk brought out an envelope bearing the proper call number and the two eagerly sat down to inspect the Will. The Will bore all appearances of the Last Will and Testament of Thomas Desmond, residing in the Townland of Ballinacurra, County Cork, dated September 16, 1878. Galvin noted that the Will was written after the death of Margaret Adams and less than a year before the death of Thomas Desmond, the Testator.

Galvin read from the Will as Quinn followed along. "The Last Will and Testament of Thomas Desmond, resident of the Townland of Ballinacurra, County of Cork. Be it known by all hereafter that Thomas Desmond, herein, of sound mind and body does hereby declare this to be his Last Will and Testament." Galvin skipped over some of the verbiage of the Will that he was not particularly interested in and again began reading aloud the paragraphs dealing with the distribution of property. "I hereby grant and bequeath at the time of my death, all right, title and interest, in and to my entire Estate to my beloved son, Jeremiah Desmond, late of Ballinacurra, who departed this beloved land, not of his own free will, for the United States of America in the year 1850, on the condition that said Jeremiah Desmond is living at the moment of my death. With that condition having been fully satisfied, said Jeremiah Desmond, my first born son shall be the heir to everything I own, including all personal and real property other than that specifically devised and bequeathed herein to my sons, William and Michael."

Galvin, with a slight tremor now visible in his hand, searched through the document to see what was specifically given to the other two sons of Thomas Desmond that would take away from the gross estate transferred to Quinn's grandfather, Jeremiah. When he found the specific paragraphs, he read both in an excited voice. "To my sons William Desmond and Michael Desmond, on the condition that they are living at the time of my death, I devise and bequeath my entire Estate only on the condition that my son Jeremiah has predeceased me and in the event that said Jeremiah Desmond, my son, has not predeceased me, I herewith bequeath to my sons William and Michael, from my Gross Estate, joint ownership of a parcel of land consisting of five hectares, being the original Thomas Desmond cottage and yard in the Townland of Ballinacurra as described in the lease dated May 2, 1859 between the Honorable Cecil Adams and Thomas Desmond."

Galvin shook his head and said, "It's clear that he did not hold either his son William or his son Michael in high regard. He gave everything to Jeremiah and a small cottage and yard to William and Michael to own jointly. Apparently there was limited communication with Jeremiah and his father was not sure he was alive when he wrote the Will. Most interesting set of circumstances. Your great grandfather gave his very sizeable estate 'en toto', basically, to your grandfather and gave a very small piece of land to his other sons. I can see the problem with the relationship between the Anglican father, Thomas, and the Fenian son, Michael, but I don't know what problem he had with William and we may never know. In any event, William appears eventually to have seen the light in the east and changed his religion, either before or after his father's death. Probably about the time he took over what had been the rather huge Adam's Estate. Very interesting that Michael was killed very shortly after Thomas Desmond died and this Will was published. The question remains as to what happened to change the distribution of the Estate because from everything I know about this matter, Jeremiah Desmond, your grandfather, should have inherited the entire Adams Estate. What we have to find out now, is why he didn't."

Chapter 29

Quinn was silent. He was stunned at what he was learning. Finally when he spoke, he said, "Believe me, my grandfather never said a word about any property or about having inherited anything. He was a poor farmer most of his life. Not sophisticated. Not stupid, but not learned in matters such as this. I don't think he would have walked away from an opportunity to return to Ireland and live a financially secure life. Ireland was all that he spoke about and by the time my parents had sufficient funds to pay for a trip back for him, he was too old to handle it. Before then, he would have done anything to be back in the country that he loved with his entire being but then he had obligations to meet, a family to support and a farm to take care of."

"Well, Quinn, with this will, there must be something of record that negates the disposition of property to your grandfather. Possibly a later will that may be recorded somewhere else would do it. In any event, the Land records will tell us what happened. It would have to happen soon after this document was written because this is dated only months before Thomas Desmond died."

Quinn recalled what he had read earlier in the day. He looked at his watch and said, "The Valuation Office should have that. We could still get over there before they close."

Galvin nodded. "I don't think they would have the records that we want. Most likely a subsequent will or other document changing the devise of land contained in this Will would be in the County Probate or Surrogate Court records which handle Decedent's Estates. That means a trip to Cork but it wouldn't hurt to first check the Valuation Office records. They're only open another hour and I would want to take my time going over what they have. Let's have a look at the Census data first and maybe we can save ourselves walking back down here to get the names of William's descendants."

Galvin wrote down the call numbers that he had written down earlier on the slips and gave them to the Clerk at the staff desk for retrieval. When they had the 1901 census records for Kinsale Parish, they located Ballinacurra Townland and noted that William Desmond was now residing in what had formerly been the Adams Family Estate. Listed as living in the Estate were William, age sixty-four, one son, Dennis, age twenty-one and two daughters, Elizabeth and Anne, ages twenty-six and twenty-four respectively. William's wife must have passed away prior to the 1901 Census. In checking the 1911 census, the only children shown were Dennis, age thirty-one and Elizabeth, age thirty-six. The daughter Ann was either married off or had passed away. The later census data was not available in the Archives.

Galvin sat back in his chair and said, "Looks like the only son, Dennis, would be the heir to the Desmond Estate. More than likely, the daughter, apparently unmarried, would have received an adequate bequest to enable her to live comfortably the rest of her life, but the brunt of the property would have gone to Dennis. He is the one you will want to follow up on in order to trace the Estate. Let's call it a day and I will meet you tomorrow morning at the Land Valuation Office. We might find something there, if not. It will be a trip to Cork."

Quinn agreed as he gathered his notes together. The two walked out of the Archives and Galvin went one way towards his bus line and Quinn headed over to St. Stephen's Green and on up Kildare Street to his Hotel. As he walked to the Hotel, he thought about what they were coming up with. At this point in time, he was assuming that they would find some document which explained the question as to why the property went to William Desmond and not to his grandfather, Jeremiah. Whatever it was, they would know by this time tomorrow. In the meantime, he decided he was going to relax and enjoy a good dinner somewhere as the events of the past few days were tiring him out. The Hotel made reservations for him at Nico's on Dame Street where he had an excellent dinner before retiring for the evening.

The following morning, Quinn was eagerly awaiting the arrival of Noel Galvin in the lobby of the Land Valuation Office. He wasn't waiting over a few minutes when Galvin walked up the steps and entered the Lobby. They went to the research room where Galvin quickly located the records for the Desmond properties at Kinsale. The only record regarding the ownership of the land was that showing transfer of title from The Estate of Thomas Desmond to William Desmond dated May 12, 1880.

The two looked at each other, disappointed that they were not finding an explanation for the transfer of title to William. Galvin shook his head and said, "Looks like a trip to Cork. I can't go down there until Friday at the earliest and that wouldn't allow us enough time in the Records Office. If you can do it, I can go down next Sunday, stay over and then be in position Monday morning early to see what we can find."

Quinn nodded. "I'm at your mercy on this one. This is all over my head. Leave a note at the Hotel as to when to meet you at the train station and I will be there." Quinn was not completely disappointed that he had a few blank days in his schedule. He had wanted to do more touring of the City and visit some of the other theaters that he had heard so much about, The Gate, The Gaity and other smaller theaters. The two parted company and Quinn headed for his Hotel noting on his watch that it wasn't even lunch time yet so most of the day was free for whatever he wanted to do.

As he walked up Kildare Street and was about to go up the stairway to the Hotel Lobby, out of the Hotel came Peter Baker. Quinn saw him first and said, "Well, look who we have here. What are you up to?"

Baker looked pleased to run into Quinn and said, "I was just checking to see if, by chance, you were around. I thought maybe we could have lunch together. I have some spare time and nothing else requiring my presence. I was in the Library and figured you were somewhere about."

Quinn stood at the bottom of the steps and told Baker that he had an open schedule because they had about exhausted their research in Dublin and were heading for Cork at week end.

"Very interesting. You'll have to tell me all about it. Sounds like you're making much better progress than I am. I know a great little restaurant only two blocks from here, called Monty's. If you've been there just say so. Not expensive and the food is excellent."

The two proceeded to the restaurant and made small talk about the weather and the places that Quinn had visited on his tour of Dublin with Anne. Baker had never been to Johny Fox's Pub in south Dublin and Quinn told him it was something that he had to do before he left. In the restaurant, the easy banter continued as they looked through the menu and after ordering, and while waiting for their food, Baker steered the conversation back to Quinn's progress in his Desmond search.

"Now you have to tell me how you are coming along. I am jealous that I'm not making the progress that you are, but then I have the interfering problem of having to work at a job while I do this."

Quinn was pleased with everything they had learned and in his excitement was eager to pass on the good news to most anyone that wanted to listen and Baker clearly wanted to listen. After his earlier appraisal of Baker as some sort of a threat to him, he had changed his opinion following their conversation in the "Duke." Baker just seemed to be a fairly regular guy with no particular agenda that Quinn could detect. Quinn went on, "I believe that I have found my grandfather's family in the Kinsale area and I'm going down there Sunday to check out some records in the Probate Court for a day or two. We found a Will where my grandfather was listed as the beneficiary and, just out of curiosity, I want to find out what happened to the Estate. Not that I have any personal interest in any distribution that occurred that long ago, but I am curious as to what happened. Very interesting facts that have come up. Anyway, it has been fun and challenging but right now I'm a little burned out on it and I'm going to get away from it for a day or two and do something else."

Baker was very absorbed with what Quinn had told him about finding his family in Kinsale. He asked a number of questions as to how he was so sure that he had the right Desmond Family and not a "record look-alike." He told Quinn that it would be best to be perfectly satisfied that he wasn't barking up the wrong tree before he made the trip south. He pointed out that he was playing the "devil's advocate" to protect Quinn from eventual disappointment as he had known many people that expended large sums of money before they realized they were on a totally wrong track in their family search. "We see Americans all the time, coming over to the Library working on the wrong family tree."

Quinn assured him that all of the facts tied together. The letters that Quinn's mother had from William to Jeremiah confirmed many of the facts that they were uncovering in the Library. It all tied together and having the assistance of Noel Galvin had saved him innumerable hours of research, in fact he probably would not have been able to do it on his own. Now, he had resolved to stay until the final gun.

Their food finally arrived, but Baker continued his questioning. "You going to look up any relatives you can locate?"

Quinn paused while he placed his napkin on his lap. "I haven't really decided yet. That would be interesting. I don't know. You know, in a sense it would be a little anticlimactic. It's the search for the facts that really keeps me going. Chasing the clues and following little leads has been, how should I say it, what this is all about. I suppose when I'm faced with the actual flesh and blood, I will enjoy the moment but then the hunt is over and that could be a little depressing. Then I'll have to find something else to occupy my time."

"I suppose you're right, Quinn. I never looked at it quite that way because my search for my branch of Desmonds has always seemed to me to be a mountain that has no top. I just keep going without really getting any place. I've had so many dead ends in my search that I can't count them. Anyway, it's interesting."

The two continued talking about Ireland and Quinn's life in the States. After they finished eating their lunch, Baker said that he had a number of appointments down in Ballsbridge, which was in County Dublin, just south of the City Center. Quinn said he had seen the area referenced on a map and one of these days, he was going to ride the Dart, the Dublin Area Rapid Transit, and visit some of the communities along the line, including Ballsbridge. Baker looked at his watch and said he had to get going. He shook Quinn's hand and picked up the luncheon bill just as Quinn was reaching for it. "No way Quinn. I was the one that suggested the lunch. I will look you up when you get back from Cork. I'm sure I'll still be here. Take Care," and he left the restaurant. Quinn looked at his watch, noted that it was not yet one o'clock and decided to take a walk around the streets of the City Center and see what the shops had to offer. He also wanted to visit the Tourist Office and get some brochures on what he was missing in Dublin.

Later in the afternoon, he stopped in at Bewley's on Grafton after buying an Irish Times from the vendor in front of the café. As he enjoyed a cup of tea and a scone, he read the paper and noted that a young man had been shot to death in Dublin in what was believed to be a revenge shooting by the Provos, the radical arm of the Unity Party in the North. The young man was very active in the "One Ireland" movement and was also believed to be a member of the INA, the Irish Nationalist Army, which was the counterpart to the Provos. Quinn shook his head as he read through the article. He could not understand why some in Ireland were so quick to solve their political problem with a gun. Fortunately they represented a very distinct minority and he was hard put to criticize the people of Ireland when he lived in a country that led the world in gun violence.

As he was about to leave, he saw Peter Baker sitting on the other side of the crowded restaurant talking very animatedly with a fellow that Quinn had never seen before. They appeared to be in a bit of an argument and Quinn watched them, out of curiosity, for some time before picking up his newspaper and heading for the door. His path to the Grafton Street exit took him right past Baker's table and as he came up behind Baker, he heard him say, "...So don't do anything stupid." At that moment, as Quinn came up to the table and Baker saw him standing there, he seemed for a moment dumbfounded and at a loss for words. After Baker collected himself, he stood up and, still obviously under some stress, introduced Quinn to his companion.

Quinn was so surprised at Baker's reaction that he never even caught the fellow's name, instead he said he was just leaving and wished to say hello before doing so. He wished Baker a good day and departed the restaurant. As he walked back to the Rockwell, he wondered what that was all about.

In the evening when Quinn figured that Anne would be home, he placed a call to her and a young boy answered the phone. Quinn introduced himself and asked the boy, who said his name was Kevin, if his mother was home. She was and in a moment or two, she was on the phone. As soon as she heard his voice, she said that she was hoping he would call. She repeated what a great time that she had over the weekend and that she would enjoy seeing him again. That was exactly what Quinn wanted to hear and the two made plans to meet the following morning, when she did not have to work and while the boys were in school.

Anne suggested that she pack a small lunch and they could drive out to Phoenix Park and find a good spot to enjoy the day. That was provided that it didn't rain or wasn't too cool. She said, "I wouldn't want you to get your shoes dirty out there, Quinn."

He just laughed and said, "They've been dirty before and they'll be dirty again." He said he did have some jeans in his bag and if that was acceptable for what she had planned, he would wear those and an Irish wool sweater that he had just purchased at Monaghan's in the Arcade off Grafton.

Anne replied with, "That had better be acceptable because that's what I wear all the time."

Quinn thought to himself that Anne would do very well in a good pair of jeans. He had missed her very much since their weekend and after they had arranged the time to meet in the Hotel Lobby, he told her that he was looking forward to spending time with her the next day.

Anne said, "Same here, Quinn. I feel like a young student again. I have been leading too much of a sheltered life for the past few years and being with you has been. I don't know. It's been like waking up from a bad dream. Anyway, thanks and I'll see you at ten."

Anne quickly hung up the phone and Quinn sat on the bed, holding the phone in his hand, wondering what she had meant. He would bring it up tomorrow if the opportunity presented itself and he hoped very much that it would.

The next day when they were together, Anne was telling Quinn her background in Ireland. "I'm from a place that you have never heard of. We called it Templemartin which really is a Parish, to the North of Bandon, down in Cork. We lived on a farm. We all spoke Gaelic as our first language. Learned most of our English in the school although we sometimes used a mixture at home. I attended U.C. Cork where I earned a degree in History. Not very marketable I found out. Then I came to Dublin and worked as a secretary, here and there until I went to work for RTE. Got the job because of my working knowledge of Gaelic. RTE had a need for it. First I was full time and then when I had the boys, I shifted to part time. That's it. Story of my life."

Quinn laughed. "I think you left out a few things, but we'll let that pass for now. I take it you met Sean in Dublin then? He never did tell me about that."

"Yes, we met in Dublin. We were both members of 'One Ireland'. I was a bit political when I finished college. I still belong to 'One Ireland', although I'm not as active as before. My history background did it, I think. Although my family was always very connected to the Republican Party. The Nationalists. Sean's political interest never changed but I think, with the boys, I sort of drifted on into other interests, although I remain sympathetic to the views of the Nationalists, but not to the point where I can't listen to a contrary opinion. Politics sort of took its toll on our marriage. Sean became more and more involved in that and less involved in being a father and husband. After a while, we just had to make a change because I was feeling like I had three children in the house and not just two. Sean was never very good at playing the role of the provider But, anyway, I've managed to be able to take care of the boys and do some things that I enjoy doing, reading. I read quite a bit. Always have. I enjoy music, classical and traditional Irish Folk Music. The Irish music reminds me of home I guess. I spend a lot of time with the boys and well, that's it. Here we are."

Quinn thought for a moment and said, "Interesting." He then told Anne about his upbringing in Minnesota, his school years, law school, and practicing law in Atlanta. "My interests are much the same as yours. I spend quite a bit of time reading, theater, what have you. I enjoy jogging and always have. When I'm home in Atlanta, I run around the lakes most every morning. Keeps me awake. I don't have a female friend right now. Haven't for quite a few years, sad, isn't it?" Quinn chuckled.

Anne asked Quinn how long he was going to be in Dublin. "I really don't know. I have no real commitments in the States, so I guess it just depends."

The two stayed in the Park talking about virtually everything until the sun began going down in the west and Quinn could tell that Anne was beginning to get a bit cold. They picked up their things and took them back to the parking lot where they both silently put things away.

They made plans to meet at the Hotel again at ten o'clock the next morning Quinn had not mentioned the fact that he had to go down to Cork the following Sunday for a day or two. He could cover that in the morning. What he would really like to do was to take her along, but he didn't think that could be worked out. If he saw a chance of bringing it up, he would do so but he thought that maybe that was pushing the relationship a bit.

When Anne pulled up in front of the Hotel, she leaned over and gave Quinn a long kiss and told him she would see him in the morning. He stood on the curb and waved to her as she drove off in the heavy rush hour traffic. As he went up to his room, he was thinking that it was going to be very difficult leaving Dublin, if and when he returned to the States. It was the first time that the thought had entered his mind of remaining in Ireland.

The following days sped by. Quinn and Anne were together every available minute that Anne did not have to spend with the boys. On Saturday evening, Anne invited Quinn to the house to have dinner with them and give him a chance to meet Kevin and Neil. They were very much the way that he expected them to be. Very polite, intelligent and musically inclined as he learned while listening to Kevin on the fiddle and Neil winging along with the concertina. Quinn told the boys that he had spent quite a bit of time with their father and as he spoke, he noticed the look of intense interest on the part of both. He wasn't sure if he was treading on sensitive ground by talking about Sean and as soon as he had a chance, he asked Anne if that was alright.

"By all means. They have a hunger to know more about their father because, really, he was just never around. He cared deeply for the boys, that I believe, but his love for Ireland, as I said, came first."

After dinner, Quinn spent more time telling the boys about their father and how he spent his time in the States. They knew he taught at the University in Atlanta, but having someone describe the school, where it was in the large city, his office, and his schedule was something they had never known. They sat listening to every word and were most interested when Quinn described Murphy's Irish Pub, in the Peachtree Mall, where all of the Irish in Atlanta hung out listening to Sean play the fiddle. Kevin, who played the fiddle, had many questions to ask, what songs did his father play, did he use an amplifier, and so forth. Quinn answered as many as he could, but he was just not that familiar with traditional Irish music to provide many details.

The boys then asked Quinn about where he lived, his family, his job and other questions that came to their minds. They were very curious and inquisitive which Quinn attributed to the fact that their parents had those qualities and had passed them on to their two fine boys. As the boys were about to go up to their bedroom and go to bed, Quinn told them how their father was loved and respected by everyone who knew him in Atlanta. He told about the service held in the pub with everyone singing Sean's favorite Irish ballads and how they all touched the casket as it was taken from the Pub. The boys were deeply touched by what Quinn was telling them and when their mother told them they had to get to bed, they each came up to Quinn and thanked him. As they walked up the stairs, first Kevin and then Neil turned and gave Quinn a smile and a wave before they disappeared from view.

Quinn and Anne sat talking and enjoying one another's company for another two hours before Quinn brought up the fact that he was going to go down to Cork to research some of the County Land Records. Anne could not hide her disappointment that he was not going to be in Dublin and immediately asked how long he was going to be down there. He assured her that he would be coming back within a day or so and would call her just as soon as he came back to town. Quinn went on to say, "I wish you were coming along and you could give me a tour of Cork City. I'm going to miss you while I'm down there."

"I wish I could go but I have to work. Maybe some other time when I have more time to plan and I can put in for vacation time. I would have to find someone to take care of the boys but that is not a problem. One of my sisters lives here in Dublin and she owes me many days for taking care of her kids. Next time, give more of a warning. For now, I want to hear how you are doing on your family history. Sean said that was the main reason that you were coming to Ireland. It sounds interesting."

Quinn explained his grandfather's background, settling in the States and homesteading in Minnesota with other Irish from the old country. He then told Anne about his progress with his research and the puzzling findings that they had made with respect to the Will, which was the main reason they were going to Cork. They were going to inspect the Land and Estate records and find out what changed the intent of his great grandfather's Will.

Anne listened attentively and then she said, "Quinn, this is a bit strange. I believe Sean was aware of something that had to do with your family in Ireland. He said some things to me that I really didn't pay much attention to because I didn't know you. It somehow was related to politics because he was so intent on your being assisted in the Library by one of the people the INA could trust."

Quinn doubted very much that Sean had any knowledge whatsoever regarding Quinn's family background, but Anne's next comment made him question that. "Quinn, you say your Desmonds came from the Kinsale area. You do know, don't you that Sean was also from down there and, in fact, I'm sure he worked in Kinsale for a number of years before going up to Cork and getting active with Nationalist Party politics. Let me run up stairs. He has some old papers up there that might be interesting."

As Quinn waited for Anne to return he could not recall if the topic of where Sean came from in Ireland had ever come up. As he thought about it, he recalled that Sean had said that he came from or lived in the "Liberties" section of Dublin. Quinn had the impression that Sean had grown up in the City. There was never any mention of Kinsale.

After a few minutes, Anne came down the stairs carrying some papers. As she sat back down on the couch next to Quinn, she showed him copies of Sean's old resume submitted to University College Dublin for his application for a teaching position. His entire work history in Ireland was detailed and as Quinn read down the list of positions held by Sean over the years, he was shocked to see, "Office Clerk, Adams Farms, Kinsale, County Cork."

"My God," Quinn exclaimed, "I'm sure that is the property my grandfather was given in the Will of Thomas Desmond." Quinn explained more of the details involving the marriage of Thomas Desmond to Margaret Adams, the surviving widow and sole beneficiary of the Adams Estate. A marriage then followed by her subsequent death, with all the Adams property being transferred to Thomas. "Maybe Sean did know something about a problem. But if he did, why didn't he just tell me about it. We were pretty close, at least I thought we were."

Anne put her hand on Quinn's arm. "Let me tell you one thing about Sean, Quinn. His politics always came first, before anyone. His wife, children or close friends. He was way up in the INA and you have to be deeply involved in the cause to hold the positions that he held."

Quinn told Anne about some of the strange experiences he had encountered in the past few months and of the people that he had come into contact with that seemed to have an excess interest in what he was doing in the Library. While he gave Anne all of the details of his encounters in the Atlanta Library, what he observed in Murphy's Pub in Atlanta, Sean's warning to him the day he was killed, Sean's death, suspicion of being followed in Dublin and Baker's monitoring of his progress, Anne sat still on the couch with a look of growing concern on her face. Quinn finished the litany of strange events with, "And now this, with Sean in a position to have first hand knowledge of something that he knew I was keenly interested in. This makes me wonder what the story is with Noel Galvin."

Anne saw more of what was probably behind the occurrences than did Quinn because she was much closer to the forces that were most likely involved. As she sat on the couch next to a man that she was becoming genuinely interested in, her fear for his safety increased as he continued talking.

"Quinn, I know how the INA operates because I lived with a man for a number of years that lived and breathed INA operations. He was sent to the States by the INA as a Regional Director. I know that because in one of his very seldom weak moments, he told me that. The INA is at war. They always have been. Some people are expendable if they come in conflict with the INA regardless of whether they are a direct threat to the INA or not. Their goal is a united Ireland. That is the goal of most of the Irish in the Republic as well but there is a difference of opinion as to how that goal is achieved. Northern Ireland has its own INA, the Provos. Same thing, different name. I don't know what's going on here, but it seems to me that you have wandered into the middle of the battle field."

Quinn interrupted Anne and said, "Look, I have no real bone to pick with anyone."

Anne's response to that was, "Sometimes innocent people get caught in the middle. Do me a favor and be very careful." Quinn assured her that he would but thought she was making more out of what was happening than was justified by the facts.

The next morning, when Quinn entered the station, he immediately purchased his round trip ticket to Cork and then proceeded to the small food counter where he paid for a cup of tea. He sat at the counter in the food service area and waited for Galvin to show up. At fifteen minutes after eleven, Noel Galvin entered the terminal and spotting Quinn, walked over to him. Galvin appeared irritated about something and merely nodded in recognition to Quinn before ordering tea and a scone. When he came back to where Quinn was sitting at the counter, he sat down without saying a word.

Quinn looked at him with a wry smile on his face, "Well aren't we happy today. What's this all about? You are not the happy camper today."

Galvin nodded and apologized for being a bit short with Quinn. "We lost a good man this week to those scum sucking Provos. Tom O'Rourke, right here in Dublin. Right under our noses. We should have seen it coming because he was involved in some sensitive business." Galvin proceeded to bite into his scone, still shaking his head.

"Oh yes," Quinn said. "I read about that in the paper but it didn't give too many details. Just said something about the fact that he was shot by the

Provos. Didn't even say how they knew that. What's the story?"

"They nailed him as he was coming out of his house. Almost got his girl friend who was with him but he apparently threw her to the side when he saw what was coming and took the full hit himself. Not real clean. They unloaded automatic fire on him. I think there was some sort of message there. Usually they are a little less messy when they do business in the Republic, but not this time. I knew O'Rourke quite well because we were about the same age and came up through the ranks in the Party at about the same time. He was a real soldier."

Quinn would have liked to know just how active Galvin was with the Party and if he was on Party business today in making this trip to Cork. His comments about this O'Rourke and his close connection to him led Quinn to assume that Galvin was more than just a loyal Party member. He was most likely active with the INA. He thought he would test him a bit. "Noel, there is no reason why you have to make this trip down here on my account. I'll be frank, I'm getting a very guilty conscience about all the time you're spending on my family history. I don't know how to bring this up, but I am in no position to compensate you for everything you are doing. I'm embarrassed to say this, but that is the reason I came over myself because I couldn't afford to pay someone here to do what had to be done."

Noel looked over at Quinn. "Relax. I have my own reasons for going to Cork so don't feel that you owe me something. I just happen to enjoy the sort of project you are involved with and that's why I'm here."

Quinn didn't totally believe that but at least it took him off the hook as far as being obligated to compensate Galvin for his expenses. They would be in Cork for at least two nights and that could get a bit pricey. As he was thinking about that, Galvin said that he had made reservations at the Imperial Hotel in Cork and that was a short walk over to the Court House.

Galvin told Quinn that Michael Collins, the Irish Free Stater, had spent his last night alive at the Imperial before he was shot to death by the Republicans south of Macroom. He also said that if they had time, they could take the train out to Cobh Harbor which, Galvin said, was where Quinn's grandfather, Jeremiah, had most likely departed Ireland from. It was a short train ride, only fifteen to twenty minutes or so from Cork and a scenic spot to visit. They also had a Famine Exhibit at the train depot in Cobh which Quinn would enjoy seeing.

Quinn had not been aware of the significance of Cork and Cobh in his grandfather's life and hearing this from Galvin increased his interest in the trip. Quinn had also admired Michael Collins, from his readings, and thought it very interesting that he would be staying in a hotel that had such significance in the life of the Irish Patriot. As he thought about it, he recalled seeing the movie, "Michael Collins", with Sean and that Sean had admired Collins even though Sean was such a staunch Republican and Collins was a Free Stater. What had Sean said, something about "time changes one's perspective." Quinn thought, it certainly must, as Galvin obviously had a positive view of Collins as well or he would not have brought it up.

The ride down to Cork on the train was interesting as it gave Quinn a view of the Irish countryside not possible from either a plane or a car. The train passed through farm lands and small country towns affording Quinn a birds eye view of life outside of metropolitan Dublin. It reminded Quinn of what country life in the States looked like in the 1950s. Quaint, peaceful with small shops, farms with a variety of farm animals but predominantly stocked with sheep. Wool was obviously the number one farm product from what Quinn was seeing. The people riding the train appeared to have a small farming town look about them. They were dressed modestly and did not have the look of sophistication one saw in Dublin.

An older man sitting across from Quinn fumbled across the beads of a rosary with his gnarled, wrinkled hands, moving his lips silently as he stared out the train window. Occasionally he would turn and look at Quinn with a look of curiosity on his face. Quinn and Galvin had to change trains at Mallow Junction for the ride to the southeast down to Cork, so, before the train came to a stop, they gathered up their belongings so they would be ready to off load. Within minutes, they were again seated on the Cork train bound for their destination. As the train pulled into Cork Station, Quinn checked his watch and noted that they had been on the train for approximately three hours. It had been an enjoyable ride.

The two men caught a cab and proceeded directly to the Imperial. Quinn was impressed with the appearance of the Hotel, with its old paintings and architectural style dating back to the 1800s. The Marble floor, high ceiling and Celtic artwork covering the wall panels. He could almost visualize Michael Collins checking in at the Reception Desk. He doubted anything had changed in the decor or furnishings of the Hotel since that fateful day in 1922. After they were assigned their rooms, Galvin said that he was going to be tied up for the evening as he had to visit some people in Cork. He would meet Quinn for breakfast in the Hotel dining room at seven in the morning if that was alright. Quinn assured him that he would be up and around much earlier than that and he would be there. Quinn wanted very much to visit Cobh but it was after three by the time he got into his room. There just was not enough time left in the day to return to the train depot, wait for a train, take the trip to Cobh and still be able to tour the Exhibit and the town. He would have to do that some other time.

Instead, he read through the City Guide Book on the desk in his room and found what appeared to be a decent restaurant not far from the Hotel. He called the number in the Guide and made a reservation for one person at seven. Later on, as he walked to the Savoy Restaurant, up on Morgan Street, he was impressed with how different Cork appeared from Dublin. It was Sunday evening, but there would be much more traffic in Dublin than he was seeing here. Far less people out and about and few cars on the street. Cork, to Quinn, from what little he had seen thus far, reminded him a bit of a large market town in the Midwest on a Sunday afternoon in the fifties. The following morning as he sat in the dining room waiting for Galvin, his view of the City changed considerably. Traffic was extremely heavy and crowds of people were moving up and down South Mall Street on the other side of the dining room window, heading for their offices to begin a new work week.

Galvin came up to the table and wished Quinn a good morning. The two asked one another as to how their evening went and Quinn told Noel that he had found a very good restaurant for his future reference. Galvin assured him that he was familiar with the place and that it was considered one of the best in Cork. Galvin then tapped the table somewhat nervously and asked Quinn if he was ready to find out "What really happened to your grandfather's inheritance."

"Can't say I'm not curious." The two finished their breakfast and began the trek to the Court House. Quinn did not mention it, but the anxiety to know what had happened had been growing since he boarded the train in Dublin. Before then, his involvement with Anne had occupied his mind to a considerable extent. The more physically removed from her that he was, the more he began concentrating his thoughts on the Will of Thomas Desmond and what had transpired in the following few months to change the property distribution from his grandfather to the other son, William. As they walked towards the Court House from the hotel, Quinn told himself, "this is going to be interesting."

CHAPTER 30

As the two men approached the Court House which was situated along the banks of the River Lee, the wind coming in from the harbor brought a chill to Quinn. He pulled up the collar of his coat to protect himself from the full blast of the damp ocean air. Galvin commented that this time of year, one could not count on comfortable weather anywhere in Ireland, but this was unusually cold for southern Ireland. Quinn replied that he hoped this was not an omen of what they would or would not find in the records.

"Don't worry about that, Quinn. With all that land, I can assure you we will find enough to keep ourselves busy for a day or two."

As they walked into the building, Galvin proceeded directly to the Surrogate Court Office on the second floor with Quinn close behind. Galvin spoke to the clerk and the two men were directed to a room in the back whose walls were lined with large aging volumes stacked vertically in rows extending around the room. Each volume had an identifying number in large print written across the binding and the clerk explained to Galvin where he could find the reference books that would lead him to whichever volume he was interested in examining.

After the clerk had gone back to his work station at the front desk, Galvin explained to Quinn how they would proceed in their examination of the records. "OK, Quinn, what we want to see are the land transfer records and also the Estate or Will records. We know the will was dated 1878 and your great grandfather died May 12, 1879 so the will was probated some time after that and we should find records reflecting that probate in that time frame. If there was something filed changing the intent of the will, it would have to have occurred between the date of the will and the date of Probate. At least that is what I am thinking. Something had to be filed, or we know the wording of the Will would have prevailed. I would suggest that we take a look at those records first."

Quinn followed Galvin and observed as he paged through the Will Records Reference Book following the dates until he located Wills filed for Probate in May, 1879. He wrote down the volume and page numbers of the wills probated from the reference book and then headed back to the stacks to locate the proper volume. After they had pulled the time worn, bound volume from the shelf, they carefully laid it out on the work table and Galvin began thumbing through the pages until he came to the wills that had been filed during the relevant time period.

Both men read over the names on the various documents filed with the Surrogate Court and bound by date in the old volume they had before them. They did not come to the Will of Thomas Desmond until they came to those filed for Probate in September of 1879. They had already read the Will of Thomas Desmond in the Archives and had no reason to read it again at this time. The two continued paging through the book, examining the records filed by date with the Court, looking for some later filing that changed the intent of the Will of record for Thomas Desmond probated in September of 1879. They continued examining the records up through the year 1881 and found nothing filed with the Surrogate Court that would change the devise of all property from Thomas Desmond to his eldest son, Jeremiah Desmond. After two hours of poring over the difficult to read documents, both men were in need of a break.

Without commenting on the failure to find something explaining why the property went to William when the Will clearly recited it was to go to Jeremiah Desmond, Galvin suggested they go downstairs to the café and get a cup of tea. The two men walked downstairs and after getting a pot of hot tea and scones, sat down at a table and relaxed.

Quinn was not overly concerned that they had not found anything that explained why the property of Thomas Desmond had not gone to his grandfather, Jeremiah Desmond. He figured that there had to be a valid reason for the change and in time they would find out what it was.

Galvin continued to remain silent as he drank his tea and ate his scone. After a while, he looked up at Quinn and said, "We should have looked at the Land Records first."

"Why do you say that?"

"The Will clearly devised the land to your grandfather. That would have dictated how the land was transferred at his death. Any change to the devise as dictated in the Will would have to be shown in the Land Records. I should have thought of that."

"Well, Noel, it wasn't as though we would have ignored the Will records regardless of what we found in the Land Records. So we didn't waste time anyway. Right?"

"I suppose so. Well, when you're done there, we'll go up and follow the land transfers. This is going to be a bit more tedious."

After the clerk had pointed out the land transfer reference books and directed the two men to another room in the building housing all of the deeds, leases, and other documents effecting transfers of land, Quinn and Galvin set their notebooks and briefcases down at one of the reading tables and went about their work. Galvin explained that they would have to go back to the original Adams Estate holdings and follow those land titles forward in order to ensure that they were going to locate the document or documents that affected the devise of the Will.

After hours of poring through a number of dusty volumes with difficult to read, hand written, land records, the two men had determined the specific parcel of land that comprised the Adams Estate up to the date of death of Margaret Adams Desmond in 1875. It was her will that transferred the land to Thomas Desmond and that will was filed for Probate before the time period examined by Galvin and Quinn in the Will Books.

"Well, anyway we've got the land description and now we really know what we're looking for. Quite a piece of land that went to your great grandfather. He went from being a tenant farmer to a very wealthy fellow. That didn't happen everyday back in those times. He must have been a hell of a guy to get the Adams Widow to sign everything over to him but then, maybe she just didn't have any other family, or maybe she was Irish to start with, and not English. You might check that out someday. That's a good question."

It was already after four o'clock and the County Records Office was about to close so the two men packed up their notebooks and walked downstairs to the exit. They made plans to meet again in the morning and to continue their review of the land records then. Galvin had other business to take care of that afternoon in the City so he left Quinn after the two men had crossed over the Lee River Bridge and told him that he would not be back until later in the evening. That was fine with Quinn as he wanted to do a little sight seeing on his own in Cork City.

Quinn went back to the Imperial, dropped off his papers and briefcase in his room and went for a walk in the area around the Hotel. He found a small store on Oliver Plunkett Street that had a number of books and pamphlets describing the history of some of the towns in County Cork. One of the pamphlets dealt with the "Corporation of Kinsale" and contained considerable information relating to the Adams family and their holdings. Quinn bought the book and took it back to his hotel where he read it in his room until he checked his watch and noted that it was getting past his suppertime. He ordered a sandwich in the Hotel dining room and was soon back in his room learning more about the Adams family and their various business ventures. Apparently Sir Cecil Adams was an only child and there was just brief mention of his having a wife named Margaret.

Nothing was said about any children having been born to Sir Cecil and Margaret Adams.

The pamphlet did not contain any information regarding the local peasantry and was devoted to the major personalities of the time and describing the economy of the area. It further brought out the fact that Kinsale was not only a market center for the area, but also a focal point for commercial trade by reason of its location at the mouth of the Bandon River where it emptied out into the Sea. The Adams Estate encompassed land on either side of the Bandon River out to the Head of Kinsale and undoubtedly profited from the trade goods coming down the River from as far west as Dunmanway. The pamphlet noted that Sir Cecil Adams had greatly enhanced the commercial holdings of the Adams Family following the death of his father. There was no mention that the huge estate was later transferred to the Irish Desmonds.

Quinn checked the publication date of the pamphlet and noted that it was written originally well before Irish Independence and during the period when the British controlled virtually all property throughout Ireland. As he put the pamphlet into his briefcase, he thought about the scandal that must have erupted in the upper echelons of English society when they learned that Margaret Adams had not only married the Irishman, Thomas Desmond, but also left him one of the larger Estates in County Cork. Maybe Galvin had a point. She may have been Irish to begin with and even a Catholic at that. It was most uncommon in those times for an English landowner to wed an Irish commoner but it did occasionally happen. That was something for Quinn to take a look at some other time. Right now, his interest was focused on what he might find in the Land Records in the morning.

Quinn ordered a light breakfast from the waitress as he sat waiting for Galvin to appear. He had found that a heavy meal was counterproductive when it came to sitting at a reading table, searching for a particular legal document among hundreds of barely legible transcriptions. What Quinn had seen the previous day bore no resemblance to what he was used to reading in land records in Georgia court houses. Those were all neatly typed and even the signatures were well drawn and always above or below a typed duplicate of the name which was easily read. The records that he and Galvin were examining were all done in flat edged ink pens by professional scribes who wrote in an italic fashion with great flourishes, particularly at the beginning of sentences. Sometimes Quinn had to study a word for a period of time before he was able to discern that it was, in fact, a word and not a name.

As Quinn sat contemplating the day's activities, Noel Galvin walked into the dining room, carrying his brief case. He greeted Quinn and sat down to join him for breakfast. "Well, my friend, ready for another exciting day I trust?"

"Yes. Actually, it should be. Don't you think? Seems to me we've closing in on the target. Hope so anyway."

"I agree. I think we could get out of here today although if you want to stay after we finish in the Land Records Office, you may want to tour around a bit."

Quinn had thought about that. There were a number of places in County Cork that he wished to visit, certainly including the old Desmond Homestead around Kinsale. Not only the Adams Estate lands but the old Desmond home before they inherited the Adams Estate. He hoped to be able to locate that when they visited the Land Records office today. That land was referenced in the Thomas Desmond Will as going to William and Michael, so they should be able to find the location of that. Also, he wanted to visit Cobh, the departure point for most of the Irish emigres but, in his thoughts at all times was his getting back to Anne.

Quinn had missed her on this trip and was in hopes that he could visit these significant sites when she was with him. That would make such a trip for him far more enjoyable than if he went alone, although he would certainly do that if she could not come along. He looked upon his trip to Cork and revisiting the old family sights as sort of a pilgrimage to a sacred place. Quinn was staring off into space and finally Galvin said, "Hey, wake up. It's time to get going."

The two men finished their breakfast, picked up their briefcases and umbrellas and headed for the Court House. It was a refreshing walk and by the time they arrived at the entrance, Quinn was wide awake and ready to get to work. They had the legal description of the lands transferred to Thomas Desmond and in no time, they were tracing the various documents affecting transfers of the land from Thomas Desmond to leasehold tenants and, in a few cases, of sales involving small sections to adjoining land owners. There was also a year-to-year lease transferring a small parcel consisting of five hectares of land described as "the Thomas Desmond cottage and yard" to "my son, William Desmond."

Quinn excitedly wrote down the legal description on the lease to William Desmond and captioned it, "original Desmond homestead." He commented to Galvin that the leased land was more than likely the ancestral home of the Desmonds.

Galvin agreed as it was a known fact that families held the same plots of land for generations until many of them lost their holdings during the Famine. He added that with Thomas Desmond serving as the Land Agent for the Adams Estate, he was in a slightly better position than other Irish tenants and was able to retain his five hectare parcel through the very difficult Famine years.

Quinn said, "He may have been better off than others, but apparently not well off enough to keep his family together. I know my grandfather never would have left if he had any other alternative." Galvin had made a few comments in the time that Quinn had known him to the effect that Quinn's great grandfather held a position in nineteenth century Ireland that put him at odds with the mass of the Irish population. Quinn had ignored the remarks for a couple of reasons. First, he knew it was true. The land agent was not loved by the tenants and secondly, Quinn had come to realize that Galvin was a true academic. If he had an opinion about anything, particularly relating to Irish nationalism, he would voice it regardless of what effect it might have on those around him. He did not do that to offend, rather it was more of a natural reaction to a stimulus of some sort. In this case, the stimulus was the fact that Thomas Desmond was able to hold onto his leased land.

The two continued paging through the land records, which were filed by date, in silence. After another hour or so, they were reviewing leases and deeds that were dated near the date of death of Thomas Desmond, May 12, 1879. Galvin commented that "We should find something here that explains why the property went to William. If not, there is a very serious title problem for William and his kids."

As they turned the pages, each expectantly studied the documents that followed, but nothing of significance turned up until October 12, 1879 when there was an entry for a Surrogate Court Order transferring the land previously described as the Thomas Desmond cottage and yard in fee title to William Desmond based on a review of the Will of Thomas Desmond and the filed certificate of death of Michael Desmond, co-grantee in the Will of Thomas Desmond.

"Interesting", commented Galvin. "We are getting someplace here. The Will has been filed and now we know that title is being transferred based on it. There should be a title transfer of all the remainder of the land coming up here pretty quick."

The two men pored over the following documents but found no further mention of the Will during the rest of 1879. Replacing that volume and taking the 1880 book from the shelves, they began carefully going over the records beginning with January 1. Finally on May 12, 1880, there was another entry from the Surrogate Court of County Cork transferring all property vested in the Estate of Thomas Desmond to his sole surviving son, William Desmond, including all lands formerly held under the Adams Estate. Both men looked at one another and said almost in unison, "Sole surviving son."

"When did your grandfather die, Quinn?"

"I know the exact date, July 30, 1932. He was almost a hundred years old and was as alert as ever. He was walking in the hot sun during the summer, which he should not have been doing, passed out and struck his head on the concrete walk."

"Let's read on." Galvin directed his attention back to the document filed by the Court. The court order read, "based upon the Will of Thomas Desmond, and death certificates on file herein, reciting the death of Jeremiah Desmond on February 20, 1879 and the death of Michael Desmond, August 14, 1879, all right, title and interest in and to all real and personal property included in the Estate of Thomas Desmond, shall vest in William Desmond according to the terms of the Will of Thomas Desmond dated September 16, 1878."

Galvin looked over at Quinn. "That's the will that we have copied. So, there was no codicil or follow on will to change that one. What the hell are they talking about though saying that Jeremiah Desmond is dead? We have to get the Court Record that is referenced in this order and see where that death certificate came from."

Both men copied up the Court File number on the document they were reading from, closed the book, returned it to the shelf and proceeded to the Court Clerk's desk to see what was in the referenced file. Within minutes, a sheaf of documents was handed to them and, after signing for it, they returned to the reading table and eagerly examined the contents.

The file contained administrative documents, a copy of the Thomas Desmond Will, Death Certificate of Michael Desmond, Statement of Survivorship completed by William Desmond and the Death Certificate of Jeremiah Desmond, a single person, showing that he died February 20, 1879 in the City of Columbus, County of Columbia, State of Wisconsin, in the United States of America. Included in the file was the Order of the Court transferring legal title to a lengthy land description that appeared to be the entire Estate of Thomas Desmond.

The two men looked at one another and the thought that entered Quinn's mind was that he possibly had been tracing the wrong Jeremiah Desmond. Noel Galvin was reviewing the same possibility and he began to run through the facts that negated that possibility. The overwhelming evidence that the Thomas Desmond that they had found in the records in the Library and the Archives was the father of Jeremiah Desmond was very convincing. Galvin told Quinn that he had little doubt that they were on the right track. The way he said it was not sufficiently convincing to Quinn and he continued to sit silently and review all of the birth, baptism, marriage and death records that they had been pouring over for the past month. The questions remained in Quinn's mind until he remembered the letters. The letters from William to his grandfather, Jeremiah, were absolute proof that they had the right person. The Death Certificate in the file was either a mistake or a fraud committed on the Court.

"Noel, the letters. They prove that we have the right Jeremiah Desmond. No doubt about it at all. The letters discuss the entire episode of Thomas marrying into the Adams Family, the sizeable Estate and the fact that Thomas inherited the property. There is no doubt. Jeremiah Desmond, my grandfather, was the rightful heir to the Estate of Thomas Desmond."

As the fact that the huge inheritance should have gone to his grandfather dawned on Quinn, he was silent for some time as he tried to absorb exactly what that meant. He had never pursued this matter with the thought in mind that he could benefit, in some manner, monetarily from the Estate. But now, the thought that his family had been unfairly deprived of property that was rightfully theirs took over his thinking. His immediate reaction was to dismiss the thought that he would interfere with the lives of living descendants of William Desmond who more than likely knew nothing of the error committed over one hundred years earlier. Furthermore, the property may well have been distributed over hundreds of descendants since that time and trying to recreate the Estate would be fruitless. Not only that but there were undoubtedly Statutes of Limitations to prevent attempts at rewriting one hundred plus years of legal history.

Nevertheless, the more Quinn thought about the death Certificate of Jeremiah Desmond that was lying on the table before him, the more he realized that it was not a mistake, it was an intentional act of fraud on the part of Jeremiah's brother, William Desmond. William knew Jeremiah was alive and well years after the date on the Death Certificate. The letters proved that as well. Quinn knew that fraud tolled all statutes of limitations and that the letters were valid evidence in a court of law by reason of the Ancient Documents Rule which gave validity to the letters based upon their age supported by the relevance of their contents.

Noel Galvin was the first to speak. "Well, this is most interesting. I would suggest that we follow the deeds on the Thomas Desmond Estate and see what happened to the property. If it stayed in the Desmond family and wasn't spread around to hundreds of people, you may wish to pursue, what looks like, your family's property."

"Noel, I haven't really thought about that, but I would like to see what happened to the Estate. Let's go back upstairs and check that out."

The two men went back up stairs to the Land Record books and continued following the ownership of the land from one generation of Desmonds to the next. William died in 1915 and passed on ownership of all lands to his son Dennis Desmond, residing at Park Ridge in Belfast, Northern Ireland. There were deeds from Dennis to a corporate owner, Desmond Enterprises with offices in Dublin and Belfast with Desmond Enterprises eventually becoming the fee title owner of all of the Estate Lands with the exception of the five hectare plat of land, described as the Thomas Desmond Homestead. That was transferred at the death of Dennis Desmond to his son, Patrick Desmond, of Park Ridge, Belfast, Northern Ireland. Patrick Desmond's name appeared on the most recent corporate documents relating to the lands and Galvin commented that he was undoubtedly the person administering the Desmond properties at the present time.

"Quinn, if I'm not mistaken, I would venture to say that the Desmond Enterprises mentioned in these land records is the same company that has a large chain of retail stores throughout the Republic and Northern Ireland. A very successful chain of stores, I might add. You must have seen them at one time or another since coming to Ireland. But now that I think of it, I don't believe there are any in Dublin City itself, only in the outskirts."

Quinn thought for a minute, "Yes, I did notice the Desmond name on stores. I saw two or three as the train passed through some of the larger towns, but I didn't think much of it because Desmond is such a common name, particularly the farther south you go. One of the fellows in the Library in Dublin was a Desmond and I asked him about it, but his family came from around Limerick."

"Anyway, Quinn. You have a good handle on who your relatives are and where they live. Park Ridge. Sounds pretty fancy to me. Maybe you'll live there some day." Galvin chuckled as he said that but Quinn ignored the jibe.

The two men sat for some time at the reading table absorbing what they had found. Quinn thanked Galvin for all of his help and said that he was ready to call it a day and head back to Dublin unless Galvin had other suggestions.

"I'm ready to go. I didn't lose anything here. I enjoyed working with you on this Quinn and hope that this is not the end. Seems to me, this could be the beginning depending upon what your intentions are."

"I'll have to work that out. I really haven't given it any thought. I suppose I'll contact this Patrick Desmond and just take it from there."

"Well, if you need some help, you know how to get ahold of me. Let's get out of here."

Within three hours Quinn and Galvin were sitting on the Express Train to Dublin and Quinn was deep in thought as to what his next move would be. He was eager to get back to Anne and he was also thinking about how he would go about contacting this Patrick Desmond. He could just grab a train and go up to Belfast, walk in and introduce himself or he could make the first contact by phone and wait for an invitation. He would work that one out later. Right now, he was thinking about spending time with Anne Flanagan.

As the train pulled into Connolly Station, the two men made ready to depart the train and Quinn again thanked Noel Galvin for all of his help. He wanted to do something to show his gratitude and made plans with Galvin to meet for lunch the following day. That way, Quinn would have time to purchase a gift of some sort and give it to him when they met. The train came to a stop and the doors slid open, allowing the waiting passengers to embark. As they walked along the ramp towards the exit gate, Galvin looked at his watch and commented that he could still make the "One Ireland" meeting and would be glad to take Quinn along if he cared to go.

The two men had talked about the "One Ireland" organization a number of times since they had met and Quinn had indicated an interest in attending a meeting. He had qualified that by saying that his interest was primarily based on his tourist curiosity and not particularly motivated by politics. Galvin said that the organization was more social than political anyway, and Quinn would enjoy the experience. Quinn said he had to make a phone call first and if Galvin could wait for that, he might be able to go along with him. Galvin waited in the lobby while Quinn went to the phone on the wall in the terminal and placed the call.

The phone rang two times and then he heard Anne's voice on the other end of the line. "I'm back. What's your schedule? I would really like to get together."

"Quinn, I would love to see you tonight, but I can't. My sister has dropped her kids off here and I'm on the hook until late. I don't have to work tomorrow though, hint, hint."

Quinn explained that he didn't expect to be back until tomorrow or he would have given her more of a warning. He then said that Galvin had invited him to attend the "One Ireland" meeting and he was going to do that but he would call her first thing in the morning and they would spend the day together.

"I would love that, Quinn. See you then, and I wish I was going to the meeting with you. I think you'll enjoy it. Depends on what sort of a program they have. Sometimes it's more political than I care for, but I know many of the people there and all of Sean's friends attend. Have a good time."

As Quinn hung up the phone, he gave the thumbs up sign to Galvin and said, "Let's go. I'd like to drop this bag off at the Hotel, if you don't mind. I don't want to haul this around all night long. You can leave yours there too, if you want."

The two men hailed a taxi and in minutes they were in the Hotel and dropping their bags off in Quinn's room. They then headed for a restaurant for a quick bite to eat and then hailed a taxi for the ride out to Ballsbridge and the meeting. Quinn was excited about attending. Sean had mentioned the group a number of times and it seemed to crop up in conversations with most everyone that he had met since arriving in Dublin.

The taxi pulled up in front of a large stone building located next to what appeared to have been a church at one time. Galvin explained that the property had been owned by the Anglican Church but had been purchased by "One Ireland" many years ago and now served as the National Headquarters and area social center of the organization. They also had other properties spread throughout the Republic and were, as Anne had said, a social and political group with roots that reached back to the days of Patrick Pearse and the Easter Rising of 1916. Pearse was said to be the founder of the group, but Galvin commented that it may have been more a case of him having been proclaimed the founder as he personified the goals and ideals of "One Ireland" and thus served as an excellent figurehead. In any event, apparently no one had complained as Quinn realized when he later saw Pearse's portrait proudly displayed in the center of the hall.

As Quinn and Galvin walked into the hall through the large wooden double doors, Quinn was struck by the fact that the building appeared much larger once they were inside. They had entered a huge room that seemed to Quinn to be about double the size of a football field. Hundreds of people milled about. Tables, staffed by young men and women, had been set up in the entry way for membership registrations, pamphlet displays, sign ups for coming events and just to answer questions from the growing throng that continued to pour through the double entry doors.

Quinn observed the crowd and noted that they were mostly young to middle-aged men and women who appeared to be a cross section of Irish society. Some appeared very well dressed, most likely professionals, and others could have been tradesmen, technicians or even farmers. They were a very gregarious group, obviously at ease and apparently quite familiar with one another. Quinn noticed a black wreathed photograph of a young man that was placed on the wall in the entry way and he inquired of Galvin as to who it was.

"That's Tom O'Rourke. The latest victim of the bloody English. That's the fellow they just shot down, not too far from here either. Bloody Provos got him, but they'll get theirs." As Galvin turned his gaze from the photograph on the wall, he grabbed Quinn's arm and said, "Interesting, there's the girl that was with him that night. She would have gotten it too, but Tom pushed her out of the way. Damn lucky girl. She's from Belfast they say, but she's not one of em. Poor girl. Took it pretty hard when Tom got it. Well, let's have a pint before it's all gone."

While they were in line to get a pint, Quinn looked back at the girl that Galvin had pointed out. She was well dressed. An attractive young woman that he figured was probably in her late twenties. Hard to tell the age of some of these girls. She must have gone through hell, he thought, but you wouldn't know it now. She was talking with a group of young men and women who were all laughing and obviously enjoying one another.

As Quinn drank the dark stout which he had come to enjoy since arriving in Dublin, he thought over Anne's comment that many of Sean's friends would be at the meeting. He looked over the crowd wondering if any of the fellows from the pub in Atlanta had returned to Ireland since the shooting. He searched for a familiar face but found none.

Quinn mentioned that Anne Flanagan, Sean's wife, was active with "One Ireland" and had commented that she would have enjoyed attending, but had other commitments this evening. Galvin confirmed that she was a member but not particularly into the political side of things. The way he said it, he made it clear to Quinn that she was not a member of the Irish nationalist inner circle. That was fine with Quinn. He was not into women with an aggressive political agenda who were constantly attempting to convert people around them into supporting their views. He had not detected any such interest on the Anne's part and if he had, he would have been long gone.

Quinn glanced through the program of the evening that he had picked up at the reception table and noted that there would be a short business meeting followed by a guest speaker, one Paddy O'Connell, who had been in the Maze Prison and was only recently released. That program was to last only thirty minutes and then a social hour would follow which would extend as long as there were sufficient people remaining in the hall.

While Quinn had been studying the program, Galvin was talking with a number of fellows with whom he was obviously well acquainted. He brought a few of them over to introduce to Quinn and, in doing so, would mention that Quinn was a friend of Sean Flanagan. Whenever he said that, Quinn noticed an immediate response on the part of whoever he was meeting. It was obvious from their reaction that these men held Sean in very high regard.

One young man in particular stayed to talk with Quinn about Sean and his life in Atlanta. As they continued talking, the young man mentioned that Joe Robbins, Sean's friend from Atlanta, was back in Dublin for a few days and would most likely be at the meeting. This came as quite a surprise to Quinn and he wondered if Galvin had been aware of it. When Galvin again joined into the conversation, Quinn asked him if he knew Joe Robbins was in Dublin.

Galvin said, "Quinn, I knew that two days ago and every time I thought about telling you, I would forget it before it came out. Old age is taking its toll, I guess. I apologize. He will be here this evening and you'll have a chance to talk with him. I think he's only in town for a day or two. I believe he has taken over Sean's duties in the States."

Quinn could tell that Galvin regretted adding the last sentence as the two had never really discussed what Sean's duties were. Quinn did know from Anne that his real purpose in being there had little to do with teaching Irish to college students. Quinn moved the conversation on by commenting, "Well when you see him, let me know. I want to say hello. I don't think Anne knows that he is in town either. I suppose he'll give her a call in the next day or so."

"Oh, for sure," Galvin added.

"There's our boy," Galvin said, taking Quinn's arm and pointing through the crowd at Joe Robbins. Robbins was surrounded by a group of apparently old friends who were glad to see that he was back in town. Galvin and Quinn made their way through the crowd and when Robbins saw Quinn, his face lit up in a broad smile and he walked over to him, holding out his hand.

"Quinn Parker, I'll be damned. Am I glad to see you. How are you? Don't answer, I can see that you are in good hands." Robbins slapped Galvin on the shoulder and it was obvious to Quinn that the two were close friends. Robbins said to Galvin, "I trust that you have registered Quinn as a life member of 'One Ireland' by now, right?"

Galvin laughed. "He's coming around. Give me a little more time. He's here, isn't he?"

"Good work, Noel. Quinn, how has your trip to the greatest city in the world been?" Robbins was obviously glad to see Quinn and he was also very obviously glad to be back in Dublin. The three men talked for the next few minutes about various topics, including the fact that Sean was dearly missed back in Atlanta and that Robbins was going to visit with Anne while he was home. He wished that he had more time to talk to Quinn to find out about his trip to Ireland, but he had a meeting in the staff room in the next building and he had to go. Quinn told him what Hotel he was staying at and Robbins said that he would contact him there. They shook hands and Robbins was gone.

In time the speaker was introduced. He was a young man in his early thirties and had served seven years in the Maze Prison in the North. He spoke about conditions in the Prison, the hunger strike that had taken place there and some personal anecdotes about fellows in the prison who were well known to the audience. As he told humorous stories about the men, there was laughter and when the tone of the story changed to the more brutal side of prison life in the North, occasional moans of pity came from the crowd for what the men were going through. To Quinn, it was an interesting talk because it gave him an insight into the struggle existing between the Irish people that he would not find elsewhere. He was glad that he had come to the meeting and told Galvin that he appreciated the fact that he had invited him along.

Quinn checked his watch and commented that it was getting close to his bed time. "What are your thoughts on heading back, or are you going to stay for a while?"

"Actually, Quinn, I was thinking that I would leave my gear in your room and pick it up tomorrow if that's alright with you. I can survive without the few things I have in that bag and I live in the opposite direction from the Hotel. Tell you what, the Dart train runs right up there and I can get one of the boys to see that you get on the train if you don't mind."

"No problem, Noel. I've ridden it before and I know exactly where to get off for my hotel, Pearse Station. It's just a couple of blocks from the hotel."

Galvin studied his watch, thought for a moment and said, "Tell you what, it's late. I don't want you wandering around dark streets on your own. I'm going to have one of the boys go with you."

Quinn protested, but Galvin insisted and walked over to a heavy set young man and spoke to him out of the hearing of Quinn. When he came

back, he introduced Quinn to the young man and said "Bryan here will
see you home safely. I'll give you a call tomorrow Quinn. Hope you had
a good time."

Quinn apologized to the young fellow for interrupting his evening, but
he only smiled and said it was no problem at all. "I'll see you back to your
hotel and then go over to the Temple Bar section where the real action is.
I don't mind this at all. Part of my job."

Quinn wondered exactly what his job was. Possibly, if Quinn asked
the right questions, in the right way, while they were on the train, he just
might find out. He was curious as to why Galvin had insisted that he have
someone accompany him back to his hotel. What did Galvin know that
Quinn did not. As they walked down the dark street to the Landsdowne
Road Station to catch the DART, Bryan was not very communicative
until Quinn mentioned that he was a friend of Sean Flanagan. Mentioning
Flanagan was like turning on a spigot as Bryan spoke of his admiration for
Sean the rest of the way to the Station.

As they were on the train for the short trip to Pearse Station, Quinn laid
out a little bait to see what type of response it would draw. "Too bad about
Tom O'Rourke. Apparently in the wrong place at the wrong time."

His comment drew an immediate response. "Provos were gunning for
him for some time. It's pretty hard to protect somebody like Tom all the
time. He didn't like to have his life restricted by having people like me on
him at all hours."

"Was that one of your assignments?"

"Yeh, it was. But not that night. One of the other boys."

Good timing on his part, Quinn thought. Walking from Pearse Station
the four blocks to the hotel must have made Bryan uneasy because he was
very quiet and constantly peering behind him and down side streets at
every intersection. Finally Quinn commented to him that he was certainly
checking everything out.

Bryan continued looking behind him as he responded. "Can't be too
careful Mr. Parker. Better safe than sorry, eh."

"I suppose." Quinn thought he would gamble a bit. "How do they
normally go about this sort of thing?"

"Usually, if they were to make a move on a night like tonight, they'd
do it from a car. Drive by, like they do in the States. It's quick and they're
outa here."

"Seems to me we couldn't do a hell of a lot about it if they came at us
right now. No place to hide."

"Trust me, there are places to hide. That's glass in that locked door right there. You'd be inside in a heartbeat and I would be doing my job from there. Then, we'd get the hell out of here before the Gardai showed up. I don't like to be interviewed by them. If I see what's coming down, nothings going to happen. That's the secret. See it coming down before it does come down."

Bryan didn't miss any part of his scan as he told Quinn how he did his job. Whatever it was that he was keeping an eye out for, Quinn was confident that he would see it before, as he said, it came down.

Within minutes they were walking up to the entryway to the Rockwell Hotel and Bryan took one last look up and down the street before bidding Quinn a good evening. He walked a few feet down the street, glanced at his watch and then shouted back at Quinn, "I trust you're not planning on going out for a walk this evening without me, right?"

Quinn laughed, "No way, Bryan. Way too late for a guy like me. Thanks and have a good one."

CHAPTER 31

Frank Baumler was just leaving the office when his secretary knocked and opened the door. "Mr. Baumler, there's a call on line two and it's Dublin. I told them you were on your way out but they say it's an emergency." Frank dropped his briefcase on the couch and picked up the phone. "Baumler here." He recognized the voice at the other end of the line as his assistant in charge of Dublin security operations.

"Frank, Ellen Desmond's friend was hit just minutes ago."

The news hit Baumler like a hammer. He fell back into his chair and swore. He had been keeping close touch on the situation involving Ellen Desmond and Tom O'Rourke for some time. It was the consensus of those closest to the scene that they had some breathing room before the Provos would move against the young man who was interfering with their drug operation on behalf of the INA. This was a complete surprise and Baumler was infuriated that his team had not seen this one coming. "You had our friends wired, I thought. What the hell happened?"

"Don't know Frank. It may have been handled by a different wing. There was nothing coming across from the bugs that indicated anything imminent was about to happen. We had wires on everything that could talk. Frank, we're as surprised as you are."

"Is Ellen OK and do you know if the old man knows anything about this? Give me the facts, what the hell happened!?"

"Frank, one at a time, please. Ellen is OK. Apparently this O'Rourke saw what was going down and pushed her aside. That is what saved her because bullets were flying all over the place. It was a drive by right when O'Rourke and the Desmond girl were leaving their apartment. Apparently the guys that did the hit were watching the place, waiting for them to leave. Our tail on Ellen Desmond was down the block and saw the whole thing happen but there was absolutely nothing he could do about it. It happened too fast. Bam Bam and they were gone. Automatic weapons that laid a spray all over both of them, but Ellen was on the ground when the full blast hit O'Rourke. We got a tag on the car and we're tracing it now, but we're sure it's stolen. Our boy on the scene says that he's sure Werner Hoffman was one of the guys firing. He had a fairly good look at the guy with the blond hair. We have called no one but you, so unless the girl has called her father, he probably doesn't know. This just happened less than half an hour ago. It's not on the news yet that we've seen. As far as Ellen is concerned, she is being sedated in her apartment and is under guard by Desmond Security people as we speak."

Frank Baumler was silent for a moment and then said, "OK. Keep me posted on what the hell's going on down there. Also, I want to know why we didn't know about this in advance. That's what the old man is going to be asking me and I would like to give some answers other than, we're just not real smart. Know what I mean?"

"Yeh, I know, Frank. We're trying to figure this one out ourselves. The Provos may have sniffed us out. I don't really know, but we'll check it out carefully. I'll be with the girl tonight. I'm sure the Gardai are going to want a statement from her and we'll stay with her until we hear otherwise from you, so let us know what you want us to do."

Frank hung up the phone, thought for a moment, looked at his watch and noting that it was almost six in the evening, called Patrick Desmond at Park Ridge. As the phone continued ringing, Baumler thought about how complicated his life had become in the last few months. Finally, a voice answered that Baumler recognized as Robert, the Houseman. "Robert, Baumler here. I'd like to speak with Mr. Desmond." Robert responded dutifully, "One moment, sir," and all Baumler could hear was the sound of Robert's footsteps disappearing down the hall. After a minute or two, Patrick picked up the phone and Baumler gave him the news of the shooting but immediately told him that Ellen was not hurt and was under heavy guard in her apartment in Dublin.

Patrick was in shock at the thought of his daughter being nearly gunned down in what he assumed was a Provo operation. When he got over his initial reaction which left him momentarily speechless, he was overcome by anger and rage at Carter who must have known that this was going to happen. He let loose with a string of expletives and when he had calmed down some, he asked Baumler the question that Baumler had no answer for. "How the hell did this happen and we not know anything about it?"

Baumler could only reply that they were investigating that right now. "They may have known about our bugs, we just don't know right now. When I have more facts, I'll give you a full report."

Patrick was concerned as to what might happen next. Did Baumler consider Ellen to be in any danger or was the attack directed solely at O'Rourke. Did Baumler have any indication that the Provos wanted to take her out as well or was her presence merely a chance happening that O'Rourke's attackers had not anticipated.

These were difficult questions for Baumler to answer. He knew that Patrick was extremely upset at hearing the news and when he had settled down a bit, he would be thinking this through more rationally and would arrive at some rather unpleasant conclusions. The foremost being that the Provos had to have known that O'Rourke was frequently accompanied by Ellen Desmond, the daughter of their most liberal benefactor. "Chief, I don't know that they wanted to take her out because I can only assume that if they had wanted to do that, they would have succeeded. They seldom screw up. Taking O'Rourke out with Ellen present may have just been an acceptable option to them. Had he been alone, I'm sure they would have still made the hit. With Ellen walking along side of him, that raised the ante quite a bit and that most likely had been considered well beforehand with approval coming from the highest levels of Unity. That is not a Dublin level decision. As to why they allowed that, I probably know less than you do. Were I to make a guess, I would say that they were sending a message to you, Ellen, Adam, or to all of you."

Patrick was now beginning to think more clearly about what Baumler was telling him. There was no doubt that his relationship with Unity had undergone a change in the last year. They had become more demanding, more belligerent towards him, less beholden to him for his contributions and that confirmed in Patrick's mind that they were receiving larger sums from some other source. Baumler's belief that their drug operations in the Republic were netting huge cash benefits could account for their changed attitude towards him. Yet, they apparently still needed him because they were an ever growing cancer in the Shipping Department of Desmond Enterprises. It seemed that their method of dealing with him had shifted from pleading for contributions to threats of reprisals of one form or another if he did not cooperate. They hadn't actually said that to him, but it appeared to Patrick that was where they were headed and drawing Ellen so close to the line of fire confirmed it in his mind.

Baumler was holding on the other end of the line and not having received a response from Patrick for some time, asked him if he was alright. "Yeh, I'm just thinking... this business is getting more complicated every day. I need some time to think. I'll talk with you tomorrow," and he hung up.

Patrick went into the study, closed the door behind him, and poured himself a tumbler full of Benedictine. He sat in the dark for a long time trying to get his thoughts together and come up with a course of action to follow with respect to Unity. He figured that whatever he did, he had to be very careful because they could turn the screw on him in twenty different ways. This Parker business was just one avenue they could take. They had virtual control over his Shipping Department and even if they hadn't, they could shut him down in a week if he didn't cooperate with them. There were many techniques they could use to attack a company that had vulnerable lines of supply to its retail stores, not to mention games that could be played with government regulations or labor squabbles that could be cooked up. Unity controlled the Unions and they could tighten the grip on Desmond Enterprises just as easily as they could the corner grocer.

Patrick's mood sunk deeper into gloom as he pondered his situation. He poured another tumbler of Benedictine and took refuge in the warm protective glow that it seemed to cast over him. The study was his fortress that gave him some protection from all the forces acting against him and when he was besieged by his enemies, he could think most clearly when he was safe behind its walls. He had to call Ellen and console her in the loss of a man that she obviously cared very deeply for. He would have to lay out his lines in advance because he was, by no means, aggrieved that O'Rourke was out of the picture. He was a threat and in a sense, the Provos had done him a favor. He was certain that was not the motive for the Provos action and it did not detract from his immense hatred of Carter for letting this happen, but it did offer him some solace at this moment.

When he had prepared himself adequately for the call, he dialed Ellen's apartment and a man's voice answered the phone. When Patrick identified himself, the person said, "Just a moment, sir, I'll see if she is able to take the call. She is quite despondent as I'm sure you understand." It was obvious that Baumler had informed the Dublin Security staff guarding Ellen that he had notified Patrick. After a pause that dragged on for a few minutes, Ellen picked up the phone and in a voice that Patrick had difficulty recognizing, said, "Daddy, I can't believe this. Who would do this to Tom? He was such a good man with a great future ahead of him. I just can't come to grips with this."

Patrick did his best to console his daughter and asked her if she wanted to return to Belfast. If she did, he would send a plane down to pick her up and she could be back at Park Ridge in a few hours. He wanted her to say yes, but he knew that she wouldn't return. That would be to run from the people that had harmed her so severely and that was contrary to her nature, but he had to ask.

She thanked him for his concern and assured him that she would be alright. She said that she had to cut the call short as the Gardai had arrived and had questions for her concerning the shooting. She added that she had nothing to offer them as Tom had violently thrown her to the ground just micro seconds before he was cut down by the bullets. She saw nothing.

She only heard the staccato burst of gunfire that seemed to light up the entire area around them. She saw Tom get hit but did not see where the gunfire came from or who was shooting. She had to go and would talk with him tomorrow.

Patrick sat quietly in the study for some time after he had hung up the phone. It was raining softly outside and there were no noises coming from the house other than the footsteps of Robert on the old wooden floor, outside the study, and later, as time passed, he heard what sounded like Adam entering the house and going up to his room. He seldom even saw Adam anymore. They seemed to operate on a different schedule and Patrick had made no effort to visit the Shipping Department since Adam went to work there. He had spoken to Frank Baumler about how Adam seemed to be under tremendous pressure the few times that he spoke with him, but had never learned anything specific that might explain his deteriorating appearance. Patrick had his own problems and Adam would have to handle his as best he saw fit.

Patrick filled the tumbler again, slowly sipped the liqueur, enjoying its anaesthetizing effect. His mind wandered over the years of his stewardship of Desmond Enterprises and as he thought about this, he could feel the eyes of his grandfather, William, boring holes through him from the portrait on the wall. With the alcohol giving him courage, he left the comfort of his heavy leather chair and walked up to the painting. "You couldn't have handled all of this any better than me, you old buzzard." He dropped his tumbler on the thick carpet of the study and made his way over to the couch where he awoke in the morning with the sun's rays shining in his eyes through the stained glass window panes.

Stan Morris had checked into the Rockwell the night before after being told by Frank Baumler that the Rockwell was where Parker was staying. He had given the clerk a twenty pound tip to buzz him when Quinn Parker reappeared from his trip. He had been in the Hotel for two days before the clerk signaled to him that he had some information of interest. When Stan walked up to the desk, the clerk leaned forward and told him in a low voice that Mr. Parker was returning that evening from his trip. He did not know when but Mr. Parker had said, that evening. Stan thanked the fellow and went up to his room. He checked the rail time table for the train to Dublin from cork and saw that one arrived in Dublin at 5:45 in the late afternoon and the next one came in at 8:15. That would most likely be the one that Quinn Parker was on and assuming Parker came directly to the Hotel from the Station, he should walk through the lobby at about 9:00 or shortly thereafter. Morris decided that he would station himself in the lobby, reading a newspaper at about that time and, just by accident, run into Quinn then.

That evening, at the appointed time, Morris seated himself on a couch in the lobby that afforded him a good view of the traffic entering the lobby and waited. He was off on the time because it was close to eleven before Quinn walked into the lobby of the hotel. As Quinn Parker retrieved his key and turned to head for the elevator, Morris, still holding the newspaper as though he was reading it, looked over in mock surprise and said, "Quinn Parker. Are you staying here?"

Quinn was surprised to hear his name called by this person who appeared somewhat familiar, but he could not place where he had seen him before. He walked over to Morris and said, "Yes, I am but I'm sorry, must be age, I just can't place where we have met. I recognize you but..."

Stan Morris held out his hand to shake Parker's, "Stan Morris, Cosmic Engineering. We met in Atlanta at the Library. I'm sorry to put you on the spot. In my business, I write everybody's name down on a note pad and when I saw you come in the door, I had to pull it out and check so I was a bit unfair in being able to come up with yours so easily. I am staying here for a day or so to do some work in the Library. You may recall, my Irish side came from Clonakilty, down in Cork and I'm still working on that from time to time. You know how that business sort of grows on you."

The two men talked for some time and Morris suggested they retire to the Hotel pub for a pint as he was about to go up to his room and would not mind a nightcap before he did so. Quinn was very agreeable to that as he had spent a long day in Cork, finishing up his work and wanted to relax. He told Morris to go ahead and get a table in the bar while he checked the desk for messages that may have come in while he was gone.

When Quinn entered the pub, Stan Morris waved him over to the table that he had secured and pushed a pint of Guinness over to him. Quinn thanked him, tipped his glass to Morris and took a drink of the heavy dark beer. He had eaten only a sandwich on the train with a cup of tea since breakfast. He was not only hungry, he was thirsty. After he had relaxed a bit, he began to ask Morris questions about his business, his travels and how he was going to be spending his time in Dublin. Morris had ready answers for each of these and told Quinn that as far as looking at microfilm in the Library he had a maximum tolerance level of two days, so he would most likely be leaving town then. He had to do some work up in Belfast for a few days and then back home to London.

After the small talk was exhausted and they had refilled their glasses of beer, Morris brought the conversation around to Quinn's research in the Library. Quinn's answers were rather short and not too informative on what he was coming up with, other than the fact that he had been down to Cork. After a while, Morris concluded that Parker was just not going to open up any further on what he was learning in his research. He decided to approach the subject from another angle and asked Quinn if he had located any living relatives in Ireland and if so, was he going to visit them. As Morris added, "That would really put the frosting on your trip over here."

Parker did acknowledge that he was very close to coming up with the names of descendants and would probably be going to the Archives in the morning to do just that. He figured that the 1911 Census would provide some information although, and then he made what Morris assumed was a slip, "my people may now be up in Ulster."

Morris considered Parker's comment very telling, but he did not show his heightened interest. Instead, he picked up the conversation without missing a beat. "Quinn, remember that the Republic didn't gain its Independence until the latter part of 1921 so Census records for the North before then should likewise be available in the Archives. In fact I've heard that the North has the records, but they are not available for research. Why, I don't know."

Parker thanked Morris for telling him that. He had just presumed that the old records for the six counties of the North would be archived up there and not available in the Republic. "Well, that's good to know. Maybe I will be able to make some progress in the Archives after all. I was thinking it was going to be wasted effort. Thanks for the tip." Parker then went on to discuss other activities in Dublin that he wanted to take in while he was here and did not bring up his research again which Morris interpreted as his wish not to discuss the matter any further. Morris found that interesting as well.

Stan Morris was not privy to the reason for his being assigned to learn about Quinn Parker's genealogy project. He had presumed that there must have been some problem regarding the Desmond family that posed a threat of some sort to Patrick Desmond but what it could be, he had no idea. Furthermore, he had no great personal interest. He would call Baumler in the morning and let him know what he had learned and maybe that would be enough to end his trip to Dublin. He would find out tomorrow. The two men sat in the pub discussing events in Ireland and in the States for another half hour and then Quinn said that he had to call it a day.

As Morris went up to his room, he thought about Quinn's comment that "His people may be up in Ulster." He would have to remind Baumler that it would be best if Quinn did not run into him around the Desmond offices. That might be hard to explain. Maybe he could work this into an Austrian ski trip.

CHAPTER 32

Back at Desmond Enterprises, Frank Baumler had informed Ted Somers of his conversation with Adam Desmond regarding the cargo containers and what might be happening to them. The two men concluded that extra containers being sent to Southeast Asia were undoubtedly being used to transport narcotics back to Belfast for trans-shipment to the Republic and Desmond Enterprises appeared to be a key player in the operation. The containers must have been receiving customs seals at the point of embarkation which gave them free transfer without inspection when they arrived in Belfast. Not too difficult to get the seals if you paid enough money for them.

The question remained as to where they were going once they arrived in Belfast. Somers stood up, walked to the door, turned and said, "I know, Boss. We'll get the answer. They have to go someplace, someplace like maybe Dublin."

Baumler nodded in agreement. "That's what I would say."

Patrick Desmond was sitting at his desk in his office when Martha buzzed him and said Frank Baumler wanted to meet with him if he was available. Patrick told her to have him come up but that he had better hurry as Patrick had to leave for a meeting with Tony Carter. Within minutes, Baumler was ushered into Patrick's office and after he had closed the door, Patrick motioned for him to take a seat. Frank got right to the point and gave Patrick the information that Stan Morris had provided regarding Quinn Parker having apparently zeroed in on Patrick.

"There are still some doubts, Chief, but it looks as though he will be contacting you shortly. I thought you would like to know this. I have one of our men staying in the same hotel in Dublin as this Parker and I don't know if you want him to stay there or not. I personally don't see that he can do much more good by staying down there as it is rather clear now that this Parker's next move will be to give you a call. You'll know more about him then than our guys will who are following him around."

Patrick thought for a moment. "Interesting. I suppose Carter knows all of this. I have to meet him down by the wharf in thirty minutes. He called me earlier this morning and maybe it relates to what you have to say. We'll see. Or, maybe he just wants more money. Anyway, this guy

Parker is tenacious and it looks like sooner or later, I'm bound to be sitting here looking across my desk at him. I wonder what he wants. So far, no one seems to know, at least they're not telling me. Maybe he just wants to say hello and we're eating our guts out over nothing. As for your guy in Dublin. Cut him loose. We're just wasting money on having him park down there. Wait on calling him though until this evening. If Carter has anything of interest, we may want to use this guy in Dublin for who knows what. While you're here, Frank, what's going on with Ellen?"

"She seems to be coming along fine. She attended the funeral for this O'Rourke and that went along without a hitch. I am told that she is continuing her involvement with 'One Ireland' which tells me that her interest in the group was not related solely to O'Rourke. I am sure there is a lot of anger on her part against the Provos and maybe this is her way of getting even. Obviously the INA would like to convert her to their way of thinking and we should keep an eye on that. As far as what counteraction we might expect for the shooting of O'Rourke, I would assume that we will see something from the INA up here but I see no risk for Ellen. She is working again. In fact, she didn't miss a day other than the day of the funeral. I am told she is doing a great job running the office down there for whatever that's worth. If you're thinking about going down there, be sure and give me a warning."

"No, Frank. I'm not planning on going down there right now. I wouldn't want to miss meeting my cousin." Patrick smiled at that as did Baumler who then stood up, picked up his notepad and turned to leave. As Baumler walked out the door, Patrick thanked him for keeping him posted and told him that if he didn't call him by five in the evening to pull off his guy in Dublin. He would just wait for Parker to contact him.

CHAPTER 33

Patrick went to meet Tony Carter down by the wharf again at the statue of King William III. There was a light breeze blowing from the fish stalls towards the parking area adjacent to the where the statue was located and the smell was overpowering. It was not raining as of yet, although the sky was overcast and threatening. Patrick stayed in his car, out of the cold wind, and waited for Carter to show up. As he sat in the car, he looked over at the shipyards on the other side of the water from the fish stalls and he could see a number of ships undergoing maintenance or overhaul at the Belfast Docks. He had not spoken with Hillary in over a week as they intentionally or otherwise worked different schedules. He had heard her enter or leave Park Ridge at various times throughout the week, but had made no attempt to talk with her nor had she with him. Patrick was aware that she had spoken with Ellen a time or two since the shooting, but Patrick had no great interest in knowing what was said. He had heard everything from Ellen and didn't need Hillary to interpret for him. As he thought about her, Patrick figured that Tony Carter more than likely had more information concerning her whereabouts than he did.

Ten minutes after the appointed meeting time, Tony Carter walked up to the Statue and came into Patrick's view. Patrick walked over to him and the two exchanged pleasantries. Carter commented on the fact that he should have suggested a warmer meeting place and Patrick agreed. There was a small tea shop down the street and the two headed over there walking in silence. When they sat down, each ordered a cup of tea and both waited for the other to speak.

As Patrick looked across the table at Tony Carter, he noticed that Carter was not all smiles as he had been for the past month or so since he had been borrowing Patrick's wife. Patrick sipped his tea and took in the changed demeanor of the Unity representative and wondered what had occurred to interfere with his enjoyable pursuit of pleasure. Patrick was almost at the point where he was not worrying about anything anymore. He was tired of it. He was tired of Carter, Hillary, Unity, his business and everything with the possible exception of Ellen and Martha. He was almost enjoying his new attitude, because he was beginning to worry less about everything he had worried about before. Patrick knew that was not necessarily a good trend and was possibly related to the fact that lately he had been virtually drinking himself to sleep at night. If he didn't, he just could not get to sleep. It was one worrisome thought after another and the next thing he knew, it would be morning.

As these thoughts were crossing Patrick's mind, Carter finally spoke, "You aren't looking real hot these days, Patrick. Anything bothering you?"

Patrick knew his appearance had deteriorated lately. His face was constantly flushed, he was putting on the pounds and Martha had told him that he had better start exercising and stop drinking so much or he wouldn't be around much longer. He reddened a bit at Carter's insolence and said, "Why hell no, nothing's bothering me. Why should it?" As he spoke, the thought of Ellen almost getting killed in the shooting of O'Rourke flashed across his mind and he blurted out, "What the hell were you people thinking about blasting that son of a bitch with my daughter standing right next to him? You knew damn well that she was most likely going to be with him. What the hell were you trying to do?"

Carter was a bit taken back by Patrick's outburst, but he quickly gained control of himself and said, "I don't know what you're talking about. I heard about it like everybody else but Unity had nothing to do with that. It was a drug related shooting. That's what the press said and that's just the way it sounds."

Patrick was angered even more by Carter's denial. "Don't give me that cheap shit. You and your people knew well in advance that shooting was going to take place and you did it right in front of my daughter's apartment. Don't bullshit me Tony. I've about had it with you bastards. I've supported your movement through the years because I believed in what you were trying to do, but lately it seems you have another agenda. Maybe it's to make money, I don't know." Patrick knew he should not have said that as it implied he might know something about what Unity was doing, selling drugs in the Republic. Having made the slip calmed him down a bit and he thought he had better keep his mouth shut. He had said enough.

Carter did not respond. He was clearly digesting Patrick's last statement and he sat staring at Patrick as though waiting for him to expand on what he had said. After a while when it was apparent that Patrick was not going to speak further, Carter said, "Well... I'm sorry about what happened to Ellen, Patrick. I really am, but believe me, we were not involved."

Patrick wanted very much to tell him that he knew Unity was involved because they had taps on their cars and phones but he would just have to sit and listen to Carter as he tried to lie his way out of being involved in the shooting. Baumler had told Patrick that Carter was one of the key people in the drug trade with the south and as such, he had to be involved in making the decision to hit O'Rourke and when to do it. It was difficult to sit there and pretend he had no further information to support his outburst, but he did. Patrick closed out further discussion on this topic by saying that if he learned that Unity was involved in the shooting, Tony Carter could kiss any further contributions goodbye.

Tony Carter just shook his head. "I hope you have solid evidence before you take that step. We need your help and frankly you need us. It's not just a one way street with you helping us. You know that, I'm sure."

"Let's just skip all that and move on, Tony. What's on your mind today that brought about this little get together?"

Carter nodded. "Fine, OK... what I wanted to tell you is that your long lost cousin is in Dublin and has been down to Cork checking out Probate records. He is accompanied by a fine fellow who we are quite sure is backed and directed by the INA. Anyway, the guy has him aimed now at the Patrick Desmond family in Belfast. That, sir, is you. Any comments thus far?"

Patrick thought for a moment. He knew all of this but had to give the appearance of just having learned of it. "So, what does all of this mean. Maybe he wants to meet me and then he'll get on a plane and go back to wherever the hell he's from."

"Come now, Patrick, you don't really think the INA would let this guy slip through their fingers without doing some damage to Unity's number one contributor do you? From what we know, the very least he could do would be to tie Desmond Enterprises in knots with litigation. I will give it to you straight. We think he is a very real threat to you. What would you like us to do about it?"

Carter sat staring at Patrick. He clearly wanted Patrick to give the green light to do a hit on Quinn Parker so that they could remind him of that in the future. Patrick had considered praying to God that this Parker was run over by a tour bus or whatever, but he had no stomach for giving the OK for a hit.

Patrick shook his head and fingering the embroidered stitching in the table cloth mumbled, "What you people in Unity do is your business. I will just wait to hear what the fellow has to say and then make up my mind. If I have to, I will just pay him off. I don't know right now."

"Patrick, it might be too late then. The INA is working this guy hard. They see a shot at Desmond Enterprises. All of it. All the property, assets and everything that goes along with it. Right now, he's just some unknown tourist, wandering around Ireland, looking at old castles. If he starts a lawsuit and files for protective orders over his anticipated properties and then has a sudden unfortunate accident, half the world will be investigating it. Now is the time to get rid of this guy."

"If you want to hit the guy, that's your business. I'm not into that sort of thing. I sell retail clothing and try to run a legitimate business. You do what you have to do, leave me out of it."

Carter shook his head. "We may have to. Your company is important to us, even if it isn't to you. Oh, what the hell, I have another meeting I have to go to."

As Patrick drove back to his office, he began to feel guilty that he had not strongly objected to Carter's talk of putting a hit on Parker. Was he, by not arguing strongly against the hit, as guilty as the guy that pulls the trigger. What kind of animal was he becoming? These thoughts plagued him as he drove through the busy Belfast streets and he knew they would join the other disturbing thoughts that came to him in the dark of night as he tried to drift off to sleep. The meeting had depressed him and he decided to stop by the Club for a little something to lift his spirits.

Patrick drove over to the Royal Ulster Golf Club, gave his car to the attendant and made his way back to the lounge. There were a few people there but Patrick did not know them so he did not have to pretend to be sociable as he made his way directly to the bar. As he climbed up on the stool and made himself comfortable, the bartender, Kenny, came over and asked him, "Absolute and tonic, Mr. Desmond?"

"Please, Kenny." When the drink came, Patrick made small talk with the bartender, asking him how business had been, how his family was and what was going on in the Club.

Kenny was not a talkative sort but he did like Mr. Desmond and he, as well as virtually everyone else in the Club, knew what was going on between Hillary and her latest tennis partner, Tony Carter. Kenny also knew who Tony Carter was and the weight that he carried in the Union Halls so, as far as Kenny was concerned, it was a good idea to stay on his good side. Kenny went along with that, but when no one was around to listen, he made it a point to let Mr. Desmond know a thing or two about Mr. Carter's personal activities. "Mr. Desmond, your wife was just in here with her tennis partner. They just left a few minutes ago."

Interesting thought Patrick. That must have been the luncheon meeting that Tony had to take off for. Apparently he didn't think it was necessary to tell me he was having lunch with my wife. Oh, what the hell do I care anyway. Patrick acknowledged what Kenny had said and commented that possibly Hillary had gone back to Park Ridge. As he thought about the fact that she might be at the house this very moment, maybe he could catch her there and discuss a few things. He ordered another to fortify himself in case she really was at the house.

When Patrick returned to the house, Hillary was not there. He assumed they had gone to his place and were, at this very moment, in some contorted position, gasping for breath. Well, let them have their fun because one of these days the shoe is going to drop. The possibility that Somer's investigation might uncover embarrassing facts that could seriously damage Desmond Enterprises, did not enter his thought process. He was so intent upon destroying Carter and embarrassing his errant wife that he did not care what it did to his own company. His hatred for Carter, Unity and Hillary had overtaken virtually every aspect of his life. All he could think of was how he was going to destroy all of them.

Martha had long ago grown tired of hearing him rant and rave about how evil the two of them were. She had told him that if he kept it up, it was like a cancer and it would destroy him. There were other, more productive ways of dealing with the problem presented by those two and it wasn't to sit in a dark corner, drinking and thinking about all of the things he was going to do to them to get even. Patrick knew that Martha was right and he had tried to forget about them, but it would only last a day or two and he would be back at it again.

Ted Somers rapped on the office door and when he heard Baumler's gruff voice, "Come in," he walked in and sat down on the couch. When he first came to Desmond, Somers used to stand and wait for Frank Baumler to tell him to have a chair but after the second or third "For God's sake, sit down. You make me nervous," Somers just entered, took a seat and gave his report.

"Frank, we've got it all set up. Adam's getting us a list of inbound shipments. We'll have our men at the dock and tail every truck load that comes off the boats. One or two of those loads are going somewhere that we don't know about. We've been wasting our time checking inventory records and we should have been checking the container inventory." Adam did a good job on this one. The two men talked about other security matters and how Adam Desmond appeared to be dealing with the events taking place in his department. Somers had spoken with him, but only off company property. He didn't want anyone in Unity to see he and Adam together.

Three days later, Somers was sitting in Baumler's office reading to him from a notepad. "Seventeen sealed containers came off the "London Belle" on Tuesday morning with Desmond shipping bills calling for delivery in

Belfast and Dublin. Ten of the seventeen for Dublin. All of the paperwork appeared to be correct and all seals were unbroken and seemed normal in every respect according to Denny. The trucks were all followed by our security staff and the ones going to our warehouses here all arrived and are accounted for. The ones going to Dublin, passed through the Republic Inspection Station, without incident. The paperwork had already been stamped by inbound customs at the wharf. There were three trucks, two with four each and one truck with two containers. Our men followed two trucks, carrying eight containers, that went to the Dublin warehouse and were unloaded there. No problem with that shipment. One truck with two containers went to a warehouse in Dublin that has nothing to do with Desmond. We're watching the place right now. The driver was, of course, a Unity man. That's it Boss. What do we do now?"

As the two men sat in silence in Baumler's office, Frank made up his mind. He would have a meeting with Patrick and lay out the facts. Unity and Carter were using Desmond Enterprises for more than a source of contributions. Desmond was a key conduit in their real financing operation, selling high quantities of drugs in the Republic. No wonder they nailed that O'Rourke. If Patrick appeared at all incapable of dealing with the realities of the situation, Frank could contact Ellen and try to bring her into the picture, but he was not sure how she would react to that. He had doubts in his own mind that informing the Royal Ulster Constabulary as to what was going on was a good idea.

They had their own political alliances and it was a known fact that Unity had great influence at all levels of the R.U.C.

The following day when Patrick passed by Martha's desk on his way to his office, Martha stopped him and said that Baumler wanted to talk with him again. Patrick said, "Send him up." As he continued on into his office, Martha checked her watch and noted that it was going on eleven o'clock. He was arriving later and later every day. She knew that he was drinking heavily, particularly when he was not with her and she had not seen him since he left the office for his meeting with Carter the previous day. Martha dialed Baumler's office and told him that Patrick was there and could meet with him now.

"Chief, we've got some info." Frank Baumler went on to explain to Patrick what Ted Somers had told him the previous day. He then went on to say, "It's obvious what's going on. The question is how to deal with it. Go to Unity? Go to the RUC? The Gardai? It's your call."

Patrick sat staring off into space trying to absorb what Baumler had told him. He spoke with an almost pleading sound to his voice, "What do you think we ought to do?"

Baumler leaned back in his chair. "Well Chief, there are drawbacks to almost any course of action that we take."

Patrick mumbled a response, "Yes, I suppose so."

Baumler explained the risks they faced in reporting the matter to the authorities. "Unity has people placed in every office of the R.U.C., and as soon as we report it, word will get back to Unity that we know what is going on. They will immediately go into their damage control mode and, most likely, attempt to lay the blame right on us. Like we were running the show. After all, Chief, there is an awful lot of evidence pointing to our involvement. Our containers, our trucks, our warehouses, and probably some of our people may even be involved. At this point, we don't know that they are not."

Patrick just sat at his desk nodding his head in agreement with what Baumler was telling him. He asked no questions, but Baumler had the impression that much of what he was saying was not totally registering.

Waiting for Patrick to inquire further and receiving nothing but silence, Baumler went on, "Now Somers and I have figured that the way they got the contraband from Thailand to Belfast was that they used the extra empty containers that are sent out of here for delivery to Thailand in case we have additional orders finalized after the ship departs. Those empty containers, that are presumably not going to be used, sit in the ship, in the harbor at Bangkok, while contraband of whatever kind is hauled onto the ship. That is all done before it is quarantined and shipping bills for the authentic sealed containers are delivered to the Captain. The ship itself is never inspected at Bangkok, only at Belfast. After departure, the goods are brought out from wherever, loaded into the extra containers, sealed, locked and the false papers are pulled out to get the phony containers through customs in Belfast. Actually quite simple. Again, no direct proof, but it has to be worked pretty much like that for extras to come through."

Patrick sat without comment for a while. "Yeh, I suppose that's how it would be done."

After a long pause, Patrick finally spoke, "I have no idea what we should do here."

"I agree, Chief, it's a tough call."

The two sat talking over various alternatives, each of which eventually ran into a brick wall. Finally Baumler suggested the possibility of going to Carter and telling him that we know what is going on. Tell him to put a stop to this now or we are going to report it to the RUC, the Press, Gardai and whoever else wants to know about it. The trade off to Carter would be that we won't report it if he pulls the operation out of Desmond Enterprises.

Patrick was silent as he pondered Baumler's proposal. He didn't say it, but he was questioning his own backbone to stand up to Carter in what would be a difficult confrontation. If Carter told him to go ahead and call in the authorities, what would he do then. All of these thoughts were working on him. He set down the letter opener that he had been turning slowly in his hands. He told Baumler he'd talk to him later in the day. He had to think.

Later on in the afternoon, Patrick called Baumler on the telephone and told him that he would follow through on his suggestion. He also told Baumler to see that Adam was protected from being set up by the Unity employees as the fall guy should the R.U.C. get involved.

Baumler assured him that he had already taken steps to ensure that did not happen. After he hung up the phone, Patrick told himself, "Well, here goes," and he called Martha on the intercom and told her to set up a meeting with Tony Carter. Fifteen minutes later, Martha buzzed him and said that she had a meeting scheduled at the café by the wharf where they had met last time. She said that Carter told her that you would know where that was. Carter would be there in an hour, at five p.m.

Patrick left the office immediately and headed for a pub that was a short distance from the wharf. No one knew him there and he had used it previously as a momentary refuge where he could have a stiff drink or two without interruption or interference. There were a few workmen sitting at a table in the pub, but no one at the bar. Patrick walked in, pulled up a barstool and ordered a vodka tonic, "Light on the tonic." The bartender recognized him from previous visits, but did not intrude on his thoughts. Patrick mulled over exactly how he was going to handle the task at hand, but every time he would come up with a scenario that he thought would be the least painful, he would think of something that would detract from it. As the minutes passed by, without coming to any set plan, he noted that it was almost time to meet Carter. Reluctantly he downed his drink, picked up his coat and left the bar. He did not want to miss Carter and go through another afternoon like this one.

There was an empty parking slot just up the street from the café, and Patrick maneuvered his car into the space, locked it and walked up the street to his rendevous with Tony Carter. He had not figured out how he was going to deal with the purpose of the meeting. As he walked towards the café, he tried his best to psyche himself up to face the man who in normal circumstances had the ability to rattle him, not to mention at times such as this. When he entered the café, he saw Carter sitting off to the side of the seating area and the only other people present appeared to be the cook and the waitress. Carter gave him a half hearted smile and waved him over to the table. The waitress came up and took his order for tea while he hung his coat up on the rack.

As Patrick sat down at the table, Carter said, "Saw your car parked outside of Gallivan's Pub so I figured this had to be important." He chuckled as he said it which further unnerved Patrick.

Patrick mumbled that he had to meet someone there that was doing some work on the house at Park Ridge. After he had said that, he was ashamed that he had let Carter get in the first direct hit. He would have to get control of himself or this was going to be a disaster.

Carter sat staring at the obviously tense Patrick Desmond, wondering just what was on the mind of the President of Desmond Enterprises that led to this meeting. As the seconds ticked by with no change in Patrick's expression, Carter became impatient. Finally, Carter looked at his watch and commented that he was short on time, "So let's get down to business. What's on your mind?"

Patrick would have preferred a few minutes to get as comfortable as possible before getting into what he had to say but he was not afforded the opportunity. "Well, uh... there are some things that we need to talk about."

"Fine, let's talk."

"You know that our Security Office has been investigating the Shipping Department for the past month or so."

"Tell me something I don't know. What the hell do you think I've been calling you about... for the past month or so. Get to the point."

Carter's attitude was even more insulting and arrogant today than usual which was destroying the last vestiges of Patrick's confidence.

"Well... they know all about it."

Carter tensed up just enough so that Patrick could notice it. "Know all about what? Get to it."

"They know how you are running drugs using the Company."

"What do you mean, 'I am running drugs'? Are you drunk?"

"They're pretty sure it's a Unity operation and that you are involved." As soon as Patrick said that, he knew it was a mistake. It told Carter that they did not have absolute proof it was Unity or that Carter ran the show. "Uh... what I mean is... that they have the whole system figured out and it has to be Unity that is doing it."

It was dawning on Carter that behind this bumbling fool, there were people working for Desmond Enterprises that had some brains and that they may have stumbled onto something. He knew Desmond Security had been hanging around the shipping area with Unity as the target, but Carter's people had been very careful.

"Patrick, I don't know what the hell you've been told. Unity has far more important things to do than to get involved in that business. Someone may be peddling some drugs that works for Desmond or maybe one of our low level troops is selling an ounce here or there. That's possible but nothing we know about. We'd can his ass in a heartbeat if we knew that was going on. Christ, Patrick. This is ridiculous."

By now, Carter was visibly angry and had raised his voice to the point that Patrick was becoming concerned that the others in the restaurant would overhear what he was saying. "Hold it down... for God's sake; let's not tell the whole world." The two men were silent for a moment and then Patrick responded.

A drop of perspiration had built up on Patrick's lip and he brushed it off. "It involves large shipments, Tony. This is not an ounce we're talking about. I would think you would know about it. You're people run the Department."

"What the hell do you mean, my people run the Department? Your own son is the Superintendent of Shipping. He runs the Department."

That remark brought the trace of a smile on Patrick's face. "We both know that Adam runs nothing. I wish it were otherwise, but that, unfortunately, is a fact."

Patrick had said enough to make Carter uneasy, but Carter did not want to appear concerned. He was fairly sure from watching and listening to Patrick, that Patrick was not completely certain about anything he had said thus far. What bothered Carter though was the thought that the investigators back at Desmond were far less unsure of what they had than Patrick. If there was any chance of putting a stop to this investigation from proceeding further, it was now.

"Look, Patrick, let's talk sense. I'm glad you brought this up. If there is any shred of truth to this, we want to know about it. With all of our men working at Desmond, we don't need any bad publicity. You don't need it either. If some of our guys are involved, tell us and we'll get them the hell out of there. You know as well as I that in every barrel, there are some bad apples. It can't be helped. They just as well could be your people, and maybe our boys can ferret them out. We can work together on this. Tell your security guy to give me a call and we'll cooperate to the fullest on this. Now, in return, I want you to call off your dogs from harassing our boys in Shipping. They can't unload a box of shirts without some jack ass peering over their shoulders. How the hell would you like it if someone was watching you all day long. Now, can I have your word on that? We've put up with this long enough."

Patrick was losing what little control he had left. He came here to get Unity to stop using his company in their drug operation and Carter was demanding that he order the investigation to come to a halt. "...Ah... Security is pretty sure Unity is involved in this drug operation."

"Patrick, you've said that already and I'm getting a little pissed. Unity is not, has not and will not, get involved in any drug operation, anywhere, so just drop it. If you're wise-ass security guy tries to put that label on Unity, you can kiss contract negotiations out the window. That's next month, you know. Also, for your information, Customs is wanting to jack up tariffs another twelve percent. We might be able to hold that down to two or three percent for Desmond, but not if your boys are out to destroy us. Patrick, remember that we both benefit when we work together. We have for years and we should for many more years to come. Look at your profits. I know what they are. I probably get the profit and loss statement before you do. Don't you want to keep those profits up there? I would. Remember this Patrick, you need us and we need you."

What Carter did not say was that he needed Desmond a lot more than Desmond needed him. This was just one more bucket of crap that Carter had to solve or he'd be back on the street, or worse. This Parker guy and now this. Both could bring him down and he knew it. The proceeds from the importation of heroin from Southeast Asia dwarfed, many fold, the contributions to Unity by Desmond Enterprises. That had always been his concern about Parker. If the INA was successful with Parker, they would lose this valuable conduit in their supply chain. They had worked years to get control of Desmond shipping. They couldn't afford to lose it now.

It was almost laughable to Carter to think that Unity was clearing a path through the maze of regulatory restrictions for Desmond Enterprises because of their annual two hundred thousand Irish Pound contribution. It was the valuable drug trade conduit that Unity was interested in protecting. Unity had assigned to Carter the primary responsibility of seeing that this conduit remained clear of obstacles and thus far he had succeeded, but there were threatening specters looming on the horizon. Carter was considerably more unnerved by this conversation with Patrick than he let on.

Ellen Desmond was another one that concerned Carter as a threat to his control over Desmond Enterprise management which was why he had ordered the hit on O'Rourke to be conducted in such a manner that it would make a lasting impression on her. He would have to wait and see if her attitude was changed by her near death experience. If not, he would have to handle the problem more aggressively.

One problem at a time, he thought. As for Parker, that problem was about to be resolved. Carter had issued the order to remove Parker as an obstacle and he expected word from the Provo Specials at any moment that the goal had been achieved.

What Carter was hearing in this meeting with Patrick Desmond greatly concerned him but as long as Patrick was president of the company, Carter was confident that he could control him and through him, Carter could control the staff of Desmond Security. If Patrick gave the word that the investigation was to stop, it would stop and Carter was fully aware of that fact.

The two sat at the table drinking their tea without further comment. Carter looked over at Patrick and thought to himself that as long as he was at the helm of Desmond Enterprises, Carter's position with Unity was secure. He knew Patrick was drinking too much, too often, and he was a bit concerned for his health. Hopefully, when Patrick had the big one, Adam could be pushed into the top slot and Carter could basically run the company with minimal interference. That plan assumed that somehow Ellen would be sidetracked from taking over the top office in the company.

Carter had initially considered Hillary to be a potential problem, but as of late, he had pretty much neutralized that one with what he viewed as his overpowering prowess in bed. She had done his bidding on a number of important staff changes as of late and as long as that continued, he was not concerned. If and when she was not cooperative, he had some thoughts as to how he could remove her as a problem. She was known to drink to excess and had already had a few close ones when behind the wheel of her Silver Shadow Rolls. He hoped he did not have to expedite her removal from the scene as he had actually enjoyed having her around.

Finally Carter looked at his watch and said, "Gotta go. Business to attend to, my friend." He reached over and slapped Patrick on the shoulder as one friend to another.

Patrick just nodded and said, "Go ahead. I'm going to have a sandwich while I'm here. I'll talk with you later." Actually, Patrick was absolutely drained of energy. He didn't think he would be able to stand up and walk out the door if he had to. He knew as he sat there that Carter had whipped him again. What would he tell Baumler. What difference did it make though. Carter was right. Unity needed Desmond and Desmond needed Unity. If we rat on Unity, assuming it is all true and provable, Unity will absolutely destroy us. Furthermore, nothing will happen to Unity. They will walk free and we'll be out of business. All we can do is try and make sure that they don't try to lay the evidence on our people or the company. They would do that if they thought the authorities were closing in. Patrick had seen it happen to other companies where Unity was involved in activities that were not completely above board.

The next morning as Patrick walked into his office, Martha said that Frank Baumler had called a number of times for him. "Should I tell him to come up?"

Patrick had dreaded the meeting with Baumler and was in hopes that he would be allowed some time to figure out what he was going to say to his Manager of Security. Unfortunately, that was not to be. Reluctantly, he told Martha, "Send him in when he gets here." Within minutes Baumler knocked on Patrick's office door and then entered.

"Chief, how did it go? I'm curious to say the least."

Patrick shook his head. "It didn't go well. He denied everything of course. Even offered to help us find out who is doing the drug smuggling. He did make it clear that if we call in the authorities, we will not only pay dearly for that, but we may be left holding the bag. I just don't know."

Frank Baumler read the look on Patrick's face to mean that he was not interested in doing anything that would put pressure on Unity for fear of what would happen to Desmond Enterprises. "Chief, we really have no choice. We have to act and we have to act now."

Patrick felt that he was being cornered. First by the threats of Unity if he reported the matter to the authorities and now by Baumler laying out solid reasons, which he knew were right.

"I don't know, Frank. I need some time to figure this thing out. I just don't know what to say and let's not do anything rash in the meantime. OK." Patrick looked up at his security chief and for the first time, was a bit concerned that his trusted aide, Frank Baumler, or some of his people may possibly take the matter to the authorities behind his back.

"Don't worry Chief. We'll keep the lid on while you sort this out. When you've made a decision, let me know." With that, Frank Baumler gathered up his notepad, turned and walked from the room. He closed the door behind him and passed by Martha's desk without his usual jovial comment. He was deep in thought as to what they were going to do now. It was apparent that Patrick lacked the stomach to challenge Unity and this could continue forever or until someone blew the whistle on the smuggling operation and then, they could all be in real trouble. Now Baumler was torn between his loyalty for his boss and loyalty to the company. In the past, he had considered them to be one and the same, but lately with Patrick's increased reliance on alcohol to solve his problems, the two were taking separate directions.

As he walked back to his office, he continued thinking about possible solutions. The company needed someone at the helm right now that had the drive, guts and brains to fight Unity. He had just the person in mind, but she was down in Dublin, working there as the office manager of Desmond Enterprises. He would have to give some thought as to how she could be maneuvered into taking over the reins of the company.

CHAPTER 34

T he morning after he attended the "One Ireland" meeting, Quinn called Anne and made arrangements for her to meet him at the Hotel at ten and they would then make plans on how to spend the day. She said the weather was not going to be great so maybe a play, or whatever, as long as it was inside. Quinn commented that maybe they could visit the archives unless she found that too boring. Anne said, "Whatever, I don't mind."

At ten o'clock sharp, Anne pulled up in front of the hotel with her car and Quinn ran down the steps and jumped in. "No sense in getting out in this weather," he said. "I haven't had a bite to eat yet this morning, how about you?"

Anne said, "You must be reading my mind. I got the boys ready for school and just had time to put things together and get over here. Traffic was heavy for some reason. You bet. I know just the place."

Anne drove north, through the City, on up to a restaurant that overlooked the Botanic Gardens. The restaurant was located on the second floor of a small hotel. As Quinn stepped out of the elevator, the dark oak paneling, the hardwood floors, covered with rugs, and peat burning in the stone fireplace presented a welcoming picture. The dining room was of modest size and quiet, with only a few other late risers having their breakfast. A perfect setting for two people who wanted to enjoy private conversation and good food. Quinn and Anne ordered their breakfast and then poured themselves a cup of tea.

"OK, Quinn. Tell me about your trip to Cork. I'm envious. I wished I could have gone with you."

"I wish you had been there. In fact, I wanted to do some touring around the City and out to Cobh, but rather than spend another day doing that, I figured I would talk to you about running down there. I want to visit Kinsale as well. So, as they say in the States, the puck is in your court."

"They say it here too, Quinn. This may surprise you, but I'm working on that. Maybe the week after next if everything goes well. How does that sound?"

"I'll count on it. The trip went fine. Very interesting. I came up with some information that I want to talk to you about. I'm in a bit of a quandary as to what to do about it and I need someone to bounce some of this off on. I hope I don't bore you with this business."

"Not at all. Fire away."

"Before I get into that, guess who I ran into at 'One Ireland' last night? Joe Robbins. Did you know he was in town?"

Anne appeared genuinely surprised to hear Robbins was in Dublin. "No, I didn't. Sean was very close to Joe, but it was a political thing and I suppose I will hear from him, but we were not all that close. That's interesting. How did you like the meeting?"

"I enjoyed it. Galvin introduced me to quite a few of the fellows there that he knew. They had a good speaker. To me, the evening was like filling another square on my trip to Ireland. Heard about 'One Ireland', now I've been there, done that. If you were going to go to a meeting, I would be glad to tag along. That sort of thing."

Quinn then told Anne about seeing the girl that was with Tom O'Rourke the night that he was shot by the Provos. Seeing the very person that had been with the young fellow that was shot, sort of humanized the experience for Quinn. As he said, "you read about these things happening, but there is no face on it. Only ink in a newspaper. Seeing her there made an impression on me. Probably much more of an impression than all of the arguments raised by Sean or Galvin or Robbins. There has to be something wrong when a young person like that has her life so radically changed because people can't resolve their differences in another way."

"Quinn, there may have been more to it than just politics. I knew Tom O'Rourke fairly well. Not close, but friends. I liked him very much, and Ellen as well, but like Sean, he was very political to the point where, I'm sure, he would do things that normally he would know enough to avoid. O'Rourke may have had some involvement with the drug trade. I don't know if he was doing that for himself or maybe for the INA. I've heard rumors. It's best not to go around discussing that sort of thing. He may have stepped on the wrong toes. The druggies play for keeps."

"Well, Anne, I'm certainly not an expert on the INA. We hear about them in the States, particularly whenever there is a shooting or something, but underneath the violence, I have the impression that they are working for the common good of the people of Ireland. In fact I had the impression that the 'war' was pretty much over. Guess not. I would be very surprised to learn that they had anything to do with the drug trade. My impression of them would be that they would be a force fighting against the drug traffickers."

"You would think so, wouldn't you, Quinn. But you have to keep in mind that there's a lot of money to be made as a result of drugs and that can be a powerful influence on how people or organizations operate. As I said, there are rumors and I don't like what I hear. Anyway, your trip. How did it go?"

Quinn then explained in detail to Anne what they had found when they went through the Will and the Land Records. He told her about how the Will transferred everything to his grandfather on the death of Thomas Desmond on the condition that he was alive on the date of Thomas' death. How William Desmond had apparently filed false papers showing that Jeremiah Desmond was dead so as to receive the entire Estate himself. Quinn told Anne about the letters that he had Sean translate which had been the seed of his interest in this business, and how they absolutely proved that the transfer to the present holders of the Desmond Estate was fraudulent.

Anne sat with her mouth open, listening as the interesting tale unfolded. "Well, is there anything you can do about it?"

Quinn explained that he could pursue the matter if he wished to do so, but he was not sure he wanted to interfere in the lives of people who undoubtedly knew nothing about what had happened. But, he was also angered at what had been done to his grandfather who would have returned to Ireland, beyond a doubt, had he known about the Will.

"Quinn, how much money was involved? Can you tell that?"

"Galvin tells me that we are talking about a very huge Estate and most of it appears to be intact at the present time. I assume you are familiar with Desmond Stores, the chain out of Belfast."

"My god, Quinn. That is the largest retail chain in the Republic."

"Well, that is just part of the Desmond holdings. There is no question that we are talking a huge sum of money here but I just don't know what in the hell to do about it. Maybe I'll give them a call or go up there and see how things go."

"Quinn, I smell a rat here. Have you given any thought to the fact that this may account for Sean's interest in your situation or the other incidents that have happened to you in recent months? It could well be that knowledge of your existence may have preceded you on your visit over here. Sean worked for Adams Farms and if I understand what you have said, that was the property of your Desmond Family, that you know, and I'll bet anything that he knew or heard something while he was there. Maybe the story of how this William inherited the Estate was not a total secret down there in Kinsale. I'll just bet you that Joe Robbins may know something about this. Maybe even the Desmonds in Belfast already know about you. Did you think of that?"

"Can't say I have. Why do you suppose Sean would be so interested in me getting back the Desmond Estate?"

"Quinn, I don't know, but I bet it had something to do with the INA or Nationalist Party politics. I'll bet anything on that. The more I think of it, the more convinced I am that is what is going on here."

"You could be right Anne. On the other hand, maybe we're just assuming too much. I'll just deal with things as they occur. That's all I can do anyway.

"Speaking of your trip, what are your plans now?"

"Good question. I would like to check out a few things in the Archives or the Library today, if you don't mind. Won't take long. Then, this evening or tomorrow, I think I'll place a call to this Patrick Desmond who seems to be the senior Desmond up in Belfast. His name is on all of the most recent Desmond property documents that we came across when we checked the court records in Cork. If he is receptive to getting together, I will hop the train and go up there for a day or two and meet my long lost relatives. Should be interesting no matter what happens."

"Are you going to mention the false papers that were filed in Cork?"

"I doubt it. I still haven't figured out how to handle that one. I'm not going to bring that up, if ever, until I've thought it through."

"Quinn, I'd suggest you get ahold of Joe Robbins and try and find out what he knows, if he'll tell you. I'd do that before I went up to Belfast."

"I've already decided to do that but I need his number."

"I can get the number. Have another cup of tea and I'll be right back."

In a few minutes, Anne reappeared in the dining room and placed a note bearing a telephone number in front of Quinn's plate. "That's it. He'll be back there in an hour or two, so give him a call then."

"You do good work. Maybe I should hire you as my secretary."

"Maybe you should Quinn. That way I could keep my eye out for you. I don't want you wandering into anything you can't handle, regardless of how well you take care of yourself."

The two sat talking about Quinn's trip to Cork and the things that they could do on their trip back there in two weeks when Anne could get away from work. Anne mentioned that they should also visit Templemartin so that Quinn could meet some of her family and see how people in that part of Ireland live. They also considered the possibility of driving through the southwest of Ireland, around the Ring of Kerry and then down the Dingle Peninsula. Those were places that Quinn had read about or heard about and he wanted to visit while he was in the country.

"Quinn, let me put it to you this way. Why don't you just plan on spending another month over here and you can take in all of these places. There are interesting sights to see over on the west coast, around Limerick and Galway, and up in Sligo and Donegal as well. The beauty of Ireland is that everything is fairly close so you aren't talking about long driving distances

"Maybe I will. I've just been so tied up in libraries and court houses that I haven't really thought about touring the country. After I make contact with my relatives here, I'll concentrate on being a tourist."

Anne and Quinn left the restaurant and then toured the Botanic Gardens before driving over to the Archives where Quinn fruitlessly searched land records looking for Desmonds that predated Thomas Desmond that may have resided on the small plot of land referred to in the Will as the "original Desmond homestead." After an hour of fruitlessly combing the ancient documents bound in the archived volumes, Quinn said he had enough of research for the day.

The two spent the remainder of the day visiting the National Gallery, The James Joyce Center and then various other sights of interest on their way across the Liffey and up O'Connell Street to the Writer's Museum. They stopped for a cup of tea and a sandwich in Eason's Bookstore after Quinn purchased a history of the Easter Rising. After they drank their tea, Anne mentioned that traffic gets ridiculous this time of day and that she didn't want to get caught up in that or "the boys'll be home before I am."

The two picked up their things and were about to leave when Quinn remembered that he should give Robbins a call. He did want to talk with him before he contacted Patrick Desmond in Belfast. The waitress told him where the pay phone was and Anne gave him her telephone card to use in the machine. While Anne waited at the table, Quinn located the phone and placed the call. After a number of rings, a woman answered and soon Joe Robbins was on the line.

The two exchanged greetings and Quinn suggested that they get together with him later this afternoon, this evening or in the morning if he was available as he was heading up to Belfast and wanted to discuss some things first. Quinn purposely explained his intention to travel to Belfast with the thought in mind that it just might expedite the meeting with Robbins. Whatever the reason, Robbins said that he could meet Quinn later in the afternoon and possibly they could have dinner together. "Fine, Joe, you tell me when and where and I'll be there."

Robbins gave Quinn directions to an Italian Restaurant just off Dame Street in the Temple Bar area. "Is six o'clock OK with you, Quinn?"

When Quinn and Anne walked out onto the street for the trek back to the parking area, a light mist was falling and fortunately both of them had brought their umbrellas. The streets were crowded with people leaving their offices for the day as well as with shoppers heading for home. The umbrellas added to the difficulty of maneuvering along the sidewalk as there seemed to be no organization to the foot traffic. People did not seem to favor a right or left side of the walkway, rather apparently preferred the converging mass approach. After a while, Quinn suggested that they walk in the center of the boulevard which was a paved area for pedestrians and had far less foot traffic.

After a short drive, Anne dropped him off at his Hotel and, checking his watch, he saw that he had about two and a half hours before meeting with Robbins at the Café De Luna. In the meantime, he went up to his room, cleaned up, took a nap and then read through the latest issue of the Irish Times.

Quinn noted that there had been a shooting in Northern Ireland that had apparently gone awry as the potential target, a Unity Party official, returning to his residence, noticed that the doorman at his apartment house was not the one that was normally there. At the same time, he saw a car parked across the street in a zone marked no parking and the warning flags went up.

The man took cover in a doorway just as a hail of bullets riddled the flagstone and the pillars on either side of where he was seeking cover. He returned the fire and the assailants realizing their plot was foiled, jumped in the waiting automobile and fled the scene. The official, one Anthony Carter, told investigating officers that his attackers were most likely small time thieves attempting a robbery. The Royal Ulster Constabulary declined comment. Mr. Carter was licensed to carry a firearm.

Quinn shook his head. Just like the Wild West, he thought as he continued paging through the newspaper, checking the stage performances at the Abbey and the other theaters in the City Center. If he did not go up to Belfast in the next couple of days, he would take in a show, maybe tomorrow night. As he thought about it, he picked up the phone book to figure out how to get telephone information in Belfast. He dialed the international operator who connected him with Belfast information and in time had the residence phone number of Patrick Desmond residing at Park Ridge Estate. He wrote the number down for later reference, assuming Robbins didn't say something that would change his mind about calling his cousin.

At fifteen minutes before 6:00 p.m., Quinn left the Rockwell for his meeting with Joe Robbins. It was already dark out and the overcast skies with a chilly light rain sent a shiver through Quinn as he headed over to Dame Street in the direction of Temple Bar. Crowds of pedestrians were scurrying down the street with their umbrellas tilted before them resulting in an occasional collision with those, similarly blinded, coming from the opposite direction. Quinn's height at times like this was a definite advantage as he could see the oncoming foot traffic from under his umbrella and avoid most of the approaching mass of humanity.

The sidewalk that ran along Nassau Street next to Trinity was the worst because it was so narrow and people were stacked three and four deep along the Trinity University wall waiting for their buses. Quinn, along with others trying to make headway in the mob of people, would occasionally step out into the street to avoid people blocking the pathway along the sidewalk. With his prior experience on Nassau Street, Quinn would look behind him to make sure that no cars were coming even though it was a one way street and only oncoming traffic was allowed in the direction he was proceeding.

After a few more minutes of making his way through office workers trying to get to their homes, Quinn turned down a side street and headed into the Temple Bar section. He soon found himself in front of the Café De Luna and saw Joe Robbins, through the front window, already sitting at a table enjoying a glass of wine. Robbins held up his wine glass in a salute and waved to him to come join him. It was still fairly early by Dublin dining standards and the restaurant was only half filled. Quinn hung up his coat, folded his umbrella and hooked it over the coat rack before walking over and joining Robbins.

Robbins looked up at him with a big smile on his face, "Looks like you've had an enjoyable trek over from your hotel."

"Just another beautiful day in Dublin, Joe. They didn't say anything about this on the travel poster. Good to see you."

Robbins poured a glass of wine for Quinn which hit the spot as he had gotten a bit of a chill from his walk. Robbins gave him time to get situated and then asked him how his trip was going. Quinn filled him in on how he had been spending his time and also thanked him, or whoever it was that lined up Noel Galvin to help him with his research. Robbins assured him that Sean was the one behind that effort and if he needed any additional assistance, Galvin had said that you were to contact him at any time. "He'd be glad to work with you."

Robbins took another sip of his wine and said, "Sounds like you guys got along quite well. Noel says that you found some rather interesting facts out about your family. Really an unusual story. Most Americans come over here and, if they're lucky, find they do have a distant cousin that barely scrapes out a living. Looks like you've struck gold."

"Joe, I really have no interest in what sort of a balance sheet my Irish cousins have. In fact, in many respects, I would prefer it the other way as I don't care for complications, which it seems as though I have run into."

From the look of disappointment on Robbins face, it was clear that he expected to find a certain amount of glee in Quinn's reaction to learning that he had, what appeared to be, a good probability of participating in a sizeable fortune.

"Quinn, from what Noel tells me, it sounds as though your grandfather was defrauded of his inheritance. I wouldn't let that just pass. Seems to me, you owe that to your grandfather."

"Joe, that's the only thing that does bother me. Trust me, if he were alive, I would do everything I could to see that he received his fair share. But, he isn't. Furthermore, the people that scammed him out of it, they're gone too. I just don't know. I'm going to talk to the Desmonds up in Belfast and just see how things go."

"God, you're more forgiving than I am. I'd be all over that Estate. If you want to talk with an attorney here, just let me know and I'll find a good one for you."

Quinn thanked Robbins for his interest and then he got down to what was really on his mind. Quinn brought up a couple of things that had been bothering him. Among which were the burglary of his house and Sean's last ominous comment implying that something sinister was involved with Quinn's trip to Ireland. He also brought up Joe Robbin's own warning, after the service for Sean, to be careful. "That didn't exactly seem very normal to me as well."

Robbins did not reply and Quinn went on, mentioning that he suspected at times he was being followed or at least periodically observed. He had seen two men in particular too often to be accidental sightings. It could be a coincidence but he doubted it. What their interests were, he didn't know. Lastly, he mentioned all the help that he had received from Sean and then the almost full time assistance of Noel Galvin which, in Quinn's mind, exceeded any level of hospitality he had ever heard of. He assured Robbins that he was not complaining and that he was very thankful, but it was unusual at least to him.

When he finished, he added, "Obviously, the fact that my grandfather was defrauded out of his legitimate inheritance seems to be the focal point of interest and, Joe, what I would appreciate knowing is exactly what is going on here and who all are involved. I have the definite impression that I could get hurt here and I don't want that to happen without knowing who or why."

Quinn finished and looked up at Robbins for answers to the many questions that had been forming in his mind over the past months. Robbins said nothing. He just stared back at Quinn and it was obvious that he was considering his options. Whatever involvement the INA had with respect to Quinn Parker, the decisions as to what he could be told were made at a higher level than Joe Robbins. Robbins was fully aware of that fact as he pondered what to say, but he was also very aware that Quinn Parker seemed to know generally what was going on. To try and deny the obvious would be harmful to the objectives the INA was trying to accomplish and occasionally soldiers had to make decisions normally reserved for the generals. This appeared to be one of those times. The two men sat in prolonged silence as Robbins thought about how he would respond to Quinn.

Finally, Robbins said, "Quinn, I'm not going to sit here and try to bullshit you about things that are obvious to you. Yes, you have been a subject of considerable interest within the INA. You are also the target of growing interest on the part of the Provos and maybe of Desmond Enterprises. Let me give you some background." Robbins explained the relationship between Desmond Enterprises and Unity in the north. He also laid out what had been rumored for generations regarding the source of the Desmond wealth and finally the ongoing struggle between Unity and the INA taking place in both Northern Ireland and the Republic.

Robbins paused and again organized his thoughts beforeproceeding. "This really involves a fight between the INA and the Provos over eventual control of Desmond Enterprises for various reasons. One of which is that Desmond is a substantial contributor to the Unity Party in the North, but that is certainly not the only reason. Now, I will say this and then I think I have to clam up because I'm in way over my head at this point already. You should be careful. The INA is interested in your good health which is the reason why you have been watched. The Provos and Desmond Enterprises would be well served if you were out of the picture, but I have heard absolutely nothing that would indicate to me that they have any such intention. So don't think you have a target patch on your back. We usually get solid indications that something is going to happen and we have nothing that relates to you, other than the fact that they are rather informally keeping an eye on you. That guy, Peter Baker, for your information, was on the Provo payroll."

That came as a considerable surprise to Quinn. He had some questions about Baker, with everything else that was happening, but Baker had always come up with very credible answers whenever Quinn challenged him. Robbins comment about Baker also told Quinn that the INA was more observant than even Quinn had suspected. He must have been under the watchful eye of the INA at all times and not just on the few occasions that he happened to spot the fellow that he figured was following him. Quinn asked Robbins about the fellow that he had observed on occasion and asked if he was with him all the time.

Robbins smiled. "Actually, that fellow was assigned to you early on but was later pulled off. The funny part of it is that it was after he was pulled off that he kept running into you. I didn't know if you had noticed that or not. You have usually been with Galvin so it's not like we need to hide somebody behind a tree to watch you."

As he thought about it, he came to the conclusion that the INA was taking care of him because they were assuming he would take care of them with respect to any claim he might have on the Estate. He had already made it clear to both Galvin and now Robbins that he had made no decision on how to deal with the Desmonds in Belfast. Up to this point, it had just not been the number one topic on his mind.

Quinn was silent for some time and finally Robbins asked him, "So, have I told you anything that you hadn't already figured out?"

"Not really. You have just confirmed a few things."

"Well, Quinn. We'd really like to work with you because we believe we have common goals here. I can understand to a certain extent your reluctance to get into a conflict with your newly discovered Irish relatives, but let me assure you, from what I know about them, they do not have your best interests at heart."

"I'm not so sure they even know of my existence, Joe."

"They do, Quinn. Of that I am fairly sure. We are certain that anything the Provos know, relevant to Desmond Enterprises, goes to Patrick Desmond. He is very tight with their security people. Now that reminds me. I don't know if you saw the small item in the news about this guy that was involved in a shooting up in Belfast. He was a Provo agent and was their contact man with Desmond Enterprises. Just a little bit of local gossip."

Quinn figured that Joe Robbins knew a lot more about that particular shooting than he was telling him. "Do I assume that the INA was involved in that shooting, Joe?"

"Who knows? I don't know. That's out of my league. As I read the article in the papers, this guy, Carter, thought it was the work of some petty criminals."

"You know, Joe. I don't know whether to run to the airport and catch a plane or ignore all this crap and just continue my trip. Now, I'm fairly sure that you know my status a hell of a lot better than I do. How about some advice. Am I at risk to stay here or not?"

Joe Robbins had to think a moment before answering. There was no doubt in his mind that Quinn was at risk by being in Ireland but Robbins did not want to admit that fact. If he was an ordinary tourist, he would be safer in Ireland than in the States. Unfortunately, he was not very ordinary. He was a potentially valuable commodity, but that depended on whether he was alive or dead. For now the INA wanted him alive. For the Provos, he would be more valuable if he were dead. Robbins knew that Quinn posed a threat to their very lucrative drug operation and to a lesser extent to their contributions from Desmond if he pursued his claims and they did not want to lose either one.

"I'll be candid, Quinn. There is risk here for you, but it wouldn't disappear if you headed back to the States. Now while you are in Ireland, you, at least, have the benefit of the INA who have taken an interest in your personal safety. You wouldn't have that in the States, or it would be far less effective than here. I would suggest that you stay in Ireland and take care of business. I will let you know if we are learning anything that you would want to know. We have very good intelligence on their 'in country' moves."

"Joe, that brings up point two. What if I go up to Belfast? Am I walking into the lion's den?"

"I'd be more careful on that one because we, obviously, don't have the freedom to operate up there that we have here. If you go up there, I'd stand right next to your Desmond relatives. I'd have that all worked out in advance before I ever went up there."

"Interesting." Quinn thought over Robbin's answer and decided that he would call Patrick Desmond first and make his decision about going to Belfast after he had considered his cousin's response. If his cousin was lukewarm, or negative, he would cancel the trip and reconsider where he was going with this family history business.

The two had dinner and then parted company with Quinn walking back to the Rockwell. He went up to his room and read a while before calling Anne.

When she heard his voice, she quickly said, "What did he have to say?"

"He admitted the INA is involved and it is related to the family history thing."

"I thought so. What did he say about you being followed?"

"He basically confirmed it. Apparently the Provos and maybe Desmond reps are tailing me or at least checking up on me. The INA as well unless Galvin is with me. I had no idea when I came over here that I was going to cause such a stir."

"Well you're just such an interesting guy, Quinn." Anne laughed and then added, "I wish that was what it was all about. You'd better be careful if you go up there."

The two talked on the phone for another ten minutes or so and made plans to get together over the weekend. Anne had received permission to take a week off and go with Quinn down to Cork and visit places that were of interest to him and also to visit her family in Templemartin which was not far from Cork City. Before she hung up, she had Quinn promise to let her know what he was going to do about the Belfast trip.

When he hung up the phone, Quinn leaned back in his chair and pulled out his note pad to lay out what he wished to discuss with Patrick Desmond. He continued to have doubts that the Desmonds even knew that he existed but his more cautious side told him that it was better to be safe than sorry. He would listen to Robbin's warnings but the real purpose of his call was to discuss family history with a cousin that would undoubtedly have similar interests.

Quinn penciled out some of the more important points in his own history that could be of interest to his cousin. As he wrote down the year of immigration of his grandfather, Jeremiah, he wondered for a moment if this Patrick Desmond had any first hand knowledge of his own grandfather's obvious trickery. If Sean had heard the rumors, would not this grandson also have been aware of the stories and followed up on them. Maybe not if he did not want to know the truth, but wouldn't that make him guilty as well. Quinn dismissed these thoughts.

Wherever the truth lay, it would come out in time and Quinn was not going to dwell on the dark side of this business until confronted by it. When he had prepared his own introduction to this long separated cousin, Quinn pulled out the notepad with the phone number of Patrick Desmond, noted that the time should be well past the dinner hour, and dialed the number.

The telephone rang three times and a very formal sounding male voice said, "Desmond residence."

Quinn asked if he could speak with Patrick Desmond and the person asked him who he should say is calling. Quinn gave him his name and identified himself as a relative from the United States. This produced no reaction other than, "Just a moment, I will see if Mr. Desmond is available." This was followed by a very long wait which made Quinn seriously consider whether or not he should hang up and call back. As he was about to do that, the same person came back on the line and said, "Mr. Desmond will be with you shortly."

After what seemed to be ten minutes or more, Quinn heard the phone being picked up and a person saying what sounded like, "Patrick Desmond here."

The words were slurred and the voice trailed off so that Quinn was not totally certain as to what had been said. He introduced himself and explained who he was and his connection to the Desmond Family of Kinsale. There was prolonged silence on the other end of the line and finally Quinn said, "Did you get that? Can you hear me alright?"

"Yes. Certainly. Very interesting. What can I do for you?"

Quinn was put out by the limited, if not total lack, of interest on the part of whoever he was talking with. After all of his research efforts, the trip across the ocean and weeks in libraries, he did not expect champagne and balloons, but a little enthusiasm wouldn't be out of place. In a somewhat irritated voice he said, "This is Mr. Patrick Desmond, is that correct?"

"Yes. That's me." It was clear now to Quinn that Mr. Patrick Desmond was either in the sauce or had a speech problem.

"And you are the son of Dennis who was the son of William, right?"

There was a pause while Patrick sorted out the lineage. "Yes, that's right."

"Well, Mr. Desmond, that sort of makes us out to be cousins. I thought you might find that interesting"

"Oh, yes. That is interesting." This followed by another long pause.

This reaction of Patrick Desmond was such a total comedown for Quinn that he was beginning to find it a bit humorous.

Quinn just chuckled and said, "Yes, yes. It is interesting isn't it?" Deciding to press ahead, Quinn went on, "I thought I would come up there and visit with you if that would not disrupt your schedule. Do you have any thoughts on that?"

"My schedule... ah ... I have that at... ah... the office. Call my secretary,.. ah... Martha and she can fix you up with that... ah."

"I take it, Mr. Desmond, that you don't have a hell of a lot of interest in meeting your relatives from the States. Is that a fair statement?"

"Yes. Yes. I... ah... think you are correct... yes... correct... ah... call my secretary, Martha, and she can take care of all of that... ah... thank you." With that, there was a click and the line went dead.

Quinn was irritated, but his attempted telephone call to Patrick Desmond made him laugh. The guy was in the bag. He was absolutely plowed and most likely would not remember the call in the morning or whenever he sobered up. Quinn sat back in his chair a bit stunned and very confused. What now? The more he thought about it, the more determined he became to confront Mr. Desmond face to face. He would call the secretary, Martha what's her name and set up an appointment. He hadn't spent the past year buried in libraries to have some drunk ruin his party.

CHAPTER 35

The next morning, Quinn located the number for the Executive Offices of Desmond Enterprises in Belfast and after being routed from one secretary to another who all insisted that they could take care of whatever it was that necessitated the call, he finally was connected to Miss Martha Blair, Personal Secretary to Patrick Desmond. In order to forestall her from summarily cutting him off, Quinn quickly explained that Mr. Desmond had instructed him to call her. He then went on and explained who he was and that he would like to meet with Mr. Desmond, possibly even that or the following day.

"Mr. Parker, I'm sure that Mr. Desmond would enjoy the opportunity to meet with you. He is not in, but if you would leave your number, I will discuss this with him just as soon as he arrives and call you back. Is that alright?"

She had a very pleasant voice and seemed sincerely interested in accommodating his request. Quinn listened carefully but could not detect whether or not she knew who he was. If she did, she had covered it up well.

Quinn told the secretary that he would remain near his phone for the next hour or two and would appreciate it if she called him just as soon as Mr. Desmond arrived. He hung up the phone and checked the train schedule to see how long he could delay his departure and still arrive in time to get together with Patrick Desmond. If he received a call by noon, he could still be in Belfast in the late afternoon and possibly have dinner with his cousin that evening, assuming his cousin was so inclined. In the meantime, while he waited for the call, he put together some of his research notes that might be of interest to Patrick Desmond and also packed an overnight bag for his stay in Belfast.

Quinn was reading a Belfast tour book when the phone rang. He checked his watch and noted that it was eleven thirty and he could still make the train, if this was Mr. Desmond's secretary.

"Mr. Parker, this is Martha Blair. Mr. Desmond would be delighted to meet with you either this evening or tomorrow, whenever you can arrive in Belfast. I assume you would come by train. We can pick you up at the Belfast Central station if you know when you would be arriving. Also, Mr.

Desmond has already made a reservation for you at a fine hotel near Park Ridge, that is his home. He is looking forward to meeting you."

Quinn wondered if his cousin had any recollection of their telephone conversation from the evening before. He had the impression that he did not which was fine with Quinn. Quinn referred to the train schedule and told Martha when he would be arriving at the Belfast Station.

Martha told him that she would be wearing a blue rain coat and would wait just outside of the passenger exit door at the Station so he should look for her after he went through security.

What the hell is this security business, he thought. There was no security guard or screening on the trains out of Dublin. This is going to be an interesting trip. When he hung up the phone, he quickly gathered his things together, locked the room and, as he passed through the lobby, he told the desk clerk that he would be out until at least the following day. The train would depart the station in one hour and he figured that if he walked at a fast pace over to Connolly Station, he could make the departure time. A taxi would not be that much faster as the traffic at this time of day was very heavy. Fortunately it was not raining which made the walk a bit easier. At least he would not have to dodge the umbrellas.

He bought his ticket just as they were announcing the departure of the Dublin Express on track five. He found an empty seat on the third car and made himself comfortable for the trip. The train was not full and the car he was riding in was similar to the one he took to Cork. Two facing bench seats with a table in between. Actually very comfortable, clean and in good condition. As the train slowly pulled out of the station and headed to the north, an attendant pushing a cart came through the car selling tea and biscuits. Quinn purchased something to eat as he had not had breakfast, not wanting to miss the call from Martha Blair. The trip north was interesting. There were coastal views just to the north of Dublin and then as they crossed the border into Northern Ireland, Quinn saw signs of the conflict going on in that country. When they passed through Portadown, he saw, what he assumed were, British helicopters patrolling at low level and outside of the town, he saw armed, helmeted, soldiers moving in a thin line, with automatic weapons at the ready, searching through the brush for something or someone.

As the train entered Belfast, he was struck by the difference in the appearance of the city from what he had seen in Dublin. Belfast was obviously more of an industrial center than was Dublin. The overcast, somewhat misty, skies added to the smoky, somber appearing factory buildings, giving the city a hard, unfriendly look. This effect on Quinn was cemented when he left the train in the terminal and armed guards with security dogs were shouting at the passengers to walk apart, in single file, so that the dogs could sniff them for weapons or drugs or whatever it was they were so concerned about. Quinn was not impressed by this welcome to the City of Belfast and he consciously hoped that it was not indicative of how his trip to the North was going to go.

As he made his way along the line of passengers through the exit doors and into the lobby, he scanned the few people that seemed to be waiting for someone coming off of the train and immediately spotted an attractive woman, wearing a blue rain coat who seemed to be watching everyone that came through the arrival gate. She was alone which gave Quinn some concern as he expected Patrick Desmond to be with her. Quinn headed in her direction and as he did so, she stepped forward, apparently recognizing him, and announced that she was Martha Blair and that Patrick had a last minute conflict but that he would meet them later at the hotel. Quinn introduced himself and told her that it was not necessary for her to have gone to the trouble of meeting his train. He could have managed to get over to the hotel on his own.

"No, Mr. Parker, Mr. Desmond insisted that someone should be here when you arrived. He intended to handle that himself, but you know how business can interfere with pleasure."

Quinn thought to himself that she was not only attractive, she was also very polished in her manners. She was undoubtedly a valuable resource in Desmond Enterprises and probably to Patrick Desmond as well. He smiled to himself as he considered the possibility that she could stay on board if he ever pursued his grandfather's claim to the company. He quickly banished the thought as a tinge of guilt reminded him that his grandfather, whose claim was involved, would not approve of such folly

Martha directed Quinn to her car, which was parked in the lot, and soon they were enmeshed in heavy afternoon traffic trying to make their way to the western part of the city. Martha explained various points of interest as they made their way out of the city. Quinn had not noticed but Martha explained to him that the railway station was just off the Lagan River that flowed into the Bay. It was the river and the Bay that had given rise to the shipbuilding industry that put Belfast on the map. Martha added that the Titanic had been built there along with many other famous ships. They drove north through the center of the City and then took Shankil Road to the west which gave Quinn a view of the Protestant inspired murals painted in bold colors on the sides of buildings. Martha told him that she was taking the tourist route which would not get them to the hotel as quickly as the major western exit route but they had plenty of time as Patrick would not be there until well after five.

When Martha ran out of things to say about the area they were passing through, she began to inquire of Quinn, his relationship to her employer, Mr. Desmond. Quinn laid out, in some detail, that his grandfather and Mr. Desmond's grandfather were brothers

"I've never heard Mr. Desmond mention that he had family in the States."

"That's probably because he was not aware of that fact." Quinn explained that once his grandfather left Ireland, he never again returned and no one else from the family had either, until now with his own visit. Quinn asked about Patrick's family and learned that he was married and had two children.

"His wife, Hillary, is Lord Fairchild's only daughter, if that means anything to you."

"Not really. We just don't follow that sort of thing in the States."

"Well here it means quite a bit because they are a very wealthy English family and have extensive holdings throughout the U.K. I will say it again, very wealthy."

"Well, now, I'll be suitably correct when we meet." He was beginning to like this secretary more all the time.

"Am I going to meet Lady Hillary or is that not in the schedule."

"Not in the schedule, Mr. Parker. She keeps her own schedule and I have nothing to do with that one. You may meet her while you are here, but that would be purely by chance. She is very busy with her own interests as well as with Desmond Enterprises and quite frankly, does all of her socializing in London."

"Well, I don't socialize there so I guess I'm just out of luck."

"Not necessarily.

The way she said that told Quinn that there was no love lost for the boss's wife. Was that jealousy or was that just plain dislike for Mrs. Patrick Desmond. He would make up his own mind later, if and when he ever met the woman.

After another fifteen minutes, Martha turned the car into a wide cobblestone drive, bordered by flowering plants on either side which curved in an arc up to the entryway of the Cheshire Arms Hotel. The grounds were immaculately manicured and perfectly landscaped to accent the impressive Greek architecture of the hotel with its heavy, fluted columns set apart at approximately ten foot intervals along the portico. Further back from the columns, another twenty or so feet, were what appeared to Quinn to be the largest brass covered doors that he had ever seen decorating the entryway to a hotel. It was an impressive sight and his reaction at seeing his quarters for the night caused Martha to say, "Mr. Desmond wants you to be comfortable while you are in Belfast, so consider yourself his guest for the evening. If you need anything while you are here, just let them know at the desk."

Martha expertly brought her car to a halt immediately to the side of the bright red carpet that extended from the brass doors out to the cobblestone drive. An attendant opened Quinn's door and addressed him, "Good afternoon, Mr. Parker. We have been expecting you."

Quinn was a bit overwhelmed by the reception that he was being given and any concern that he may have had regarding his Northern Ireland cousin was rapidly diminishing. As he got out of the car, Martha told him that she would park the car and then meet him in the lobby. In the meantime, the porter that had taken his overnite bag out of the trunk of the car was waiting to take him to his room. Quinn carried his briefcase and followed the fellow through the mammoth double doors and into the lobby of the hotel where the porter stopped to point out where the dining room, bar and concierge were located.

As Quinn stood in the foyer, taking a closer look at the ornamentation on the doors, his attention was drawn to the artwork that extended across the ceiling of the lobby, consisting of brightly painted Celtic designs that bore a striking resemblance to the artwork he had seen when he viewed the Book of Kells at Trinity University. He stopped to study the grandeur of the lobby which was tastefully decorated with heavy Mediterranean furniture, chairs, tables and couches placed on huge rugs embroidered with what appeared to be Norman scenes. The windows in the room were similar to the entryway doors in dimension, running from just above the floor to a height of fifteen or twenty feet, arched and recessed, with leaded glass panels permitting only soft light to enter the large room from the outside. The sense of power which the design of the room and it's furnishings conveyed, while certainly not subtle, still could be effective in convincing a person not to contest his host's authority. The thought came to Quinn that the choice of this particularly impressive hotel was not accidental.

Quinn followed the porter to his room which was again, elegant. Two huge windows looked out on the lawn which extended as far out as Quinn could see. Huge trees, obviously very old, were situated sporadically across the green landscape which blocked the view of any road, building or other sign of civilization. The impression for the guest was that he was staying in an uninhabited pastoral setting and not in a hotel some fifteen miles from the center of Belfast. Quinn received a brief explanation of the room's amenities, received the key and put his things away before returning to the lobby to meet Martha. She was just walking into the foyer when Quinn stepped out of the elevator and he met her as she continued on into the hotel.

"How do you like your room?"

Quinn smiled and said, "Not bad at all. Really, it is very nice. It was not necessary. I have quite modest tastes and this is much nicer than I am used to."

"Patrick insisted, seeing as how you may be a cousin from the States. Let's go in the bar and have a drink. Patrick should be here shortly."

As they walked towards the doorway to the lounge, Quinn figured the room would be done in heavy, dark oak with thick red carpeting to be in keeping with the rest of the Hotel's decor. He was almost correct. The carpet was more of a burgundy color. They found a table and ordered their drinks while Martha explained the history of the hotel. Apparently it dated back two or three hundred years and was considered the finest hotel in Belfast. It had suffered some damage in the bombings of World War II, but that had all been restored and, unless one was an expert, a person could not tell what had been restored and what dated back to the original construction.

"Now, do you mind if I call you Martha?"

"Please do, but understand I will have to refer to you as Mr. Parker."

"Only if you insist. Now, how about Mr. Desmond's family. You mentioned he had two children."

Martha told Quinn about Ellen and Adam, their respective ages, and their jobs, now that they were both out of school, working for Desmond Enterprises. She spoke at length about Ellen and how well she was doing in the Dublin office of Desmond but said very little about Adam, other than the fact that he worked in Shipping in Belfast.

Quinn was interested in the fact that Ellen lived in Dublin and suggested the possibility that he could meet with her before he left for the States.

"When are you planning on returning?"

"Good question. I didn't think I would be here this long, but one thing just led to another."

"Well, here comes Mr. Desmond."

Quinn looked over to the door to see a man entering the lounge that seemed to be about his age. Grey hair, slightly balding, mottled skin, rounded shoulders, reddish eyes and nose, all of which combined to present a basically dissipated appearing individual. Another man, stockier, more substantial appearing, came through the door behind him and Martha muttered, "well." She paused. "He has a friend with him."

Quinn made no comment, rather stood to meet his Irish cousin. He was curious as to who it was that Patrick Desmond had seen fit to bring along to this meeting. Quinn had decided, even before getting off the train in Belfast, that he was going to play the part of the American tourist with no particular motives in mind, other than meeting his Irish relatives. Pursuing this line, Quinn stepped out to shake hands with Patrick Desmond, giving him his most cousinly smile.

"Patrick Desmond, this is a pleasure. Sort of an historic moment, don't you think?"

Patrick had a nervous and somewhat confused look about him, but he managed a smile and took Quinn's hand to shake it. "Mr. Parker, this is a friend of mine, Frank Baumler, who I am dropping off at his apartment. I hope you don't mind if he sits in on our get together."

"Not at all." As they were taking their seats, the waiter stepped over and asked Mr. Desmond if he wanted "the usual." Patrick nodded and his companion, Mr. Baumler, ordered a soft drink for himself.

There was a long pause in the conversation while the group waited for their drinks to arrive during which time, Martha looked over at Patrick Desmond and said, "Mr. Desmond, if there is no reason for me to attend this meeting, I will leave, but if you needed me for anything, I can certainly stay."

Patrick appeared not to know what to say and finally blurted out, "Well... ah... stay for a while... ah... if you don't mind and ah..."

Martha just nodded and leaned back in her chair as though to wait out the next opportunity to exit the gathering. Again, there was a long pause, finally interrupted by the waiter bringing the drinks. He first served Patrick Desmond who immediately rewarded himself with a long sip of his vodka tonic. After he set the glass down, he smiled at his friend Baumler and commented that he had needed that as it had been a long day. Baumler just nodded in affirmation and glanced over at Martha. It was apparent to Quinn that Martha and Frank Baumler were at least good friends but from the other signals passing around the table, the President's secretary seemed to belong to the President.

After another sip or two of what Quinn assumed was basically vodka with a twist of lime, Patrick Desmond seemed to loosen up considerably. He asked about Quinn's immediate family in the States and the line of work that he was involved in there. He seemed to raise his guard a bit when he heard that Quinn was a lawyer, but that seemed to pass by the wayside after another sip or two of his drink. "Now Mr. Packer, tell me what you know about your grandfather's family. That sure is interesting."

Frank Baumler leaned over and said, "Parker, Mr. Desmond, Parker."

"Oh yes. My apologies," and he leaned over and gave Quinn a pat on the back. "Long day."

It was apparent to Quinn that it may have been a long day, but it was going to be a short night at this rate. He had best get on with at least laying out the relationships so that his host could deliver whatever message he had in mind, before the vodka took its toll. Quinn briefly explained that his mother was the only child of Patrick Desmond's Grand uncle, Jeremiah. That Jeremiah had emigrated to the States and that he spoke about Ireland until he died in 1932. While Quinn recited the lineage, Patrick nodded as though in agreement but seemed more interested in the glass sitting in front of him than in what Quinn was saying. Quinn was beginning to get the picture that his Irish cousin had decided to entertain him for the evening and possibly bid him adieu the next day and forget about him. Consequently, he decided to probe a bit to see if he could get some reaction from his host.

"Now, I take it you are aware of my grandfather's emigration to the States, right?"

Again, there was a pause which seemed to precede anything requiring a response from Patrick. "Yes... ah..." glancing over at Baumler, "er... ah.. .no. Not really. No, never heard the name. The family was not very good at passing down information. You... ah.. .Americans seem a lot more interested in dead ancestors than we do over here. Ah, I don't know why, but that is true, right, Frank?"

"Right, Mr. Desmond."

"Well, then Mr. Desmond, I don't suppose that you know about your grandfather's other brother, Michael, who was murdered down at Kinsale shortly after your great grandfather passed away."

Again after a long pause during which Quinn could almost see the wheels turning, Patrick said, "Ah... yes. I heard something about that when I was a young boy, but that was about it."

"Well, I have some newspaper articles that discuss it and you might find those interesting."

Patrick shot a glance over at Baumler who sat stone faced looking at Quinn. It was apparent to Quinn that they were unaware there was a newspaper article discussing the murder of Michael Desmond. It was also clear that, at least Patrick, was concerned as to what the article might have said. Not knowing was obviously unnerving for him. Patrick took a long sip of his drink and then waved to the waiter to send in another round.

"Ah... yes... Mr. Packer... Packer... er Parker. Sorry. I would like to see those. Do you have them with you?"

Quinn said that he did, but that they were in his room. Having the impression that he was at least getting Patrick's attention, Quinn decided to press on. "Mr. Desmond, I understand that your great grandfather had a will. Did you ever have occasion to see that? It is very interesting."

Patrick quickly emptied the remaining contents of his drink and looked over at Baumler for help. Receiving no assistance from his friend, he looked back at Quinn. "Well, no. I never had occas... ah... I never saw it. I didn't know there was one. I suppose there had to be one, but... ah... no."

After another somewhat embarrassing long pause, Frank Baumler spoke up. "Mr. Parker, it would probably be beneficial for all concerned if we met tomorrow at Mr. Desmond's office. Would that be acceptable, Mr. Desmond?"

"Why yes, Frank. No problem."

Frank Baumler looked over at Martha and asked her to suggest a time that would be available for a meeting and she replied that the calendar was clear for anytime in the morning. Baumler suggested ten a.m. and Quinn said that he was available then or anytime. They all agreed and Frank Baumler suggested that he had to get back for another meeting and had to leave. Patrick immediately suggested that he could drop him off and the two men shook hands with Quinn and rather quickly left the lounge. Martha was apparently forgotten in the rush to depart and Quinn offered to join her for a drink if she could spare the time.

"Yes, I could use one."

Quinn ordered the drinks and the two sat in silence for a few moments.

"Patrick has been having a bit of a problem with alcohol."

"I see that."

"It has just been getting worse, especially over the past year. He is under a lot of pressure."

"I suppose, running a large company can put strain on anyone."

"No, that is not what is causing his problems. It is everything else. Actually, Hillary makes the major decisions and she passes the tough jobs on down to two or three vice presidents to handle. Patrick, frankly, has very little to do in the company."

Quinn wondered "what else" was causing his problems but thought it best to not inquire. He waited a moment and said, "If it would be possible, I would like to meet his son and daughter."

"When you are at the corporate office tomorrow, you could bring that up to Frank Baumler, the fellow that was just here. I'm sure that he would introduce you to Adam. Frank is Head of Security at Desmond but he is more than that. He is really Patrick's confidant and a very fine man. As for Ellen, she is in Dublin, as you know, and I would suggest that you just call the office there, in Ballsbridge, and speak to her directly. I'm sure she would be glad to meet you. I think you will run into a more normal situation sitting down with her than what you have experienced here."

"What do you mean by that?"

"Patrick is just having major personal problems as you can see. He is really a very fine man and I just hope that we can get him back on his feet again."

Quinn just nodded. "Yes, that's too bad." He didn't consider it his place to criticize his host.

The two talked about their respective jobs and about Quinn's visit to Ireland. After the two finished their drinks, Martha said that she had to get home as it was getting late. Quinn walked her to the parking lot and thanked her for picking him up at the airport and for her conversation.

"Why you're welcome Quinn. That reminds me. I have to pick you up in the morning. Say, 9:30. How is that? I'll just pull up in front of the lobby and you can hop in."

Quinn protested that he could take a taxi, but Martha would not hear of it and besides, as she said, Patrick would want it done that way.

After she had driven off, Quinn walked back towards the lobby. It was a cool night but it was clear and the stars were out. Actually very pleasant after the rather tense meeting in the lounge with Patrick. Quinn thought about his cousin. Very uptight and he seemed to be confused either as a result of alcohol or maybe he was confused all the time. Quite a contrast from what Patrick had expected. He had envisioned Patrick as being robust, somewhat arrogant and loud. The total opposite of what he had encountered in the lounge. If his cousin's problem was alcohol, Quinn would have trouble being sympathetic because he had always considered that a self inflicted wound. Well, tomorrow should be an interesting day.

The following morning, as Quinn stood on the Hotel portico, he saw Martha drive through the entrance at exactly 9:30. Within fifteen minutes they were passing the huge ship building dry docks along the bay and turning into the Desmond Enterprises parking ramp. Martha maneuvered her car up four levels to executive parking and swung into a slot that had

Ms. Martha Blair painted on the wall facing them as the car came to a halt.

"Very impressive, Ms. Blair."

"I'm glad you are impressed Mr. Parker. Not everyone is."

He followed her as she walked at a rapid pace, checking her watch and noting that they had four minutes in which to arrive at Quinn's meeting on time. As they walked down the hallways of Desmond Enterprises, Quinn had the distinct impression that everyone they passed, those at their desks and those walking down the hallway, were wondering who he was and why he was being personally escorted by the President's secretary.

The Desmond employees looked for clues as he passed but he was obviously not one of the financial consultants, business advisors or attorneys that would occasionally visit with Mr. Desmond. Not dressed as he was. Well worn tweed sport coat, over a sweater with no tie, faded leather patches on the elbows and shoes that were either off white or formerly white. This attire, contrasted with his rather distinguished physical appearance, increased their curiosity as to who he was. They would have to ask Martha later when she came down the hall to refill the coffee and tea containers.

When they came to the President's Office, Martha stopped at her desk which was just outside and pressed a button on the intercom which transmitted a light beep on the phone at Mr. Desmonds desk. Quinn heard Patrick's voice over the intercom, "Yes, Martha?"

"Mr. Parker is here Mr. Desmond."

"Send him in."

When Quinn walked into the office he saw that Frank Baumler was already present, sitting in a chair to the side of Patrick Desmond's large desk. The room had a look of antiquity about it, from the obviously very old desk to paintings along the walls and some of the memorabilia placed on tables and stands as well as on the desk itself. Patrick Desmond stood and seeing that Quinn was taking in some of the more unique aspects of his office, walked around the desk, took Quinn's arm and explained some of the artwork. Patrick explained that the large colorful plaque hanging on the wall was the Adam's Family Coat of Arms. It consisted of an upright sword on top of a full faced metal helmet in the center of a shield. Patrick further explained that the depiction of the helmet as full faced and not a side view denoted the possessor of the crest was a knight or a prince. He went on to say that side views denoted lessor rank.

Quinn didn't know whether to congratulate him or be polite. He chose the latter. "Interesting."

"Here, Quinn. We give our customers these table coasters that have this crest on it. I know this is not your family line, as you understand it, but it may be a matter of some interest for you. As a matter of fact, you may see the crest on some Desmond label products as we have used it for years. The Adams family, before we entered the picture, were in many enterprises and they used the crest on everything they dealt in, so we are not being irreverent. I have found it stamped on old books in the house, silverware and even some pieces of furniture. It was obviously a badge of honor for them and they used it liberally.

Quinn took the pack of colorful table coasters and examined them briefly. The gold sword standing upright in the center of the shield was truly impressive, as was the silver, full face protecting, helmet. He looked for a motto or verse but found none. He was curious why there was none, but didn't want to get into a long winded conversation about something that didn't particularly interest him. He thanked Patrick and put them in his briefcase.

Turning his attention to his desk, Patrick told Quinn that it had belonged to his grandfather William and had been used by the President of Desmond Enterprises for over one hundred years. Quinn studied the ornamental wood carving and hand craftsmanship that had gone into making the large oak desk and commented that whoever had built it, was truly an artist.

"I wish I knew who it was. It was one of the many secrets that my grandfather kept to himself, unfortunately. Please have a seat. May I address you as Quinn? Call me Patrick, please."

"By all means. Thank you." Quinn then acknowledged Frank Baumler who added, "Frank, Frank Baumler, please."

Patrick seemed much more composed this morning than he had appeared the previous evening. The change in his demeanor was so different that it was obvious to Quinn that the two men had formulated some sort of plan for the meeting this morning. Patrick sat down behind his desk and placed a notepad in front of him before looking directly at Quinn.

"Quinn, I had a rough day yesterday and I may not have been as good a host as I should have. My apologies."

"Believe me, Patrick. None are necessary. I am most appreciative for your hospitality."

"Well, anyway, let us all be candid today. First of all, welcome to Northern Ireland." Patrick then gave Quinn some facts concerning the history of the family from the time that his grandfather had left Kinsale and moved his business offices to Belfast. Patrick explained that he, like Quinn, was not from a large family, and this was a matter of considerable interest to Quinn who was curious as to the existence of other cousins with common ancestry. Patrick described the old homestead down in Kinsale and said that it was still owned by the family. Quinn was invited to visit the farm which was now open to the public and preserved as a typical nineteenth century Irish homestead.

Patrick then inquired of Quinn's family and the life that his grandfather had followed upon immigration into the States. Quinn told about the life on the farm in Renville County in the State of Minnesota and the fact that others from the Kinsale area also settled there, presumably at the same time. This was of interest to Patrick as he was aware that there were some Farrells and O'Learys still residing in Kinsale.

When these amenities were concluded and the relationships had been explained, Patrick inquired of Quinn as to what he had found in his research while in Dublin and Cork. Quinn could not recall that he had told Patrick that he had visited Cork for the purpose of reviewing records, but how he knew that was not particularly important. By now Quinn was aware that most everyone had a pretty good idea of what he had been doing since he arrived in the country.

Just then, Martha rapped on the door and entered with a pot of tea and cups for the three men. They all took a break from the conversation to pour their tea and the respite gave Quinn a moment or two to gather his thoughts on how he was going to respond to Patrick's question. He decided to lay the facts out as he knew them to be and deal with whatever issues resulted.

"Patrick, my research basically verified everything that I have told you about the relationships. There is no doubt that my grandfather is the one and the same Jeremiah Desmond that was the brother of your grandfather, William. That, of course, was something that I wanted to be very certain of. The primary proof for that being the old Gaelic letters that I have in my safe in the States. I have brought copies of the originals in Gaelic as well as the translations with me and I would be glad to share those with you. I am sure that you would find them to be of considerable interest."

Quinn then went on to explain the existence of the Will by Thomas Desmond, father of William and Jeremiah, wherein all of the property was to go to Jeremiah, the eldest son, and Quinn's grandfather. Quinn took careful note of Patrick's reaction to this assertion and seeing none, concluded that Patrick had apparently verified this for himself.

Quinn told about the murder of the other brother, Michael who was named in the will as a co-beneficiary of William in receiving the old Desmond homestead, but made no comment on the coincidental timing of

Michael's convenient death. Finally he laid out with great specificity, the finding of the Court Order granting the entire Desmond Estate to William based upon the death certificate filed by William, showing that Jeremiah was deceased and William was the sole heir.

"That is basically what I have discovered in my rather extensive research which began well over one year ago. It has been a most interesting endeavor."

Patrick nodded. He had been making notes of most everything that Quinn had been saying and when he put his pen down, he looked over at Frank Baumler and asked him if he had any questions that he wanted to ask.

"Excuse me for a moment, Frank. Before you ask, let me explain your involvement here so that Quinn understands." Patrick then told Quinn what Frank Baumler's position was with Desmond Enterprises and why he was sitting in on these meetings.

"Anytime someone has any claim, to anything involving Desmond Enterprises in anyway, Frank is brought in. Let me assure you that you are not the first person to come to contact me, or my family, and claim to be a descendant of the mysterious Jeremiah Desmond. That is a claim as sought over as some of the notorious buried treasures in your country. It is a story told over and over down in Kinsale that this Jeremiah was defrauded by his own brother out of the huge Desmond Estate. Every now and then someone shows up here in Belfast with proof. We have seen certified birth certificates, certified marriage certificates, verified will copies, you name it, absolutely proving that the person sitting in the very chair you are in now, is a descendant of the defrauded Jeremiah Desmond. Furthermore, they are always the only living heir of Jeremiah, which I can only assume that you are. Now, I don't wish to insult you, I am only explaining to you our side of this business. As I am sure you are aware, we must be careful and protect ourselves from false claims that have all of the apparent proof to support them. You say that you have letters that absolutely prove your case. I believe that you do have letters, I do not know if they are genuine letters or if they are forged letters. Quite frankly, they could be either and it would be virtually impossible to prove which they were."

Quinn was stunned to hear this from Patrick. He had expected that he would have to prove everything that he had alleged regarding the relationship, but he had never considered the fact that anyone would challenge the authenticity of the old letters that had been stored for years in his basement. He had just assumed they would be accepted as fact and now he saw that was a mistake. He should have anticipated that. As he sat in silence, he considered what other support he had for the relationship other than the letters. He knew, as did Patrick, that there were hundreds of other Jeremiah Desmonds that emigrated from Ireland in the approximate time frame that his own grandfather had. He had seen that very same name probably over a couple of hundred times while looking at microfilm of just one parish in County Cork. It would not be very difficult for any of their descendants to lay the very same claim as he. As he sat there, he felt a bit foolish for not having anticipated this very reaction. After all, Quinn was a lawyer and by training should be expected to challenge even the obvious. He had failed to do that in his own case. What was that old saying, a lawyer who represents himself has a fool for a client. So true.

Patrick, seeing that he had won this round but not wanting to alienate Quinn, continued. "Please don't think that I am accusing you of anything, Quinn. You don't strike me as the type of person that would claim to be someone you weren't. In fact, you very well could be the grandson of our Jeremiah Desmond, but how do we know. In the meantime, I hope you have enjoyed your stay at the Cheshire Arms. Now, if you don't mind, I'm sure Frank has some questions that he would like to ask about what you have come up with to support your claim."

Frank Baumler asked a number of questions regarding Quinn's research. He made notes regarding what was known of Jeremiah's immigration into the States. Where he had lived in Minnesota and when he died. Baumler also requested that Quinn leave copies of relevant birth and death certificates with him as well as copies of the old Gaelic letters that Quinn had brought along on the trip. As he finished his questioning, Frank Baumler said that he would drive Quinn back to his hotel and then he could get copies of the research papers, letters and certificates that he had requested.

When Baumler finished talking, Patrick stood up at his desk indicating to Quinn that the meeting was over and that he had to get back to his regular duties, whatever they were. Quinn was still somewhat stunned by the turn of events and just thanked Patrick for his hospitality before picking up his briefcase and heading for the door. As he was about to leave the office, Quinn turned back to Patrick and said that he would like to meet Adam before he left if that could be arranged.

Patrick looked at Baumler as though for assurance and Frank said he would be glad to take care of that on their way out of the office. As the two men left Patrick's office, Quinn stopped to thank Martha for her assistance and told her that he would most likely be leaving that afternoon for Dublin. Martha seemed a bit surprised but wished him well on his trip and hoped that she would see him again in the future. As Quinn walked down the hall with Frank Baumler he doubted very much that he would be returning.

Quinn followed Frank Baumler as they wound their way through the huge building, taking elevators and stairways, until they were down in the depths of the structure, a number of floors below street or ground level. After walking another long distance, through narrow hallways, they entered a huge, noisy, dusty room which was obviously the main receiving area for inventory items arriving from various points for further distribution to Desmond stores. Baumler raised his voice above the noise of the forklift trucks carrying pallets of merchandise and said, "His office is on the far side, so watch yourself. These guys don't always look where they're going. Also, let me warn you. Adam is a bit different."

Quinn had heard that before but did not know what it meant. Everyone was different but apparently Adam was very different. He would just have to wait and see. The two men walked to the far side of the storage room which Quinn estimated was two to three times the size of a football field. There were five or six offices built along the back wall with glass windows running the length of them so that Quinn could see the clerical workers, inside, staring at computer screens and inputting data. In the very end window, there was a single person sitting behind a desk and talking on the phone. It was a young man and Quinn guessed from his appearance that he was in his mid twenties and, unless he was wrong, that had to be Adam Desmond. His suspicion was confirmed when Frank Baumler said, "That's Adam in the end office."

Baumler made his way back to Adam's office, rapped lightly on the door and when Adam saw who it was, he waved the two men in. He was still on the phone working out an inventory problem with one of the stores that had received a shipment that was short on what the shipping documents described. When he finished the call, he stood up and smiled as he offered Frank a cup of tea. He then looked quizzically at Quinn and waited for Frank Baumler to make the introduction.

"Adam, this is Quinn Parker, who believes that he is the grandson of the Jeremiah Desmond that was the brother of your great grandfather. You may have heard your father mention that name. Anyway, he wanted the opportunity to meet you. He is from the states."

Adam seemed a bit puzzled by the introduction and Quinn had the definite impression that Adam had never heard the name Jeremiah Desmond before. Adam stood for a moment with a blank look on his face and then seemed to gather himself together.

"Have some tea, Mr. Parker, and make yourself comfortable. I am afraid that I don't know a great deal about the Desmonds. I have followed the Adams line with a bit more interest and doubt that I can give you any information. My father may have more to tell you, but I doubt that as well. He is not into his Irish roots, so to speak."

Quinn spoke up, noting the discomfort in Adam at the somewhat strange circumstance of his visit. "I did not expect any information. Actually, I just wanted to meet you to satisfy my curiosity about my Irish relatives. I did speak with your father and I believe I may have been much more familiar with the pedigree than he was."

Adam smiled and said, "I don't know that I would use the word pedigree with the Desmond line. You know, down in Cork, they joke about the intermarriage of the families. Seems like back in the 1800s that was quite common. Now, the Adams Family, on the other hand, their line goes back to the fourth or fifth century. Much royal blood there. Also, my mother's line, the Fairchilds, are of very aristocratic lineage. I prefer to concentrate my interests on those lines."

It was not only what he said, it was the haughty way he said it that made Quinn instantly dislike the young man and made him respond in kind.

"Yes, I suppose you are right. But at least with the Irish, you usually knew who the father was."

Baumler immediately entered the conversation and suggested that they should move on as Adam was obviously busy with inventory matters. Quinn agreed as he had seen all of Adam that he cared to see. His curiosity was satisfied and now he could return to the Hotel, pack and be on his way. It had been an interesting trip and he wanted to return to Dublin and reevaluate his position.

On the drive back to the hotel, Frank Baumler said very little. Quinn had already figured out that Baumler was, by nature, not a talkative person so he did not take offense at the lack of conversation as they drove through the heavy traffic. As they neared the grounds, of the hotel, Baumler did ask him when he was going to depart.

"In the morning, Frank. Just as soon as I can grab a train for Dublin."

"I'll have Martha call you first thing in the morning and she can run you to the station."

"No need, Frank, they have a shuttle at the hotel that handles the Dublin travelers. I've already put my name on the list, so don't bother Martha with that one. Thanks anyway."

When they pulled up in front of the hotel, Quinn suggested that Frank park and meet him in the lobby while he had copies made of the papers that he had requested.

"God, I had forgotten about that. Fine. I'll meet you in the lobby."

After Quinn copied the papers, he found Frank in the lobby waiting for him and suggested that if he had the time, they could have a beer. Baumler was agreeable to that suggestion and the two men were soon seated in the lounge as two frosty, cold beers were being placed in front of them.

"Cheers, Frank. It's been a most memorable day." There was a touch of sarcasm in Quinn's voice as he raised the glass.

Baumler smiled and tilted his glass in Quinn's direction. "Who knows, Quinn, we may meet again."

Now it was Quinn's turn to smile. "I believe we just may."

Up to this point in time, Quinn had been in a fog trying to figure out what he was going to do, whether to pursue his Desmond claim or to just drop the matter. Patrick's assertion that Quinn was just one of many who had been to see him with the same claim had stopped Quinn in his tracks. Particularly after Patrick's comment that there was no way to tell if the letters were genuine or were forged. Quinn had not thought for a moment that others may have focused on this method of gaining entry to the Desmond fortune. The thought that anyone would stoop to such activity had just never entered his mind. However, as the day had progressed and he had the opportunity to visit with the insolent Adam Desmond, he began to analyze, more critically, Patrick's words.

If others had focused on Jeremiah Desmond as their ticket to the promised land, why had no one else mentioned it. Sean said nothing and seemed never to challenge Quinn's assertions as being anything but statements of truth. Noel Galvin never mentioned that others had made similar claims and he should have been aware if such claims were being made from his work in the National Library. Even Adam seemed to be unfamiliar with the name, Jeremiah Desmond. The more that Quinn thought about what Patrick had said, the more he began to think that it was nothing more than a defensive move on his part.

"When do you think you will be returning to the States?"

"I keep changing my mind about that. I have things to do in Dublin and possibly back here so as I sit here, I really don't know."

Frank Baumler made no reply, but Quinn could tell that he was very curious as to what further work Quinn was involved with in Dublin. After a moment or two, Baumler probed with a statement.

"I'm going to be looking over your papers in the next few days and may wish to get ahold of you if I have any questions. Do you have a phone number where I can contact you?"

Quinn wrote the Hotel name and number on the back of one of his old business cards and handed it to Baumler. "Frank, for your information, I have other data that supports what I told Patrick regarding my grandfather. I have no doubt that my grandfather is one and the same Jeremiah Desmond that was a brother to Patrick's grandfather. I will be candid with you. I was a bit offended to have what I consider quite convincing evidence of the relationship to be dealt with so summarily without further examination. If you or Patrick were in hopes that this story of numerous other Jeremiah Desmonds making similar claims would cause me to fold up my tent and leave, I think you may be mistaken."

Baumler began to speak, but Patrick held up his hand to indicate he was not finished. "I think it would have been much wiser on your parts to seriously consider what I had to say and then to review the documentation. For your information, up to this point in time, I have had no great interest in finding a pot of gold over here in Ireland. That was never my intention, although you people obviously think that it is. On the other hand, since reading the will and seeing what I believe to be a fraudulent death certificate filed at about the time of the mysterious death of the other brother, leads me to believe that my grandfather was defrauded out of his rightful inheritance."

Baumler again began to speak, but Quinn went on. "I feel that I have some obligation to correct that wrong but as to how I go about that, I do not know. I intend to return to Dublin and decide on where I go from here. So, the long and short of it is, let's all drop the bullshit and deal with facts. If you have facts which negate what I am coming up with, let's see them. If not, then maybe we can talk about where we go from here."

Baumler nodded. "Makes sense to me. Let me assure you, though, Quinn. You are not the first person to approach us with a similar story. If you go down to Kinsale and talk to some of the older folks down there, the mystery of Jeremiah Desmond is fairly well known, especially around the older locals, and it is appealing to some people as an easy way to win the lottery. We are spring loaded to distrust stories such as yours. If we offended you, I apologize. Now, on the other hand, we have treated you quite well and, for your information, we treat anyone, who arrives here with decent documentation of their relationship, to a very comfortable night or two at the Cheshire Arms Hotel. Oh, you're not the first one to get the pack of Royal coasters either." With a chuckle, Baumler added, "we figure that one of these days, the real descendant of Jeremiah Desmond will show up and we don't want to be accused of being bad hosts."

"No, I can't complain about the quarters. Very comfortable. Thank you, by the way. You are good hosts. If you ever visit the States, I will try to reciprocate but I don't think we have anything comparable to this around

Atlanta."

The two engaged in friendly banter while they finished their drinks and then departed the lounge. Quinn shook Frank's hand at the entrance and told him that he would most likely contact him again before he left for the States. Baumler wished him well and departed the hotel.

Quinn had dinner in the hotel dining room and later in the evening placed a call to Anne. He described his meetings with Patrick and his brief visit with Adam. Anne listened quietly as he described Patrick's comments regarding other people claiming to be descendants of Jeremiah Desmond.

"You know, Quinn, I may be wrong on this, but I faintly recall that Sean may have mentioned something about this to me, years ago. Maybe when we were in one of the Desmond Stores. It would not be something that would get my attention which is probably why I don't recall the exact conversation. But, as you tell me this, it sort of rings a bell. He was right there, working for the Desmonds and would be in position to hear the story. I'm surprised that he never brought that up to you."

"I thought of that myself, particularly after Frank Baumler told me it was fairly common knowledge down in Kinsale. Sean must have heard it. Maybe he didn't want to offend me by bringing it up. He had the letters and they may have just blown aside any thoughts about the claims of others."

"Quinn, did you give him the originals or copies for him to translate?"

"He had originals. Why do you ask?"

Anne paused before answering. "Did you have copies of what you gave him or did he have the only copy?"

"He had the only copy. That made me a bit nervous because he had them for quite a while and I was worried they would get lost."

Anne was quiet for a moment and then said, "Interesting."

"What are you thinking?"

"I don't know. This whole thing is very strange. Sean had his own agenda, you know."

"Hmm." Now Quinn's mind was racing. "Well, that opens up a whole pile of things to think about. Anyway, I have to get my things together and figure out when I'm leaving here. I'll call you from the hotel tomorrow."

Quinn took the shuttle to Belfast Central Station and was soon on board the express bound for Dublin. The train was over half filled and this time, Quinn found that he was joined in his compartment by an elderly woman and a fellow who appeared to be a businessman, deeply involved in reading the Belfast Times. On the trip back to Dublin, Quinn thought over the events of the past two days. There had always been blank spots in what he knew about his grandfather's life in Ireland before he emigrated to the States. Before Quinn had the letters translated by Sean and before he began his research he knew virtually nothing.

Since coming to Ireland and working with Noel Galvin he had learned a great deal that seemed to tie in with the letters and confirm the relationship between Jeremiah and William. Yet, there would always be doubts and that was what Patrick was playing on. The inability of Quinn, or anyone else, to absolutely prove the relationship in the absence of the very people involved. Patrick, for all of his apparent deficiencies, had been successful in momentarily making Quinn question his own findings but those doubts were now rapidly receding.

As the train made its way south to Dublin, Quinn went over all of the details that he had assembled in his research. From the translations of the letters to the findings in the National Library and the records in Cork. It was a convincing array of evidence that spun a reasonably tight web in Quinn's mind proving that Jeremiah Desmond's rightful inheritance was stolen by Patrick's grandfather. For Quinn to sit back and do nothing about it would be the same as helping William Desmond succeed in defrauding his own brother.

Patrick's apparent lack of interest in righting the wrong along with the insolent behavior of his son, Adam, added additional fuel to the fire that was beginning to burn in Quinn's mind. By the time the train pulled into Connolly Station, Quinn had decided that he would pursue the matter and even take it to court if that became necessary. He had not decided what, if anything, he wanted from the Desmonds, but he did want the truth to be known that Jeremiah Desmond had been swindled out of his rightful inheritance.

CHAPTER 36

Patrick sat waiting for Baumler to arrive. He was very nervous this morning and waiting only made it worse. He looked at his watch again to see how long it had been since Martha told him that Frank wanted to see him. He couldn't believe that it had only been a matter of minutes. It seemed like hours.

"God, if it isn't one thing, it's another. Why didn't he just tell me over the phone what the hell he wanted to talk about?"

Patrick's hands were moist from the tension and twice the letter opener skittered out from his fingers and landed on the floor. He held his hands out, extending the fingers, to see if he could make them stop shaking. He could not do so. He knew the liquor was poisoning him but it was about the only thing that he trusted anymore. He was no longer sure even about Martha. True, she had never betrayed him or failed to answer his call when he wanted her, but he thought that she was a bit too friendly with Frank. He didn't think she was screwing Frank. That wasn't it, because Patrick just could not envision Frank Baumler screwing anyone. They must be conspiring about something more serious than that.

Patrick had been aware of the fact that in the last few months, Adam had been a regular in Baumler's office. Patrick had been there once or twice himself when Adam came by and it was obvious that he was much closer to Frank than to his own father. Possibly Baumler, Martha, and Adam were conspiring to replace him in the company. But with who. It would have to be a Desmond and Adam was the only one that those two could manipulate as they wished. Ellen was too tough for them and Hillary never listened to anyone else except for Tony Carter. No, Adam would be a likely target if anyone wanted to unseat him as President of Desmond Enterprises. As he sat waiting for Baumler, Patrick decided that he would not let them know that he was aware of what was going on. He would just bide his time. Possibly he could work some sort of a deal with Tony Carter to protect his interests, but he would have to be very careful about that. Just then Martha's voice came over the intercom.

"He's here"

"Send him in."

Frank Baumler entered the office, notepad and pencil in hand. He took a seat and waited for Patrick to give him the go ahead. His boss looked terrible this morning. As he waited, he concluded that Patrick must have spent the entire night drinking. His eyes were deep set in his face, more than normal, bloodshot with puffy dark bags under his eyes. His face had a pallid, almost waxen, look about it causing Frank to wonder just how much longer he would be able to function as President of the company. As he pondered these thoughts, Patrick finally got himself organized.

"What's on your mind, Frank?"

"Just wanted to report on our findings respecting your cousin's letters and his research."

"I'd rather you didn't call him my cousin. Just say Packer or Pecker or whatever the hell his name is, OK. So, go ahead. Let's hear it."

Frank looked over his notes and began. "Our attorneys in Cork handled the entire matter. They checked out the allegations concerning the Will, the dates of death of all principals, the newspaper articles on the brother, Michael, and the Death Certificate covering Jeremiah Desmond. On all of those items, they checked out as Mr. Parker described them to be. With respect to the Death Certificate on Jeremiah Desmond. It appears to be an authentic, American, Death Certificate issued by a proper County office. That, of course, does not mean that it is for the right Jeremiah Desmond. Proving that is going to take some time and, the attorneys tell me, it may never be proven. Apparently half of the people that emigrated in the middle nineteenth century were named Jeremiah Desmond. There was no shortage of them in the States."

Through the fog of his memory, Patrick could see the letter from the attorney in Illinois and the circle around the one Jeremiah Desmond whose Death Certificate was the subject of Frank's comments. He had suspected at the moment that he first read the letter that his grandfather was up to no good and now as he listened to Frank, he was even more convinced. But wait, his grandfather may have recognized the town that was referenced and just circled it as the one where his long lost brother lived. That could be it. He'd better not throw a monkey wrench in the mix by telling Frank about the letter. The only other person that knew about it was Robert, but he was just a houseman and beyond a doubt, didn't know what he had been looking at. Maybe the letter could even help his case. He would have to think about that after Frank left. Patrick realized that Frank was continuing to speak and what he was saying sounded positive.

"The attorneys suggested to me that the difficulty of proving that this is the right Jeremiah Desmond on the Death Certificate is not necessarily our problem. The job of challenging the Death Certificate is for Mr. Parker.

You don't have to prove anything. It's the burden of proof business, Chief. Mr. Parker has that burden, not you. Again, they tell me that proving it to be authentic or not could be very difficult, or, if Mr. Parker is lucky, it could be relatively easy depending upon the lengths that he wishes to go with his claim."

"Well, that's not exactly reassuring."

"Good points and bad points, Chief. You know how lawyers are. Anyway, the next item on the list is the letters purporting to be from your grandfather to Parker's grandfather. The content of the letters that we have seem to tie out to his facts. Also, the attorneys had a Gaelic scholar review the wording and he tied it back to the time period and the region. You know, Gaelic was spoken and written differently from place to place, particularly back then. Now, as to the age of the letters themselves, this is another tough one. We do not have the originals, nor do we have all of the letters that Parker claims to have. Consequently, we can't verify that they are genuine. Again Chief, this is one of those things that can't really be proven absolutely. What I mean is that you need the originals to verify their age and even if the age is verified, there is still a question as to whether they are genuine or not. Remember though, that is Parker's problem."

"How in the hell can you tell how old they are? Maybe Parker had them written three months ago."

"I guess there are ways. The attorneys said that old paper was made quite differently from paper now a days, and that can be determined fairly easily. The problem is that you can buy old paper today from specialty houses and I think the same goes for the old style ink that didn't have some of the fancier chemicals in it that are put in ink today. Remember though, Parker would have the burden to prove that the letters and the writing was genuine."

"Well, maybe he should just pack up and go home."

"Well, I said something like that to the attorneys and they said that Parker's case, if he pursues it, depends on the entire picture and how convincing that looks. He may lack absolute proof of one thing or another, like the letters, but if the letters appear genuine and their content ties in with known facts, then the burden may slide over to us to prove that they are not genuine. That may be an impossibility for us. I hope I'm making all of this clear."

"Yeh, so what do we do?"

"We sit and wait to see what he comes up with, if anything."

"This is driving me crazy, Frank. Either this Parker is for real or he has done a very good job of preparing a phony claim. The other's weren't this good. What if he is for real, did you talk to the attorneys about that?"

"As a matter of fact, I did. They said that, if true, it would most likely be an enforceable claim and could be for a very large sum of money. They did say that was a very preliminary opinion and there were many unknown factors involved that could change the entire picture, so again, we just have to wait and see what develops."

"They love complicating things, don't they."

Baumler smiled, "That's what they're paid to do."

When Baumler left the office, Patrick placed the call to Tony Carter on his secure line that did not pass through Martha's control panel. After two rings, Carter's secretary answered and said that he was in. She did not ask who the caller was because she immediately recognized the voice. There was a pause and then the secretary came back on the line and said that Mr. Carter would be with him shortly. This exasperated Patrick because he was certain that Tony Carter was readily available but was playing one of his many games of one upmanship. After another long wait, he was about to hang up the line when Carter answered.

"Yes, Tony Carter here."

Patrick knew that it was another one of Carter's tricks to pretend not to know who was calling him. Nevertheless, Patrick played the game according to the rules.

"Tony, it's me, Patrick. I'd like to have lunch. How's your schedule?"

"Just a minute, I'll check." Another minute passed and he was back. "I can make it at one. How's that?"

"Same place. Down by the wharf. Is that OK?"

Patrick had two hours before they met. Just enough time to clear out of the office and have the necessary fortification at the pub. He needed a drink anyway and the anticipation of meeting Carter only upgraded the desire for a drink from a need to an absolute craving.

As he walked out of his office carrying his coat, Martha looked up from her desk and asked when he would be back. That always irritated Patrick, the need for her to insist on knowing where he was all the time. Why the hell couldn't he have some time of his own. She knew he was going out to have a drink and this was her little way of jabbing him about that. He tried to cover up his anger but there was an edge to his voice.

"About three. Some business to take care of."

"Patrick, Adam just called and he wants to meet with you."

That stopped Patrick in his tracks. What the hell did he want? He never wanted to meet with Patrick in his life and certainly not in the last five or so years. Adam had obviously made it a point not to even cross paths with his father. Patrick had heard him moving through the house at times, but always when Patrick was just getting up in the morning or already in his room for the night. Now he wants to meet.

Patrick turned around to face Martha. "Adam wants to meet me?"

"Not so loud, Patrick. Others will hear you."

"What in the hell does he want?"

"I don't know. How about later this afternoon?"

"Make it five o'clock and tell him to be on time."

"I'll tell him five o'clock, Patrick."

Patrick made no comment, just spun around and resumed his course towards the elevator that would take him down to the garage. Jumping into his car, Patrick's growing irritation caused him to drive faster than normal in the direction of the pub by the wharf. Recalling that Carter had spotted his car there the last time they met, he circled the block and found an open spot on the side street where he could park the car. Patrick found the walk to the pub to have a calming effect on him and he thought that he should try getting his life back in order with some exercise. As he entered the pub the thought of taking up exercise disappeared as the overpowering aroma of ale and spirits brought him back to reality. He headed straight for the bar, took a seat and was a bit surprised to hear the bartender ask him if he wanted his usual, vodka and tonic.

"Uh… yes.. please. Uh… light on the tonic."

"I know." The bartender clearly had Patrick's number. Down to the fact that Patrick did not like to talk so he placed the tumbler of vodka, ice and a dash of tonic in front of him and left him alone.

As the calming effect of the vodka took over, Patrick tried to focus on the day ahead. He had two thoughts running through his mind. He had to figure out what he was going to say to Carter and he was wondering what the hell Adam wanted to see him about. He tried to put aside the latter thought until after the meeting with Carter, but it kept interfering. After another drink, he was able to think in a more structured fashion about the meeting. He asked himself, just what was it that he wanted to accomplish. After further thought, he concluded that he had to get out from under the pressure. He pursued that notion. The pressure came primarily from this Parker business. That had to be resolved one way or another. Carter would have some ideas on that and possibly some immediate solutions. An immediate solution was what he needed.

The other source of pressure, as he saw it, came from the fact that he knew he was losing his grip on the Company. Others were moving in. He could just feel it. Maybe that was what Adam wanted to meet with him about. If it was, he would fire the son of a bitch. He could still do that. No, back to the Carter business. He could not waste his time with Adam right now. He checked his watch and saw that he still had fifteen minutes before the meeting. He ordered another drink, downed that one and paid the bartender, including a sizeable tip to ensure his future privacy. The bartender thanked him and Patrick made his way to the door. He noticed that he was a little unsteady on his feet and he would have to do his best, when he met Carter, not to let that show. The walk back to the car would help.

Patrick purposely parked his car a good distance from the café to get the blood flowing to his brain before he sat down with Tony Carter. He should not have had the third drink. He must have had close to a half a pint of vodka in the three drinks that he had and now, he recognized, that was a mistake. As he walked towards the café, he questioned which was worse, not being able to think straight or being cowed by that ass hole. Certainly the latter was the more painful and with some effort, he would get his thoughts together. Just take my time. That's the answer. Don't let your mouth get ahead of your brain. Also, gotta remember to smile. Makes me look more confident. As he approached the door to the café, his heart began to race and he could feel the breath leave his lungs. There was no longer any sign of a smile, only an apprehensive look on his face as he walked in the restaurant and spotted Carter reading the Belfast Times at a table in the back of the room.

As he walked in, Carter looked up, smiled and spoke first. "Good day, Patrick. My, you are looking chipper today." The sarcasm was dripping from his words as he set the paper down and motioned for Patrick to take a seat.

"Not feeling very chipper today, Tony." Patrick pulled out the chair and sat down heavily as he motioned to the waitress for a cup of tea. "I'm sure you know through your network of spies that Mr. Packer… er Parker came to visit. My so called cousin."

"Now Patrick, you know I have no spies wandering around Desmond Enterprises. They are needed for more important projects than that." Carter let out an audible chuckle and went on. "It so happens that one of the staff at the Cheshire Arms told me that you had a guest there and when I learned his name, I figured out who it was. That must have been an interesting visit."

"Oh, it was. Tony, I'm worried about this guy. The attorneys tell me that he may be for real and if he is, I am in serious trouble." Patrick paused and went on. "That is what I wanted to see you about. I need some ideas.

Actually, I need solutions. This thing is getting to me. I can't sleep. My nerves are killing me. This guy could ruin me. I'm too damned old and sick to put up with this crap."

"Easy, my friend. We can take care of Mr. Parker any time. This might be a very good time, before the notoriety of it all leaks out. Then the press would focus in on him and it would be too late. You say the word and Mr. Parker will take the big trip. Is that what you want?"

"Tony, I don't know what I want. I don't want to have a guy put away. I don't know if I could handle that. Why don't you just do what you have to do and leave me out of it."

"Oh, I see. You want us to carry the entire load while you sit back in the comfortable lounge chair. Oh no, Patrick. If we do this, it is for you. I want you to understand that."

Patrick wished he had another vodka sitting in front of him right now. It would help him deal with Carter. "Tony, I want the problem to go away, period. I want your help on this. You know what this is doing to me. Do what you have to do."

"OK, Patrick, we will take care of this for you." Carter spoke slowly and clearly as he said, "I am taking what you are saying as your request to us to see that Mr. Parker is no longer a problem for you, and to do whatever is necessary, is that correct?"

Patrick looked down. He was trembling all over and he knew that it was evident to Carter. After a long pause and in a voice barely audible, he said, "Yeh. Take care of it."

"Louder Patrick, I didn't quite hear you."

"Yes, god damn it. Take care of it."

"OK, Patrick. We will do this and we are doing it for you, do you understand that?"

Christ, I'll bet he has a wire on him. I know he is recording this, the son of a bitch. "Yes, I understand it."

Softening his voice, Tony Carter went on. "Now, is there anything else that I can help you with? You're becoming a full time job, Patrick."

"I have other problems, but I think I'll handle them myself, at least for the time being.

"Well Patrick. Just don't wait until they're all screwed up before you call me. It's easier to solve minor problems than major ones, you know."

"I'll keep that in mind. How's my wife, by the way, I haven't seen her lately." God, where did I get the nerve to say that. Must be the vodka.

"Oh, good sense of humor, Patrick. As a matter of fact, I'm playing tennis with her in exactly one hour. I'll be sure to say hello."

"I'd appreciate it. That was all I wanted to talk to you about, so I think I'll leave. I'm not hungry and I have to get back to the office. Rather a busy day."

Carter said he was going to stay and have lunch. As Patrick prepared to leave, Carter stood and said, "You can relax about your cousin, we'll take care of it."

"I assume you're referring to Mr. Parker, the fellow from the States."

"Oh, that's right. If something happened to a cousin, that would be worse than to some stranger from another country. I'll try to remember that."

Patrick glared at him, said nothing, turned and left the café. As he walked back to his car, he took in the cool, fresh air. It had a cleansing effect on him after sitting in the small café in the company of Tony Carter. Unfortunately, the breeze coming in from the harbor also had a slight odor of decay with it, from the tide being so low, and it reminded him of what he had said to Carter about taking care of the Parker problem.

Patrick tried to convince himself that he had merely acquiesced in having Tony Carter work on solving the dilemma posed by Parker's claim. No matter how he tried to twist the conversation around to that interpretation, the words spoken produced another meaning. There was no doubt that Carter was talking about putting Parker away, permanently, and Patrick had obviously agreed to that as a solution for his own problems.

Patrick rung his hands as he thought, God, I can't believe I've sunk this low. I have got to get my head together before they do anything. I have time and I could warn Parker. No, I can't do that. He'd go to the police and then I'd be in more trouble. Well, at least I'm not involved in what Carter does... or, am I? Am I as guilty as he is if he gets rid of Parker? I don't think I could handle that. God, I need another drink. Then I'll be able to think this thing through. Carter isn't going to do anything today, or in the next day or two, I wouldn't think. I have some time to figure this out.

Patrick drove towards his office, taking a less traveled route, looking for a pub that he had never visited before. He had to pass two or three before he found one that he had not been in, at least that he could recall. He was now in a warehouse district and there was little sign of life anywhere other than that given off by a small neon light above the door of the pub. He parked down the street from the pub, but not too far because he didn't know the neighborhood and didn't want to expose himself to other dangers. He had enough to deal with the way it was. As he walked into the pub, he had to get his eyes accustomed to the dark interior before he could find where the bar was. There were a number of people in the bar and they were a rough looking crowd. Most likely from the factories and warehouses that surrounded the area. He thought about turning around and leaving, but he knew that would look foolish and probably even invite trouble. There was an open stool at the bar that he climbed up onto and ordered vodka and tonic.

"Out a vodka and don't have tonic."

Jesus Christ, Patrick thought. Where the hell am I? "Make it gin, straight up. Some ice."

The bartender walked to the end of the liquor cabinet and pulled out a bottle with a label that Patrick did not recognize. He poured straight from the bottle into the bar glass, grabbed a couple of ice cubes with his grimy hands, threw them into the glass and placed the drink in front of Patrick.

"In here, everybody pays before they drink." He eyed Patrick's fine suit of clothes and said, "three pounds."

Two of the men sitting down the bar from Patrick laughed.

"Shut up you two or I'll throw yer ragged asses out on the street."

Patrick dug three one pound coins out of his pocket and laid them on the bar. The bartender scowled at him as he picked them up and placed them on the till. He didn't bother to ring up the sale.

The gin was terrible but Patrick figured he'd better drink it down or he would be insulting the bartender. After the first few sips of the acrid tasting liquid, it began to go down more smoothly. When he had finished about half of the drink, he realized that it was hitting him like a hammer. He thought about not finishing the drink, but the state of euphoria it was producing beckoned him onward. He looked over at the fellow sitting next to him. He was about Patrick's age, maybe a bit younger. Hard to tell. The fellow needed a shave and either he or his clothes emitted an odor that reminded Patrick of the barn at the homestead. The fellow just stared straight ahead, but the gin was creating an interest in Patrick for conversation. Any kind of conversation. He was also losing the fear that had come over him when he entered the bar. These were just working class lads and what the hell did he have to fear from them.

"You work in the factories here?"

The fellow said nothing and continued staring straight ahead.

Patrick put his hand on the fellow's arm and repeated, "You work around here, my friend?"

The man turned towards Patrick, took his hand and slammed it down on the bar. "Keep your fucking hands off me, mate. I'm not your friend."

"Sorry, Christ, I'm sorry." Patrick gulped down the remaining gin in his drink, stood and staggered towards the door. As he did so, the two men from the end of the bar also stood up and opened the door for Patrick to make his way through and out into the open air. As he looked up and down the street, his blurred vision told him that he and the two fellows who had followed him out onto the street were the only three people around. He turned around, intending to make his way back into the bar, but his route of flight was blocked by the two.

"Eh, Mate. C'mon. We know another good pub down the road a piece. Right, Billy?" His friend agreed and with one on each side of him, basically carrying Patrick, they proceeded down the street and turned into the alley.

Patrick knew he was in trouble, but saw no way out of his predicament. He couldn't have run even if he was able to break loose, which he was not. He was petrified with fear and all he could think of was how stupid he had been to get himself into this situation. He looked down the alley and there was nothing but trash, the backs of buildings and no sign of a refuge of any kind. The alley just dead ended into another dirty brick wall a hundred feet or so from the entry. "Wait, my car is back there. We can drive to the pub." The two men stopped in their tracks. They had not thought about whether this guy might also have a car for them.

"Where's the car?"

Patrick explained that it was just down the street and he said, "If you'll let go of my arms, I'll show you the keys." They did and he pulled the keys out of his coat pocket.

"What kind a car?"

Patrick described the car and one of the men fished the keys out of his hand. Meanwhile, the other began going through Patrick's suit pockets, taking his wallet, cash and a pocket knife that Patrick had carried since his youth. Patrick made no attempt to resist, having sense enough to know that if he did so, that would just make matters worse and they would take his money anyway.

When they had cleaned him out, they pushed him up against the brick wall of the building. The one, Billy, put his face close to Patrick's and said, "Ya Papist bastard. Ya stopped at the wrong pub, din ya." Patrick began to protest but the words never left his mouth before the first punch struck him square on his jaw, smashing his head back against the brick wall. He felt nothing after that as his body went limp. The two men did not stop there. One held him up as the other pummeled him mercilessly until he fell into the dirt and rubble unconscious.

"Billy, we might a killed him."

"Ee's a Papist anyway. Who the hell cares. We should really finish im off." With that, Billy delivered a powerful kick into Patrick's unconscious body and seeing no sign of life in him, they pulled him down to the darkest part of the alley and covered him with debris so that he would not be discovered before they had made good their escape. After one last look to make sure they dropped nothing, they fled to the alley entryway and then took up a normal pace down the street looking for the car. Moments later they were comfortably seated in Patrick's Bentley with Billy driving and his companion searching the glove box, storage trays and rear seat to see what else they had been able to make off with after this day's work.

Two days later, the car was tagged by a police officer in Londonderry for being illegally parked. Eventually it was towed to a storage lot and the Vehicle Identification Number was scribbled down on a notepad by a clerk in the constable's office so that a notice could be mailed to the owner that the car was being held pending payment of the fines and storage charges. Unfortunately, in her haste to get out of the office and meet her boyfriend, she entered a zero instead of the letter O and the notice that eventually went out one week later, went to the wrong party. Seeing that the notice did not involve her car, the woman, who it had been sent to, crumpled it up and threw it in the waste basket. The follow up notice was not sent for another two weeks.

The following day, Martha dialed Frank Baumler's office. The phone rang two times and then Baumler answered.

"Frank, I am wondering about Patrick. He missed his meeting with Adam yesterday afternoon and he hasn't come in yet. Do you know where he is?"

"No." Baumler thought a moment. "That doesn't sound like him. Do you want me to call the house?"

"Better you than me. Let me know what they say."

In about five minutes, Frank was again on the line with Martha. "They haven't seen him since he left for the office yesterday morning. Robert said that his overnight bag and personal items were in his quarters so wherever he went, he didn't pack for it."

Martha explained his departure from the office the previous day and suspected that he might have gone to meet Tony Carter although Patrick did not say. "He knows what I think of Carter." She suggested that Frank talk to Tony and find out if he knew where he was.

"Not my closest friend, you know."

"Nor mine, Frank. Here's his number." Martha gave him Carter's office phone number and told him to let her know if he had any information. "This is beginning to worry me, Frank. It's not like Patrick to just take off.

He plans everything."

"I agree. I'll get on this right now."

Carter was out and his secretary did not know how to contact him but he had said he would be returning to his office later in the afternoon. Baumler told her to have Carter call him immediately as it was very important. He left his number with her and then sat back in his chair to try and figure out what he should do next. It was a little soon to be calling the police. Maybe Patrick had gone someplace to drink and just got a little too far into the bag. Maybe he was holed up in some hotel someplace trying to dry out from a very rough night. Frank knew that Patrick had stayed overnight on other occasions because of his drinking, but he was always in the office the following day at his regular time, mid morning. He called Martha back to report to her on his call to Carter. She just said to call her as soon as he heard from Carter and she said that she would check Patrick's office and see if there were any notes on his desk that might explain his absence. She would let Baumler know if she found anything.

As Baumler mulled over the possibilities that could explain Patrick's disappearance, he kept coming back to the conclusion that this was not like Patrick at all. Even in his most drunken moment, he always had displayed a reserve of common sense that seemed to surface and keep him out of trouble. Frank was aware, however, that Patrick had been deteriorating rapidly especially in recent months and maybe he had stepped over the line. Frank thought for a moment and dialed Ted Somers on the phone.

In less than a minute, Somers was seated in Frank's office. Baumler explained Patrick's strange absence and what investigation they had pursued thus far. Somers listened quietly and then added, that based on his knowledge of Patrick's personal habits, this was very unusual for him.

"What do you think, Ted? Any ideas?"

"Carter's sort of key here, Frank. If you want, I'll go over to his office and search him out. You know how he is. He just might not return your call."

"Good point. Do it."

Ted Somers was soon in his car, speeding towards the wharf area where the Unity offices were located. He pulled into executive parking, flashed his expired police badge at the attendant and asked where Mr. Carter parked his car.

"That's it right over there, officer." Somers glanced over at the parking spot and saw that it was occupied.

"I take it that's his car?"

"Yes sir, that's it. He just came in a few minutes ago."

"Fine, where can I park while I'm upstairs?"

"Anyplace that does not have a name on it, Sir."

Somers wheeled his car into an open spot, marked guest, locked the car and asked for directions to Carter's office. He then headed for the elevator and was soon stepping out on the twelfth floor and walking towards a reception desk with large blue letters on the back wall spelling out, UNITY SECURITY. There was a very attractive, young woman wearing head phones and a mouth piece, and wearing an identification tag with the Unity emblem and the name Fiona.

"Fiona, my dear, I would like to see Tony Carter."

"Who should I say wishes to see him?" The rhythmical way she said that and with her one eyebrow raised ever so slightly, made impure thoughts run rampant through Somers head.

"Fiona, tell him it's Jones from the R.U.C." Somers had called on Carter before and had spent what he considered excessive time waiting in the lobby for him. He didn't particularly care for that.

Within thirty seconds of making the request to see Mr. Carter, Tony Carter came wheeling out of the hallway and was well into the lobby before he spotted Somers. He immediately came to a stop and was about to retrace his steps when Somers had him by the arm. Somers pulled Carter tight against him so that he could feel the bulge of Somer's Glock against his ribs.

"How good to see you Mr. Carter. This is indeed a pleasure. Where would you like to talk?"

Carter coldly and calmly turned to Somers. "Obviously wherever you would like. You should check your toy at the door before coming in here. You could hurt yourself."

As the two men separated, Carter continued. "I would think they would have taught you some manners over at Desmond. It's polite to give your correct name when you come to our offices."

"We used to do that but we found that we spent an unusual amount of time studying your cheap paintings and that seemed like such a waste of our time. Now where would you like to talk?"

"Before we get down to whatever it is you wished to speak to me about, Mr. Somers, let me tell you that one of these days, I'm going to give you a new face. How would you like that?"

"Mr. Carter, you are so sweet. Let's have our little meeting and then maybe we can discuss those more enjoyable pastimes."

Without further comment, Carter walked back down the hall, with Somers following him, to his office which was located on the corner of the building. The location of his office gave him a sweeping view of the wharf area, the docks and the shipyards. He walked around his desk, sat down in a huge leather chair and told Somers to have a seat.

"Lovely office, Tony. You've done quite well since we were kids."

"Yes. Some of us have."

"Brutal, Tony. Down to business. Have you talked with Baumler since you returned to your office?"

"No. I see there is a note from him, but I've been busy."

"I'm sure. Our problem, Tony, is that Patrick has disappeared. We can't find him anywhere and he has been gone from the office since yesterday noon."

Carter was obviously surprised to hear this. He thought for a moment and then said, "We had lunch. No, that's right. He didn't actually have lunch, but we had met to have lunch and he was there only about a half hour or so. Down by the wharf. A small café, soup and sandwich sort of place. I think the name is O'Brien's, but I'm not sure. Right by the statue of what's his name."

"King William, or was he a Prince?"

"Whatever. Yeh, that one. Just to the south of that. He didn't say where he was going when he left. He looked terrible by the way. Said he hadn't been sleeping well lately. He probably went to have a drink some place."

"No doubt. What did you fellows talk about, if I may ask?"

"Sorry. Confidential stuff. Nothing that would help you find him. Just some family business. I think he said he had to get back to the office, but I had the definite feeling that he was going to stop and have a drink or two first."

"Not unlike him. Any ideas as to what might have happened to him?"

"None. If I hear from him, I'll let you know. Now if you don't mind, I've got work to do."

"You're a hell of a guy, Tony. Tell me something before I leave. You don't hold it against me for beating the shit out of you when we were kids do you?"

"You have a bad memory, my friend. You know where the door is. Good day."

Somers stood to leave and stopped. "Oh, by the way Tony, who won the tennis match yesterday?"

"Well, you do get around, don't you."

"That's my job. See you."

Carter watched him as he moved out of the office. Nosey bastard, he thought to himself. He's a tough one though. So is Baumler. Too bad they weren't on our team. Now, what the hell happened to Patrick. No sense in wasting time looking for him. Baumler would take care of that. What if something happened to him though. That could seriously complicate matters. Carter thought about placing a call to Dublin to cancel the job on Parker, but decided not to, at least for now. He would wait and see what developed with Patrick. He was probably passed out in some flea bag hotel, working out the cobwebs from a serious drunk. He would turn up eventually.

When Somers left the Unity parking lot, he did not head for the Desmond Office Building, rather went in the opposite direction towards the wharfs. Soon he was driving slowly past the Statue of William III, and searching down the street to see if he could see the café where Patrick and Carter had met. As he proceeded north, he noticed a sandwich shop just a few doors east of the street he was driving on. He swung a left turn and soon found a parking place. When he entered the café, there was only one patron having a cup of tea. The waitress and cook were in the back talking and Somers walked back to talk to them. He described the two men and asked if they had been in their café the previous day.

The waitress remembered the two because she thought the one had been drinking although he was not unruly, only that she could tell he had been drinking. Somers asked her a number of questions as to where he may have gone, what time he had left and his appearance when he left. She answered them as best she could, but had no information of any significance that would assist Somers in the task at hand. She did confirm that Carter had stayed and had soup with a sandwich. He left the café about twenty to thirty minutes after Patrick.

When Somers returned to his car, he pulled out a street map of Belfast and found the location of the café. He then drew a straight line from there to the Desmond Offices. Staring at the line, he tried to envision what route Patrick may have taken. The obvious route was to follow the M2 south into the City Center and then over to the offices. Assuming that Patrick intended to have a drink or two first, where would he have gone. He could have gone out to his club, but that would involve a lengthy detour and Baumler said that Patrick had a meeting scheduled at the office. He would only go to the club if he was not returning. There were probably fifty to a hundred small bars and pubs on side and cross streets between the café and the City Center that he could have gone to. Probably most of them were not even in the telephone book so locating them would most likely have to be a hit and miss proposition.

As he sat in his car, staring off into space, Somers tried to recreate

Patrick's thought process. Let's see, he gets in his car. He had to be parked facing the west because you can't park across the street. Baumler had told Somers a number of times in the past how Carter was able to intimidate Patrick, so Somers figured that following the meeting with Carter, Patrick was very ready to have a drink someplace and he intended to stop and have one even before moving out of his parking space. He would drive some distance away from the café before stopping and it would have to be off the beaten track so that he was not seen. He would not want Carter to see him going into a bar because that would be humiliating for him. Assuming that these were reasonable assumptions on his part, Somers then located a through street on the map that paralleled the M2 and probably had bars situated on it or on cross streets that might afford Patrick anonymity.

Somers drove down the street he was on in an easterly direction until he located the through street, Nelson Road, and then turned south in a direction that would lead him into the City. He searched both sides of the street for bars or pubs and quickly glanced down side streets for the same. He hadn't gone two blocks when he saw his first pub located mid block on a side street. He stopped at the corner and searched the street on both sides for Patrick's car. It was not in sight. Somers maintained this routine without success until he was on the edge of the business center of Belfast. He was fairly certain that Patrick would not stop that close to his own offices and Somers then abandoned the project.

When Somers walked into Frank Baumler's office, he first asked if there was any news on Patrick. Baumler only shook his head and asked Somers what, if anything, Carter had to say. Somers explained their conversation and then the follow up visit to the Café. He also told Baumler about his search along the through street for any sign of Patrick's car.

"Good thinking. You are most likely right. If he doesn't turn up this evening, we have to call in the police. I would then suggest that you get a team together and check every pub and booze joint within a mile range either side of Nelson Road. I think you can count on hitting the one where he at least stopped for a drink. Some of those areas up there are a bit rough and maybe he went into the wrong one. You'd better double up your teams with add-ons from Shipping. Make sure the Security guys carry protection. No weapons for those birds from Shipping. Some of those guys are liable to blow their own foot off."

Baumler thought for a moment. "Have Martha run off about thirty copies of Patrick's corporate photo and pass them out to your guys. She should have a current one around. I'll take care of the R.U.C. I've talked to Martha and she is setting up a command post that will be manned until we find out what happened to Patrick. The number is her direct number, so make sure your guys have that in case they come up with something. Last but not least. This is all confidential. Impress that on your guys. This could just be one of Patrick's bad moments. We don't want to scandalize him if that's what it is. I will be available through that command post number if you have to talk to me. If you don't have any questions, let's get moving."

After Somers had left the office, Frank Baumler sat back in his chair to figure out where they went from there. Patrick had been getting dangerously deep into the bottle lately and if this turned out to be just an extended drunk on his part, it would be hard to keep this episode out of the public eye. Too many people were now involved in the search for him. On the other hand, as Baumler thought about it, he hoped the other, more likely, alternative was not the answer to the mystery of what had happened to Patrick.

CHAPTER 37

When Quinn returned to the Hotel after his trip to Belfast, he first checked his messages. There was a note from Joe Robbins to call him as soon as he returned. Quinn went up to his room and placed the call. A woman answered and said that he was not in, but would return in an hour or two. Quinn left his number for Robbins to call him when he came back and then Quinn ran out for a quick sandwich in a small shop on Nassau Street.

When he returned, he sat down at his desk and began writing out a summary of the facts that he had accumulated supporting his grandfather's right to the Desmond inheritance. There was no doubt that the key to all of his arguments was the packet of Gaelic letters. Anne's questions concerning Sean's access to the letters had bothered him ever since their conversation. The letters were out of Quinn's possession for over a month, during which time Sean apparently made a return trip to Ireland.

Sean never mentioned the purpose of the trip and never discussed what he had done while he was back in Ireland. As Quinn thought about it, he wondered if Anne was even aware of Sean's trip back to Ireland. She had not mentioned seeing Sean in that time frame, but then maybe she had just not thought about telling him. Quinn made a mental note to take a close look at the letters when he returned to Atlanta.

Fortunately, Quinn had the foresight to secure the originals safely in his rental box at the bank so that they would not be lost by theft or a fire. Since the break in, he had become quite careful in how and where he stored his research materials and had duplicate disk copies of virtually everything that he had done. He had also password protected his computer files, but he knew that any good teenage hacker could bypass that barrier with ease.

As he sat thinking at his desk and making notes in his summary, the ringing of the telephone startled him. He had forgotten about the call from Robbins and had to think for a moment who he was talking with on the other end of the line. "Joe, good to hear from you. Where are you at? I thought you were heading back to the States."

"I'm leaving the day after tomorrow, Quinn, and if you are available, I would like to get together, either tonight or tomorrow."

Quinn paused a moment before answering. He was tired from his trip to Belfast but also wanted to visit again with Robbins before he left. He just might have some information that Quinn would find useful. "Either one, Joe. It's your call."

The two made plans to meet at a pub in Temple Bar in a half an hour. Quinn made disk copies of his work and buttoned up the computer before leaving the room. It was already dark out on the street but many people were on the sidewalks which he always found reassuring. It was a chilly walk as he made his way past Trinity University and over to Dame Street but fortunately, it was not raining. As he walked into Gogarty's in Temple Bar, he saw Robbins standing at the bar talking with another fellow. When Robbins saw him, he pointed to an empty booth and the two men were soon seated and ordering a pint.

"Quinn, how did your trip go? I heard you went to Belfast. I'm anxious to hear about it."

Quinn ran through all of the events of the trip from the pickup at the rail station to the return trip to Dublin. He told Robbins what Patrick had said in their final meeting in the offices of Desmond Enterprises but made no comment as to what he thought about it. Robbins smiled. "I'd say he was trying to bullshit you. From what Sean told me, those letters that you had Sean translate more or less said it all."

"I agree. They did keep copies of what I had come up with, including copies of some of the letters. If they were not somewhat receptive, they would not have kept anything. But, the long and short of it was that they put the puck back in my court. I will do something, but I don't know what. I just haven't made up my mind."

"Quinn, why don't you talk to a lawyer? An Irish lawyer. I've got a good one for you. Guy's name is Jerry Donahue and he's been around quite a bit. Also knew Sean. Don't let those bastards get away with it."

"Joe, I'm not so interested right now in getting anything out of it. I may feel different about it on down the road but right now, I just want the truth of what happened to get out."

Quinn was silent. He didn't want to argue the issue just now and he knew that Robbins and the others wanted anything that would hurt their opposites in the north. He remembered Martha alluding to the fact that the Unity Party had an interest in protecting one of their benefactors, but, she also said, there was another reason for their interest, but she wouldn't tell him what it was. As he thought about it, he wondered if Robbins could put some light on that subject.

"Joe why would Unity have an interest in what I have been doing?"

A very faint smile crossed Robbin's face. "Patrick Desmond is their number one contributor through Desmond Enterprises."

"Is that it?"

Quinn could see the wheels turning as Robbins thought about what to say. "Well." He paused. "I would assume that Unity may be benefitting in other ways from Desmond Enterprises and they don't want that interfered with."

"What other ways could we be talking about, Joe?"

"Well, maybe they're into something like, drug trafficking. Who knows?"

Robbins had a smile on his face as he spoke that indicated to Quinn that he knew what he was talking about.

"Joe, wouldn't that be a little stupid for the Desmonds to get involved with."

"Not in the north if Unity had anything to say about it. They pretty well run the show up there."

Quinn thought over what Robbins had said and was about to speak when Robbins went on. "Also, Unity pretty well runs Patrick Desmond from what I know. His wife is very active with the company but she has other interests, one of which is a Unity exec, who, by the way, was the one that someone tried to take out a week or two ago."

"Interesting. No one mentioned that when I was up there, but I don't suppose they advertise that business. By the way, do you know this Frank Baumler who seems to be in charge of Security for the company?"

"I know of him. Very competent guy. He came out of the R.U.C., Royal Ulster Constabulary. Was in charge of Security there. No dummy. He's been with Desmond about ten years, maybe more. I take it you met him?"

"Yes. Forgot to mention that. He was with Patrick Desmond whenever we met. I thought he was very professional. I agree, no dummy."

"Quinn, you know my thoughts on this. Go get 'em. We'll back you up and we'll provide the horses. They deserve it and you deserve it."

"Well, I haven't noticed that you had security on me lately."

Robbins smiled, thinking about their guy sitting in the same compartment with Quinn on the ride down from Belfast. "Our fellows are pretty subtle, Quinn."

"Good, I don't like it when people are looking over my shoulder."

Robbins told Quinn that he would talk to him again in the next few days. Either from Dublin or when he was back in the States. The two men sat in the pub for another hour or so, discussing various subjects, including

Anne Flanagan. Robbins had spoken with her on the phone but had not made a visit to the house. He had been very busy but hoped to get in touch with her before he left.

Quinn knew that Joe was taking over Sean's duties in the States and that was what was keeping him so busy. "She would enjoy seeing you before you left, Joe." Quinn then told Robbins that he had been seeing quite a bit of Anne since he had arrived in Dublin. From the lack of any reaction from Robbins, Quinn figured that was not news to him.

Robbins walked part way back to Quinn's Hotel with him, then the two men shook hands and promised to stay in touch. Quinn genuinely liked Joe Robbins. Quinn was well aware that Joe had a higher calling that required a greater loyalty than anything he could have for a mere friend, but, in that respect, he was very much like Sean.

As a result of what he had learned, Quinn no longer had the high level of trust for Sean that he formerly had, but he didn't hold that against him either. He was beginning to understand the psyche of people such as Sean and Joe Robbins, fully engaged in the Nationalist struggle. They had their own hierarchy of loyalties and it so happened that loyalty to friends was down the list from loyalty to the cause.

As he walked back to his hotel, following his meeting with Robbins, he checked behind him a number of times but never saw any sign that he was being followed. He smiled as he thought that maybe his "protection" was one more thing that he was being told, that he should question.

A few nights later, Anne invited Quinn to attend another "One Ireland" meeting. His interest in attending was focused primarily on being someplace with Anne and a "One Ireland" meeting secondary.

As they walked into the Hall, Quinn thought about Joe Robbins and asked Anne if he had called. She said he had, but that he regretted he was not going to be able to stop by before he left. "That's no problem anyway, Quinn. I was never that close to Joe. He's as deep into Irish politics as Sean was and we just were not alike in that respect."

Quinn looked around the vast hall and saw that there was an even larger crowd than was present at the other meeting that he had attended. They walked on into the huge room and Anne said hello to people that she knew. Quinn also recognized a face or two from people that Noel or Joe had introduced him to, or that he had met in the library. As they made their way through the hall, Quinn recognized the woman that had been identified to him as the woman that was with Tom O'Rourke the evening that he was killed.

Quinn pointed her out to Anne who quickly responded, "that's Ellen

Desmond, Quinn."

Quinn thought a moment. "She's not the daughter of Patrick Desmond of Belfast is she?"

"Quinn, I think she does work at the Desmond offices here in Dublin. Desmond is such a common name here, I don't know."

"She must be Patrick's daughter. They said she was here, in Ballsbridge. I'll be damned."

"That would fit. Quinn, I've met her before. Let's go over there and I'll introduce you. You can ask her."

"I don't know if I want to, her brother was such a twit."

"If you don't, I'm going over there and point you out to her."

"I guess I'd better."

Anne walked on over to Ellen who smiled when she saw Anne and said she would be with her in a just a minute. "Business, you know." When she concluded the conversation, Ellen stepped over to Anne, took her hand and said how sorry she was to hear about Sean.

"And Tom." Anne said. "You have to wonder what kind of a world we live in. When will it end?"

"Soon I hope, Anne. I believe that. If we all work at it."

Ellen looked over at Quinn who was listening to the two women. Seizing the moment, Anne quickly introduced Quinn as "a friend of mine and Sean's. He was wondering if you and he may be related, which you may find interesting."

"Well now. This is interesting. Tell me about it." Ellen was obviously, genuinely interested in hearing that this distinguished appearing gentleman was possibly related to her. The only relatives that Ellen had ever met were all from the Adam's or the Fairchild families. With only one exception, they were too stuffy for her tastes. The exception was Sir Charles Fairchild, who she viewed as a certified lecher.

Quinn wasn't sure where to start but quickly collected his thoughts. "If Patrick Desmond in Belfast is your father then we may well be related."

"That he is. This is interesting. I have one of the few families that seems not to have any relatives, particularly in the south. Please explain."

Quinn explained that Jeremiah was the brother of her great grandfather and left it at that. He did not expand. This was not the time nor the place.

Anne was clearly interested in what Quinn had to say. "Well, this is interesting. I would like to discuss this at greater length. How about lunch or dinner sometime?" Ellen looked over at Anne. "Look, Anne, I'm stealing your friend."

Anne laughed. "That is why I brought him over here to you. I'm sure you would enjoy hearing what he has to say. It's very interesting."

Quinn made arrangements to meet Ellen for lunch in the City Center at La Meza Luna on Dame Street. Ellen had a number of other people waiting to talk with her so Anne and Quinn said their goodbyes and walked on through the hall.

As they made their way through the hall, Anne said, "I have always heard good things about Ellen. She has been here in Dublin for about two years now and is very well liked. You probably think that she is tied in with 'One Ireland' because that is where you have seen her, but the word is that she is not political. She was pretty hooked on Tom O'Rourke and he, more or less, brought her into the group."

When Anne dropped Quinn off at the hotel, she said, "Now don't go running off with Ellen, Quinn. Remember, she's your cousin."

Quinn laughed and said, "The family's from Cork, you know."

"Oh, you are nasty."

"I try to be every now and then."

"Call me tomorrow night." Anne waved to Quinn as he looked back at her from the hotel steps and she sped off into the evening traffic.

At exactly one o'clock, Quinn walked into the dining room of La Meza Luna. He looked over the crowd of young professionals busily discussing business matters and spotted Ellen Desmond sitting at a table off to the side. He motioned to the Maitre D' that he saw his dinner companion and could find his own way to the table. As he approached the table, Ellen started to stand and Quinn told her to stay seated.

"I'm not quite so old that attractive women have to stand when I approach them. Wait another twenty years, please."

"I only do that for cousins, Quinn. It has nothing to do with age."

Ellen told Quinn about her job at Desmond in Ballsbridge until the waiter brought their carafe of wine and two glasses. After they had ordered, Ellen told Quinn that she had spoken with her father this morning and he related to her the gist of his conversation with Quinn. She lowered her voice and put on a mock serious look as she said, "Pretty serious stuff you're involved with here, Mr. Parker."

"Well, maybe it is and maybe it isn't. I frankly came over here from the States just to see if I had any relatives around. I didn't know it was going to turn into this sort of a situation."

"Daddy says that others have raised this claim before which is, quite frankly, news to me. I was not aware of it. Now, tell me more about what you are relying on that has you so convinced you are on the right track."

Now that Ellen was aware that there was a problem with the title to the Desmond Estate, Quinn held nothing back. He told her about the Will of Thomas Desmond, the Death Certificate that Quinn was certain was fraudulent and, again, more detail regarding the letters and what they contained that related to proven facts.

"Quinn, it seems to me that everything you have depends upon the authenticity of the letters. Are you certain that they are genuine? Don't get me wrong, I'm not questioning you, I'm wondering about the letters. That is Daddy's concern and I think he has a valid point."

"The letters have been in my family's possession for around a hundred years Ellen, and I can only assume they are what they purport to be." Quinn did not mention that Sean Flanagan had done the interpreting of the letters and had possession of them for approximately a month, something that was of growing concern to him.

"Well, regardless of what happens with all of this, I would like to know about your Desmond family after your grandfather emigrated from Ireland."

Quinn went through the history of the family on down to the present time and explained to Ellen that he was now the sole living descendant of Jeremiah Desmond in the States. That was one of the reasons why he had sought out other cousins in Ireland.

"Well it's too bad Quinn that we can't ask our ancestors all of the questions that come to mind after they're gone. I have always been curious about the Desmonds but never knew any of them. My grandfather, Dennis, was the only son of William and he died when I was just a small child. I would like to see pictures some time, if you have some of your grandfather, I would like to see them. You know, we have an old painting of my great grandfather, William and it would be interesting to see if there is any similarity there."

Quinn had never even thought of that. He had one or two pictures of his grandfather, but they were back in his room. As he thought about Ellen's suggestion of looking for a comparison between William and Jeremiah Desmond, brothers that were very close in age, he wished that he had brought that up when he was in Belfast. He was excited at the prospect of seeing if there were visible similarities.

"What a great idea, Ellen. If you have any pictures, please send them to me and if you would, take a picture of the painting. Good idea. I should have thought of this myself. I will send you pictures of 'Grampa' Desmond. He lived a long life, ninety seven years. Sharp right up to the end. A very personable guy. Great idea."

"So, Ellen, what is your time line for becoming president of Desmond

Enterprises?"

Ellen smiled and said, "Now, Quinn, that's an easy one to answer. My time line is right now. Better yet, yesterday. If I have the opportunity to move up, I am taking it."

"Quinn, I have to ask you this. If you are able to prove that your grandfather was, in fact, defrauded out of the Desmond Estate, what would you do about it?"

"Good question. I just haven't figured that out yet. I will say this, though, I would very much like to know the truth."

"Interesting. Well, keep me informed. Maybe I should start looking for a job."

Quinn laughed. "Ellen, from what I have run into so far, I would promote you immediately to CEO of the Company. Let me assure you, I have no interest or aptitude for running anything remotely similar to Desmond Enterprises. That is not what I am about."

"Speaking of running the Company, I'd better get back and do just that. Quinn, this has been interesting. Stay in touch while you are here in Ireland. I'll get you those pictures within the next week or two and send them over to the Rockwell. If you leave, let me know."

As Quinn walked down Grafton Street, Ellen's final question continued to linger in his mind. What if he was successful in arguing his claim? What would he do? He would have to figure that one out.

CHAPTER 38

After Somers left Baumler's office, Frank Baumler dialed the Shipping Department. A clerk answered and soon Adam Desmond was on the line. Within minutes, he was seated in Frank's office wondering just what was up.

"Adam. I'll get right to the point. Your father has been missing for the last day and a half. We do not know where he is and, frankly, we are very concerned about him. We are organizing a search team as we do know where he was last seen yesterday afternoon. Also, if we don't have word from him by seven this evening, we are notifying the R.U.C."

Adam went white. "I assume this has something to do with the Provos or the INA, right?"

"I don't know, Adam, but I rather doubt it. Your father was not a particular threat to either one and I think they are fully aware of that fact."

"I didn't tell you, Frank, but I went to see Father yesterday afternoon, but he didn't show. I wanted him to help me financially in getting out of here. I have to tell you I'm scared of what is going to happen to me if this drug business gets out. They'll know that I ratted on them and they are a damn mean bunch. I have the feeling that one of these days word is going to get out on their operation and when it does, they'll look for a fall guy. That's me, Frank. I know it."

Baumler sat behind his desk studying the young man. Just like his old man. No guts. He isn't even thinking of his old man, only himself. "Listen, Adam, I'll know well before that business collapses, so don't get panicky. I'll see that you are out of the picture before the word gets out. In the meantime, I'm busy on your father's case. I just wanted you to know that he is missing and this could be serious. We do not know where he is. Now, if you don't mind, I've got to get working on this."

"He's probably on a toot someplace. He's been living in the bottle for the past year and everyone knows it."

"Maybe. Nevertheless, we have to find him. Have a good day."

After Adam left, Baumler placed a call to Ellen in Dublin but she was not there. He left a message on the answering machine for her to call him at his office number when she returned.

Somers had his men out combing the bars and pubs before nightfall settled over Belfast. They moved methodically and carefully, scrutinizing the streets within walking distance of any drinking establishment, looking for the Bentley, and then into the bar or pub to see if the bartenders recognized the photographs of Patrick. The hours passed without success and finally at eleven o'clock, Somers called off the search for the night. A number of his teams had reported increasing difficulty in leaving some of the establishments safely and besides the bartenders were very busy and didn't want to waste their time talking to them.

Somers figured that they could resume their search the following day at about the time that he figured Patrick had left the café. If that search proved fruitless, he would send them out again to recheck the places they had gone to during the night. Many of the teams reported that the bartenders working the evening shift were not the same ones on duty after the lunch hour and consequently wouldn't know if Patrick had been in their bar during the afternoon.

That evening, after a cold sandwich in his office, Frank Baumler called one of his contacts at the Royal Ulster Constabulary to report that Patrick Desmond had disappeared. A formal report was prepared and a bulletin issued to the uniformed patrolmen to conduct a search in their areas of jurisdiction for Patrick and the Bentley. There was to be no press release until the family members had all been informed and that might not happen until well into the next day. That would give Frank one more day to keep the information out of the press in case Patrick showed up. In the mean time, as he waited for word, Baumler assumed that at least the car would turn up. It was not exactly the sort of vehicle that would blend in with others in the parking lot.

Baumler's contact in the R.U.C. assured him that he would let him know as soon as they found anything. It was two o'clock in the morning when Frank left his office and there was no word from anyone that Patrick or the car had been located. Now, Baumler was becoming convinced that something very bad had happened to him. He would have to call Ellen in the morning, at work, if he didn't talk with her this evening. He believed Hillary was in London on a shopping trip and would be back in two days. He could leave word with her secretary over at Fairchild but that could wait until tomorrow. Hillary probably didn't give a damn anyway.

The following morning when Frank Baumler arrived at his office, there was a message from Martha that Ellen had arrived early in the morning by chartered plane and was in her father's office. She had been told by the houseman, Robert, during the night that her father was missing. Baumler went up to the office and found Martha, Ellen and Adam sitting in Patrick's office waiting for word on his disappearance. Frank had called the hot line earlier and learned that nothing had been found, not even the Bentley. The R.U.C. had called during the night and received the Vehicle Identification Number and description of the car. They also indicated that they would be expanding the search throughout Northern Ireland if nothing was discovered by noon.

Ellen asked if Hillary had been informed and Martha said that she had contacted Hillary's secretary and they were trying to locate her but Hillary was notorious for not telling people where she was going. Nevertheless, the secretary was confident that she would be able to find her by noon. Adam looked like a nervous wreck as he sat dwarfed in the oversize leather chair. He was pale and he kept moving about the chair, trying to get comfortable. He would occasionally glance at Baumler and then shake his head. Only Frank knew that his real concern was for his own well being. Adam figured that he was next on the hit list.

After a long period of silence, Ellen looked up at Baumler and asked. "What do we do now, Frank?"

"We have our own people out trying to retrace his steps, Ellen. I'm fairly confident that we will find something out, at least by early afternoon. I'm puzzled that we have not located the car. It's a little hard to camouflage a Bentley. I'm sure whoever has the car has taken it far out of Belfast. The R.U.C. should have figured that out by now. At this point, Ellen, there is nothing to do but wait. Both our people and the R.U.C. are looking for your father and sooner or later, something will be found."

Later in the afternoon, when they had still not heard anything, Ellen took one of the company cars and drove out to Park Ridge to get some rest. She had been up all night and was not in any shape to help in the command center. Shortly after she had departed, Somers called Frank Baumler and told him that a couple of their men had visited a pub in a very seedy part of town, not far from the wharfs, and while everyone there denied ever seeing Patrick in the place, the team had the definite impression that they were lying about that. The Desmond men were not about to challenge what they were being told as they considered their situation to be a bit precarious. They acted as though they believed what they were being told and left the bar, but strongly suggested that someone should go back with more horsepower than they had and get the real story.

"Ted, get a couple of your best guys and I'll meet you downstairs at my car. And I want them armed."

The four men were soon heading in the direction of the pub and some fifteen minutes later were motoring slowly down a narrow, dark street, littered with garbage and debris. Somers drove around smashed wine bottles, tin cans and what appeared to have been garbage can lids and other debris strewn along the roadway. The grime and smoke darkened building walls gave the appearance of an old industrial area with, every now and then, a sign of life when a person stepped out of a doorway or a light shone through soot stained windows.

Somers was leaning forward, huddled around the steering wheel as he peered out the window, searching the buildings they were passing. It was now getting dark and there were no street lamps to illuminate the area which made it very difficult to distinguish where one grimy building ended and another began. All the structures had the same finish and texture. Old brick covered with dirt and soot. Somers slowed the car to a crawl as he moved further down the street. "It has to be right around here, but I don't see anything that looks like a pub. Least, not a pub I'd like to hang out at."

After driving slowly down the same street and on into an even less inhabited cluster of unused buildings, Baumler shouted out, "There it is. Next to the building without the roof. Right by that alley over there."

Somers parked near the entrance to the pub and, on Baumler's suggestion, the men all loosened the strap on their issue nine millimeters before leaving the car. As they were getting out, Somers said that the team that preceded them had mentioned that the place appeared to be closed, but it was not. "I can see what he meant."

There was no light coming from the only window in the pub that was visible from the street, but it was impossible to tell if that was due to the combination of dirt and soot on the window or for some other reason. The four men walked up to the door which appeared to be slightly ajar and Somers pushed the door open and entered the room first with Baumler right behind him. The stench of the room was overpowering. A combination of stale beer and urine spilled on a wooden floor that was never cleaned.

There appeared to be five or six men sitting around at tables or standing by the bar. There could have been more but it was difficult to see across the room with smoke from cigarettes and cigars blanketing the room. The only light came from a single, dim, bulb hanging in what appeared to be the center of the room.

One bartender was working the bar and he was now studying the four as they slowly entered the bar. It was obvious to the bartender that the four had not come by for a drink of his fine whiskey. Two of the security men placed themselves with their backs to one wall so that they could best observe the patrons who were all now focused on the new arrivals. Somers and Frank Baumler walked up to the bar and sat down at two stools that were vacant.

The bartender said nothing. He just stared at the two, waiting for them to order something to drink. Neither Somers nor Baumler had any intention of ordering anything. Baumler said nothing. He had worked with Somers before on similar projects and he had complete confidence in his assistant. Somers just stared at the bartender. Eye to eye. With just the trace of a smile. Not saying anything. Just a cold, hard stare. The seconds that passed seemed like minutes. No one in the room was talking. The patrons were now watching what was happening at the bar. Nothing was happening but everyone knew that something was about to happen but they couldn't figure out what it was going to be.

"What do you guys want?" The bartender knew that neither of the men sitting in front of him wanted any of his rot gut booze, but they wanted something and they apparently wanted it from him.

Somers waited to answer. "I'll tell you what we don't want."

"What's that?"

"We don't want bullshit."

The bartender didn't know what to say. He was rapidly associating these four with the two that were in earlier in the day. These weren't going to be as easy as the others were but he had one thing going for him here. They were on his turf and he knew he was not alone in the room. He had been leaning on the bar with his arms outstretched and his hands visible on the graffiti carved top of the bar. He now began slowly sliding his right hand along the inside bar rail while he spoke.

"No reason to get nasty, boys. I'd be glad to help you out. What do you need?" As he spoke he reached behind him for a bar rag and then wiped both hands. When he finished that task, he replaced the rag, wiped his right hand on his filthy apron and then began to reach his right hand under the bar. As he did so, he observed both security men simultaneously reach inside their coats with their right hands. The bartender immediately began withdrawing his hand and placing it back on the bar.

Somers smiled. "That's much wiser. I see you are an intelligent man. That is the kind that we prefer dealing with."

Two of the men in the back of the room stood up and started towards the bar. One of the security men called out, "Sit down. Nobody is to move around while we are here. Stay in your seats and there'll be no trouble." They still had their hands inside their coats and the message they were giving was not hard to read. The two men returned to their chairs and glared at the four intruders.

"Now, my friend, down to business." Somers pulled out the photo of Patrick Desmond and placed it directly in front of the bartender. "Have you seen this fellow in here?"

The bartender studied the photo for some time and said, "I don't think I've ever seen him here before. I could be mistaken, but I don't think so."

"I think you're a lying sack of dog shit. What do you think about that?"

"I haven't seen the guy. Now, get the hell out of here."

"You've got quite a collection of rot gut whiskey back there. How would you like to have it lying in a heap on this pig sty floor of yours?"

"I never seen the guy."

In the blink of an eye, Somers picked up an empty glass sitting on the bar and wiped out two bottles of cheap whiskey on the end of the rack behind the bartender.

"Now, let's go over this again. Have you ever seen this guy in the bar before?"

This time, the bartender thought a bit longer. He looked past Somers at the two security men standing along the side wall. It was clear how the game was about to be played. If he did get to his gun, it would be the last thing he did as a living person. He could deny having seen the man and he would lose more whiskey, or he could admit having seen him and maybe not lose any whiskey. As Somers began reaching for another glass farther down the bar, the bartender spoke up.

"Yeh, I think he was in here a couple a days ago. Came in alone."

Somers had him say what Patrick was wearing to ensure that he had actually seen Patrick. What the bartender described seemed to confirm that it was, in fact, Patrick Desmond who had been in the bar. "What time of day was it when he was here?"

"Early afternoon. We'd only been open an hour or so."

"Who was in here at the time?"

"Just some guys that work or spend time around here."

"Any of these guys?"

The bartender looked over the crowd and a couple of the men turned their gaze away from the bar and down to the floor or to each other. "No, none of these."

The bartender continued. "He wasn't here long. Just had a drink and left."

"Who left with him?"

"He was alone."

"You know what I mean. Who left with him?"

"I don't think any..." Somers began reaching for the glass and this time pulled it over in front of him.

"Remember what I said. We don't want any bullshit. Now, you know what happens when you bull shit. I'll ask you again, who left with him?"

"Two guys went out at about the same time, but I don't know if they went with him. I don't know who they were. Only time I'd ever seen `em."

"OK. Now, let me tell you this. You obviously don't have a license to run this booze shack. If you are giving me any bullshit, we will not only shut you down, we'll also destroy this place. Every bottle, table, chair and even that one lousy light bulb up there. Do you understand that?"

"I'm not lyin."

"You'd better not be, my friend. Now describe those two guys to me and, trust me, we will get them anyway, with or without your help and if the guys who got to Patrick don't match your description, you, my friend, are out of business. Understand?"

The bartender then gave Somers a fairly complete description of the two men that had left with Patrick. When he had finished, Somers gave the bartender his card wrapped in a twenty pound note and said there would be more if he came up with any more information. He then stood up and looked over the patrons sitting around the room. He said that he hoped he and his friends had not interrupted their conversations and that they were now going to leave. "I trust you gentlemen will see no reason to accompany us out of here." With that, he allowed his jacket to fall open just enough to reveal the black grip of the Glock. While Somers and Baumler walked to the door, the other two security men kept a close watch on the clientele. Seeing no movement on the part of anyone, the last of the foursome quickly exited the room.

As they left the bar, they walked out and proceeded towards their car. It was an overcast night and, had the bar not been so poorly lit, their eyes would not have adjusted so quickly to the darkness outside. Even so, they had to walk slowly so as not to stumble over debris along the street as they found their way out into the road. There was virtually no light other than what was reflected from a lone street lamp some four blocks down the road and the faint glow from a night light in one or two buildings in between. As they made their way to the car, the two security men kept a close watch behind them to make sure that no one tried to follow. After they were seated in the car, Somers turned to Baumler and asked, "What do you think?"

"I wouldn't bet a hell of a lot of money on it, but I think he was telling the truth."

"I do too. Well, what now?"

"I'll send the descriptions to Connors at the R.U.C. and they can compare them to what they have. Maybe they can come up with something. He picked up his cell phone and dialed the contact's number. When he had completed the call, he looked up and down the street and suggested that they check out the area around the bar. They drove past the alleyway that was a short distance from the bar, stopped and shined their spot light slowly over the length of it. Nothing there but debris and garbage. There was no sign of the car and Somers continued moving down the street at a very slow pace. They covered the road they were on as well as parallel roads either side of it and all intersecting crossroads. There was no sign of Patrick's car.

When they had thoroughly canvassed the area for any sign of the Bentley, Baumler mentioned that it was close to one a.m. "No sense in prolonging the agony." He called the command center to see if anyone had come up with anything that they should pursue that evening. The clerk on duty said all reports were routine. No one had made any requests for additional follow up of leads and most of the teams had retired for the night.

Baumler shook his head. "Take us back to the barn, Ted. We'll regroup in the a.m. and figure out where we go from here. The car has me faked out. They must have ditched it in a lake or the big pond."

A week and a half later, two events occurred almost simultaneously. The R.U.C. office in Donegal called the main switchboard at Desmond Enterprises to say that they had a late model Bentley, four door Sedan, license plate number BKK746, registered to Patrick Desmond that had been in storage at their facility for the past two weeks and when was someone going to come and pick it up. According to their records, the owner listed on the V.I.N. number had been notified when the vehicle was impounded. The message was placed by the Desmond switchboard operator in interoffice mail for delivery to Frank Baumler. He received the message some four hours later.

Two hours after the vehicle was located, Ted Somers received a call from the security office secretary who said there was a fellow on the phone that wanted to speak with him.

"Who is it?"

"I can't understand him when he says his name. I don't know. Sounds like a kook."

Somers took the call and it turned out to be the bartender from the bar that they had visited. Somers had the same problem understanding what the fellow was trying to say to him but eventually got the hang of it.

"I think I've got some news for you."

"What is it?"

"We think we know where the fellow is that you are looking for."

Somers tried not to sound excited. "Where is he?"

"What's in it for us?"

"I'll see that you're taken care of. Where the hell is he?"

"Two hundred pounds."

"I'll see it's delivered today if you're not bullshitting us."

"OK. He's just around the corner in the alley. One of the guys that drinks here passed out right by the alley and spent the night there. The next morning the stench woke him up. He knew what the smell was because he'd been in the war, so later, he and another guy went in there and, sure enough, they found a body. They came and got me and I went out to look. Can't tell much what he looked like. Pretty bad shape, but those were good clothes, like the guy wore when he was in the bar. Most likely him."

"We'll check it out and if it's him, you can pick up the money at my office. The address is on the card. You'll read about it if it's him."

Somers asked if the bartender or his contacts had reported any of this to the police and they had not, so Somers said he would take care of that. The bartender said he would appreciate it if nothing was said about the bar being there or who had found the body as nobody wanted to be talking to the cops. They were going to shut the bar down for a few days until this blew over. Somers said, not to worry.

Since the visit to his office by Somers, Carter had been mulling over whether he should cancel the hit on Parker or not. Parker was an unknown quantity and, as such, to Carter he was potentially a greater threat to the lucrative drug operation than was Hillary and far more than Adam. In Carter's mind, the situation resembled a horse race. Patrick was still in the running as the President of the company, but as the days passed, without any sign of him, he was fading fast.

Carter still had some thoughts that Hillary would take over the company if Patrick was no longer around and, if she did, there was an outside chance that the very dark horse, Adam, would eventually take over the reins. Ellen was always hovering in the background but Carter had it pegged that Hillary might find Ellen's competitive spirit a little hard to take. She could order Adam around much easier. Carter was always assuming that the call would be Hillary's to make and never considered the possibility that such was not the case.

Carter remained in this fluid state of mind regarding the hit on Parker for some days after learning Patrick was missing. What made up his mind, rather quickly, was when Hillary informed him that she had no ownership interests in Desmond Enterprises and stood to gain none in Patrick's will. Everything would go to Ellen and Adam with Ellen gaining the lion's share.

Carter knew he would have trouble with Ellen. He then realized that he had made a serious mistake by ordering the hit on Parker when he could have waited a bit longer. He quickly placed a call to his Dublin contact and told them to put a stop order on the Parker hit. To his relief, the office said that they had not yet received any word the job had been completed. The only hitch was that the Stazi agent handling the assignment had just called in last night and was not expected to check back in until the following evening. No one knew where he was operating as he was either locating Parker or keeping tabs on him and waiting for an opportune moment. Carter told the contact, "Find him. This is important. Cancel the assignment."

The contact said, "We'll try our best," and hung up. Carter thought what an impudent group they had down there in Dublin. Hadn't they discovered cell phones yet? He again chastised himself for sending the hit order out especially when he knew at the time that Patrick had not been seen by anyone for twenty some hours. That was a little extreme, even for Patrick.

Tony Carter learned of Patrick's death about an hour after Somers did when a contact in the R.U.C. called his office and told him that Patrick Desmond's body had been located. Learning what he had suspected for the past week put Carter into a deep slump. He had made mistakes before, but this could end up being the blunder of his life.

There was a flurry of activity in the Desmond offices for the next two weeks with people busy with the funeral and also with everyone trying to figure out who was going to assume the position of president of the company. Hillary had taken over Patrick's office but she made it quite clear to everyone that she did not intend to take over Patrick's role at Desmond. She said that she had better things to do with her time. Martha stayed at her desk and continued to function as the president's secretary, which a number of people in the company found interesting and somewhat amusing.

While those people may have found the close working relationship of Hillary and Martha a matter of intense interest, it did not seem to affect the two principals involved. Hillary passed out more directives in one hour than Patrick had done in two weeks and Martha enjoyed the heightened level of activity. For once she felt as though she was performing at the level required of the position that she held.

When Frank Baumler called Martha to tell her that Patrick had been found dead, Martha felt no immediate reaction. Their relationship was one of convenience. She provided a certain amount of companionship for Patrick and he provided her with the security and material things that she needed to make her life reasonably comfortable. In recent years he had seen to her future well being so that when the time came that he was no longer around, she would be able to continue living as she had before. For this, she was very grateful and she did her best to make Patrick's time with her as enjoyable as possible.

Patrick was more involved emotionally with Martha than she with him. He had told her many times that if and when he was able to do so, he would like to formalize their relationship with marriage. That was never an issue with Martha and her somewhat aloof response to these promises of his further aroused his desire for her. It was as though he sought a visible sign of her dependence on him to reassure him that she would never leave him. He never received it, at least to his satisfaction, and that cemented the long term nature of the relationship.

As a result of what Patrick had provided for Martha financially, her working for Hillary did not create a tense situation at least for Martha. Hillary, likewise, could have cared less. She had always looked upon Martha as a handy relief valve for her boring husband. There was never animosity on her part. She believed Martha, who she thought was not too bright, was doing her a favor.

Consequently, it came as somewhat of a surprise for Hillary to discover that Martha was quite a capable person. Martha was also very familiar with Patrick's daily duties at Desmond as she was the person who actually accomplished them. As a result, there was little, if any disruption in the performance of the president's duties.

After Hillary had spent a week and a half at Patrick's desk taking care of her own business while dealing with the day to day problems that came her way, she called Martha into her office.

"Martha, I've had enough of this crap. You obviously can handle this on your own. No, you're not going to be the new president of Desmond Enterprises... or maybe you are. No, you wouldn't want the job. You probably know more about who's in the running than I do."

Martha was surprised at what Hillary was saying. She had assumed that if anything happened to Patrick, Hillary would just take over.

Seeing the look on Martha's face, Hillary said, "It all depends on what's in the will, you know. I'm sure I'm not in there. I would assume that the two kids will get the stock and it depends on what they decide. They're getting a little too old to run to their mother for decisions, but if it were up to me, it would be an easy decision. I'd put Ellen in there. She is young but she has more brains than I have and, frankly, I think she would be great. Patrick was not totally stupid. He occasionally did some things right and he thought the world of Ellen. I'm sure he had that taken care of."

Martha said nothing but she was taken back a bit by Hillary's candor. It was true what she said, but some things were better left unsaid.

Hillary continued talking, apparently unconcerned whether Martha was listening or not. "I think the two of you would work together very well. I even thought of trying to get you over at Fairchild Investments as my secretary, but the gal I have there would shoot you, me or both of us. In the meantime, I want you to prepare a memo for the staff that you are to handle matters in my absence. I'm sure they all think that I control everything now and until they learn otherwise, we can do as we please. Just don't do anything drastic without telling me. Do that now, as I am leaving here in minutes. Now, do you have any questions?"

Martha was surprised at what she was hearing. Up to this time, Hillary had given no indication as to whether she approved of Martha's performance as a secretary or not.

"Well, thank you. I consider this a great compliment. I have very much enjoyed working with you. It has been an enervating experience. If Ellen does come in, I know she would be a great president for Desmond Enterprises. I have always thought of her as taking on that position some day. Now, just one question. If something comes up that you should be made aware of, how do I contact you?"

Hillary gave Martha her cell phone number and cautioned her not to give it to anyone else. "Only three people have that number." Hillary threw some papers in her brief case, stood up and said, "The office is yours until the president is appointed. Enjoy yourself, Martha."

In the next instant, Martha was sitting alone in the office. She sat down behind Patrick's desk and immediately prepared the memo. Best to get this out right away or people will assume that I am taking advantage of a situation. She drafted the memo as issued by Hillary Fairchild Desmond, added the current date, made copies for the department heads and sent them out for distribution. There were certain matters that required attention and Martha laid out a "to do" list and immediately went to work.

Hillary was right in her predictions. The stock went to the two children of Patrick Desmond with a majority share to Ellen. Clearly Patrick did not want there to be a deadlock over any business decisions and he clearly favored Ellen's business sense over Adams. Ellen had not been in the office since Patrick had been found but a few days after the funeral when the will had been read, she walked into the Executive wing of Desmond Enterprises and on into Patrick's former office. Martha was seated behind the desk and immediately rose and began gathering her papers to take them out to her secretarial desk.

Ellen took off her coat and sat down on the couch. "You don't have to rush out of here, Martha. I just stopped in to talk to you. I will be here tomorrow to get down to work, but I thought I'd visit with you while I was in the area. Have a chair, you make me nervous, standing there."

Martha sat down as Ellen continued talking. "I am exercising my stock and taking the position of President of Desmond Enterprises. I am going to need a lot of help and mother tells me that you have the brains and experience to help me out during the learning process. I want your very involved support during this period and I also want you to stay on as the secretary to the president. I have no intention of replacing you, if that was a matter of concern."

"I really hadn't thought much about it Miss Desmond."

"One more thing, Martha. When you and I are alone, it's 'Ellen'. When formalities require, 'Miss Desmond' is just fine. OK?"

"Yes, that's fine." Martha was going to have to learn how to say "Ellen". It was not easy for her under the circumstances.

"Now, I'll be in tomorrow morning at nine and I would like for you to brief me on the general operation of the president's office. What my father usually accomplished here and what my mother did while she was here. She may come in from time to time and when she does, I would defer to her requests, should she make any. Just make sure I know what they are. If I have a problem with them, I'll take it up with her."

Ellen thought a moment. "After our little briefing, I would like for you to schedule a meeting of the department heads so that I can introduce myself to them. Some of them, I have never met. Then, I want a tour of Desmond Enterprises. I am fairly familiar with the physical setup of the company, so I want the real tour. You know. That guy over there knows what he's doing. That one doesn't. That sort of thing. Martha, I want complete candor at all times. You will get the same from me. In the meantime would you send out a memo that I am the new corporate president of Desmond Enterprises and will be serving in that capacity commencing tomorrow morning. Anyone that wishes to speak with me about company business is welcome to do so. OK?"

Martha had been busy writing down everything that Ellen was saying and when she was sure that Ellen was done talking, she looked up and said, "OK. I'll see that the memo goes out within the hour. I will prepare a briefing covering the departments and what I know about the key personnel in the company so that you have some idea of who is here, what they do and how well they seem to do it. And, I will be very candid in my dealings with you. I, also, believe that is the way to do business. Is there anything else... Ellen?"

Ellen smiled at the way Martha had added her name and Martha did as well. Ellen added that she liked to drink tea and wanted it available at all times. She also spent a great deal of time working but that Martha was under no obligation to work the same hours. Other than that, they would each learn about the other as time passed. With that, Ellen picked up her coat, and said, "See you in the morning."

After she had left the office, Martha said, "Phew. What a change from her father. This is going to be different."

In the morning, Martha had a lectern set up in the president's office to hold her notes while she briefed Ellen. As soon as Ellen arrived, Martha poured her a cup of tea and set it on her desk. When Ellen told her that she was ready for the briefing at any time, Martha walked over to the lectern, arranged her notes and commenced her briefing.

Martha covered general statistical data first. The number of employees, executive staff, clerical staff, total payroll and that sort of thing. She then described the general operation of the corporate offices, keeping in mind that Ellen had a fairly good understanding of the company from her time working in the Dublin office. She covered all of this in ten or so minutes so as not to bore her new employer.

Then Martha began explaining the separate departments in the Belfast office of the company with a brief appraisal of the department head. Most of these were men and she had known all but two for an extended period of time. She had not formed opinions regarding the two new ones and told that to Ellen. Regarding the others, she provided her own informal evaluation which she believed represented a consensus of the opinions of the office staff. If a fairly general consensus was not available or there was some disagreement among the staff as to the effectiveness of one of the managers, she mentioned that to Ellen as well.

Adam was also a department head and Martha saved him for last. Pursuant to Ellen's request that she was to be candid at all times, Martha said that the general consensus regarding Adam was that he was in over his head. But, the Shipping Department was an unusually difficult department to manage and would challenge a far more experienced person than Adam. Martha said that had to be kept in mind. The entire briefing lasted close to one hour with Ellen's questions included. Shortly before ten, Martha announced that the Department heads were assembling in the executive briefing room and would be waiting for her there.

Ellen stood up, took a quick look at herself in the washroom and said, "We'd best be on our way. I don't want to keep them away from their work."

The next few days Ellen spent going over department financial reports and discussing some of the specifics with Martha. When Martha was unable to provide necessary information for Ellen, she called in the people that could. As the days passed, her understanding of the company and the people responsible for the day to day operation grew. She had been serving as the company president for exactly one week when Martha called her on the intercom and said that Tony Carter wished to meet with her.

Martha then added, "Maybe I'd better tell you about this fellow before we confirm a date and time, OK."

"Sure. Come on in."

Martha filled Ellen's tea cup and poured one for herself before sitting down on the couch.

"I assume you generally know who Tony Carter is." Martha did not know if Ellen knew about Carter and her mother and first wanted to find out what Ellen knew.

"Yes. I know he is with Unity. He made a few trips to the Dublin office and visited the Shipping Department. Other than that I don't know a great deal about him. Oh, I think he is also a friend of my mother's. They play tennis together."

"OK." Martha tried to figure out how to handle this hot potato. She explained that Carter was basically the money man for Unity and as such he called on Patrick periodically for contributions to the party. She also explained that Patrick did not like Carter for whatever that was worth. "Now the tricky part is that there seems to be a tie in between the company contributions and labor union negotiations. That primarily affects the Shipping Department as that is the only department that is unionized. So, keeping this Carter happy was one of Patrick's more difficult tasks. Seems that no matter what you would do, Carter always wanted more. He is a hard guy to deal with, Ellen. He is right out of the Belfast slums, according to Patrick, and it's like he has an ax to grind with respect to the Desmonds personally. So, anyway... that's about it." Martha felt guilty about not laying out the entire picture, but she just had to give that more thought. She continued sitting in the couch to see if Ellen had any questions on what she had said.

Ellen had already picked up on Martha's actions to tell when she was uncomfortable about something and after a brief pause, she looked over at Martha and said, "Is that all about this Carter, or is there more?"

Now Martha began to get a bit nervous because she was not sure if Ellen knew all about her mother and Carter and was testing her or if she was just asking if there was additional information. Martha decided to lay it out and try to be as discreet as possible under the circumstances.

"There is more, but I don't know that I should be bringing this up."

"Remember, Martha, the word is candor. I don't want to learn things the hard way."

"Well, according to Patrick and others around the company, your mother and Tony Carter are very close, if you know what I mean. I bring that out only because it is relevant to your situation as the president of the company. Carter has obviously used that relationship to further his interests in Desmond Enterprises. Your father was never able to deal effectively with Carter and it was really your mother's input that put limits on what Carter was allowed to do. Unfortunately, she gave him fairly wide latitude."

Ellen was taken back a bit by the disclosure regarding her mother's private life, but made no comment regarding that issue. "What interests was Carter trying to further in the company?"

"I'm not totally sure as to what was going on but he managed to stack the Shipping Department with his Unity people even well before it was unionized. He has tried to put his people into the executive offices as well, particularly accounting, but Hillary has been able to keep him out of there. I suppose he wants to know the company's profit picture or God knows what.

"Well, go ahead and set up the meeting. You've got my calendar."

"Will do, Ellen. Sorry to bring out this business with your mother, but I think it is important that you are aware of that as the company president."

"I agree, Martha. Don't worry about it. I'm glad you told me."

Ellen had seen little, if anything of Adam, either at home or around the Company. After a while, she concluded that he was trying to avoid her for one reason or another. She told Martha to call Adam and have him come up to her office. It was close to one hour after Martha had called him that he showed up in the Executive wing of the building. She brought him right in to Ellen's office and gave the two of them a cup of tea before leaving and closing the door.

"Well, where have you been hiding?"

"I've been busy."

"We all have. Now why have you been keeping yourself so scarce?"

"I have my reasons."

The two bantered back and forth for some time until Ellen blew up and said, "Look, Adam. I've got things to do and I don't have time to screw around trying to get my own brother to tell me what's bothering him. You are also a Department head and from what I hear, you need my help and that of others in the company. I'm not going to let that department go down the drain just because you are my brother. Fess up or I'll start treating you like anyone else. Then you will be in trouble."

"I want out of here."

This surprised Ellen. She had assumed that the best refuge for her brother, whom she considered socially disabled, was Desmond Enterprises. "Why in the hell would you want to do that?"

"They got Dad and they'll get me next."

Ellen thought for a moment that her brother had gone mad. Her father had been killed for his watch, credit cards and some pocket money. Oh, yes and the Bentley as well. Whoever did that did not know Adam existed. "Who are you talking about?"

Adam then let loose. His hands were shaking and his eyes were wide with fright. He sat on the edge of the couch and spoke rapidly, stopping every now and then to catch his breath and organize his thoughts. He told Ellen about the smuggling operation that Unity had been running using Desmond shipping and that Baumler had been working on the problem for months. He told her how, he was sure, he had been brought into the department because they figured he would be easily controlled. They had threatened him that if he told anyone what he knew, that they would kill him. He figured they were the ones that had killed Patrick.

"Who the hell are *they*? The people doing this."

"Unity, Ellen. Unity controls the shipping area and they can do anything they want down there. I'm just a figurehead."

"Have you reported this to anyone? Did your father know about this?"

Adam explained how he had reported it to Frank Baumler and the investigation that had gone on for weeks under Ted Somers. "They had figured out how the operation was being done and, as far as I know, had reported it to Patrick. They were waiting for his OK on what to do about it when he was killed. That's why I know that when it breaks, which it will someday, they'll come after me."

Ellen was stunned. She had no idea that this was going on. The longer she sat silent, thinking over what Adam had said, it came to her that the Dublin office was being manipulated as well. Unity had virtually controlled the shipping department there from well before the time that she went to work in Dublin.

"Adam, I had no idea. I'm going to find out what this is all about. Stay working there until I know what is going on. Trust me, Adam. If your life is at risk, I will see that you are sent out of the country. You could go to England and work for the Fairchilds, I'm sure. Leave me now while I figure this one out."

Frank Baumler was seated in Ellen's office within minutes. He had not spoken to Ellen since the funeral of her father when he had expressed his condolences. He was not avoiding her, rather he wanted to give her time in her new job before laying the Shipping Department bombshell on her. Martha had told him that Adam had been up there so the cat was most likely out of the bag. Ellen wasted no time in confirming that assumption.

"Frank, what in the hell is going on in shipping?"

"Quite a bit. I could write a book. I will be very blunt about this, Ellen. Your father and your mother, to some extent, have allowed Tony Carter and his Unity people to infiltrate and take control of our shipping departments. Both in Belfast and in Dublin. I'm sure you are aware of problems in Dublin."

"I am. Why wasn't I told about this before now?"

Baumler explained that Patrick had been sitting on the decision as to what to do about the matter and then with the funeral, Ellen's taking over the job and getting situated, he thought it would be best not to burden her immediately with a problem that had existed for years.

"I intended to speak with you in the next few days after you were somewhat situated here. Believe me, all of us in Security have been frustrated by the lack of interest from Patrick in getting these scum balls out of this company."

"Bring me up to date on this, Frank. I only know that Unity had stacked their people into the shipping jobs in Dublin, but I had never heard that they were up to anything like this. Give me all the details, right from day one."

Baumler spent the next hour and a half explaining the drug trafficking operation, the people involved, the investigation run by his department and the meetings with Patrick discussing how to handle the matter. Ellen asked a number of questions from the number of shipments involved to where the drugs were being taken. She learned that the main storage point was a warehouse in the Phibsbourough section of Dublin, fortunately not owned by Desmond Enterprises. That would have been the ultimate insult.

"What do we do about this Frank? Seems to me that by doing nothing, we are implicating ourselves."

"I agree. I say we move on this right now. We have to be careful in how we go about it because, at this point in time, we are in a difficult situation." Baumler went on to explain to Ellen that Unity was in this business for the money and there was a lot involved. If Desmond caused them to lose that income, there could be hell to pay with Union problems. If the government got involved, the company itself could be charged as a coconspirator in the drug operation and severely fined, or worse.

"Details, Frank. What do you think we should do?"

"I say that we go to Carter and offer him a deal. Martha has probably explained our contributions to Unity. Maybe we double those for a period of years. Tell them we won't blow the whistle on what they are doing, but that they knock it off, immediately. If they don't, we blow the whistle. If we did, we could hurt ourselves more than Unity. Keep in mind that Unity runs this government, from top to bottom, and they could do us a lot of damage. I can't even imagine how disastrous it would be to have both Unity and the government gunning for us. We would have to comply with absolutely every one of their thousands of regulations which, as we all know, no one does, nor could anyone do so for long." Baumler smiled at the thought and went on.

"Compound that with union shutdowns. In order to avoid that alternative, we may have to just keep sweetening the deal until Carter takes it. I hate to say that because the guy is an absolute scum ball, but that is the situation we're in. That's why Patrick sat on this as long as he did. If he had acted ten years ago, we wouldn't be in this position today."

Ellen was quiet for a moment as she took in what Baumler was telling her. "OK. Let me think this one through. I want to meet with this Carter. I never have actually met the guy, although I've heard enough about him. I want to get my thoughts together and then you and I'll meet before I meet with Carter. You might give this a lot of thought yourself. Meetings over unless you have anything else."

"Nothing other than the fact the R.U.C. still has no lead on the two guys that are believed to have taken out your father. I'll let you know if that changes. No clues found in the car to speak of. They must have just driven it to Londonderry and dumped it."

Ellen was quiet for a moment as she thought about how terrified her father must have been when he was alone in the alley with the two men. Strangely enough, she had no great interest in the investigation to determine who the men were. They were non issues as far as Ellen was concerned. No matter whether they were caught by the police or not, her father was gone and there was no way to bring him back. She would just have to move on with her own life and try to make more of it than her father had made of his.

CHAPTER 39

Quinn met with the attorney, Jerry Donahue, that Robbins suggested he talk to. But, after Quinn explained to the attorney that at this point in time, he had not yet decided on what course of action regarding the Desmond Estate he wished to take. However, he did have something else on his mind that he wanted some assistance with. "Do you do wills?"

It was days later before Anne brought up his meeting with Donahue. He had not mentioned it. Finally her curiosity got the better of her. Quinn had placed a call to her from his hotel room.

"Well, how did your meeting with the attorney go?"

"Fine. Didn't really commit to anything. I thought he knew what he was doing but I haven't decided yet on what I'm going to do."

"So... what happens now?"

"I really don't know. Trying to decide. Anyway, let's talk about when we leave for points south. Cork, Cobh, Kinsale and where was it that your family lived? Templemartin, right?"

"Oh, you have a good memory or do you have that written down someplace. No matter. I can leave the day after tomorrow. I have my sister ready to move in and take care of the boys. So, whenever you are ready, so am I. Now, Quinn, I can only miss one week of work but if we leave Friday after work and return Sunday, that will give us close to nine days."

"Plan on it. We'll grab the evening train for Cork and I'll make reservations at the Imperial for Friday and Saturday evening. We can rent a car after that and visit Kinsale and your old home, up around Bandon."

Quinn arranged with the Rockwell to check some of his personal items in their storage room until his return so that he didn't have to take everything with him. He planned on checking out of the hotel in view of the fact that he would be gone for approximately eight or nine days. Whatever he did, he didn't want to be paying for a vacant room for the amount of time he was driving around the southern part of Ireland.

Quinn longed to see the ancestral home and considered himself very fortunate, more so than most Irish-Americans, to be able to visit the very home where his forbears had lived and worked. He could walk the hallowed ground, see inside the very same home where his grandfather,

Jeremiah Desmond, spent his early years as a boy and then a young man, living in Ireland.

He would go to Cobh, the port of embarkation for the emigrants leaving for Quebec or New York, or wherever they landed in the New World. He had read about how the emigrants last view of Ireland was the church high on the hill in Cobh and how they wept as the church faded from their view as the old sailing vessels moved away from the coast. What a painful experience for people who, very likely, had never ventured over twenty miles from their homes.

Friday afternoon, Quinn had arranged to meet Anne at Connolly Station a half an hour before the five o'clock express for Cork. He arrived at the station early, purchased two coach round trip tickets and had a cup of tea while he waited for Anne to arrive. At exactly four thirty, she walked in the main entrance carrying her suitcase. Quinn waved her over to where he was standing and went up to her to take her bag.

"No problem, Quinn. I can handle this quite well. I made sure I did not load it down seeing as how we're going to be moving around all the time."

"Smart girl. I tried that but I brought some books along and they weigh a ton."

"OK, we'll make a deal. You carry your bag and I'll take care of mine."

Just then the announcement came over the loudspeaker that the Express for Cork was boarding on Track Four. The two hurried through the gate as there was already a crowd heading for the train. Anne had told Quinn that the train would be filled with business travelers finishing their work week as well as people on holiday, so they should board early. She was right as he found out when they entered the rail car. There were only a few empty compartments and they were rapidly filling up. Quinn and Anne spotted a seat that was available and while Anne reserved the seat for the two of them, Quinn stored the two bags in the rack at the end of the car. Even that was already almost full as Quinn crammed the two canvas bags into the remaining space. When he walked up to where Anne was sitting, she made way for him to slide over next to window, saying "I've made the trip a hundred times, Quinn. I know what it all looks like."

"Well, I've done this before as well, but it was on the other side of the car so, thanks"

When Quinn was seated, he looked around the rail car to see who else was making the trip south to Cork. It appeared the car was filled about half way with businessmen carrying briefcases and the other half probably from a variety of backgrounds. Farmers, trades people, families and people that Quinn presumed were retired, most likely returning to their homelands for a brief visit.

As he looked over the men and women sitting in the car, he wondered if any of them were making the trip to keep an eye on him. As Robbins had mentioned, their people were very subtle and Quinn would most likely not recognize that he was being watched. No one seemed to be paying him any heed so he soon dismissed the matter and returned to staring out the window at the passing scenery. He found the trip south to be more interesting than his train ride up to Belfast. The scenery was more diverse with rolling hills, white sheep on green fields, and an occasional small town with people bustling around, oblivious of the train speeding past them. In a little over two hours, the train pulled into Kent Station and soon they were getting off, carrying their bags down the concrete boarding lanes towards the terminal. Outside, Quinn hailed a cab and within minutes they were standing at the registration desk in the Imperial Hotel and the clerk was looking up his reservation.

While the clerk was busy booking the rooms and locating the keys, Quinn looked down at Anne and said, "I reserved two rooms but if you think you could deal with it, we could get one room with two beds. Whatever you decide on is fine with me."

Anne began to laugh. "Quinn, I thought you would just get one room with one big bed, a water bed or one with one of those large circular things. No, really Quinn. One room is fine provided you don't snore. I can't handle that."

"Not that I know of." Now Quinn laughed. "I've never had any complaints."

"Well, let me tell you. I'll complain if you do. Get one room, two beds and…" with that, Anne punched him lightly in the arm, "we'll see how things go."

"Oh, now you're being nasty." They both laughed as Quinn motioned to the clerk and changed the reservation to one room, two beds. The clerk looked at Quinn, then over at Anne, and selected one of the sets of keys which he gave to Quinn.

Here you are, Sir. Third floor, to the left from the elevator. Quinn told him they didn't need any help with their bags and they were soon in their room unpacking. The room had one large, queen size bed and a smaller single along the wall. Anne immediately threw her bag on the larger queen bed while Quinn was hanging up his coat.

"Say, Miss. Just what do you think you're doing? That bed has Quinn

Parker written all over it."

"Quinn, it's a big bed. Look how wide it is. I could sleep over on this side and you could sleep over there, on that side. What do you think?"

"I think that's a hell of a good idea."

One hour later, the two of them were seated in a small Italian restaurant just down one of the side streets off South Mall and within walking distance of the Hotel. While they were having a glass of wine and finally relaxing after all of the activity, they laid out a very loose schedule for the week that lie ahead. They would visit Cobh by train while continuing to stay at the Imperial Hotel in Cork.

It was only a twenty minute train ride to Cobh from Cork and a day, or at the most two, spent there would, according to Anne, be plenty of time for Quinn to see everything he wanted to see. Quinn was most interested in seeing the places and sights that would have been viewed by his grandfather while he was in the port awaiting the departure of his ship.

"Quinn, they have a very interesting Heritage Center right at the rail station complete with a well done diorama that depicts the emigration during the Famine. You will really enjoy that."

Quinn listened as Anne described Cobh and the places that she thought he would like to see. "The old dock is still there that the emigrants used for boarding their ships. It's falling apart now from age but there is enough of it remaining so you can still envision the emigrants boarding the ships and waving back at relatives, or friends, who were not leaving with them. The town and harbor are beautiful and I'm sure every one of the emigrants that left from there intended some day to return."

Quinn grew silent as he thought about his grandfather coming from Kinsale, most likely staying at Cork for a night or two and then to Cobh to wait for his ship. Quinn had read about the charlatans and schemers who had preyed upon the naive and inexperienced travelers. Renting them boarding rooms, that were hovels or nonexistent, at exorbitant prices and selling them supplies for the voyage, that were never delivered as promised.

Cobh back then was teaming with opportunists eager to take advantage of the unsophisticated laborers and farmers who had virtually nothing in the way of funds to provide them with what they needed for sustenance. Their passage was, for the most part, arranged before hand. Either with the assistance of their landholder who was eager to remove them from his estate or his or her own family who sacrificed what little they had to send a son, daughter or husband to the New World in hopes that they would send money back to help support those that didn't, or couldn't, make the trip.

As they sat in the comfortable Italian restaurant with its lit candles, darkened lamps and dark wood interior, the nineteenth century decor contributed to the vision that Quinn depicted in his mind of the travelers carrying their limited worldly possessions with them as they made their way through Cork and on towards Cobh. He almost expected to see them, through the rain streaked café window, passing by on the darkened wet street, eyes deep set from hunger and bent over from fatigue.

When the waiter served him the hot plate of Lasagna with the aromatic flavoring of spices and herbs, it brought him out of his reverie. None of the emigrants had food such as this. He looked up and smiled at Anne as the waiter placed a dish of Fettuccine Alfredo covered with a delicious Parmesan cream sauce in front of her. The fragrance of fine Italian cooking permeated the small café and when the cook stepped out of the kitchen to ask them if they were satisfied with their dinner, Quinn thought about how times had changed since his grandfather passed through this city, so many years before.

Quinn refilled their wine glasses from the bottle of Chardonnay and tipped his glass to Anne. "Before I get too tongue tied from this wine, I would like to thank you for coming along with me on this trip. You are a wonderful tour guide, as I have known for some time, but you are also very enjoyable to be with. Thank you."

"Oh, you are a smoothie, Quinn. Why, thank you. I enjoy your company or I wouldn't be here. I must say, I'm also anxious to visit my family home. I think you will find it interesting as well because they have retained many of the old ways of doing things and, as I told you once, they still speak primarily in Gaelic. So don't think we are talking about you when the three of us forget that you don't speak the language."

"Well, if you all talk in Gaelic and then look over at me and start laughing, I'll certainly get suspicious."

"I doubt that will happen Quinn." The two finished their dinner and then went to a pub over on Tuckey Street. It had stopped raining and while it was a fair distance from the café, they decided to walk rather than to try and catch a cab. When they arrived, the pub was crowded with locals and traditional Irish music was playing in the back. It was impossible to find a place to sit and after having a drink, standing at the bar, they were both ready to return to the hotel.

It was now getting fairly late and all of the stores and shops along the way were closed but there were still quite a few people out on the streets. As they walked back to their hotel, a car with two men drove slowly past them and then sped up. Anne did not seem to notice as she was talking about something that had happened during her childhood on the farm at Templemartin. Quinn, on the other hand, did take notice of the car because one of the occupants seemed to be staring at them. Quinn could not see the fellow clearly because the street was dark and there was very little light illuminating the fellow's face. The incident reminded him of how Sean was fatally shot and, as he walked down the sidewalk, he thought about Sean until Anne asked him why he was so quiet.

"Oh, just thinking about some things back in the States."

"I hope you're not thinking about returning permanently."

"No thoughts about that. I like it here." When they arrived at the hotel, they stopped in the lounge for a nightcap and as they sipped their brandy, they mapped out their plans for the coming day. They decided to get an early start, walk over to the train station, which was a fair distance, and then take the short train ride to Cobh, spending the day there and returning to the Imperial.

When they returned to the room, the two went about preparing for bed as though they had done this for years. When Anne finally hopped into bed next to Quinn, they talked for a while and then made love. It was not a wild, passionate, affair, rather a natural joining together of two people who genuinely cared for each other. No embarrassment or tension on the part of either one, and when they finally separated, Anne said, "That was very nice, Quinn. I needed that." Quinn quipped that he was a bit out of practice but further training would take care of that. The two lay in bed talking and laughing about this and that event in their lives and after a while, the words came slower and finally the room was silent.

The next morning, after a long walk from the Imperial to Kent Station, the two boarded the train for the twenty mile trip to Cobh. It was an interesting trip. There were only a few people on the train, some tourists and what appeared to be locals. The train moved slowly on its eastbound route to Cobh, making a number of stops along the way to pick up or discharge passengers. When it came to a stop at Fota, Anne explained to Quinn that there was an excellent wildlife park there and many people from Cobh brought their children to Fota for a day of viewing the animals. After a number of passengers disembarked, the train was soon on its way again to Cobh.

Once in Cobh, they spent a couple of hours in the Heritage Center which was in the same complex of buildings as the train station. Quinn found the diorama of the Famine emigration very interesting with the lifelike depiction of the emigrants on board the sailing vessels and the horrible conditions that they had to undergo on the crossing. Outside the building, they took pictures at the bronze statue of the young emigrant mother with her two children and then walked down the quay to see the very dock that the emigrants had finally departed Ireland from.

The old pier and pilings supporting it were disintegrating from age and exposure to the elements but there was enough of it left for Quinn to form a mental image of Jeremiah, carrying his possessions and looking back at his family or friends. He took pictures of Anne standing by the pier and also of the harbor which was formed by the expanse of the river Lee which flowed out to the ocean from Cork and points further east.

The weather was unusually pleasant for this time of year in Ireland and the harbor was filled with sailboats from the clubs over at Crosshaven, on the other side of the water. Quinn looked out towards the Harbor entrance and the sea beyond and he thought of Cobh being linked to the two great maritime disasters, the sinkings of the Lusitania and the Titanic. The Lusitania was sunk within sight of Cobh and the Titanic made its last port of call at Cobh before striking the iceberg in the North Atlantic. Anne and Quinn walked down the pier watching the variety of boats transiting the harbor. Ships, tugs, sailboats and fishermen all vied for the choppy, wind-swept, waters of the harbor.

Anne asked Quinn if he knew the name of the body of water along the southeast coast of Ireland. He ventured that it had to be either the Atlantic or the Irish Sea but Anne only shook her head. "Wrong. You now owe me lunch. It is the Celtic Sea, my friend."

Quinn had never heard the name before and joked to her that she was telling him tourist stories now. "Whatever it is," he said, "I like the smell of fresh, salty ocean air. Reminds me of food. Lunch is a good idea." They went across the street to the Commodore Hotel and, being a bit early, found a table next to a window looking out at the harbor. After they had ordered, Quinn walked around the room to study the old photographs of the Lusitania sinking that covered the walls. When he returned to the table, he commented. "Very interesting place, Anne. The place just reeks of its history. I almost expect to see my grandfather walk in and order a pint."

"That's why I wanted you to see it Quinn. Wait until we walk up to the church. It is absolutely beautiful."

After they finished their sandwiches, the two of them walked up the steep hill to St. Colman's Cathedral and as they stood before the massive structure with its prominent location on the highest ground anywhere around the harbor, Quinn marveled at the architecture.

"Beautiful. I don't believe this was here when Jeremiah left Ireland, but I assume another, smaller church was and the departing emigrants would have seen that as well."

"It was built in the late 1860s, Quinn, so your Grandfather didn't see this one, but he would have seen its predecessor. Wait until you go inside, Quinn. Check out the ceiling."

When they walked through the massive doors, the size of the interior exceeded what Quinn had expected. There was a group of older women reciting the rosary in the front pews with one woman leading with the Hail Mary in Gaelic and the others responding with the Holy Mary in English. They appeared to be local women and most likely this was a daily event for them. The interior of the church was lit only by the daylight passing through the old stained glass windows and a few candles up on the white marble altar. The view inside the church was very impressive with the fine statuary, the stone columns, wood carvings decorating the confessionals and the ornamental side altars, all bathed by the soft light coming through the different colors of the stained glass panels. As Quinn took all of this in, his eyes went up to the ceiling. He could only imagine the work that must have gone into the intricate layout of the woodwork on the ceiling. The arched ceiling was finished with narrow strips of dark wood, laid together, forming a symmetrical pattern that complimented the other features of the Cathedral.

The two walked around the building for some time without speaking. They were both visibly impressed although this was not Anne's first visit to the church. When they finally left the building, neither said a word until they were out on the walk way that took them back down to the street below.

Quinn was the first to speak. "Seeing Cobh first hand and not just reading about it, has been quite an experience. It's amazing that my grandfather never spoke about Cobh or his actual departure from Ireland. I think it was just such a painful experience for him that he pushed it out of his mind."

"Part of my family left as well, Quinn. I assume that they left from Cobh as that is where most everyone from County Cork departed. I remember my first trip here and I think it had the same effect on me as, I am sure, it did you. My regret is that we lost touch with our family that left just like the Desmonds that stayed here in Ireland apparently did. I'm sure that the parents, brothers, and sisters of the emigrants stayed in touch, but after that, contact in most cases was lost. I've talked with many of my friends about it and they have no idea what happened to their grandparent's family members that went to the States or to Australia. If it weren't for the strong interest of the descendants of emigrants, there would hardly be any contact. That is really too bad."

"I agree, Anne, and the sad part is, that it is really an interesting challenge to become involved in the search for your ancestors. Sort of like detective work. You can dig for hours, days, months in the library and when you are about to hang it up, bingo. You strike gold and find something. After that you are keyed up again and ready to go for more hours, days and months of searching records, court documents, or what have you. It's been fun for me."

"And a little exciting too, eh, Quinn?"

"You could say that. I hope the exciting part is over."

"I hope so too, Quinn."

They took the train back to Cork and agreed that they had seen enough of Cobh for this trip. They would rent a car in the morning and take off for Kinsale and points west, to return around the end of the week or however long it took them. In the evening, they mapped out a route that they intended to follow but if something looked more inviting elsewhere, they would just redraw the route.

The following morning, they rented a car from the Budget office, just down South Mall and were soon prepared to head southwest on the N71 towards Kinsale. As they put their bags in the trunk of the car, Quinn suggested that he drive and Anne handle the map. This brought a chuckle from Anne who said, "It's common knowledge around here, Quinn, not to let the American do the driving."

"Now, I might take offense at that. I'm an excellent driver."

"You might be but out in the countryside of Ireland, the roads are very narrow, curvy, the drivers go way too fast and, last but not least, we drive, as you say, on the wrong side of the road. Put it all together and it spells accidents for people who aren't used to that. We have enough of our own, believe me, without the help of the American tourist. So, Quinn, here is the map. Oh, one other thing for you to watch for. The roads are not marked really well out here in the country, but you'll get the hang of it after a while."

Quinn, as the passenger, sat in what was normally the driver's seat in the States and began studying the map to see what looked like the best route to Kinsale. It appeared to Quinn from looking at the map that the trip to Kinsale would not take very much time. "We ought to be able to make this in about thirty minutes. I thought it was farther than that." Anne did not respond.

They drove in silence for some time as the road they were on, N71, was wide, smooth and fairly straight. Before they came to Bandon they had to turn to the south to catch another road down to Kinsale. Quinn was eagerly peering through the windscreen looking for the road marker to the south but never did see it until Anne had turned onto what he thought was an access road for a grocery store. She made more turns that took her around the backside of the store and onto a narrow, windy, rough tarmac road that seemed to proceed more westbound than to the south.

"Just how in the hell did you know to turn there? I never did see a sign."

"There was a sign." Anne laughed and then said, "This is really going to test our relationship. If we aren't yelling at each other by the end of the day, we are made for each other."

"Just where in the hell was the sign?"

"Do you want me to show it to you?"

"Yes. I do. I don't think there was one."

Anne slowed the car down and turned around in a driveway. Soon she was headed back towards the grocery store and as she approached the place where they had gotten on the smaller road, she slowed almost to a stop. Sure enough, there was a very small white sign with three faded numbers painted on it, just behind the telephone pole.

"You have got to be kidding me. Is that what I am supposed to be looking for?"

"That's right, Mr. Navigator. Have fun."

After again turning around, they proceeded down the very rough, narrow road passing through a number of unmarked intersections that Anne seemed to negotiate without undue concern. After a while, Quinn had to inquire.

"I assume you know where you're going, because for the record, I'm lost."

"I think I do, Quinn, but you can't be sure until you finally see the town." She drove on and finally, coming over the crest of a hill, the town almost magically appeared before them. Now they could see the water, the boats and the colorful homes and buildings surrounding the harbor. As they entered the town they soon found themselves immersed in slow moving traffic that occasionally came to a complete stop for no apparent reason. The streets were narrower than any that Quinn had seen thus far on his trip, but fortunately the busiest streets were restricted to one way traffic.

They drove through the town, turned around and reentered, looking for a parking place somewhere near the business center of the town. From what Quinn could tell, it appeared to him that the hotels, restaurants and retail stores all occupied a very small area, five or six various shaped city blocks all clustered together, and the rest of the town consisted of the harbor and single family residences.

They found a parking place and then walked over to the Tourist Office to find out how to get to the Desmond Family Farm. When they walked into the Center, there were brochures displayed on stands around the room and while Anne stood in line at the information desk, Quinn browsed through the displays. Prominently displayed on one of the racks was a folder entitled, Historical Irish Farm, owned by the Desmond Family, founders of Desmond Stores throughout Ireland. Quinn recognized the logo on the front of the brochure as the Adams Family crest with its raised sword alongside the Knight's helmet. A map of the location with respect to the town of Kinsale was drawn on the back and Quinn hurried over to Anne to show her.

"Look what the ace navigator found. This should get us there."

Anne looked at the brochure and complimented Quinn on his find but suggested that they book a room through the Tourist Office before heading out to the old homestead. After speaking with the young woman at the information counter, they were soon booked into White's Hotel situated right in the center of the downtown activity and were heading back for the car and the drive out to the farm.

With Quinn reading from the brochure and shouting out directions to Anne, the two of them finally located the farm after a few wrong turns and reversals of course. The area where the farm lay was to the northwest of the town of Kinsale, a distance of approximately four or five miles. The countryside that they passed was very picturesque although it did not appear to be well suited for farming. The land, for the most part, was hilly, covered with scrub, stone, small trees and built up only sparsely with single family homes.

As they rounded a curve on the narrow, tree covered road, the view opened up to a lush, green expanse of relatively flat land. Off to the right were the disintegrating remains of walls from what appeared to have been a large house located a short distance away from the entry gate to the "Desmond Family Farm". A sign on the gate announced, "Public Welcome." The entry gate led into a surfaced road that went approximately one hundred feet up to a small, white stone cabin with a thick, tightly woven, dark, rounded thatched roof. There were also small outbuildings, built in similar fashion, located behind the cabin. It was apparent that the small cabin was at one time the main dwelling for the family that lived on the farm. Before they drove in the entry gate, Quinn told Anne to stop as he wanted to take some pictures.

"I'll just bet you, Anne, that the remains of that large house across the way belonged to the Adams Family. You can tell by the stonework that it dates back to the same time as the Desmond home does. This is really interesting." Quinn took a number of pictures, both of what he presumed to be the Adams home and views of the Desmond cabin and grounds. He then got back in the car and they drove into the parking area just outside of the cabin.

There was an older woman inside the cabin who was the caretaker and guide for the visitors. She had Quinn sign the visitors log and charged each of them two pounds to tour the facility. She explained the purpose of the outbuildings and the fact that the Desmond family grew potatoes and raised a few farm animals on the five hectares of land that comprised the homestead.

Noting that Quinn was an American, she added that five hectares would be about the same as twelve American acres. Quinn made no mention of the fact that he believed he was standing in the home of his grandfather. He did not wish to draw any more attention to himself while in Ireland than he already had. He did ask if the old home across the road was the Adams home and the guide confirmed that it was. She commented that Quinn had apparently read up on his local history and he just replied that he had done some reading.

As the guide continued to describe various features of the cabin and grounds, Quinn absorbed everything she was saying. In the meantime as he stood in the cabin, he thought about how every square inch of this small room had most likely been imbedded forever in his grandfather's memory.

The cabin consisted of one room approximately twenty feet by twenty feet. The large fireplace was located on one wall with a large iron pot holder that swiveled out from the wall permitting the person cooking to position it over the peat fire smoldering in the fireplace or to swing it out, away from the fire. There was scant furniture in the room and only one picture on the wall. The picture, the guide explained, was found in every Irish cabin in the nineteenth century, The Sacred Heart of Jesus. She made no mention of the fact that the Desmonds that married into the Adams family abandoned their Catholic faith and became members of the Church of England, in order to come more in line with their new economic status.

In one corner of the room, Quinn's great grandparents, Thomas Desmond and Catherine O'Brien, had their very simple bed located. The guide explained that the children, presumably Jeremiah, William and Michael, slept on the other side of the room on bedding that they placed on the floor every evening. It was known that the pigs and other farm animals kept by all of the Irish families back then, shared the interior of the cabin with the family. The guide also explained the diet the family existed on and how the potatoes were grown, stored and finally served as the primary form of sustenance for all who lived there. Quinn was amazed at the quantity of potatoes the farm laborers would devour in a day. Nevertheless, they always appeared tall and lean in old photographs or paintings which indicated how demanding their lifestyle was.

After the guide had exhausted her knowledge of the farm and the Desmond families that had lived there, Quinn and Anne toured the other buildings on the property and then took a brief walk around the grounds. The caretakers had planted long rows of potatoes using the methods of the nineteenth century and Quinn again envisioned Jeremiah bent over the growing plants and tilling the soil.

Like most people searching their ancestry, Quinn regretted that he had never asked his grandfather about the twenty some years he had spent on this very farm. His mother and his grandfather had only spoken about the good times back at Birch Cooley in Minnesota. Apparently life on this farm for his grandfather had been extremely difficult but there had to have been good times as well. Most likely, it was the pain of remembering the beauty of the country and the good times that prevented Jeremiah from discussing the specifics of where he had lived and what his life was like back on the farm in Ireland. There was no doubt that his longing to return to Ireland was foremost in his mind during the years that Quinn had known him.

After they had covered every square foot of the Desmond farm, Anne and Quinn headed to the car and retraced their drive back to Kinsale. In fifteen minutes, they were back in the outskirts of the town and again enmeshed in slow moving traffic. Anne had already received the directions to the Hotel and wound her way through the narrow streets finally arriving at the front door to the small Hotel. There was absolutely no place to park or unload, so Quinn jumped out to talk to the hotel keeper while Anne waited with the car in an alley way hoping that no one would want to pass through. Quinn was out and back in the car within a minute or two with directions to go around behind the hotel and there were some reserved spaces back there for hotel guests.

As Anne drove down the street, Quinn was taking in the sights and looking in all the shop windows. Their car, moving slowly in the traffic, passed a small café and Quinn saw what he thought was a familiar face sitting at a table next to the window. The person he was looking at turned his head at that moment to look out at the street and their eyes met for a fraction of a second. He quickly turned the other way so that Quinn was not able to get a better look at him. Quinn was sure that he had seen the man before, but he could not place where it was. Seeing the man bothered him because there was something about him that was unfavorable in some respect but Quinn could not dredge it up from his memory.

As they unpacked the car, checked in and took their things up to their room on the second floor of the building, Quinn hardly said a word as he continued to worry about who the fellow was. Finally Anne asked him what was on his mind.

"Nothing. I saw a fellow in the coffee shop across the way and I think I know him from some place, but I can't think of where. Somebody from Atlanta, I think. Bugs me that I can't think of who he is."

"Well, why don't you go over there and talk to him? I can take care of these things."

"I think I'll do that, if you don't mind. I'll be back in a few minutes and then maybe we can head over to the Blue... whatever it is... pub across the street and kick back with a pint."

"Sounds good to me."

Quinn walked downstairs and out onto the street. The café was about a half a block away on the opposite side of the street from the hotel. He couldn't put his finger on it, but for some reason he was a bit apprehensive about searching the fellow out. As he walked down the street on the opposite side from the café, he continued to try remembering where he knew the man from but he just could not recall. He decided that he would walk past the café and see if he was still sitting where he was before. There was still quite a bit of traffic and as he drew abreast of the café his view was intermittently blocked by passing cars. Not seeing any sign of the man, Quinn waited for an opening in the traffic and dashed across the street. When he entered the café, he saw that it was very small and the only area for customer seating was in plain view of the entry way. There was no sign of the man and Quinn breathed a sigh of relief at not having to confront someone who, for some unknown reason, made him feel very uneasy. As long as he was in the café, he decided to have a cup of tea and took a seat at a table that faced the window and gave him a view of the passing traffic.

Quinn was beginning to dismiss the matter from his mind and think about his visit to his grandfather's home when he saw a car pull up at the curb and out from the front passenger seat stepped the man he had been searching for. At first, the fellow was looking down and speaking to the driver so Quinn could not get a good look at him. He could only see that he was wearing a cap and had an athletic build. When the man turned around and began walking down the street in the direction of the hotel, Quinn had almost a full face view. It was then that he saw the blond hair from below the line of his cap and his memory clicked. He was again looking at the same person as the one in the club who had been staring at Sean and who was the same fellow as the one he had seen running at the lake. The conversation that Quinn later had with Robbins immediately came to mind where Robbins said that he thought the fellow Quinn had described to him was a former Stazi, or East German Security Agent, now working for Unity.

Quinn sat petrified in his chair. He had almost dropped his tea cup when he realized who the fellow was. He replaced it in the saucer and continued to watch as the man walked down the street, apparently keeping his view focused on Quinn's hotel. The man came to a stop directly across the street from the hotel entrance and looked back at his companion who had managed to find a place to park the car. The two exchanged a hand signal and then the blond fellow leaned against the wall of a restaurant directly across the street from the hotel entrance and pretended to be reading a paper. Quinn could see that the fellow would periodically glance up to check for movement around the hotel entrance.

Quinn sat in his chair wondering what to do. The fellow waiting in the car most likely knew what Quinn looked like, so there was no chance that Quinn could walk down the street in that direction without being spotted. The blond fellow had the other direction blocked so Quinn called the waitress over to the table and asked her if they had a back door to the café. She gave him a strange look and said they did, but it did not connect to an alley or street for a considerable distance. Quinn said that was no problem and left an Irish pound coin on the table and asked her where the door was. He followed the waitress to the rear of the building, past the curious stares of the cook and made his way out of the building.

The waitress was right. The back door led to a narrow passageway between buildings for a distance of a couple of hundred feet before intersecting what appeared to be an alleyway lined with a row of uninhabited, boarded up buildings. Having walked down to the intersection of the alleyways, Quinn looked down to the end of the next lane where he could see people walking and automobile traffic passing in both directions. He was very nervous as he made his way down the alley, which was lined with solid brick walls on either side with an occasional, boarded up and chained metal, door.

There was no place to run or hide if he was spotted. He desperately wanted to find a telephone and call Anne to warn her that not only his life was in danger but hers as well. He had to get out of the alley and find a public telephone so that he could call her and then call the police. He figured that the blond fellow was on the corner of the street that he was approaching and he would have to be careful when he came out of the alley that he not be seen.

As he approached the cross street, he peered around the corner of the building searching for the blond haired fellow. He was no where in sight. Now Quinn had no idea where his adversary was. He could be on the very street that Quinn was entering or he could have returned to the car and his waiting companion. Quinn thought about running over to the hotel without making the telephone call, but that was too risky. He looked down the street, in both directions, and spotted a small cafe a short distance from where he was standing. He again looked around for the blond fellow but there was no sign of him in any direction. He walked over towards the cafe, fearing that if he ran, he might attract attention.

Once inside, he found the coin operated phone and after looking up the number in the telephone book, dialed his hotel and asked the clerk to ring his room. After a ring or two, Anne picked up the phone.

"Where have you been? I was about to start searching for you."

"Anne, we've got a problem. The guy that got Sean. I think he's here in Kinsale and I know he's after me. He knows I'm in the hotel and I'm sure he knows you are with me. We have got to get out of here."

Anne said nothing for a moment as she tried to grasp what Quinn was telling her.

"Quinn, is this for real?"

"Yes, damn it. He was out in front of the hotel just minutes ago, watching the entry, and I don't know where the hell he is right now." Quinn told her where he was calling from and suggested that she stay right in her room with the door locked.

"Quinn, what are you going to do?"

"I don't know. I think I'll try to make my way over to a police station if there's one around here. I'll call you later."

"Be careful, Quinn."

Quinn thought about calling the police and having them come to where he was but he did not know what sort of response that might bring. If the station was close by, it would be better if he made his way over there. He asked the waitress if there was a police station close by and with a somewhat alarmed look on her face, she told him there was a small substation around the corner and up the block.

Quinn had learned some time ago that when an Irishman tells you something is "up the block," that may mean in the very block he was in or in some block up the street somewhere. He tried to get a more specific description of the location of the substation, but it kept coming out as "up the block." He decided that he would take his chances that the substation was in fact just around the corner a short distance.

Quinn knew what the Gardai emblem looked like and that it was always prominently displayed over their station doors. He went to the door of the cafe, checked in both directions, and went in search of the police station.

Quinn walked up the street at a pace that was rapid, but not one that would stand out from other pedestrians. The sidewalk was crowded with tourists and locals doing their shopping and looking at what was displayed in the windows of the retail stores. He maneuvered around them as best he could, but they occasionally brought his progress to a standstill as they stopped in front of him or formed a wall of pedestrians that he had to walk around. His heart was beating furiously and he could feel the perspiration building. He had never been so frightened in his entire life and for once was contemplating his own imminent demise.

There were things he yet wanted to do with his life and he didn't want those dreams to be frustrated by his being drawn into a war that he had little or no interest in. Yet, here he was, virtually running for his life in, of all places, the birthplace of his grandfather, Jeremiah Desmond. Quinn thought to himself as he searched the buildings for a sign of the Gardai emblem, maybe it is prophetic that I, the last living descendant of Jeremiah, should meet my maker where he was born. I suppose there are worse places to pick for your final departure.

Quinn continued to check around for any sign of the blond fellow and as he progressed up the street, his confidence was gradually returning. He stepped into a bookstore and asked the clerk where the Gardai substation was located. The clerk pointed in the direction that he had been proceeding and again said, "Just up the street."

"How far up the street?"

"Not far at all. Just up there a little ways."

Quinn resumed his walk and was now making better time as the sidewalk was less crowded. This was both good and bad. He was moving faster but he was now more visible to anyone that was looking for him. As he proceeded up the street, he looked ahead and on the very next block, he could see the white globe and the black emblem of the Irish police, the Gardai. He breathed a sigh of relief and began thinking about what he was going to say to them. He was afraid that they might consider him some looney fellow that was making up stories and throw him out of the station and into the clutches of the agents for Unity.

As his mind raced, laying out the explanation that he would have to give to whoever he spoke with, his eyes were now focused on the white globe growing ever closer. He did not see the sedan that had come up behind him, nor hear its engine slow down as it pulled over to the curb just slightly ahead of where he was walking. He finally looked over in the direction of the street and right into the eyes of a familiar face holding a machine pistol with what appeared to be a silencer on the end of the barrel, all pointed directly at him. Quinn could not believe what was taking place yet in the moment of time that he had to think, there was no doubt in his mind that he was about to die. It was too late to run and there was nothing to hide behind. Later witnesses said that he had shouted out, "Why" just as the first muffled report of the gun was heard.

All that Quinn saw was a bright flash coming out of the muzzle. He felt as though he had been hit with a hammer in the chest and there was no longer any air in his lungs to draw upon. There was no pain, only a numb feeling that seemed to shut everything down. Strangely, the sidewalk was rising up and about to strike him. It did but he felt nothing. His vision closed down to a pin hole and he thought about Anne for just a moment as he saw her face. He tried to speak and may have but then the numbness throughout his body was complete.

CHAPTER 40

When Baumler left the office, Ellen walked out to Martha's desk and told her she would be out for the rest of the day. She had to supervise the disposition of Patrick's personal items out at Park Ridge and she could be reached there if something came up. Most of his things would be given away but personal items and memorabilia had to be gone over and preserved or disposed of, depending upon their value or interest to others in the family.

Thirty minutes later, Ellen was seated in the kitchen at Park Ridge having something to eat and going over what needed to be done with Robert. She had tried to enlist Adam in the sorting project but he claimed to have some very important matters to take care of in Shipping and just couldn't tear himself away. As a matter of courtesy, she had told her mother what she was going to do but her mother said that she was occupied as well.

The chauffeur and the gardener were busy on other matters but Robert had arranged for the yard boy to come and do the heavy lifting when that was required. Ellen had spoken to her mother about taking over Patrick's room and receiving no objection had moved many of her things in there that had been shipped up from Dublin. Most of her personal items had stayed in her room at Park Ridge and had never been taken to Dublin so the move primarily involved hauling from one room in the house to another. Unfortunately, before that could be done, Patrick's things had to be removed and the room rendered spotlessly clean before it was acceptable to Ellen.

The closet was tackled first with Ellen calling out the disposition of the various items of clothing with most going to charity and a few going to certain family or staff members to dispose of as they saw fit. Those going to charity were boxed up and hauled to the storeroom to be shipped out later. Next were the bureau drawers and personal items on tables and shelves. Virtually everything in the drawers went to charity and personal mementos were boxed and placed in the kitchen for selection first by family members and after a few days by the staff.

There was an old, roll top, desk in the bedroom that was locked and neither Ellen nor Robert was able to locate a key for it. Finally Robert mentioned the personal items that had been in Patrick's possession when he was found. There was a small key ring with just a few keys on it and possibly one of them would fit the desk. Those personal affects found on Patrick that had not been summarily disposed of were located in the basement of the house and subjected to lengthy soaking in a strong detergent and then repeated scrubbings before the stench was finally removed. They had been laid out on the work bench where they were still lying when Robert went down to look for the key. He took the key ring up to Patrick's room, tried two keys which did not open the lock, but the third one did. He removed the keys from the lock and rolled the desk top up to disclose a pile of old letters, bills, pens, corporate memos and other materials most of which could have been disposed of long ago.

Ellen went over each item carefully to make sure it was something that could be thrown out. After she had examined every piece of paper and had tossed virtually every one into the waste basket, she began looking in the storage drawers of the desk itself. There was nothing in the smaller bins, but as she opened the large bin in the center of the desk, she pulled out a wooden box, obviously hand made, with a fine oiled finish.

"Robert, look at this."

"Yes, I made the box. Your father wanted it to keep some of the old papers that we found when we redid the library. He may have put other old papers in there besides the ones we found in the library, I don't know."

"Well, this is something. I'll look at this later." Ellen put the box back in the bin, rolled the top down and locked it. She put the keys in her pocket to remind her to take a look at the contents of the box. The thought that it contained old notes or other papers from years gone by intrigued her. Soon, however, those thoughts were lost as she got back to the task at hand.

After another two hours of cleaning, moving, packing and unpacking, Ellen was finally moved into the room that had been her fathers. She dismissed Robert and sat down in a chair by the large window overlooking the back of the estate. This was why she had chosen to move into Patrick's room. The view of the lawns and trees extended to the edge of a wooded area that bordered Park Ridge. It was a beautiful view and most relaxing. The window itself was a work of art. It stood as a reminder of the age of the house with its lead-oxide English glass that had been cast in a mold and held in strips of lead in a metal frame. The clarity did not compare with modern glass, but the effect surpassed any modern window for beauty. Ellen sat for some time admiring the view and looking over her new abode. She was pleased with her choice, but exhausted from the work. She checked her watch and noted that it was almost time for supper.

The kitchen staff had become accustomed to not preparing any supper whatsoever as Hillary was usually gone and the other two, Patrick and Adam, either ate somewhere else or didn't eat. Having Ellen back in the house lengthened their day, but neither the cook nor Robert complained. She was a breath of fresh air in a house greatly in need of her upbeat personality and energy. Ellen called down to Robert on the intercom and said that she would like something to eat about seven. "Just a sandwich. Maybe some soup. Any kind, and tea. I'll come down so don't bring anything up here. I don't want to spill in my new room."

Robert said that it would be ready when she came down. In the meantime, Ellen tried out her new shower, put on some clean clothes and visited the library. She knew that was one of Patrick's favorite places and being in it reminded her very much of him. She missed her father and regretted that she had not been able to spend as much time with him as they both would have liked. She also would have liked to have said goodbye to him and to thank him for everything that he had done for her.

Ellen was well aware that Patrick was a very vulnerable person and that he sought refuge in drink. That did not detract from her affection for him and, if anything, left her with questions in her own mind as to what she could have done to prevent his final outcome. Maybe if she had spent more time with him, this would not have happened. She tried to dismiss these thoughts, but they kept coming back.

Ellen sat at the library desk and opened the drawers to see if there was anything there that needed to be thrown out or pursued. There were only pencils, paper clips and some note pads but nothing of any consequence. She looked about the room and understood why it was that Patrick was so comfortable here. It was warmer than the other rooms and the stained glass windows cast a hue about the sumptuous furnishings in the room. As she was relaxing in the comfort of the chair that Patrick had sat in so many times, she found herself staring at the painting of her great grandfather, William Desmond. He, in turn, seemed to be staring back at her with a cold, stern look.

His eyes seemed to follow the movements of her head as she moved from side to side to see if what they said about the painting was true. Patrick had told her that he seemed to watch you, but she had never tasted the experience. It was eerie. She stood up and walked about the room but the eyes never left her. She thought about how William had spent much time in this very room himself, according to family legend, and he most likely had instructed the artist to paint the eyes so that they had that special effect. In that way William could be the eternal watchdog over Desmond Enterprises.

Ellen thought to herself, it's a wonder Daddy didn't take it off the wall and put up something more relaxing. She studied the painting and thought about Quinn Parker's claim that William had falsified the death certificate of Jeremiah Desmond in order to acquire the estate. "Did you do that, Gramps? You look like you could have." Well, I think we'll find out one way or another. Ellen checked her watch and saw that it was almost seven.

After her light supper, Ellen went up to her room to read and relax after a difficult day. She had been thinking over her conversation with Frank Baumler regarding the situation in the Shipping Department but she had not resolved the specifics of a plan of action. She had concluded, even during the conversation with Baumler, that to delay confronting Carter and Unity would only make matters worse. She would come up with a suggestion to discuss with Frank tomorrow. In the meantime, a good book and early to bed would provide some relief after the last two weeks. When she was in her room, she cleaned out her pockets and laid the articles on her dresser.

It was then that she saw the keys to the roll top desk. She selected the key that Robert had used and went over to the desk and opened it. She pulled out the wooden box and first examined the workmanship that had gone in to its construction. Ellen admired the way the separate pieces of wood were intermeshed at the corners. They were fit together so smoothly that she could not feel the edges when she ran her fingers along the joints. So like Robert, she thought, to put all of this effort into a simple box for Patrick to store papers.

Ellen opened the top carefully so as not to damage the small brass hinges that kept it in place and began taking out the smaller pieces of paper. After she had examined and removed a number of them, she noticed the larger, letter size paper lying in the bottom of the box. The large, black lettering of the law firm name across the top of the letter immediately raised her interest level in what the letter contained. She next noted the date, January 15, 1880 and the fact that the letter was addressed to her great grandfather, William Desmond. As she read through the letter and noted the circle drawn, obviously by William, around the Jeremiah Desmond that had passed away in Wisconsin in 1879, she was at first confused as to the import of the letter, but not for long.

Unless she was mistaken, it appeared that her ancestor, William Desmond, was apparently looking for a person with the same name to claim as his brother that had emigrated to the States. He must have laid out the criteria that he needed to the attorney in Illinois and this was the response. The Jeremiah Desmond that he needed could have no wife or children. That was very clear from the letter she was reading. Otherwise there would be heirs that would have priority for the Estate that were ahead of William. Ellen was stunned.

She then began to think about what she should do with the letter. Her immediate reaction was to copy it and send it to Quinn Parker. As she pondered that, a cold chill ran down her back at the thought of what might happen to the company. She didn't want to do that, but could she live with herself if she didn't. Her mind raced searching for something to counter what her conscience was telling her to do.

What if she was misreading the letter and this was actually the brother of William and he had circled it to identify which one was his brother. That was a possibility. Was it her job to prove that the inheritance had been fraudulently transferred. The more she thought about it, the more she thought that for the time being, she would say nothing about the letter to anyone. She had to give this matter a lot more thought.

No sense in giving away "the farm" unless she was absolutely certain of what had taken place and that is exactly what could happen. She carefully placed the letter back in the box, along with the other old bills and notes, closed the cover and slid the box back into the large bin. She then rolled the desk top cover down and locked it. She placed the keys in her purse and thought about other things to dismiss the matter from her mind. She selected a book from her own collection and tried to bury herself in a romance novel but the circled name, Jeremiah Desmond, kept appearing on the page she was reading.

The following morning, as she drove to the office, she decided that she had to find out about this Jeremiah Desmond whose name was circled. The first thing that she did was to call Frank Baumler and get a copy of the death certificate that Quinn Parker alleged was fraudulent. Baumler had a quizzical look on his face as he brought up a copy from the estate file that he had in his office but, as a good subordinate, he asked no questions. Ellen thanked him and directed her attention to other matters which was Frank's clue to leave.

As soon as Baumler was out of the office, she opened the file and to her dismay noted that the date of death on the filed certificate matched that in the letter, February 20, 1879. She had already planned the next step and that was to call an attorney in Madison, Wisconsin, which was the closest large city to Columbus, and hire them to check out this Jeremiah Desmond.

There might be something in other court records to prove or disprove his relationship to William. She thought about asking Frank if he had done that already but she hesitated to do so as he might ask her what she was worried about. Ellen was fairly sure that her father had not shown the attorney's letter to Frank for the same reasons that she was not advertising its existence.

She checked her watch and noting the time difference between Ireland and Wisconsin, she figured that she had better wait until around three Belfast time before placing the call. Ellen went to the Reference Room and found the name and phone number of a highly rated attorney who specialized in Probate and Inheritance matters. She wrote the attorney's name and number down and then returned to her office.

In the meantime, Ellen began focusing on how to deal with Tony Carter. She pulled out her note pad and laid out the alternatives in columnar fashion. On one side of the page, she wrote down what she could offer him if he stopped using the company as a conduit in their drug trafficking. At the top of this column she wrote "denial". She had to anticipate that he would deny either his own knowledge of such an operation or that Unity was involved, or both. She would have to prepare for that and lay out the irrefutable evidence so that they did not waste time arguing and could move on to the solutions. She would lay that out when she finished drafting the alternatives.

Ellen agreed with Frank that they would be better off to pay good money than to face the wrath of both Unity and the government. She studied the last five years operating statements of Desmond Enterprises in order to figure out what they could possibly afford. As she did so, she wrote down, "tax benefits" on her notepad. Carter could probably work it so that all payments to Unity were deductible. That way, the company could afford to pay more and it gave her more leverage with Carter. One thing she would not do, that he might insist upon as a trade off, would be to permit further infiltration of Unity into the company. Her long range plan, which she did not need to write down, was to rid the company of Unity's influence all together.

Ellen worked on this project the better part of the day and became so immersed in what she was doing that it was 3:45 before she again thought about calling the Wisconsin attorney. She closed the door to her office, dialed the number and after explaining where she was calling from and what she needed, was soon speaking with the attorney. Ellen did not lay out what the basic problem was that had initiated her call. Rather, she told the attorney that she wanted to know if there were any records that showed the parents, siblings, spouse or children of Jeremiah Desmond who had died February 20, 1879 in Columbus, Wisconsin.

In order to prevent her request from landing on the desk of some new hire in the office, Ellen made it clear to the fellow that whoever she hired had to know what they were doing and would be compensated accordingly. "I don't want this passed down the hall to an underling. I have noted your credentials and I want you to handle the matter or tell me now that you can't. I also want it done within the next few days. I will send you a retainer right now if you can take care of this. If your schedule doesn't permit this, tell me now. What do you say?"

There was silence on the other end of the line for a moment or two. Then he spoke. "My hourly fee is four hundred dollars an hour and if I am going to do everything in connection with your search, I will need a retainer of three thousand dollars. I have to advise you that someone with less experience and much less expensive, could do the job as well. It's not rocket science."

"The retainer will be sent by private courier this afternoon." Ellen confirmed his mailing address and gave him her private telephone line as well as the line at Park Ridge and told him to contact her immediately when he found any family connections. When she completed the call, Ellen sat back and pondered the situation. She had to prepare herself in the event that the attorney confirmed that the death certificate was fraudulent. Even if it was, she was not sure that it was her responsibility to tell Quinn Parker about it. She would have to think that one through.

The following morning, Ellen called Frank Baumler into her office to decide on a plan for dealing with Carter. It was agreed that she would go ahead with presenting the two alternatives and see how Carter reacted. The negotiations could extend over two or more meetings and nothing was cast in stone until a final agreement. What she really wanted to talk to Baumler about was the issue of Adam's safety in the Shipping Department. She told him about her meeting with Adam and her concern that he could become a target. Frank Baumler agreed that there was risk to Adam, if for no other reason than to show Ellen that Unity meant business.

"So, I think that before I meet with Carter, we should get Adam out of there."

Baumler paused and said, "I agree. I would not only get him out of there, I would get him out of Belfast. I'm sure that Unity has a pretty good idea that it was Adam that led to the investigation of Shipping by Somers. Have you thought about a replacement as the head of the Shipping Department?"

"No, I haven't. Any suggestions?"

"I'd put Somers in there for the time being. He can take care of himself and he also is quite familiar with how the department operates from his tour of duty down there."

"Good idea. Tell him it may only be temporary, if it is not something that he would want to take on permanently. I'll make that change today, unless you have other ideas."

In the afternoon, Ellen called Hillary and told her that she had to talk to her about an important matter as soon as possible. The two made plans to meet for dinner and when they were seated at the table, Hillary asked what was this all about. Ellen laid out the facts of what Unity was doing in Shipping at Desmond Enterprises.

Hillary was at first taken aback by the knowledge that she had been used by Tony Carter, then the anger began to rise. "That son-of-a-bitch. Ellen, we'll throw him out on the street where he belongs. What really gets me is how good I've been to that guy. Are you positive about all of this. I can't believe he, or Unity, put this one over on me."

Ellen explained that everything was confirmed. There was no doubt about anything that she had told her mother. Ellen went on to explain the proposed solution that Baumler and she had decided upon and Hillary immediately said that she wanted to be there for the meeting.

Ellen then dealt with the matter of Adam and Hillary said that she would take care of that. They would find something for him in the Fairchild offices in London and he could live in Hillary's apartment there. The two women then agreed upon the time for the meeting with Carter for the following afternoon at Ellen's office.

At two sharp, Tony Carter came down the hallway of the Executive Offices and dropped his business card on Martha's desk. Ellen told Martha to send him on in. Hillary had not yet arrived but it would give Ellen a chance to know a little bit more about the man that seemed to be her number one problem at the moment.

When Carter entered, he flashed a wide grin for the new corporate president and walked up to the desk to shake hands. Ellen stood up, returned the courtesy and offered Carter some tea. He accepted and while she was performing the honors, they engaged in small talk to relieve the tension. Carter had a pretty good idea that this just might be a continuation of the last conversation that he had with Patrick. He knew that this one would be more difficult than the last and he would just have to feel his way along.

When Ellen mentioned that Hillary would be along any moment, that temporarily unnerved him. This could well be the end of a very enjoyable relationship if Hillary was privy to everything that Patrick had brought out in their meeting. That would also compound the forces aligned against him in this meeting and make his task just that much more difficult.

"Ellen, I want you to know how terrible all of us in Unity feel about Patrick's untimely death. You just have to be so careful these days." After he had spoken, the thought came to him that Ellen may think that Unity was somehow involved. He quickly added, "Patrick and I had such an enjoyable conversation when we were last together and I will dearly miss him. Although we argued over many things, as I'm sure you know, there was always deep affection and respect between the two of us. A dear fellow."

Just then, the intercom beeped and Martha announced that Hillary was coming down the hall. Ellen said to send her right in, as though Hillary needed an invitation. In less than a minute, Hillary entered the room and acknowledged Carter's presence with an icy smile and a greeting that let him know that he was in trouble.

"Tony, my dear friend. You're color is not very good. You need more rest. Maybe it's time to retire." This was followed by a rather frigid chuckle.

Ellen would have preferred if her mother had skipped the witty jab as the tension in the room was going to rise without the help of anyone's gratuitous remarks. When she had the two of them seated, Martha made the rounds with hot tea and then departed the room, closing the door behind her.

"Tony, I don't enjoy having to discuss what we are here for today. I am not going to mince words as I would like to get this over with as quickly as possible. She then proceeded to lay out what was known about the illegal shipments that were coming into the country under the cover of legitimate Desmond products and, further, the use of Desmond facilities and transport equipment to support the operation.

Carter tried to interrupt. "May I say something?"

"Not just yet. When we are done. We really have little interest in what you have to say about this. We have decided to tell you what we intend to do about it. That is why we are having this meeting. You can stay and listen or you can read about it in the papers."

That last comment made Carter sit up a little straighter in the chair. He doubted that the two women would try to confront Unity publicly, but he was not totally sure about that. Knowing Hillary as well as he did, he considered anything possible. Ellen, he was not sure about. He decided to be patient and hear them out.

Ellen laid out the alternative proposals that she had agreed upon with Frank Baumler. When she had finished laying out the terms, she concluded. "We are replacing Adam Desmond in Shipping effective right now. Ted Somers is taking his place and your misuse of our Company and our equipment is terminated as of tomorrow morning. Any further misuse of any Desmond property by Unity, or its people, will be reported to the R.U.C. and the press, if and when it occurs. That's all I have to say." Ellen told Carter that if he had anything to say, now was the time.

"Well, you two ladies seem to have everything figured out. Patrick brought this up as well and I'll tell you the same thing I told him." What followed was the standard Carter denial coupled with a threat. "If you try to publicly label Unity with this, let me assure you that you are grabbing a tiger by the tail. I strongly advise you that you will be the loser, not Unity."

Ellen smiled and said, "Tony, we are not going public with this. That is up to you if you try to resist us by not getting all of your scum out of our Shipping Department. Trust me, we will get you out one way or the other. The decision as to which way it will happen is up to you."

"Ellen, the shop is unionized and you can't throw the union out. You'll spend the next ten years in court."

"We are throwing out any and all people involved in this. They are receiving their notices this very moment. Baumler and Somers had their termination notices prepared yesterday and the slips are in their boxes right now. The investigation is continuing and more slips will follow. If you want to take those cases to court, go ahead. The press will find the matter very interesting and will undoubtedly conduct their own investigation. Our photo records may be appearing on the front page of the Belfast Independent."

Carter appeared angry but said nothing.

"Tony, the meeting is over."

Carter was obviously confused as to how to deal with the situation. As he stalked out of the room, he turned and said, "I have to report this to our people at Unity and they will decide what to do about it."

"Fine, good day, Tony."

Hillary raised a clenched fist. "Good job, Ellen. I don't think he'll do a damn thing. Are those notices really in the boxes right now?"

"You bet they are. I wouldn't have said it if they weren't."

The two women talked for a few more minutes and then Hillary said that she had to get over to Fairchild and make sure they were set up for Adam. When she was gone, Ellen sat back in her chair and breathed a sigh of relief. She thought to herself that nobody had told her the job would be easy, but she didn't know it would be quite like this.

As she sat at her desk, trying to relax from the meeting, she looked about the room and realized that one of these days she had to redo the office and get rid of some of the archaic furnishings that had been there since her grandfather's time. The desk she would keep as it was a beautiful piece of work. The Adam's Family crest on the wall with its upright sword and helmet represented a key part of the company history and that would stay, but some of the other artwork had to go. She looked at the worn brown carpeting that had been on the floor ever since she could remember and with that, she picked up the phone and told Martha to come on in.

"Well, how was your meeting?"

"Oh, it was fun. I hope every day isn't like this one."

"Mr. Carter looked very unhappy when he left."

"Good. That means we accomplished what we set out to do." Ellen then told Martha she wanted a new office. "Find a decorator with some taste and see what they can come up with. The desk stays. The crest stays and everything else can go. Carpeting, walls, lighting, everything. Get me some suggestions and it better not be pink."

As Ellen was about to leave her office for the day, the phone rang and it was the receptionist. She said that she had a long distance call from Madison, Wisconsin, in the States and the caller would only speak with Ellen Desmond. Ellen told her to put it through.

"Ms. Desmond. I have some information for you. Do you want me to mail it, fax it or what?"

"First, tell me what you came up with, then you can fax me a hard copy."

"There is a will from the father of this Jeremiah Desmond devising to him a parcel of land. The will identifies the grantor as his father and the Jeremiah Desmond that you identified to us sold that very same parcel about a year before he died, so we know we are talking about the right guy. That was the last sign of him on any public record other than the filing of his death certificate. I assume it is the same as the one you have."

"What was the father's name?"

"Andrew Desmond and he was from a town in County Kilkenny, Ireland, that I am not sure I can pronounce. It is spelled I-n-i-s-t-i-o-g-e. That is referenced in the will. There are other children of this Andrew other than Jeremiah."

"What are their names?"

"Seamus, Mary... and..."

"That's fine. Send me the report. You can send that by regular air mail."

Ellen asked him if he had received the retainer and he said he had. There was no additional charge and Ellen thanked him and hung up the phone. She sat back in her chair and went over what the attorney had told her.

There was no longer any doubt that the death certificate that William Desmond had filed was fraudulent and William knew it. The question remained, however, as to what happened to the real Jeremiah Desmond. Quinn Parker's case appeared very strong but was it her job to disclose the false filing of the certificate or was it Parker's to discover. She could not make up her mind on that point and would have to give it more time. She didn't want to rush out and do something stupid. Time would help put it all in proper perspective.

In the meantime, she decided that she would proceed as though nothing had changed since the last time she spoke with Quinn Parker. She had found two old photographs of William Desmond that she had promised Quinn she would send to him. She put those in an envelope, and addressed it to Quinn Parker at the Rockwell Hotel in Dublin.

Two weeks after deciding to redo her office, Ellen sat behind her desk, admiring the new furnishings and waiting for Frank Baumler to come up. Gone were the archaic paintings, worn carpeting and dull colors, all replaced by what she referred to as trendy traditional. Thick burgundy carpeting, heavy off white drapes and dark oak walls which gave the office a warm but professional appearance. Particularly, when the centerpiece of the large room, the massive carved oak desk, had recently been refinished to show off the intricate art work of the builder. Placed immediately between the desk and a credenza, built to compliment the desk, was a very large red leather chair that Ellen was learning to enjoy more every day.

Some of the wall pieces that had been in the room since the time of Dennis Desmond remained. Among them, the Adam's Family crest, which Ellen had sent out for refinishing along with the desk. The upright sword had been regilded and the full face knight's helmet was given a fresh coating of high grade silver. The wooden shield forming the backdrop of the crest was cleaned, sanded and very carefully repainted making the crest a conversation piece whenever visitors entered the office. Ellen told Martha that the Desmonds owed a certain amount of gratitude to the Adam's family for what they had done for them and the least they could do was to maintain the crest with a certain amount of dignity. It was the first time in generations that the crest had ever been repaired or refinished.

As Ellen sat waiting for Baumler to arrive, Martha called her on the intercom and announced that "Mr. Baumler is here to see you."

"Send him in Martha."

Frank walked in, notepad and pencil at the ready as was his usual custom. "Very nice, Chief. It beats the hell out of the old office. Pardon my French but it really does."

"Thanks Frank. How's Somers coming along? Is he getting stir crazy down there or can we keep him there a bit longer?"

"He's doing fine. We see no sign that Unity is trying to run anything through our warehouses anymore, but we should keep him there just to be careful. I'm sure you have heard that Carter has a new job. Not one that he would want. Seems that they want him out on the street again, as an organizer. Apparently no more cocktail parties or tennis games for Tony Carter. Seems as though the people that run the Union thought he had screwed up one too many times."

"Yes, Frank but I think their idea of a screw up and ours is quite different."

"Right, Chief. Losing the transportation system for their main source of income really wasn't his fault. It really wasn't. Sooner or later it would have fallen apart anyway. What probably got to them was his eagerness to have anyone taken out that he considered a potential threat. Unfortunately for him, Unity or somebody in government thought the benefits derived didn't justify the bad publicity. Personally, I think the heavy hitters in the parliament let the Union chiefs know that it was time to clean up their act and Carter was sent to the showers. Can't say I miss having him around."

"I agree, Frank. Yes, I was wondering what happened to dear old Tony. There's another guy from the Union that has been calling for an appointment. I assume that's his replacement. I'm expecting to be tapped big time when I meet this guy. Any suggestions?"

"That's your call, Chief. Keep in mind, they can shut us down whenever they want so you have to keep them somewhat happy. What's the guy's name?"

"Samuel Cosgrove. Sounds like a banker."

"Maybe he is. I don't know him but we can get a file on him before you meet. Give me a day or two and I'll have a file on your desk by that time."

"I'll give you time. I have to leave for London in the morning. I want to see how mother is getting along now that she is living there permanently. I'm sure she's doing fine. She never cared about living in Ireland. Very British, you know."

Frank laughed, then nodded in agreement and Ellen went on, "I hope she and Adam aren't at each other's throats. That arrangement won't last very long, but at least Adam had a place to run to when he left here. He seems to enjoy London quite a bit. A little more in tune with his style, if you know what I mean."

"Yes, Chief. So far things have worked out better than I expected. I thought Unity might have landed on us with a carload of bricks when you gave Carter the word, but I am starting to believe that cooler heads prevailed when they saw that your were serious. We may have benefitted by a general pulling back of Unity as well. I hope we've weathered the storm."

"I certainly hope so. God knows, they are a brutal bunch. That reminds me, I have to give Anne Flanagan a call. I still can't believe what they did to Parker."

"Chief, Unity may possibly be taking a bad rap on the Quinn Parker business."

"What do you mean?"

"The word on the street is that it wasn't Unity that did it."

"Well, Frank, who else would have? Unity apparently had a reason. No one else did."

"Not sure, Chief. That's just what I hear."

Baumler picked up his notepad, gave Ellen a wave and left the office.

CHAPTER 41

The large cardboard box with the heavy packing tape had been sitting in her living room for two days. Anne had received the box with a letter contained in a shipping envelope describing the contents as personal items belonging to Sean Flanagan that the school had collected from his apartment and from his desk at the University. Anne did not feel up to going through the personal mementoes that represented the sum total of her former husband's life but she knew that eventually she was going to have to tackle the distasteful job. As she began her third day of having the box in her living room unopened, Anne resolved that when she came home from work and before the boys were home from soccer, she would take on what she knew would be an emotionally difficult task.

That afternoon she left work an hour early so that she could hopefully accomplish the task of sorting through the materials in the box in an effort to determine what should be kept for the boys and what could be disposed of. She wanted to complete that job before the boys came back because she knew that they would want to keep absolutely everything in the box. She would like to grant their wish in that respect, but they just did not have room in their small apartment for everything the large box contained. She would be careful to retain anything that could provide the boys with any insight into their father's life that would have meaning for them when they were older, but the rest could go.

After she had opened the box, she could see that whoever had packed it had just cleaned off Sean's desk or dresser and thrown the papers into the box. There were some items that appeared to have been kept in some orderly fashion, but most of the papers, reports, letters and notes had no arrangement whatsoever. School papers were with laundry receipts or tax records, consequently, Anne had to briefly glance at every scrap of paper in the box.

After an hour of pulling papers out of the box, examining them and assigning them to one pile or another, she had three stacks of papers lying about the room. One was for materials to be saved for the boys, one related to unfinished business of Sean's that should be completed and the third was for the trash barrel.

Some of the materials in the box, that were somewhat organized, were segregated in files or smaller boxes. Sean's political files were well organized as were files of correspondence, particularly involving Anne or the boys. There were a number of books of a political nature that were of no particular interest to Anne, but she could donate those to "One Ireland", so she stacked them off to the side of the room. As she neared the bottom of the box, there was a letter size box of papers with the name "Parker" written in felt pen across the top of the cover. Anne pulled the box out and took it over to the dining room table so that she could more easily see what it contained.

Inside the box there were a number of blank sheets of smaller letter size paper, each sheet of paper individually wrapped. Anne removed one sheet of the paper from its wrapper and found it to be very brittle and discolored from age. This paper was obviously very old. Also in this box, Anne found photocopies of the translations that Sean had done for Quinn.

There were copies of both the original Gaelic version and the English translation. Further down in the box, Anne found what appeared to be original letters in Gaelic addressed to "Jerm" and signed by a "Wilm". Sensing that something was not right with what she was seeing, Anne's attention was now riveted on the contents of the box.

As she studied what were obviously the originals of what Quinn had referred to as the Gaelic letters, it was obvious to Anne that Sean had not returned all originals to Quinn. He had kept four of the letters for some reason, but surely Quinn knew how many letters he had given to Sean. It was then she understood the meaning of the blank letter paper. Sean apparently had removed four of the original Gaelic letters, located very old paper, and had four revised Gaelic letters prepared by someone capable of duplicating the ink, the flourish, and the style of the original writer.

As Anne thought how Sean could have accomplished the substitution, she realized that he must have done that when he was in Ireland on his last visit. According to Quinn, he had possession of the letters then and he must have brought them with him. Anne looked at her watch and noted that the boys would be back shortly. She replaced the letters and old sheets of blank papers in the box, secreted it on the top shelf of her bookcase and quickly cleaned up the mess on the floor so that they would not notice the fact that the large box and its contents were no longer in the room.

Later in the evening, after the boys had been fed and their school assignments were completed, Anne ushered them upstairs to get ready for bed. They complained as usual that it was too early to go to bed but Anne told them to get about their business as she had matters to take care of and wanted to get to sleep herself. She did check her watch and noted that she was being a bit unfair to them this evening, but her curiosity about the contents of the box had been growing all through the evening.

Anne had concluded that Sean had been about his political business in this matter but in what way, she could not figure out. She would have to read all of the letters in Gaelic and see if she could determine the ones that were fraudulent. Without the originals of all the letters, the authentic and the fraudulent, there was no way she would be able to tell for certain which four copies were fraudulent.

She could still hear the boys playing around upstairs and her curiosity was building by the moment. She called to them again to speed it up as she reached up into the bookcase and pulled the box down. She set it on the kitchen table just as Kevin walked down the stairs.

"What's in the box, Mom?"

"Just some of my papers. What are you doing down here? Get up to your room and into bed."

"I just wanted a drink of water, Mom. Look at the clock. We're still early."

"I know, Kevin, but I've got things to do here. Now get a move on so I can get to work. Sleep tight and give your Mom a kiss."

As soon as Kevin scrambled up the stairs, Anne began laying the English translations of the letters out according to the number written on each one. She assumed that Sean had numbered the letters in the order in which they were written as she noticed that none of them were dated. She then laid the copy of the original Gaelic version of the letter alongside the translation and found that the number of translation copies equaled the number of Gaelic copies. Exactly ten copies in English and ten copies in Gaelic. The four original Gaelic letters had no translated counterpart and had obviously been removed from the stack of ten letters that Quinn brought to Sean and replaced by four Gaelic letters written by Sean or his associates and copies of which were now on the table facing Anne. The problem was, which four had been switched?

Anne began reading the photocopies. The Gaelic version first and then Sean's translation in English. After having reviewed all of the photocopies, Anne could surmise which four had been switched. Six of the photocopies in English dealt with mundane matters on the Desmond farm as did the four originals in Gaelic that she found in the box of Sean's things. The other four photocopies in English, and their photocopy Gaelic counterparts dealt with specific facts relating to the Desmond Family and purported to be the last four letters sent from William to Jeremiah.

The first of these four letter copies began with a commentary regarding the marriage of William's father, Thomas Desmond, not mentioned heretofore, with Margaret Adams, the wife of his former employer, Sir Cecil Adams. The following two letters dealt with the death of Margaret Adams and then the death of Thomas Desmond. The last of the four suspicious letters severs the ties between William and Jeremiah.

Anne studied the lettering in the presumed forgeries very carefully and could not discern any differences from the writing in the letters believed to be authentic. Whoever had done the forgeries had done an excellent job as far as she was concerned. It was obvious to Anne that when Sean saw the letters that Quinn had left for him to translate, he saw an opportunity to lay claim to the vast Desmond holdings. It was well known to everyone in the INA that Desmond Enterprises was a prime contributor to Unity and Sean was uniquely familiar with the mystery regarding Jeremiah Desmond, the rightful heir to the Estate.

Anne thought that at first, Sean must have had high hopes that Quinn was, in fact, the rightful heir to the Desmond Estate. However, after reading the ten authentic Gaelic letters, he discovered that, although they did not disprove Quinn's relationship to the real Jeremiah Desmond, they did not provide any support for a claim either, other than the fact they were signed by a William to his brother, Jeremiah.

There were presumably hundreds of Jeremiah Desmonds with a brother, William, that had emigrated from Ireland during the Famine. On the other hand, with a few careful changes in the letters, Quinn could be made to appear as the sole heir to the rightful claim of his grandfather. Furthermore, Sean realized that Quinn was motivated to seek out his grandfather's family in Ireland, if they were still living. It was a situation made to order for Sean and he took advantage of it. Unfortunately, it eventually led to a tragic result.

Anne knew that Sean would never have gone ahead with the scheme if he knew what would eventually happen. He more than likely had assumed that if the forgeries were carefully done, Quinn's basically honest demeanor, and belief in his claim, would carry the day. If by chance, the fraud was discovered there would be nothing that would tie Quinn to it, so either way Quinn would not be hurt. What Sean had not counted on was that he was setting Quinn up to be drawn into the intertribal rivalry taking place in Ireland with its web of intrigue and murder.

It was obvious to Anne that Quinn's claim, which had appeared so convincing when he had explained it to her, rested almost entirely on the validity of the Gaelic letters. With that cornerstone removed, the claim fell of its own weight. Anne put the papers back in the box and was going to discard it along with the other papers that had been sent to her but then decided to keep the box of letters in the event that the issue ever came up again. She covered the box and placed it on a high shelf in the closet along with some of her other school and personal papers which had been stored there for safe keeping. As the days passed, Anne thought no more about the fraudulent claim and more or less dismissed it from her mind as another painful chapter in her life as the wife of Sean Flanagan.

Six weeks passed during which Anne tried to get her life back in order. One evening, as she was cleaning up the dishes and trying to see to it that the boys accomplished their homework, she received a telephone call.

"Anne, this is Joe Robbins. I'm in Dublin for a few days and I have some news for you."

Anne was surprised to hear from Robbins, but not pleased. Hearing his voice took her back to the fateful day when Quinn was killed. The key events that led up to his death flashed before her from the moment that she ran out of the hotel following his phone call to finding him laying on the sidewalk trying to speak. She had tried to see who was in the fleeing car but only caught a glimpse of the man pulling his weapon back in and rolling up the window. The man had features familiar to Anne, but she had dismissed the thought as preposterous. However, when she knelt down by Quinn's side, she thought that he had looked at her and mumbled "Rob...". He never finished what he was going to say before he died. Since then, the thought that Joe Robbins was the person she saw in the car kept recurring in her mind but she would always dismiss it as a figment of her imagination. Yet, it kept coming up and it bothered her to think that she was suspecting a long-time friend of hers and Sean's of having committed such an act.

"Anne, are you there?"

"Oh, yes, Joe. I was finishing up something here."

"I would like to come over, if I may, either this evening or sometime in the next day or so. I have some interesting information for you."

"I can't imagine what that would be, but you could come over right now if that's convenient."

Within twenty minutes, Joe Robbins was standing at her door. Anne brought him into the living room and got him a cup of tea After they were seated, she asked him what it was that he had to tell her.

"First of all, I'm sorry to hear about Quinn. I had heard that Unity had him in their sights, but I didn't hear about it soon enough. I would have put more people on him. Anyway, Anne, Quinn had a will done when he went to see Jerry Donahue. This may come as a surprise, but he left everything he had to you. He has a small home in Atlanta and a decent stock portfolio that won't make you wealthy, but it will allow you the freedom to spend more time with your boys and enjoy your life a bit more."

Anne was stunned at this news. She began to cry. Quinn had never mentioned that he was even thinking about doing a will. Anne knew that he had no family left in the States but never connected that with what he might do with the modest estate that he had accumulated.

"I can't believe this. I'm a bit overwhelmed. Yes. I could use almost anything. We are barely squeaking by here, but we are getting by. What a wonderful man he was. I truly cared for him and I believe he cared as much for me. I wish he was here so that I could thank him."

Anne was still overcome by emotion and Robbins waited a moment for her to gather herself together. Anne, you have to sign some papers in Donahue's office and then there are things of Quinn's that you should pick up at the Rockwell Hotel and anything else that he may have brought to Ireland with him. I assume that you have the items that he had with him when he was in Kinsale?"

"Yes, I have them in a box in the closet and I still have to go through those things."

"Anne, there is one more thing that we should discuss. I don't like to bring this up at this time, but I'm talking about Quinn's claim against the Desmonds." Robbins paused a moment, for the import of what he was about to say, to sink in.

"You are the heir to Quinn's property and as such, Donahue tells me, you have the right to proceed with legal action on that claim. Were the courts to recognize that claim, you would never have to work another day in your life."

Anne said nothing as she listened to Robbins lay out the reasons why she should take Quinn's place in pursuing the court case. The thought angered her for a number of reasons. She was now of the opinion that the claim was fraudulent and Robbins had to know that it was. Secondly, pursuing the claim had resulted in Quinn's death and she had two boys to raise without subjecting herself and them to unnecessary risks. With Quinn's will, she more than likely had sufficient security to handle the basic needs of her family for some time to come.

"Joe, I'm not interested in getting involved in that mess. Look what it did for Quinn. I don't want that to happen to me."

Robbins spent the next fifteen minutes trying to reassure Anne that she and her family would be protected were she to proceed. The more that he talked, the more she questioned his involvement in Quinn's death.

"Joe, who was it that killed Quinn? I assume that you know that."

"Anne, we have reason to believe that it was a German fellow by the name of Werner Hoffman who worked with Unity. We know he was in Kinsale that day and we now know that he was under orders to take out Quinn."

"Joe, if I remember correctly, he's the blond headed fellow that Quinn had mentioned before. Isn't that right?"

"Yes. That's the guy."

"Well, there was no blond headed guy in that car that drove away after the shooting. I caught a glimpse of the guy that did the shooting."

Robbins tensed up but quickly regained his composure. "What did he look like?"

"I hate to say it, Joe, but he looked like you."

"Rest assured, Anne. It was not me. Why would I want to take Quinn out? Besides, as I believe you said before, Quinn told you that the blond fellow was after him when he called your room."

"I don't recall exactly what he said. Right now I'm very confused about the whole business and I don't want to make any decisions one way or the other."

Robbins then laid out the reasons why she owed it to the Nationalist movement to pursue the case. "It's our way to get back at Unity, Anne and it won't cost you anything. The party will cover all of the costs."

"There's one more problem, Joe, and I think you know it already. The claim is fraudulent. I know it is and I can't stand before some judge and pretend that it isn't."

"Anne, where did you get that idea?"

"Sean forged some of the translations and I find it difficult to believe that you don't know that."

Robbins was now silent. He was well aware that Anne knew how closely he worked with Sean, both in Ireland and in the States. To argue that he didn't know the letters were forgeries would only irritate her.

"Anne, I can't admit or deny that Sean had them forged. That's party business. All I can say is that the party wants you to go ahead with the claim and they will stand behind you financially and otherwise. Remember Anne. This is a war and sometimes we have to do unpleasant things. Think it over and let me know."

As Robbins left the apartment, he reminded Anne to call Donahue in the morning and see that the necessary papers were signed so that she could pick up Quinn's personal items at the Rockwell. Donahue would also take care of getting Quinn's property in the States transferred over to her name. As Robbins walked towards his car, he knew that she would never proceed with the claim. How the hell had she ever learned that the letters were forged. The forgeries were virtually perfect. Maybe Sean had told her what was going on when he was in Dublin. Who knows.

In the following days, Anne signed the necessary papers at Donahue's office so that she could pick up Quinn's personal items at the Rockwell. The Hotel had boxed everything up and after proper arrangements had been made, the box was shipped to Anne's apartment. Rather than have the box constantly reminding her of Quinn, she immediately went through it, categorizing the various items for further disposition. The box contained mostly clothing that Quinn had not taken with him to Kinsale as well as some personal items, including a letter from Ellen Desmond which contained two photographs of her great grandfather, William Desmond. Anne studied the photographs and thought how Quinn would have liked to compare them to photos of his grandfather, Jeremiah Desmond. Anne saved the personal items, including the photographs and placed them along with the other materials in her closet. The clothing items, she packed up for pickup by Charity House.

A few days after Robbins visit, Ellen Desmond called Anne to express her condolences and to see how she was getting along. After hearing about Quinn's death, Ellen felt guilty that she had not disclosed the fact that the death certificate filed by William Desmond was on the wrong Jeremiah Desmond. Now that Quinn was dead, there was no longer any pressure on her to keep that information to herself. She was well aware that Quinn had left no relatives to survive him back in the States and carry on the suit. As she dialed Anne's number, she had herself convinced that she would have disclosed that information regardless of what had happened.

"Anne, Ellen Desmond here. I wanted you to know how sorry I was to hear about Quinn Parker. What a delightful man he was. It just never stops does it. How are you doing."

The two talked about Quinn's murder and the widespread rumors that Unity was behind the shooting. Ellen mentioned that she had been successful so far in distancing Desmond Enterprises from Unity but she added that it was an ongoing battle. Anne did not mention the fact that she had some doubts as to who had done the actual shooting. By now, she had figured out that Robbins must have known through Donahue that Quinn wasn't going to try and gain control of any part of the Desmond property. He had only wanted to determine his grandfather's rightful claim to the Estate, not to exercise the claim. Maybe Robbins and the others figured that with Quinn's will, which was drawn by Donahue, she might be easier to deal with. She could now see a motive for the INA to murder Quinn but doubt remained that people close to her could have done that.

"Anne, I have a confession to make. I discovered through a bit of investigation that the death certificate that my great grandfather was relying on for the transfer of the Estate to him instead of to his brother, Jeremiah, was for another Jeremiah Desmond. Quinn was right in his assertion that it was either fraudulent or at the least a gross mistake. Now we don't know what happened to William's brother, Jeremiah Desmond, who emigrated. We only know that the one referenced in the filed Death Certificate was not the right one. The right one could well be Quinn's grandfather, but we just don't know. Maybe time will tell. Anyway, I wanted to tell Quinn that but never had the chance. We learned this only recently."

Anne thought about mentioning the forged letters but thought it would be better just to forget the entire matter. Quinn would have been interested in what Ellen was saying but, now, it meant little if anything to Anne.

"Thanks anyway, Ellen. I'm sure you've heard the last of this business with Quinn gone."

The two continued talking about "One Ireland" matters and, before they hung up, Ellen said that she would be sure to call her when she was next in Dublin.

Some time later, Anne was cleaning out her closet and took out Quinn's briefcase that she had brought back from Kinsale. She had never opened the case as it brought back memories that were just too painful for her to bear. She took the case to the dining room table and opened it. Inside there were a few travelers checks, maps, pens and pencils, writing paper and miscellaneous materials of no particular value or interest to anyone. There were also two old photographs that had penciled notations on them, "Grampa Desmond." Obviously photos of Quinn's Grandfather.

As Anne studied the photos of Jeremiah Desmond, she was struck by the similarity with the photos that Ellen Desmond had sent of William Desmond. She went to the closet and pulled the two photos of William out of the box where she had stored them and placed them side by side with the photos of Jeremiah. The comparison was amazing. Anyone not familiar with the history of the photos would have said the two men were twins. Ellen shook her head and thought to herself that it just had to be a very unusual coincidence and put everything back in the closet.

There were also some keys in the pockets of the briefcase with identification tabs glued to them. There was a key to Quinn's house in Atlanta and one marked "S.D.Box Nations Bk." She had heard him mention the safety deposit box in Atlanta and she removed this and the house key for safe keeping. The attorneys had told her that she would have to make a trip to Atlanta to finalize matters there and she would need both of these keys while she was there.

As she continued removing things from the closet, she came upon the box containing the Gaelic letters and she placed that on the dining room table along with other materials from the closet. Before replacing the box on the shelf, her continuing, though now lessened, interest got the best of her and she again removed the letters from the box and arranged them on the table. She reread the copied Gaelic versions and then examined the four Gaelic originals. From what Anne could tell, from examining the copies, the forgeries were written on the same size and style of paper, as were the four originals that she had from the box of Sean's things. She assumed that the four forgeries were done on the same paper as the blanks that she had in front of her. Comparing those blank sheets to the four originals, that Sean had not returned to Quinn, she noted that they were identical in weight, tint and texture. Very clever, she thought, of whoever put these forgeries together. Not the sort of detail work that Sean would have excelled at.

Out of curiosity, she held one of the sheets of blank, old writing paper up to the light to see if she could see any difference between that and the four original Gaelic letters. She could see the faint lines in the paper from the wires used in the fabrication process that was in vogue in the nineteenth century. Based on her study of the old blank papers, Anne concluded that any examiner with knowledge of paper would have to admit that the forged papers were truly very old and dated back to the time of the events depicted in them. Looking at the paper through the light, she could make out the watermark of the paper maker which appeared to be a chalice or cup of some kind. Now wondering what the watermark was on the four Gaelic originals, she held one of them up to the light.

She could faintly discern the wire marks on the paper and there was some sort of symbol which she assumed was the watermark. It was difficult to discern the pattern of the watermark through the heavy flourishes of ink forming the words placed on the paper by the writer. She had an old work lamp in the storeroom that Sean used when he repaired something, which was very seldom, and after she had replaced the bulb with the largest bulb she could find, she hooked it up next to the dining room table. Anne then held the old authentic letter up to the bright bulb, not so close as to burn it, but close enough so that it brought out more of the detail of the watermark.

Anne was now able to make out the rough pattern of the mark and drew it out on a piece of paper. When she was done, she looked at what she had drawn and it seemed familiar to her. She had seen the diagram somewhere before, but she could not recall where it was. She put the materials back in the box but kept her drawing out on the dinner table so she could study it further.

The boys came home from school and Anne then set her mind to getting dinner ready for the three of them. They were all seated at the dinner table and Anne was passing out the food for the boys to put on their plates when Kevin looked over at the drawing on the paper lying in the center of the table.

"I could've done a better job of it than that, Mom."

"What are you talking about?"

"Well, who drew this?" he said as he held up the drawing.

"Oh, that. Just something I was working on."

"Why didn't you just trace it?"

"From what?"

"From those things that Mr. Parker left here."

"What are you talking about, Kevin?"

"Here, I'll get one of 'em." Kevin left the table, went into the kitchen and returned with one of the coasters that Quinn had slipped into the cupboard in the kitchen. "This."

Anne was stunned. She remembered that Quinn had described the coaster as the Adams Family Crest. She had never paid a great deal of attention to it as it didn't particularly concern her. Now that she was looking at the coaster with its upright sword and Knight's helmet she realized that it was the same basic diagram as was printed on the old original Gaelic letter as a watermark. It basically proved Quinn's case and Sean must not have ever noticed the watermark on the originals that Quinn delivered to his office. Had he noticed, he obviously would not have gone through the trouble of forging a look alike when the original would have better served his purposes.

Anne changed the subject over to soccer and did not mention the significance of the drawing. After dinner, she cleaned up the kitchen, went through the boys homework with them and ushered them off to their rooms to get ready for bed. When the house was finally quiet, she poured herself a small glass of wine and sat down on the couch to get her thoughts in order regarding Quinn's letters. There was now little doubt in her mind that Quinn's grandfather was the true heir to the Desmond Estate and now she was the lawful heir to that claim.

Regardless of finding the new evidence virtually proving the claim, Anne had already made up her mind as to what she would do. If she went ahead with the claim, she would certainly become a target for someone.

As she had learned from Quinn's death, the threat to her could come from any direction. What if she went ahead with it and then changed her mind? Would she suffer the same fate as Quinn? No, she didn't need that.

Donahue had connected her to an attorney in Atlanta and they had estimated her net proceeds from Quinn's estate as sufficient for her to live quite comfortably the rest of her life. There was also enough to see the boys educated so the thought of putting her life and that of the boys at risk for political reasons was something she could do without. There may be a war going on, but she was pulling herself out of the ranks.

She was tired of the indiscriminate killing and this was her opportunity to pull out of the fray. Robbins had obviously passed the word that she knew the letters were forged and had no interest in pressing on. She could tell that from the looks of top level party people at "One Ireland" social gatherings. They were no longer overly interested in her, as they had been when they considered her a somewhat pliant tool, that would be willing to serve the Nationalist cause. As long as they thought her case rested on forged letters, she had a good argument to keep them away from her door. That understanding on their part would take the heat off of her provided no one ever found out that the original Gaelic letters would have proved the case. Those letters were still in existence.

Anne had looked forward to making the trip to Atlanta but when she left the E concourse at the Atlanta Airport and took the escalator down to catch the underground to the main terminal, she found the throngs of people to be intimidating. The trip into the city had no calming affect on her as she gazed in wonder at the complex of modern tall buildings clustered in the city center. Her attorney had arranged a room for her at the Metro in Buckhead and she had given the information to the driver as to where she wished to be taken. Anne was pleased to observe that her taxi was taking her on through the city and away from the hustle and bustle of downtown Atlanta. After another fifteen minutes or so, the taxi pulled up in front of the Metro Hotel and soon she was in her room and unpacking her bag.

Anne did not intend to stay in the States any longer than necessary as she did not want to burden her sister more than necessary in caring for Kevin and Neil. Quinn's house was placed on the market for sale and while all of the furnishings remained in the home, his personal belongings including his computer, books and other items had been placed in storage. While she was in Atlanta, one of her tasks was to go through all of the stored items and select out those that she wished to have shipped to Ireland. The day after she arrived in Atlanta, she began the difficult task of going through his things. Most everything that she looked at she consigned to charity with the exception of his computer equipment which she knew the boys could use and some personal mementoes that she would keep in remembrance of him. By the end of the day, she was exhausted but she had accomplished that difficult job.

The following day, she went to her attorney's office and signed numerous documents that were needed to probate the Estate and to authorize the attorneys the power to enter into purchase agreements for the house should someone make an offer. They had also scheduled a brief appearance in court for the purpose of documenting her status as the lawful heir to Quinn's property. She would need the court order for transferring stock over to her name and closing Quinn's bank accounts in the Atlanta area.

After leaving the court house, with the signed court order in hand, Anne proceeded to the Nation's Bank, Peachtree Branch, where Quinn had his checking account, safety deposit box and two Certificates of Deposit. Showing the proper authorizations to the Assistant Manager, Anne was delivered the balance of the funds in the account and the Certificates of Deposit were transferred over to her name.

As her final task to accomplish while in the bank, she presented the safety deposit key to the clerk that had been assigned to assist her in closing out the accounts and she was shown to the vault where the deposit boxes were all secured. After signing the entry authorization book, with the clerk making a notation regarding her status under the court order, she was taken to the safety deposit box assigned to Quinn Parker. The clerk inserted her key in one of the locks and Anne inserted hers in the other and soon the tray containing various papers was taken by the clerk to an examining table and she was left alone to go through the documents.

There were papers relating to the house, including a warranty deed and a title insurance agreement which she set aside for the attorneys. There was an old will copy, which predated the one in Ireland by some ten years, in which Quinn bequeathed everything to one Charity or another. As the attorneys had explained to her, any prior will to the one in Ireland would be invalidated. The two certificates of deposit with the bank were evidenced by bank documents and she put those on the stack with the will copy.

In the bottom of the tray were the letters she was seeking. Ten original, brittle, faded letters with Gaelic writing on them and ten originals of the translations done by Sean. Anne carefully placed all of the letters in Quinn's old briefcase that she was now using, together with the other documents that she had removed from the box. When she departed the vault, she went to the desk and closed out the safety deposit box. She was now ready to return to Ireland but she first had to take care of one more piece of business.

Anne took a taxi over to Quinn's home. She told the driver to wait and went into the backyard where he had his barbecue pit. She took the four ancient letters that she had brought with her from Ireland and put them with the ten Gaelic letters that she had taken from the safety deposit box. All of these she placed in the bottom of the grill pit, lit a match and set the letters ablaze. As the flames consumed the old papers, she began to relax. No longer did she have to worry about someone finding the originals of the Gaelic letters and learning that she held the key to the Desmond Estate. Her life was now her own and she and her children could no longer be used as pawns in the strife that had gripped Ireland. As the last of the letters went up in flames, she felt a great relief knowing that they no longer existed. As she took one last look at Quinn's home, she knew that he would approve of what she had done. She was now ready to go home.

We hope you enjoyed THE GAELIC LETTERS by R. Thomas Roe.

For further reading, please go to our catalog online at:

http://www.signalmanpublishing.com

Signalman Publishing